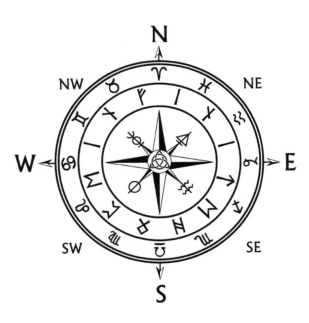

BOOK TWO IN THE **ARMEGEDDON'S WARD** SERIES

IRREGULAR MAGIC

T.J. KELLY

PERSISTENCE
PUBLISHING
Fort Worth, Texas

Library of Congress Control Number: 2018963369

ISBN: 978-1-948744-03-4 (hardback)
ISBN: 978-1-948744-04-1 (paperback)

Any references to historical events, real people, or real places are used fictitiously. Names, characters, and places are products of the author's imagination.

Manufactured in the United States of America

First Edition 2018

Cover Art by Len Jennings
For more information regarding reproductions of works by Len Jennings, please contact artist care of Persistence Publishing, addressed "Attention: Permissions Coordinator," at the address below.

Persistence Publishing
P.O. Box 6663
Fort Worth, Texas 76115
info@persistencepublishing.com

www.persistencepublishing.com

www.tjkellybooks.com

For my friends.

CHAPTER ONE
Dreams

DREAMS AREN'T ALWAYS DREAMS for a magician. Sometimes, they're messages from the dead.

I was back in the ring, fighting the Taines at the end of the trials. Flashes of light illuminated the spectators in the stands as they cheered and screamed and booed in reaction to the battle we waged below. In the Taine family suite, instead of sitting with my family where he belonged, stood my boyfriend, Chas. Hands braced against the windows, banging his fists, shouting and pointing somewhere to my right. The noise of the audience and the glass between Chas and the stadium floor where I stood made it impossible to hear him.

A spell exploded near my feet. I needed to pay attention or else the Taines would win the competition. Wait. Would they? Didn't I already beat them?

Another fireball tore through the darkness, and I ran off, ducking and dodging as explosions of light burst around me. Scrambling for something, anything to protect myself, I searched my battle uniform pockets. Nothing. No crystals, no spells, not even my pocket knife. What happened to my plan? What did I do wrong?

Accepting the inevitable, I turned to face my enemy.

Oberon Taine wasn't there. Instead, the field was empty, and I stood alone in the middle of the stadium, staring up at the Taine family's suite. Chas was still there, struggling against the glass, shouting something. My name formed on his lips and a bolt of longing seared through me. Pain crushed me, and my knees collapsed. I fell in the dirt, unable to tear my gaze from him.

What was he saying? I could almost make it out now that he was repeating only two words.

Lia. Run.

Chas pounded on the glass separating us. Streaks of blood coated the windows, his hands, his broken knuckles.

Lia. Run.

Desperation surged through me and I sprang to my feet. Whatever Chas wanted, I would give him. If he wanted me to run, I would run with all my heart.

I turned and sprinted in the direction he indicated. But the ground shifted and the stadium disappeared leaving only a pit in the darkness, glowing red and orange. Waves of heat warped the air in front of me, but still, I ran straight at it. My feet following the order from Chas, giving him all I could, anything I could. Even if it meant dying.

Before I got to the pit, a figure emerged from the shadows, blocking my way. I stumbled to a halt. Only one person could stop me when I was trying to fulfill the wishes of the guy I loved.

Chas, telling me to run.

My mother, telling me to stop.

"You must be careful, Lia," she said. She sounded warm, firm, clear. A voice I thought I would never hear again after the car accident took my parents. Magicians were protected and guided by their ancestors, only a thin veil between the loved ones who had passed and the living. But they guided us with feelings. Intuitive leadings. I never expected to actually see her again.

Red, pulsating heat glowed in the pit behind her. My mother, trying to block my path, asking me to stop.

Chas, telling me to run.

My chest heaved as I struggled to catch my breath. It wasn't the scorching air that seized my lungs, or the run across the stadium floor that snatched it away. My body jerked from the sobs I was fighting to hold back.

"Lia, you can't trust him. No matter what he says, don't believe him."

My battle for control failed, and the tears flowed. I could believe in Chas. He sacrificed himself for me. He was bound by an unbreakable spell, an oath bound with blood to serve his father Oberon. But I would save him. The way he saved me.

"Mother. I don't know what to do," I sobbed, stumbling towards her. She held out her arms. My feet struggled, heavy and slow as if they were dragging through tar.

Finally, I reached her. I was there. A sweet floral scent enveloped me. I had forgotten how much I loved her perfume. My thoughts skipped into the past to when I was six. I had scraped my knee, and I hugged her as I cried. She was touching my hair, telling me I would be okay. Her perfume surrounded us.

Then the memory faded and I was back in the present, my parents dead. Before me yawned a pit, fiery red in the dark. The perfume remained, but my mother was gone.

I was alone.

CHAPTER TWO
Aftermath

MY EYES SNAPPED OPEN, the image of my mother still haunting me. Reaching for me, calling to me, separated from me by the surrounding darkness.

Not the best way to start a day.

Shaking off my nightmare, I decided to get up. I might have tried to sneak in a little more sleep and skip breakfast, but the last thing I wanted to do was re-dream that hot mess, even if I did miss my mother. It was her, too, not a typical dream. She was giving me a warning.

Darkness and fire. Fabulous.

I slipped out of bed and wandered over to my dresser. I was finally settling in. The last several months were a blur of studying and practicing and recovering from injuries, so I never got the chance to put my personal stamp on the elegant room my aunt Peony had set up for me. I shoved aside the stack of notes I had taken the week before so I could check the clock. There were so many papers, they were blocking my view.

It was eight in the morning. Way earlier than I planned on getting up but on the upside that meant I would have time to luxuriate in the giant claw-foot bathtub in my private bathroom before I had to meet everyone downstairs.

I had always lived in large, elegant homes, provided for by the fruits of my family's company, Rector Enterprises. And by our ancestors, who had an uncanny ability to multiply our fortune throughout the centuries, making us filthy rich.

Rectors believed in helping the poor and worked with multiple charities. It saved us from the hatred and jealousy of the masses. Instead, we were hated by other businesses. And dark magicians, who we regularly vanquished on behalf of the Council.

Until I came along that is.

I sighed and grabbed a fluffy towel out of the small linen closet near the bathtub and turned on the water. Then I dumped an extra dollop of my favorite bubble bath under the faucet. Fresh strawberry and basil filled the air. Nice.

After pinning my dark brown hair onto the top of my head, I climbed into the tub. I shampooed it the night before and didn't want to go through the drama of drying it out again. After sinking up to my neck in the near-scalding water, I sighed as I closed my eyes, resting my neck against the curved edge of the tub.

A flash of fire played across the inside of my lids. Scowling, I shook it off and forced the reminder of my nightmare out of my mind. I wanted to relax, not worry about some kind of portent of doom. Instead, I slipped into a light meditative state to avoid the fiery images and reconnect with the elements.

It felt great to have complete access to my magic. Finally.

I created tiny whirlpools all over the tub that were better than having jets. I had no problem getting the element of Water to respond. I had a connection to all the elements once I became a magician. It had taken a lot of effort, not to mention a ton of help from my uncle and his agents, but eventually, I crossed the threshold from magicless child to powerful woman of magic. My nose wrinkled. It felt so odd to call myself a woman since I was only seventeen, but "teenager of magic" sounded stupid, even in the privacy of my head.

I let my thoughts drift for several more minutes before I finally stopped the tiny underwater storms I had brewing and drained the tub. I dried off while I magically whisked the condensation off the mirror. My bun was sloppy and damp around the edges, but it looked cute enough that I left it alone.

My favorite outfit was easy to find in my closet despite my aunt stuffing the vast space to overflowing. Even though I had plenty of my own clothes when I moved in with them, Peony was always buying clothes she said enhanced the gold in my hazel brown eyes. I had loads of new outfits. Instead of wearing one, I tugged on some navy yoga pants, which sort of matched the navy and teal plaid of my shirt, and then slipped on hot pink house shoes.

Peony wanted me to dress a little nicer since we had visitors coming in and out of the castle all the time. My uncle, Armageddon, had been sticking close to home because I was still a new magician and in danger from a ridiculously long list of enemies. He was an important man, so everyone came to him. I just couldn't make the effort to dress up. Comfortable clothing made my days seem more bearable.

It started with the frantic race to train me in time to win the competition for Rector Enterprises. Chas, the love of my life, betrayed me during the trials. He said it was for my own good, but sometimes I wondered

Forcing that disloyal thought from my head, I tugged on my socks. I had spent the last couple of months trying to find a way to free my boyfriend from the terrible deal he had made with his father, Oberon Taine. Well, I guess I was supposed to call Chas my ex-boyfriend, but that thought still hurt too much.

Not again. I swiped at the tears in my eyes, refusing to cry.

Chas said he did it for me. Even if I thought his sacrifice was stupid and misguided, I didn't want him to pay for his actions for the rest of his life. And I had hope. If I freed him, we would be together again. I could endure anything for him. I already made it through two agonizing months without him by my side. If I could do that, I could do anything.

I glanced at my clock, still surrounded by piles of notes and books and parchment and the little silk bag I made during the spring equinox - and snorted. The only thing personal about my bedroom was the complete wreck I had made of it.

Kind of like my life.

It was nine-thirty. I took longer in the bath than I realized. Since I didn't have enough time to do anything else before breakfast, I headed downstairs and across the castle. It was a little early to have a meal, considering magicians slept late due to our midnight spellwork. But there was probably somebody already lounging around, waiting for the rest of us to show up for the quick meeting we held before we ate. Somebody who was bright and chipper and annoyingly awake despite the late-night work we did the evening before.

Somebody like my best friend.

Sure enough, Peter was in the study, flipping through a magazine as I walked through the door. He grinned when he saw me.

"Rough night?" he asked.

"Ha. I assume that means I look like death warmed over." I wasn't fishing for a compliment, but the sweetheart would probably give me one, anyway.

"You're crazy."

I laughed. "True."

"No, let me finish," he said. "You're nuts if you think you're anything less than beautiful." Peter was the best at making me feel good about myself. He tossed the magazine aside and stood up, brushing the wrinkles out of his khakis. He had on a gray polo that matched his eyes, also thanks to my aunt's shopping habits. "Come on, it'll be at least another fifteen minutes before anyone else shows up. Let's see if we can get to the mini muffins before Ged arrives."

I was down with that. My uncle, who we all called

Ged because the name Armageddon was so pompous, was engaged in a long-standing war with me over who got to eat the chocolate banana mini muffins, when available. And it didn't stop there. We always snatched each other's best treats. He started it, though.

We made our way into the dining chamber. It was humongous, able to seat over five-hundred diners, although only one small table was set for the five of us. The empty chair where Chas used to sit gave my heart a twinge, but I turned my back and focused on the buffet.

The food was there, hot and ready for us. It didn't matter what time we arrived, it was always waiting and perfectly cooked. Almost as if by magic. I narrowed my eyes and concentrated until I made out wisps of orange transparent light curling around the chaffing dishes that held our food.

Definitely by magic.

Not a surprise. The best chefs in the world were all magicians. Mundanes - humans without magic - didn't stand a chance against somebody who could toss five ingredients on a plate and have it turn into a masterpiece. Magic inserted itself into every part of our lives, effecting everything we did. My father once told me mundanes resented us because magicians couldn't help using magic to beat our competition. He said it gave us an unfair advantage. Not that it was all bad. I liked food that was always hot and ready to eat.

"No mini muffins," I said. "What a bummer."

"Tut tut, don't look so disappointed. The peach shipment must have arrived from California. Look at those individual cobblers."

I followed the direction of Peter's outstretched finger until I saw them. "Well, hello there peachy goodness," I purred.

Peter laughed and grabbed some plates. "Come on, let's eat them while they're hot."

He slipped two cobblers onto each plate before handing me one. I walked along the length of the buffet until I reached the meats. Something about sweet flavors always made me crave salty foods, so I grabbed a couple of slices of ham. I shifted each muffin-size cobbler onto a slice and wrapped them like a burrito. Then pressing down gently, I caused the peaches and crust to spread evenly along the ham. I caught Peter shaking his head out of the corner of my eye.

"Don't knock it until you've tried it," I said. I plopped a slice of ham onto his plate, and he obliged, making himself a ham-and-peach-cobbler burrito. We leaned against the table instead of sitting down, trying to avoid making a mess that would give away our premature breakfast-buffet raid.

Peter took a huge bite. He was such a good sport.

"Wow," he mumbled around the food in his mouth. "I'll never doubt you again. This is amazing." I knew he meant it when he scarfed down the rest of the burrito.

"I know. I'm awesome, right?"

Peter choked when he laughed. "Yeah, yeah, I couldn't live without you and all that jazz." He studied me and then lost a little of his smile.

I braced myself, hoping what was coming next wouldn't be too bad. "What's up?" I asked. I couldn't stand how long he was taking to tell me what was on his mind. The Dark inside of me, which was almost evenly matched to the Light, took over and my mood changed.

Even though my light nature placed me on the side of good at the Ascension Ceremony when I became a magician, darkness never had a problem overbalancing me. Peter needed to share the bad news he was hiding before it set me off.

"Hey, it's okay," he said. "I was only wondering when you're going to visit Rector Enterprises. You're not just the figurehead for the next few years, you're also a champion and the last Rector."

Peter pulled the plate out of my hand and lay it on the edge of the table beside his. He tugged me into his arms, and I went willingly. I had discovered over the course of our friendship that nobody gave a hug like Peter Makenna.

"Sorry, I didn't mean to go dark on you," I said. My voice made a muffled echoing sound against his chest. I soaked in a bit of his Light, the elemental source of his magic humming strong beneath his skin. I stepped back once I settled down and looked up at him, smiling a little. "Uncle Ged's planning the visit. I'm still under threat of extinction, so he wants protection spells set all along the route as well as inside the buildings. My parents set up spells at the facility but never put them anywhere else. Uncle Ged said that's why they were targeted on the night of the accident. They drove straight instead of using a transition spell to transport themselves. That left them vulnerable."

I don't know what he saw on my face, but Peter's brows furrowed in response, making him look older than his nineteen years. "We'll keep you safe," he said, intensity pouring off of him like an aura. "I promise."

"Easy there, Killer. I know you will," I replied, keeping my voice light and even. He was so serious, but I understood. He worried about me. Everyone did. If it wasn't because they thought somebody would hurt me, it was because they knew I could accidentally blow up the world.

Peter snorted and his natural amiableness returned. "Come on, let's go hide the evidence of our early morning snack and get the meeting out of the way. Those mini-cobblers were great, but they've barely made a dent in my appetite."

Typical Peter, eating like there was no tomorrow. Not like I was any better. Who could help themselves when Peony employed one of the two best cooks on the planet? The other being my own cook, who stayed behind with the other servants at my manor house in San Francisco when I had to abandon my life there. Because I was much safer at Castle Laurus.

A thought about how many times I had been rendered unconscious over the last few months flitted through my head. So maybe not safer so much as the fact I had a better chance to stay alive if my family and friends surrounded me.

Shaking off my darkening thoughts, I concentrated on the present and my best friend. We tucked our plates into the sink in the kitchen, just down the hall and around the corner from the dining chamber. It was my favorite room in the castle besides my workshop. My aunt stocked it with both ancient and modern appliances, including every ingenious device my uncle's Laurus ancestors purchased over the last thousand years or so.

The old wooden countertops glowed with the patina of ages past, dark and worn and wonderful. I was always running my hands along them because they felt so good. I could probably spend all my time in that kitchen, but duty called.

Armageddon and Peony were sitting together in the study, their knees touching, heads close as they worked on a spell. I loved the contrast they presented, an outrageously tall man with black and silver hair married to a petite blond woman with radiant blue eyes. My aunt's embroidery hoop lay nearby. The buzz of magic surrounded them like a cloud. I was going to ask what they were up to, but before we could even greet them, Mort popped straight into the room in a flash of light.

Transitioning into a crowded area could have been a disaster if done incorrectly. He must have been in a hurry since it wasn't that long of a drive from the front gates. Nobody could transfer into the castle unless they were already on the property. Another of my uncle's security precautions.

"Wow, Mort. Living dangerously," I said. Besides transferring into a room full of people, he also wore no vest or belt pouch, which meant he wasn't dressed for battle the way he usually was. Instead, he went casual, wearing jeans and a forest green button shirt that made his eyes glow. It was different enough from how I normally saw him that I realized he was pretty fine for an old guy.

Mort's eyes narrowed. "Well, hello there to you, too, Lady Lia. You look nice today. For a pipsqueak barely out of diapers."

Peter and Armageddon choked back their laughter. I scowled. I had forgotten to shield my thoughts from Mort, who I recently learned possessed the ability to read the minds of the unaware. After he secretly used that skill to manage my training, of course.

Not that I was complaining. Mortem Impii, or Wicked Death, was the best teacher on the planet if anyone wanted to know how to fight dirty. Which I did.

My aunt glided across the room and took the bundles Mort brought with him. I hadn't even noticed his hands were full of brown paper-wrapped packages. It was the first time I had ever seen him without his battle gear, and it had really thrown me off. Where he had been that he felt he didn't need it?

"Thanks, Mort," Peony said. She hustled towards the door. I loved how energetic she always was. My aunt had so many things going on, she would probably have been drowning in them if she wasn't so capable. She caught a lot of flack in society about it, since most of magicians valued the cool, sophisticated look of boredom to her active interest. Even though she was a member of my family, I had heard all the gossip about her anyway. People thought she was a little dim. Or weak. Just because she didn't act like a snot the way they did.

Boy, were they wrong. And I was pretty sure she was as powerful as my uncle. But they didn't spread that around. No need to put her on the Council's radar, too. They were already suspicious of the rest of us. Although, she was the only female member of the Irregulars, besides myself, so they should have caught the clue bus. There weren't any stupid or weak agents in my uncle's employ.

"No problem, Peony," Mort said. The tone in his voice made my eyes narrow. I hated feeling left out, and it was obvious they were studiously not talking about something. My aunt left with the packages as Mort flopped down on a chair, breathing a sigh of relief.

"Rough trip?" Armageddon asked. He raised an eyebrow.

"Yes. It doesn't get easier. But at some point, I think she'll come around." Mort didn't indicate who he was referring to. So annoying.

"She might. Then again, we expected her to before and look what happened," Armageddon said.

"True," Mort answered.

My gaze swung back and forth between the two men as I followed their cryptic conversation. They had to be messing with me. And it was working. My curiosity was off the charts.

"Besides, you know she won't hurt you as long as you're unarmed." Were Armageddon's eyes glittering with humor? I thought maybe they were.

Mort nodded gravely, but I was positive I saw a twinkle in his green eyes, too. "That's true," Mort said. "It doesn't matter if she's softening. She'll still cry foul if I showed up with even one spell. And then what would Peony do?"

"What indeed?" Armageddon asked. "I must think about that. I loathe monopolies."

Mort nodded absently.

Before I rose to the bait and asked what and who and why, Peter butted in and ruined my timing.

"What's on the roster, boss?" he asked. The corners of his lips twitched. That rat. He diverted the conversation on purpose.

"It looks like a slow week," my uncle answered. "I've got a few investigations running, but we're focusing on teaching Lia self-control."

I sighed. I had assumed when I connected with my magic and won the competition to retain ownership of my family's company, I could finally live my life as an ordinary magician. Instead, my magic turned out to be a real problem. Their focus was still on me.

And I was getting sick of being in the spotlight. Not that I blamed them. A small, silver star necklace was the only thing that stood between me, my thoughts, and the obliteration of the entire planet. That was enough to keep anyone on their toes.

Mort laughed at my disgruntled scowl. "Cheer up, Lia. You can take out your angst on me in the practice ring. I'll teach you another trick for throwing a larger opponent. Peony particularly likes this one," he said.

My aunt was shorter than I was, so whatever she liked would probably be a lot of fun on top of being useful. After I mastered it. Unfortunately, learning something new usually meant that I would spend a few hours in the infirmary, sore everywhere and possibly with broken bones. Yet I couldn't wait to do it anyway.

They were driving me insane.

Mort cracked up. Yeah, I guess I had broadcast that thought instead of hiding it. Whatever.

Peony bustled back to collect us, and we made our way to the dining chamber. Armageddon eyeballed me when he saw there were only a couple of mini peach cobblers left on the buffet table. I gave him a cheeky grin.

"Don't think I didn't notice those shortbread crumbs on your sleeve," I said, excusing my early morning buffet raid. "I know you took the last shipment."

My uncle winced. "I thought I brushed them all off. I better ask for help next time I want to hide evidence from you."

I winked and turned to make myself a sandwich. I couldn't stand to eat a traditional breakfast in the mornings, and the castle chefs always had a wide variety of foods available. Magicians were often on strange schedules and ate what their appetites demanded, not what convention dictated. Especially the Irregulars.

"So what's in the packages?" Peter asked as we took a seat. Bless him. I didn't want to be the first to crack. Not during the week my uncle said they were teaching me self-control, anyway.

"They're the ingredients I need for a spell I think will help Lia," Armageddon answered. He looked so pathetic as he stared at the empty dessert platters. My heart softened and I slipped the mini cobbler I had hidden under an extra slice of bread while he had his face turned away. "I want her to be able to sleep without inadvertently doing magic. Relying on mechanical charms like her necklace is dangerous."

Because my necklace could get lost. The chain

18

could break. It could slip off while I was asleep. An enemy could take it. Anything like that would be a disaster. I had tried for so long to access my power. Now, I was desperate to put the lid back on. It was like a cosmic joke.

"Please don't tell me I have to drink something nasty," I said. My uncle knew I would do anything to keep from hurting everyone around me, but that didn't mean I wanted to choke down something disgusting. Or worse, slimy. Ugh.

"Nothing so unfortunate, niece of mine. This spell will take a long while to create, but once it's complete, I'll toss it over your head. It'll help you learn to control the space between thought and reality. No indigestion required." It said a lot about the nature of magic that I was so relieved to hear that.

After a quick knock, a messenger entered the room. She was tall and lanky, probably around eighteen or nineteen. She took her responsibilities seriously, made obvious by the way she walked so confidently despite my uncle's intimidating reputation.

Mort was my uncle's partner and second-in-command for the Irregulars. That meant by contract, he could collect or pay business debts and read all messages. He was the one who handed the messenger a small charm to thank her for her work and accepted the creamy white envelope.

Magicians rarely tipped with money. Magic complicated the rules governing employment, caretaking, and income. Merely handing a few dollars to somebody working in an official capacity could butt up against some of the harsher spellwork that bonded their contracts.

19

It was especially dangerous when interacting with messengers, who were usually new apprentices and inexperienced enough to fall for all sorts of tricks that crueler magicians liked to pull. Handing over mechanical spells and charms was acceptable payment, and far easier for the messenger to tell the difference between dangerous and beneficial.

For instance, Mort handed the young woman a Fleet-foot charm. Not only would she be able to travel faster for the month it lasted, but she would recover twice as fast from the effects of the transitions between one location and another. That was better than a twenty-dollar bill any day.

"It's for you," Mort told my uncle. Armageddon hastily finished his breakfast. He started gulping his food down as soon as the messenger arrived, probably assuming the message would be for him and would take him away from his meal.

That happened a lot. Powerful magicians could be petty, and they would often hold off until an inconvenient time to send a message. Or start a war.

I suspected that was why we were supposed to ascend into our magic on our seventeenth birthday. They were so enamored by the idea of ruining a good thing that instead of having a big party to celebrate reaching legal adulthood, we had to dress in formal clothes and perform the Ascension Ceremony. It really sucked.

Armageddon glanced at me. "I'll try to be back in time for our practice session," he said. "If not, Mort will handle it."

My uncle discovered the dessert I had smuggled

onto his plate. He winked at me as he scooped it up and popped it into his mouth before heading out. Mort handed Armageddon the letter. My uncle swerved to give Peony a quick kiss on the cheek, then disappeared in a flash.

Peony sighed. I glanced her way, and she smiled. "No rest for the wicked, right?"

"Right," I responded as I stood. I reached over and gave my aunt a little squeeze before clearing away my dishes.

She and my uncle had been planning some much-needed alone time together. Armageddon had come for me when my parents died, straight from a long-term assignment. Then we spent months frantically training for the trials and keeping me safe. He and Peony didn't get to spend much time together even though he was around the castle more than usual. I felt bad about my role in that.

I hoped my uncle wouldn't get dragged into another war or something. Magical corporations always tried to find a new way to steal market segments. That usually involved tons of negotiation and at least one or two outright battles, sucking up a lot of time. My aunt and uncle deserved a vacation.

Peter slipped out of the room at the same time I did. I turned to wave goodbye and saw Mort shake his head in response to something my aunt had asked silently. It made me wonder what she felt she couldn't ask out loud.

CHAPTER THREE
Training Session

I ALMOST MADE IT to the top when a black boot swept my feet out from under me. Plunging down a short rock face, I hit the pond with an icy splash. What a lame way to start one of our training sessions.

"Got you again, kiddo," my uncle said. He was still trying to keep things lighthearted. When I first arrived at Castle Laurus, he had concocted an entire strategy to keep me cheerful and upbeat. It had taken months to connect to my magic. In the meantime, I had been vulnerable to magical forces and the age-old battle between light and dark. And he didn't want dark to win.

Back then, he didn't know I would ascend into my magic with a near-equal balance no matter what they did. It was the nature of Rector magic. But at least I managed to come in on the side of good. That was a relief to us all and one reason I was still alive. The Council had assassins on staff, and they would have made sure I didn't stick around if they felt I was a danger to them.

Of course, nobody was all that certain I wasn't still a threat. The element of Dark always threatened to overwhelm me and tip my balance to the dark side. So my uncle continued his attempts to tease me into better moods. Either that, or he was trying to drive me insane. Some days, it was a tough call.

"You know how much I hate being in the water," I said, trying not to let it annoy me. The worst part was getting wet while still fully clothed. Plus, I absolutely hated water in my ears. I wasn't really angry or had a phobia or anything. I had spent a long time underwater during the trials to win back Rector Enterprises, and I just didn't want to be reminded of it all again.

"But you're so good at it," Armageddon teased. "The drowned-rat look is cute on you, too."

"Ha, ha," I said. I tried not to roll my eyes, but it happened anyway.

"Come on, let's take a breather. I'll conjure up some hot chocolate with tons of whipped cream. We can talk strategy." My uncle held his hand out, and I used it to steady myself as I climbed up the slippery bank. The pond was located at the center of the castle in the arboretum my aunt had designed to grow many of the herbs and flowers they used in the products for my uncle's business, Laurus Commodities.

While my uncle magically raided the kitchen, I shuffled over to one of the benches lining the outer rim of the battlefield. Mort had helped me create what I thought of as a "moon module" on our practice grounds. We all decided that we liked it enough to use the structure as a practice dome for future mock battles. It was kind of ugly and positioned in the middle of the garden. But since it kept the damage to a minimum, Peony let it stand.

We had been training in a section of the module with rundown brick walls and large ponds and puddles when Armageddon knocked me down. I guess it was better than landing on a pile of bricks. My aunt had told him she didn't want to treat me for another concussion. He must have decided landing in water would help avoid one.

I was suddenly dry. I looked over my shoulder and caught the light teal trace of the spell my uncle used to tug the water out of my clothes and back into the pond.

"Hey, thanks!" I said with a grin. He had even remembered to dry out my boots. I hated squishy footwear. "So how's the search for a spell to help my self-control going?" Maybe he would give me more details.

Armageddon flopped down on the bench beside me. He held two large ceramic mugs with homemade whipping cream piled high above the rim, extra firm, exactly the way I liked it. He handed me the blue one. I didn't know how he knew it was my favorite, but that was always the one he gave me.

"We may have solved it. But it's only temporary. I think if you have a chance to slow down for a few months, you'll be able to work things out on your own."

"Yeah. Maybe." I wasn't sure I believed that, but I would give it a try. It was that or accidentally destroy the world or something. I tugged the handkerchief I always carried with me out of my vest pocket and wiped my mouth. I loved whipped cream, but I never managed to eat it without getting it all over my face.

"Come on," Armageddon said as he set aside his mug and stood. "There are a few more techniques I wanted to squeeze in today before lunch. I think you may be sufficiently warm and dry to avoid catching a cold. If I get you sick on top of everything else, your aunt will never forgive me."

I huffed a small laugh at that thought. Peony was terrifying when she was protecting the ones she loved. He was probably scared of what she would do. With good reason.

"I'll be fine," I said. "What are we working on now?"

"Stick-work. Staffs can help extend your reach, and most magicians don't use them anymore." We were taught basic staff training in the lower grades, but nobody really stuck with it. "That could be to your advantage."

I nodded to myself. All the times someone had attacked me raced through my mind. A big stick would have been useful.

We arrived at a clearing near the center of the practice dome. Armageddon waved his hand, and the large boulders lining one side of the field shifted further to the side, widening the battle area. Then with a snap, two staffs appeared. He handed me the shorter one. Staff length depended on height. A shorter staff was better for control.

"Thanks," I said as I hefted it, checking the balance.

"Let's run through the warm-up routine and the first ten forms. That will help me assess where your weaknesses are and work out a training schedule. I'll have Mort pitch in on my busy days. He needs to know your skill level, too."

"Nothing I've learned will be good enough to stop Mort," I laughed. "I could be at expert level, and he'd still kick my butt." I stretched, using the staff to stabilize myself as I tugged my foot behind me.

"Which makes him the best combat training instructor on the planet." Armageddon finished his stretches and twirled his staff back and forth in large, lazy circles, warming up his arms. "The life of an Irregular isn't easy. If there were another way to keep you safe from the Council, I would do it. Unfortunately, though, being an agent protects you from them at the same time it makes you an even bigger target with everyone else. Although I think you are an excellent addition to the team."

Our staffs clashed with a loud snick as we started the forms. "That's not your fault," I cut in abruptly. "The Council always thinks powerful magicians are a threat. I wish I knew what my father did to keep them off his tail. No, I'm grateful to you for all of this. And I should know how to fight, anyway. You're the one who told me that my enemies will attack me physically since I'm short and a female. I want to learn everything I can to give me an advantage."

Armageddon ducked as my staff swung exactly where his head had been a second before. He slid sideways, twirling in a neat little circle, and almost knocked me off my feet again. Fortunately, each form was a routine. We knew what was coming, and I didn't need to pay too much attention to his next move. At least, not at the lower levels.

"I want you to be able to protect yourself, but I'll

always be here for you, too. When you call, I'll come to your aid." Armageddon's words sounded reassuring, but there was also a deeper thread woven into his voice as if he were casting a spell. It reminded me a little of his promise to help me if the worst happened during the trials.

Ducking to avoid his next blow, I slipped on the soft sand near the edge of the field and almost landed on my butt. Quickly recovering, I managed to swing in time to make Armageddon jump over my staff at the expected moment.

"Why didn't you intervene while I was in the ring? Things got pretty bad." My breath came out in huffs, causing me to speak with little pauses between each word. Armageddon had promised to tear the stadium down to protect me if needed. I was curious what he had meant by that since being skewered in the leg by Oberon's knife seemed like the right time to interfere. I wanted to know why he held back, although I didn't think about it much at the time. I was too busy trying not to die.

"Oh, that," he said casually before he grunted from the force of his staff striking the ground near my feet. "You had to win on your own merits. I would have stopped the knife from killing you if needed. It wasn't."

I rolled to the side, performing the second step of the ninth form. "Well, someday I'd like you to show me how you monitor things like that. I want to know how to protect my charges from a distance."

"Sure thing, sweetheart," Armageddon said as he slammed his staff into my shoulder. Or he would have if my staff wasn't there to block it. "It's an advanced skill. You have to focus to the exclusion of almost everything else, so it's not used often."

"Oh. Like the time the Taine's attacked me when I went off castle grounds? You made the pain go away." I rolled again, weaving my body to avoid his blows.

"Close. That one takes more concentration. The spell I used at the stadium allows for me to perform protection spells on myself simultaneously."

I knew it. My uncle had put himself in danger to keep me alive after I was attacked by the Taines when I was outside of the castle borders. He had made himself vulnerable around our enemies to save me.

I dragged myself off the ground and wiped the sudden onslaught of grateful tears off my cheeks. Since they were coated in sand, I pretended I had gotten a few grains in my eyes and needed to flush them out. We had completed all ten forms and it was time for a short break anyway.

"That's just one more thing I want to learn when the time comes," I said. It wasn't even funny how much I needed to learn. I didn't connect to my magic until months after my seventeenth birthday. My parents had taken me from school to school before that, trying to make it work. There had been no time to learn many of the basics like the other magicless students. I was so far behind I wasn't sure I could ever catch up.

Armageddon held out his clean handkerchief for me to dry my face when I was done splashing it with water from one of my bottles. I didn't like how the sand felt coating my skin and wanted to get it off as soon as possible.

"You're doing fine. In fact, you are the hardest working

apprentice I've ever had. And I've turned out some highly competent magicians, even if I do say so myself." My uncle handed me my staff after I stuffed his handkerchief into my pocket so I could wash it before giving it back. It was the polite thing to do.

"Thanks," I said. My feet rose a little higher as I strode towards the middle of the field as if the lift in my spirits had also lightened my tread. "It's not so bad, though. I really like a lot of the bookwork. There are so many questions that have driven me crazy for years. Now that I have my magic, I can try the solutions and work out for myself what's real and what's just superstition." Ancient texts were filled with both wisdom and foolishness, almost in equal measure. I wasn't sure why, but that was another question I could ask. When I had more time.

If I ever had more time.

"All right, let's do this thing," he said. "I'm getting hungry." Armageddon tapped his staff on the ground, marking his challenge. I sighed, knowing I would get my butt kicked. But I had a plan. It involved a lot of running and hiding.

Hey, if it worked in the trials, it would work in the real world.

I bellowed and twirled my staff as fast as I could to force my uncle to step back, which he did, and then when it came time to lunge, I instead turned and ran.

"I'm hungry, too, but I won't let you take me out that quick," I shouted behind me.

My uncle laughed, but then the area grew silent. So quiet that the lack of noise lay on my ears heavily. Great.

He had disappeared.

"While I have your attention," my uncle said from the rock formation in front of me, startling me into jumping about a foot off the ground. "I wanted to check in with how you are doing. We haven't had the chance to talk for a while now. I feel like I'm losing touch."

I dove to the side as he arched his staff, slamming it down where I had been standing moments before. I didn't like where the conversation was heading and just grunted my response.

A muffled boom sounded in the distance. There was no ceiling above the arboretum where we practiced. Clouds gathered above us in the sky, indicating that my uncle was as serious as he had ever been.

"I'm fine," I ground out as I tripped over a small pile of bricks. "Lessons are great. I'm great. Everything is great." I looked for something to use as a distraction and ended up burying my uncle in dead leaves and grass, swirling them around him with a miniature tornado I created using a little of the Air element.

"Honey, we worry about you. You can trust us. Let us in, okay? You don't need to go through this alone."

And by this, he meant my breakup with Chas. Or really, Chas betraying me to his father. He said it was for my own good, but who was he to make that choice for me?

I pushed aside my resentment and then reminded myself that Chas was my epic first love and that kind of thing came with a lot of big gestures and sacrifice. And I had vowed to save him. So we could work out the details when he was back at Castle Laurus with us where he belonged.

"It's fine," I insisted through gritted teeth. I scrambled up a small slope near the swampy area, using an extra burst of speed to round a corner so my uncle would lose sight of me. The truth was, I didn't want to think about how I was doing. It was hard to keep the faith when Chas hadn't tried to contact me even once since he left.

"But how do you feel, Lia? Peony and I want to know how you're handling his loss. Blood oaths can't be broken."

Like I needed to be reminded. It was like Armageddon wanted to start a fight again. But I was sick of arguing about Chas. That had led to disaster before, and I would never repeat something like that again.

Just when I thought it was too late, I finally found the rock pile that had a small hollow beneath it. Small, but large enough for me to slip under and hide.

I remained silent so I could lie in wait for my uncle to pass by, but it also gave me time to come up with an answer. I guess I should have had one by now, but I didn't. I had no idea how to feel. I had no idea how to break an unbreakable spell. I had no idea how to accept defeat and walk away from a guy I swore to save so we could be together forever.

What did epic love mean, anyway?

The time for thinking was up, so I launched myself straight at Armageddon's knees to knock him down. He caught himself on his staff and swung around, almost as if he were dancing, and slammed both of his feet into my chest. Or would have if he didn't stop short before making contact. Instead, he tapped me lightly on the shoulder and I dropped my staff, defeated for the day.

"I don't know how I feel anymore," I confessed. It was

31

as close as I could come to admitting that I was starting to have doubts. And I was too tired to use a little magic to push them out of my mind the way I usually did.

Armageddon squeezed my shoulder, acknowledging my feelings. He took my staff and set them both aside on one of the benches as we walked out of the dome and back into the castle proper. "I'll tell your aunt we're done practicing for the morning. Hit the shower. We'll eat when you're ready. I need to get cleaned up, myself."

I nodded, grateful he didn't press me to admit anything more. Maybe he was thinking about the last time we fought about Chas, too. Shuddering at the thought of the entire field of birds being obliterated by my thoughtless anger, I trudged up the stairs to my room. A long, hot shower was just the thing I needed to distract me from the thoughts swirling around in my head.

Like was love really love when they volunteered to leave you forever?

CHAPTER FOUR
Teachable Moments

SOMETIMES I SPENT HOURS talking to my uncle in his office, late in the afternoons after heavy reading assignments. We would talk about strategy and philosophy, magic and murder.

"We suspect the Taines were involved. Stage one is proving who did the actual deed. Stage two is when we discern whether it was a hit job or solely at their instigation. Although, it's possible the assassins had support regardless of who instigated." Armageddon finished making a note in one of his black leather-bound journals and then set his pen aside. He used the cheap ballpoint again instead of the gorgeous ceremonial quill resting beside the crystal ink holder. I did the same thing. Quills got messy, and my hand was always covered in ink before I had gotten done with one page of notes.

I heaved a sigh and shifted deeper into my favorite squashy chair. Peony hated it, and the worn out pea-green upholstery left a lot to be desired. But it was comfortable, the dip in the seat cushion allowing me to touch the floor. The fancy chairs were a smidge too tall, and my feet dangled. As if I were seven instead of seventeen. My aunt, who was shorter than I, understood the value of a chair that fit. So the chair remained hidden away in my uncle's office.

"I hate them," I said. Again. I probably said that about the Taines a hundred times a day, and yet it still wasn't often enough to express my loathing.

Armageddon heaved his own sigh, then rocked back in his chair. "I know you do, sweetheart, and I don't blame you in the least. I can't stand Oberon myself. There are dark magicians in this world who have enough Light inside them to make them redeemable human beings. But not him. I sense the Light, but it's obscured in a way that is unusual and difficult to decipher. After all these years, I can only conclude his will is set for the dark no matter what."

His voice reeked with discontent. Armageddon was arguably the most powerful magician in the world. He had ways of discerning a magician's source magic that were uncommon and useful, especially for the head of the Irregulars. But Oberon was a Taine, and the Taine clan perverted Light to use for dark magic spells. Chas had told me that before the trials to give me an edge. I toyed with the idea of telling my uncle, but I swore to Chas that I would never reveal his family secret. It made me uncomfortable to hide things from Armageddon, but I kept that bit of knowledge to myself.

My promise wouldn't stop me from using it to destroy them, though.

"Do you have any leads?" I asked, wondering if some of the messengers going in and out of the castle had been carrying information about the car accident that had killed my parents.

"Nothing solid, but there are rumors." My uncle shifted, leaning over his huge antique desk. His silver eyes glittered with suppressed emotion. I would hate to be on the receiving end of his anger. Even knowing his fury was on my behalf, my heartbeat still sped up. I had never feared my uncle, but my imagination was stellar and an image of Armageddon's enemies realizing their time was up rose strongly in my head.

"Good thing the Irregulars deal in rumors," I quipped. I smiled, trying to shift my mood before I took a turn toward the dark and lost my inner balance.

"Indeed. At some point, the threads will form a cohesive picture, and then we'll bring the perpetrators to justice. Until then, I've got feelers out." That meant my uncle had his connections sorting through conversations and messages they had intercepted months before and after the car accident.

The Irregulars kept track of all the intelligence we received, but since any Earth user could tap into computers or phones or any device with metal or crystals in their basic components, our intel was written and tracked on paper. By a lot of smart, dedicated analysts.

I wasn't sure how many agents were full members of the Irregulars. Beyond the people who directly reported to Armageddon, there was a huge network of spies and informants, support staff and vendors. There were so many moving pieces and parts that I didn't know how my uncle kept up with it all and still manage to shield us from the Council. They believed powerful magicians were a threat that occasionally needed to be removed.

As in, assassinated.

"Why are there so many dark magicians on the Council, anyway?" I asked. It was a rhetorical question - I already knew there had to be a balance, just like everything else related to magic.

"There's been a shift," Armageddon said, shocking the scowl off of my face. I jerked my eyes to his, and he gave a little nod. Apparently, I had earned the right to hear a bit more about the inner workings of the organization. "There are still as many dark magicians as light running the Council, but the balance is tilting into darkness. I'm not sure who's behind it."

I picked at a loose thread on the arm of the chair. I was the most junior agent in the Irregulars. Although I was my uncle's ward, that didn't grant me additional access or privileges. Which meant he told me because I needed to know about the shift of power. I really, really hoped it wasn't related to me, but considering how much my uncle was telling me, it probably was.

"Do you think that's why my parents were killed?" There was still a hitch in my voice every time I talked about them. They hadn't been gone very long, and my recent dream about my mother made the loss feel more present. Everything about her had been so real. Her black hair, the same as Armageddon's but without the silver that came with age, flowed down her back. Her gold-and-brown hazel eyes glowing with an inner light as she reached out for me. Tried to warn me. I had smelled her perfume again, and I wanted very much to know who stole her from me long before her time. I hadn't seen my father, though. Somehow, that made his loss even worse.

"I'm fairly certain it's all connected. The time isn't ripe, but soon we must use memory spells and see if anything happened in your presence that can help."

Ah. So that's why I was being told so many details. Armageddon wanted me to know why I was going to have to relive the worst part of my life. I wasn't sure I was up to it, or how much help I would be. But if there was a chance to bring their killers to justice, I would do anything. And my uncle knew that.

"Just tell me the time and place," I said. I was rewarded by the glint of approval in his eyes.

"This isn't easy for me, either," he admitted. My uncle folded his hands together, tapping his index fingers against his lips. He sometimes did that when he was concentrating on a particularly difficult problem. "But you don't need to worry about that. Or any of this. I'll eventually ferret out all the magicians involved." Thunder boomed outside in response to the intensity of his feelings.

"I know." There wasn't anything else for me to say. The light had dimmed in the room because of the storm my uncle's anger had summoned, but I was afraid some of the darkness was coming from inside of me, and I didn't want to make it worse. Or lose control again.

"I admit there is a possibility the Taines aren't behind it."

My head jerked up as I gaped at my uncle in shock. "Seriously? I thought they were the ones?" I couldn't even form a coherent sentence.

"They likely are. But we have to be careful about assumptions. They color our perspective and can lead us in the wrong direction. Agents must keep that in mind if they want to find the truth."

Oh. That was what some of my fellow students had called a "teachable moment." Well, I was Armageddon's apprentice. He shared his little nuggets of wisdom with me sometimes. They were always worth jotting down in my own journals.

"Thanks, Uncle Ged."

"Come on, let's shake off this heavy stuff. Your aunt will kill me if the flowers don't get enough sun because I'm irritable."

No matter how much control my uncle had, his stronger moods were always reflected in the surrounding weather. Peony would sometimes tease him into better humor so the gardens would get enough light. Laurus Commodities made the best beeswax products, but the fields of flowers and clover needed to be healthy to attract the bees.

We headed towards the door. I moved to the side so he couldn't come out from behind his desk without knocking into me. His step hesitated to let me pass, but his eyes narrowed. I tried not to smile, but I didn't completely succeed.

As soon as I cleared the desk, my uncle shifted his stance, and before I knew what had happened, he was in front of me. For a tall guy, he sure was light on his feet.

I doubled my pace, trying to catch up, but didn't quite get there before we hit the door. His movements slowed, blocking the exit so it was my turn to wait on him, and I couldn't help it. I laughed.

Sometimes, Armageddon was a bigger brat than I was.

"Sounds intense," Peter said. We were walking along the inside border to my uncle's land, hanging out and catching up on the last week. I could hardly wait for him to return from a short mission to tell him all about my conversation with my uncle the previous afternoon.

"Oh, it was. You know Uncle Ged. He's about as serious as they come." But was he really? A passing thought about the two of us racing each other to see who could get out the door first made my words almost sound like a lie. But the good kind.

"Well, it was about your parents." Peter shifted closer and our arms brushed. Warmth and Light radiated off of him and into me.

"Yeah. But it just occurred to me that Uncle Ged teases me a lot more than anyone else." I didn't say Chas's name, but Peter knew my statement included him.

"I was only five when Ged took me in," he said. "But I can still remember how intimidating he was. Man, he looked like a giant when he pulled me from the wreckage after my parents died. But he was so gentle and kind. I wasn't scared for long. But yes, he acts a little silly when you're around. We noticed that right away when you arrived."

Wincing at the memory of how I fell head over heels in

love with Chas the moment of my arrival at Castle Laurus, I latched onto Peter's statement like a lifeline. "Is that why you guys were always looking at each other? It used to drive me crazy when you would give each other significant looks but never tell me why."

Peter laughed. We veered away from the border and walked into the shade of the trees. There was a small pile of rocks nearby, and we liked to sit there sometimes.

"Pretty much. Although shortly after you arrived, Ged had a talk with us." Peter brushed loose pebbles and twigs and dried leaves from the flattest rock in the pile and then gestured for me to have a seat. "He told us to do what we could to keep you happy and upbeat. He wanted to make sure the dark wouldn't set inside you permanently when you ascended."

During the Ascension Ceremony, a magician's nature was set for good or evil - which we called light and dark. That's when we also brought over the elements we would use to perform magic.

Rectors had always used the elements of Light and Dark, which weren't in common use because they could affect a magician's balance, even after ascension. Our clan balanced between good and evil almost equally with a slight tilt to the side of good. We had to work hard to maintain our place in the light. Our control over the element of Dark gave us the ability to vanquish evil magicians in a way no other family had achieved. The struggle was worth it.

I had been especially vulnerable before my ascension. My parents had just died and I was left alone for days before my uncle arrived. Then I completely humiliated myself in front of all the prominent magicians in the City. Darkness still crept across the edges of my vision every time I thought about it and the competition I faced after.

"Does that mean you guys were looking out for me or manipulating me?" I mused.

Peter tossed a few bits of dried grass into the wind and watched them float to the ground as he answered. "A little of both, don't you think? But if it was necessary in order to save you from the dark, then I say it was justified. And worthwhile."

He looked so serious as his gray eyes stared down into mine. A shaft of sunlight highlighted his face, and I noticed for the first time that there was a ring of green around his pupils. They were really quite beautiful.

My nerves jangled inside of me. "And that's how an Irregular works, right? Doing what's right by any means possible?" I was practical enough to understand their methods, but that didn't mean I always had to like it.

Peter blinked and then shrugged, dusting off his hands as if he had just completed a monumental task. "We have permission to do whatever we judge necessary to get the job done. You ascended on the side of light. Doesn't that justify the silliness and teasing and fun?"

"If that was all you did? I guess so. I mean, as long as none of it was fake." I hated the thought that everyone was only pretending to like me. Or had to force themselves to be nice. I looked away from Peter, turning my body until my back was to him.

"Oh, come on. You know good and well nobody can resist you. You're awesome. I know you know this." Peter's voice dripped with humor and intensity, and the corners of my mouth rose in response. He slipped his hand around my arm and gently tugged until I turned to face him again. "Another reason you'll make such a great agent. You're unstoppable."

"Ha." I heaved a sigh and walked deeper into the woods. We spent a lot of time there, mostly because I wanted to avoid the silent field that used to be full of birds. I still had nightmares about how they disappeared in a moment of anger, which was probably for the best. That way I would always remember the consequences of my loss of control. And maybe stop me from doing worse. "I'm not even sure I'll make a good agent. Uncle Ged enrolled me in the Irregulars to protect me, but I suspect I'll end up being an agent in name only. Think about how many times I lose my temper or get all moody. How can I be an impartial judge when I'm out on assignment? How will I know if I'm doing the right thing or just throwing a tantrum?"

I caught a slight movement out of the corner of my eye and turned my head in time to catch Peter staring up at the sky as if asking his guardians to send him strength. "Oh, please," he snorted. "You need to learn to have more faith in yourself. Besides, are you certain you aren't just scared to face me at practice? Is all this self-doubt really a cover for your chicken-hearted nature?"

Laughter shattered my pensive mood. Yeah, right. I had been taking lessons with Armageddon and Mortem Impii. I was already holding my own when Peter and I faced off. "Dream on," I said. "In fact, I think it's time to show you a few of the dirty tricks I've learned." Peter was offering a way to distract me, and I was happy to take him up on it. It was better than feeling like such a fake.

"Whatever, Rector. We'll see." Peter shifted his weight and suddenly seemed a lot more threatening than before.

"Ha. Nice stance. I'm so super scared now," I said, sarcasm dripping from my voice. "But it's your turn to be the target. So scram, man."

Peter chuckled. Before I could say another word, he was gone.

"Ready and set," I whispered to myself as I prepared to chase him down. "Go."

CHAPTER FIVE
Practice Makes Perfect

I SPENT THE NEXT several hours chasing Peter all over the property. We were careful to stay within the boundaries of the protective spells along the borders of my uncle's land, but that still left a lot of room to work with.

After a few rounds in the forest, Peter shifted gears and stalked me while I was tracing the spell he set off near the castle door. He was playing the role of the enemy, but he probably shouldn't have used a stupid Debilitating-skunk spell where anyone walking out would have to deal with it. It was so childish.

On the other hand, the spell required a minimal amount of magic, making it difficult to trace. Peter also used the element of Light to set it off, which was harder for me to track because my affinity was for Dark. It was doubtful any of our enemies would use Light against me since I was a light magician. Nobody knew how Rector magic worked and would never think to use Light when trying to battle against me. But the Rectors were renowned for our ability to control dark magicians, and at some point, one of them might be desperate enough to try it.

In fact, it was almost guaranteed that Chas Taine's family would do that considering they infused many of their spells with Light.

A bolt of pain ripped through me. I really wished I hadn't gone there. Thinking about Chas, even peripherally, still hurt.

Shaking off my sadness and frustration with effort, I dug in deep and managed to spot the tiny thread of a pale, sickly yellow left behind by Peter's spell. I had lost it a while back and wondered if I went the wrong way. Tracing spells was finicky work, but Peter was talented and knew my magic well enough to trick me. It was a real pain. But also kind of fun.

Call me crazy, but I liked challenges.

I skirted the trees until the spell trace led me into the woods. There was a small stream nearby and tons of hiding places. I sensed that spot would be a great place to ambush an enemy so I slapped on a spell to make my skin impervious.

Just in the nick of time. Peter launched a surprise attack using his Air element to blast me with water, creating a miniature hurricane to douse me. I got soaking wet. I should have shielded my clothes, too. But at least the spell helped me stay on my feet.

If a magician successfully found the source of a spell and nullified it, the next course of action was almost always a fight. Sometimes they tried using mechanical magic and

45

threw crystals, or it got physical. And since I was a small female, most attackers would use brute force. Once Peter broke my spell, he played that out.

I should have been paying better attention to my surroundings. My mind had wandered, wondering if one of the indirect magic books I had been reading before I connected to my active magic contained a trick I could use against Peter. Most of the ancient texts had entire sections on counterspells. I still spent a lot of time studying them, hoping to make up for lost time.

Peter swung his leg around and swept my feet out from under me. I snapped out of my reverie as I fell. Hard.

He let out a shout of triumph as he knocked me to the ground. Recalling Mort's techniques well, I rolled my body over to the side, trying to avoid Peter landing on me when he followed up with several of the tricky moves Mort especially liked. He had trained Peter, too.

My best friend was a better fighter than people gave him credit for. Since Peter's magic was ultimately controlled by his artistic abilities, he usually stood back from the center of the battles so he had time to draw the marks that triggered his spells. Most magicians thought that meant he was weak because the strongest fighters were always positioned in front. To their detriment. Peter kicked butt.

"Oof," I said eloquently.

Before I could roll any further, Peter was on me, pushing my arms down and holding them against the ground above my head. Since I was still learning, and training to take out some potentially nasty characters, every practice session I had ultimately led to a fight to the death. Neither one of us held back.

I brought my head up, trying to smash it into Peter's face, but he was ready for that. It was a pretty basic move. But I really did it to use his dodge, which lightened the pressure on my arms, to free one of my hands and press it against his chest. I dimmed the strength so I wouldn't actually incapacitate him, but the bolt of power I zapped him with was enough to throw Peter onto his back and knock the breath right out of him.

I climbed to my feet and then pounced on top of him, using gravity to drive my knee down into his solar plexus. Peter couldn't recover quick enough to dodge the invisible ties I conjured to wrap around his wrists. I also used them to muffle his magic. All I had to do was to keep out of physical range.

Of course, Peter never gave up. He rolled to his side and knocked me down with his feet. Again.

My head slammed into the ground, knocking me for a loop, turning everything watery and wavy. Peter hurtled himself onto my abdomen, his elbow digging into my ribs as he swung his tied wrists up and then back down again, hitting me in the face.

We were practicing, so he barely touched me. But we both acknowledged it as a win. A hit like that from an enemy would have knocked me out. I was going to tell him he did a good job, too, as soon as the world stopped spinning.

"Are you all right?" he asked.

I wasn't sure if I formed any coherent words when I answered him. Luckily for me, when the game was up, I let my spells drop, and that allowed him to shake off the wrist ties keeping his hands bound. Peter moved his arm and my head suddenly cleared. He must have drawn a mark straight into the mud to work magic.

"Smelling-salts?" I asked, trying to identify the spell.

"Yeah. Are you okay?" Peter pushed himself up so his weight was no longer shoving me into the softened earth near the edge of the stream.

"I am now. Hold still a second," I said. I placed a hand against his chest and the other into the ground and then pulled a flow of magic out of the Earth, through myself, and into him. It not only healed what I suspected was a mild concussion from my fall, but it also steadied his heartbeat, which was off rhythm because of my earlier power burst attack.

"Okay, that's a nifty trick. I wish I had a better connection to Earth," he said.

Magicians could learn to use any element, but most of them only had a strong affinity for one or two. Those were the only ones they carried over with them in their Ascension Ceremony. After that point, they never used the other elements.

"Do you think you can develop an affinity for Earth now that your magic has been set?" I asked. Our ascension solidified our magic and the amount of light and dark within, but I wondered if it really stopped us from developing our powers in other ways.

"I don't know. I've never thought about that before." Peter stood, then leaned over to help me off the ground. "Have you seen something in your books that would indicate we can?"

I used a tiny surge of magic to pull the water and dirt out of my clothing and returned them to their place in nature. It was only polite to respect the elements, but it also meant that I was no longer wet and dirty. "I think so. Some of my studies are a blur from when I was cramming so hard, but I'm going back and rereading most of the books. They're so fascinating. When I come across the information again, I'll let you know."

I flicked my fingers and pulled the dirt and water from Peter's clothes as well. He had leaves in his hair, so I stirred up the wind and blew them away.

"Thanks," he said. He then reached out with his sleeve tugged over his hand and brushed it against my cheek. I guess I didn't get all the dirt after all. "You ready?"

"Yeah," I said, grinning like a fool. "That was awesome. Except I need to ask Mort to train me how to dodge your evil feet."

Peter laughed. He held out his hand, and I placed mine in his. It was a habit we had fallen into while working with magic, and I liked it. Touch made me feel more connected to the people around me even when I wasn't performing spells. I had been so isolated before my parents died that I appreciated every hint of connection I could get.

He tugged and the two of us launched towards the castle on a wisp of Air. It was a trick Peter learned when he first apprenticed and was the only display of magic he made without drawing a mark. That gave me the idea we could change his reliance on art for spellwork, but I let that thought go for a later time so I could enjoy being pulled along behind him. I loved practicing with Peter. By the end of our sessions, it always felt like I was flying.

We were hanging out in the kitchen again. It was comfortable and had easy access to snacks. It occurred to me that the cook was never there when I wanted time to myself, but the thought slipped out of my head when I saw the massive stack of cookies Peter had scrounged.

He was on a break between assignments, and I was taking advantage of every moment I could spend with him. There was no telling when he would be sent off again.

"Milk?" he asked. I nodded since my mouth was already full of warm chocolate chip cookie. Peter poured two mugs, sliding the blue one to me before sitting beside me at the small kitchen table. "How are the lessons going, anyway?"

I took a quick sip to wash the cookie down. "Good. Things aren't as frantic as they were before the trials and I'm retaining more. I have so much lost time to make up for it scares me sometimes."

Peter nodded absently as he thought about my answer. He always made this little grimace with his mouth when he was mulling things over, and I could see his crooked bottom tooth. It was kind of cute.

"Ged will catch you up in no time. You'll get your shot at fieldwork soon enough," he reassured me. Except it didn't. Because I was scared to go out into the field. I wasn't remotely ready.

"I'm also still concerned about the investigation into the car accident," I blurted, trying to veer the topic away from my abilities. Or lack thereof. I set the rest of my cookie aside, no longer hungry.

"Why, what's wrong?" Peter put his mug down and rested his hand on my elbow. I closed my eyes and took a deep breath, pulling in the calming influence of Peter's Light through his touch. Another habit we had formed, to my benefit.

"There's just way more to it than hunting down the people who are responsible. Because it's probably the Taines, but they work for others all the time. So now we have to go search out a boatload of leads to see whose idea it was." I was babbling. Anything to avoid what was really preying on my mind.

"Ged will figure it out. He always does. And then he'll take care of them," he said.

Peter was right. It didn't even matter if the Taines worked on behalf of the Council. Armageddon would punish the people who took away my parents. My mother was his sister after all.

I broke my cookie into pieces, then smooshed the crumbs under my finger. That way I wouldn't have to look at Peter when I admitted my weakness. I sighed, deciding I couldn't avoid it any longer. I needed to confide in somebody, and he was my best friend. "It's not just that. I'm upset because I can't control my magic. The darkness keeps overbalancing me."

For any other magician that would be a considerable issue. But for me? Lack of control meant I might destroy the world or something equally awful. It was dangerous to admit it out loud, but Peter had always taken my side. Even against Armageddon, and my uncle was the only father he had ever known. Peter was safe.

"We'll work on that. You're still a new apprentice. You have time to learn control." Peter slipped the cookie plate away from my destructive smashing and handed me a paper towel. I wiped off my fingers, then crumpled it up and tossed it in the trash.

"Maybe. I wish my father were here. He could tell me how to control the Dark better than anyone else in the world. He was born to do it. He made it look easy. I never saw him lose his temper, not once."

Peter slipped off his chair and put the plate and our mugs in the sink after rinsing them out. "Which only means you'll be able to as well. You were born a Rector, too, and you'll conquer the Dark just like all the other Rectors have before you. At the very least, have faith in that. It's in your blood."

He looked so intense. His eyes mesmerized me, fascinated by the hint of green hiding in the gray as they glittered.

"You know what? I think I believe you," I said, bemused by our interaction. Usually, we weren't so serious.

"Of course you do. I'm Peter Makenna. I know everything."

My laughter broke the tension, and I shook my head as we shuffled out of the kitchen. "Right, right. That must be it. You know everything."

We headed in opposite directions, but I thought he said something under his breath. It sounded a little like, "about you." But that didn't make much sense, so I shrugged it off and ran upstairs to my room.

CHAPTER SIX
The Definitely-Not-Lazy Summer

WE WERE EATING LUNCH as a picnic again. It was too gorgeous to remain indoors, and since my uncle and Mort had been roped into another assignment, the rest of us were a lot less formal about our meals. It seemed excessive for the kitchen staff to make a bunch of food for my aunt and two teenagers.

"I can't believe what a beautiful summer this is turning out to be," I said. Armageddon would occasionally fiddle with the weather for us, but in general, he left things alone. And it definitely wasn't all blue skies and sunny days in the Pacific Northwest without him.

I popped an orange slice in my mouth and sighed with contentment. Peter tossed the blade of grass he had been playing with at me. He used his connection to the Air element to guide it over to tickle my nose before releasing it to drop onto the blanket next to me.

We sat under a tree so I could energize both Light

and Dark in the dappled shade the branches cast down. We could see Castle Laurus in the distance, always an interesting sight. Sandy-beige stone formed the walls, the center taller than the wings on each side by at least another story. Sunlight glittered off the glass windows lining the three upper stories, and the angle of light made hazy rainbows shine in the ones on the ground floor. Armageddon transported the small castle along with the stable, barn, armory and various other buildings. There was a moat with a water wheel and bridge, and a ten-foot wall surrounded the entire thing. Who could ever get bored gazing at a fairytale?

I was tired after a long morning of combat training. Peony had taken me in hand and showed me the nifty trick she favored since Mort left with my uncle. I wasn't sore any longer, but only because she healed me as soon as she could. Otherwise, I might not have been able to walk.

She had also given me a bloody nose.

That part was an accident. Neither one of us knew how it happened, but Peony got me good right in the middle of our mock battle. Luckily, she always had a handkerchief on hand, and we stopped my nosebleed from getting all over my fighting clothes. Sure, they were dark and didn't show blood, but it wasn't safe to leave drops uncontained when there was an enemy who wanted you dead. Or a thousand enemies. I didn't know how many were after me, but I was positive it was more than one.

"Is it? I've been too busy to notice the weather," Peter said. He leaned back on his hands, his outstretched legs parallel with mine. We faced opposite directions out of habit. Even though we were still on Laurus land, we kept an eye out for danger anyway.

"Hilarious. It's the laziest and sunniest summer ever, and you know it. Aunt Peony said the world must be on hiatus because outside of routine stuff, Uncle Ged and Mort are the only Irregulars busy." To emphasize my point, I flopped onto my back and folded my hands behind my head. I stared up through the leaves, reveling in the quiet, calm day.

"That's true. This is the first summer I haven't been in some hellhole trying to help people dig their way out of some nightmare or other. Ged asked me to stay near you while he was gone, and I gladly accepted. How was I to know you'd be bigger trouble than the Mongol hordes?"

"Yeah, yeah, and that all started because of a woman, too," I said, referring to Genghis Khan's wife, Borte.

Peter laughed. "I didn't mean it that way, but you know she was a wicked powerful magician. So I just complimented you. You're welcome."

I snorted. I turned towards him on my side, and Peter also shifted position until his head lay near my stomach. We could still keep a lazy eye on our surroundings, but it was easier to talk.

"Okay, fine. Thank you, Peter the Great. You deserve a treat for being so nice and heroic and stuff like that. I know! I'll reward you with the ice cream I smuggle out of the kitchen." I pushed myself up and dragged the basket closer. I murmured a short string of words and the freezing shield I had set around the ice cream dropped. "Here. Chocolate strawberry cinnamon surprise." I handed him the small container.

"What's the surprise?" he asked, eyeing the carton suspiciously as he sat up.

"Oh, don't be such a chicken. You know I've never steered you wrong before." I tossed a spoon at him, which he caught easily.

"Fine." Peter took a bite. "Wow. Caramel. Nice." He ate in earnest while I pulled out another container. I tilted it so he couldn't see it held plain vanilla. I had a reputation for crazy foods to maintain.

"Aunt Peony's going to show me how to handle the family business," I said between spoonfuls. Laurus Commodities would go to my cousins Richard and James, but I was still related through my mother, giving me an heir's claim. But only because I could do the required magic for their spells.

Not that I wanted their company, especially since they would have to die before that happened. Magicians inherited magic from only one side of their bloodline, and I definitely took after my father. But Rectors were versatile, enabling me to manage the Laurus line of spells. It turned out that way sometimes. At least I could help them out and feel like less of a freeloader.

My aunt was practical, so she taught me Laurus spells just in case something happened to my cousins. They were on a long-term assignment so deep undercover there was a real possibility they might disappear. They may be excellent agents, but it could happen to the best. Irregulars were always in danger.

"I thought I saw you near the beehives the other day

when I got back from town. Were you learning to harvest the honey?" Peter licked the extra caramel off his spoon.

"Yeah. The whole process is nuts. But I taught my aunt the spell I found a few months ago to make skin impervious. We didn't need to wear those bulky suits or anything."

"Man, you sure are convenient to have around." Peter grinned. "I'm going to start asking you to solve all my problems. It seems to me your oddball brain has a spell for everything."

I gave him a regal nod, then popped another spoonful of vanilla into my mouth. Heaven. "How did your errands go?" I asked. I wasn't sure what he had been up to. Even if he wasn't on an assignment somewhere else in the world at the moment, he was still doing Irregular business. Sometimes he would discuss his activities, but other times they were a secret. I found that annoying.

"Fine," he answered. Something about his tone and posture, the way his eyes slid away from mine, put me on alert.

"Oh, yeah? Then what's up with the cold shoulder?" I asked. I hated being locked out, and Peter had unconsciously raised shield. My stomach clenched in response, vision growing dim.

"Ah, sorry. I'm used to blocking questions about the Irregulars. You know that," he said. The expression on my face softened his resolve. He set his empty ice cream container aside and heaved a sigh. "Look, it wasn't agent business I was trying to protect you from. I just didn't want to hurt you."

Oh. He must have seen Chas. A familiar bolt of pain

lanced through me. I tossed my ice cream back into the basket and jumped to my feet.

"What was he doing?" I asked as I paced. Since Chas had signed a blood oath, he was forced to do family spells. The Taines walked a fine line between pure darkness and legitimate business. Most of the time, whatever they were doing was shady. The Council left the Taine clan alone because they used their services occasionally. Unpleasant ones, like assassinations. It was sick, and why Armageddon kept a close eye on them, shielding as many Irregulars as he could. The Council could decide one day we were too dangerous and use the Taines to take us out.

In fact, the Council wasn't entirely convinced of my loyalty or the amount of control my uncle had over me. That's why they didn't order the Taines to stop targeting me. Just in case it turned out I wasn't willing to leave the status quo well enough alone, and they were better off with me dead.

"Chas was out to dinner. That's all. Not a big deal."

Peter was trying to reassure me that there hadn't been a confrontation between the two of them, an idea that had obsessed me for weeks. I didn't want him to get hurt by Chas's family. And they could require Chas to do something mean and nasty. I was worried he would break down and turn evil. Oberon was that good at manipulation.

Then I remembered nastiness existed in many forms. "Was Clarissa there?" I asked. I loathed the woman Chas had been Promised to as a child. Their connection had been severed when he was banished by his father, but now that he had returned, part of his deal to save my life had been to start that back up again.

There was no way Peter missed the sound of my voice cracking. So much for acting casual. He stood and reached his arm out to squeeze my shoulder, then shook me a little, ducking his head so he could look me in the eye.

"Yes, she was. His brothers were there, too."

I grimaced. They had tried to kill me both before and during my time in the ring. Darkness clouded the outside edges of my vision. Thinking about Chas hurt.

But it also felt good. If Chas was out to dinner, he wasn't held captive somewhere being tortured. I cared about him. I wanted him to be safe until I could break his blood oath to his father. His needless, worthless, stupid oath.

"Did he look happy?" I asked. Conflicting emotions warred inside me. I wasn't sure if I hoped he was or wished he wasn't. I was still angry he didn't have enough faith in me to believe I could win without his help, but I didn't want him hurting any more than he had to. Chas made his deal with his father to save me. Maybe if I reminded myself of that often enough, it wouldn't make me so angry anymore.

Peter's hand squeezed my shoulder again. "No. He didn't. I know him better than that. He had a smile on his face, but it was for the benefit of the others. When he realized I was there, he couldn't keep it up. He looked away really fast, though. I think he was trying to keep his brothers and Clarissa from following his gaze and noticing me."

The peace of a simple afternoon disappeared. The darkness inside me rose up and the world dimmed. The sun faded, and everything around me was bathed in my own personal twilight. I tried to gain control, but my emotions were in too much turmoil.

Shadows crept along the corners of my eyes, like bugs or rats trying to find the best way to attack me. Just when I thought I figured out the trick to maintaining my equilibrium, something bad happened to prove otherwise. Sometimes the Dark made me sad, other times, angry. There were times I could cling to the Light. Sometimes, the darkness won.

The cloud blinding me was pierced by a tidal wave of Light. It surrounded me, warmed me. Then the veil lifted, and Peter was there, glowing with power. He had his arms around me, his hand cupping the back of my head, murmuring three words into my ear.

His magician's name, Armalucis. Weapon of Light. My new magical name, Praelia Nox. Battles the Night.

Peter was chanting our names to pull me out of the pit. Creating a spell made of Light and the power of our friendship. I couldn't sense his levels like I could with others, but he had almost no darkness within him. Even though the Makennas were an ancient family of evil, Peter was good. My aunt and uncle took him in when his parents died during a battle. He withstood the Dark, rejected it, proving to the world we are more than the circumstances we are born into.

Fortunately, he had enough Light to occasionally give a little to me.

"Thank you," I said. When I leaned into him, he tightened his arms until I almost squeaked. But I needed the contact to keep me from sliding under the Dark again.

I rested my cheek against his chest and snaked my arms around his waist. As I took a deep breath, my nostrils filled with the scent of cinnamon from the ice cream he ate and pine from the trees we hiked through on our way to the picnic spot. I was flooded with happy memories of Eostre, the celebration of the magical new year, when I gave him a sachet made with the same scents. Peter was such a good friend. He steadied me.

When I was ready to stand on my own, our arms dropped. We cleaned up the mess from our meal and packed the blanket and leftovers. I imagined the basket sitting on the side counter in the kitchen and sent it there with a surge of magic.

Peter held out his hand, and I took it gladly. I wanted to go home. I needed to pull myself together before the darkness found its way out again.

When in doubt, I take a nap.

It didn't always work, but I was still riding the high from Peter's infusion of Light, so I wasn't worried I would have any more nightmares. Although, it would be nice if I saw my mother in a dream again. Maybe get a chance to see my father and ask him about guys and their stupid ideas about duty. Or he might have pointers on how to smash through the blood oath Oberon forced on Chas.

I slept right through tea time, but woke early enough to take a shower and wash my hair before supper. I felt grungy from sleeping in the clothes I wore to the picnic, and I needed the heat to chase away the coldness that came with the Dark.

I almost put on a tattered pair of sweat bottoms, but at the last moment decided that I wanted to look nice. Bolster my confidence with a little lip gloss and a cute outfit.

Good thing I did. When I entered the study near the dining room, my aunt had company. Besides Peter, three other men occupied the chairs, and a woman close to my aunt's age leaned against the sofa.

"Lia, dear heart. You look lovely tonight," Peony greeted me by the door. "Come in and meet more of the Irregulars. This is Reginald, one of your uncle's earliest recruits. Reg, this is Lia, our niece." She gave me an approving glance as she took in my outfit. I chalked that up in the win column for the day and my earlier gloom eased.

My aunt's use of our informal names told me we were among friends. Peony knew I wasn't up on the inner workings and politics of the Irregulars yet, and there was always the possibility of a Council spy. Agents often used subtle verbal clues to communicate relevant information in an instant.

I shook Reg's hand firmly. Of the three men, he was the closest to Armageddon's age, although Reg's hair was already completely gray. Restless energy combined with the magic that hummed inside him, making his rich, mahogany skin glow with vitality. His dark brown eyes were kind, and I liked him right away.

Soon after my ascension, a new talent emerged, enabling me to sense the source elements used by other magicians when I touched them. My uncle could do it, too, but we kept the information about our abilities to ourselves since most magicians couldn't. Advantages were more useful if they remained secret.

Reg used Earth and Air, and he tilted to the light side. Probably only a third darkness. Enough to keep him from being employable in law enforcement and security, but the Irregulars had an entirely different set of criteria. Armageddon had welcomed him.

"It's nice to meet you, Reg. You seem familiar. I think I've met you before," I said.

"Yes, it was my pleasure to help with the final practice for your battle in the trials. We didn't have much time to talk."

"That's right," I said, my memory of him solidifying. "You're the one with that wild sandstorm maneuver."

"You got it. I'll show you the trick of it sometime if you'd like," he offered, his white, even teeth showing as he grinned.

I perked up. It would be a good night if I finagled a promise to learn more spells.

"Lia, Reg and the others will be here for a few weeks," my aunt said. "We're supposed to swap skills and information. Ged had planned some assignments, but he's running a little late. We'll start without him, and he can add more when he's back." Peony sounded bright and cheerful as usual, but there was something in her eyes that made me uncomfortable.

"Awesome," I said, shelving my disquiet for later. "So we can work on the sandstorm in the next few days?" Nothing would deter me from learning as many spells and techniques as possible. Not even my uncle's absence. I was his apprentice, but I could still learn from others while he was gone.

"Sure," Reg agreed. "I call it the Sand-stinger."

"Cool." I grinned back at him. Reg was already becoming one of my favorite new people. He had a lot of bright energy inside him, and it made me feel lighter just talking to him.

Peony continued with the introductions, gesturing to the woman. "And this is Reg's wife, Tian," she said.

She was gorgeous, her eyes as close to violet as I had ever seen, curly ebony hair cascading down her back. I could sense through our handshake that Tian wasn't nearly as powerful as Reg, which explained why she wasn't an agent. But there was something interesting about the way the element of her power source, Fire, interacted with the light inside her. I could almost see it glowing in her bright eyes. No wonder Reg was attracted to her. There was so little darkness, it was hard to believe she was real.

My aunt introduced me to the final two men in the room. They were younger, probably in their early twenties. One had dark hair, and the other light, but they were the same height and looked similar enough I could tell they were brothers.

"This is Seth and Harris," Peony said. Seth was the brother with dark hair and eyes. "They're from the Andersson clan."

Ah. That would explain it. The Anderssons took after the Karls or the Nils, the two major families who merged back in the 1200s to form a new clan. Every generation had an even number of children and they were split into groups that looked like one original family or the other. I suspected there was some kind of spell behind that although why they would care how many offspring had light or dark hair was beyond me. The answer would be shrouded by confidential magic. Magicians loved their family secrets.

Seth gave me a smoldering, mysterious gaze. That probably worked for him with most girls, but I thought he looked a little silly and I had a hard time not laughing. When I shook his hand, I could sense he used Fire and Air. He was only about a quarter dark, which was enough to keep him edgy yet render him trustworthy. He could have gotten just about any mainstream magician job, but there had to be more to him for my uncle recruit him. There was a steady hum of strong magic inside him, which could have been the reason, but knowing my uncle's quirky nature, there was likely something else special about him.

As I turned to shake hands with Harris, I heard Tian and Reg stifle a laugh. I glanced their way and caught Tian slipping a coin to her husband. I shot her a curious glance but Tian only winked, so I turned back and greeted Harris, the light-haired brother. His eyes were also lighter than Seth's, a pale blue ringed with gray, and he seemed to think his innate charm was enough because there was no affectation of mystery or smoldering about him.

Water and Earth elements ruled him although it was hard for me to read him at first because he pumped my hand up and down with such exuberance it made my teeth rattle. Finally, he settled down. Despite his difference in personality, Harris had the same amount of darkness in him as his brother.

Reg handed Tian the same coin as I turned back to my aunt. Before I could ask what they were doing, Peony led us to the dining chamber where a massive spread lay on the sideboard. There was probably three times as much food as usual, and I wondered how many cooks worked at the castle. I had only met two, and they were a productive and hard-working couple. But even magicians couldn't pull off something like that without a small army to help.

Peter nudged my arm while we stood behind the guests as they filled their plates. I looked at him with my eyebrow raised in query.

"Don't do it," he whispered.

"Do what?" I had no clue what he was referring to.

"Quit acting innocent with me. I've seen your table manners. You know I meant 'don't swipe anyone's dessert.' Or other tricks."

Oh. That. "Hey now," I said, a little hurt. "You don't think I'm a total barbarian, do you? I can behave. I'd never do that." I let out a huff, honesty overtaking me. "Until I got to know them better."

Peter laughed. I gave him a wink, and since we were at the end of the buffet by that time and nobody was looking, I swiped his caramel tart. Just on principle.

CHAPTER SEVEN
Wobbly Air Net

THE NEXT WEEKEND PASSED in a blur of combat training, studying, and getting to know the visiting agents. I avoided all mention of Chas, which helped. But at night, thoughts of him far away in the clutches of his father, made it difficult to enjoy my summer entirely. If only I could see him, or talk to him. Make sure he was okay. Give him hope.

I didn't get to spend as much time with Reg and his wife Tian as I wanted, but we ate meals together, and I grew to love their humor. I also learned a little about how powerful magicians used their magic when Reg told me about how he created the Sand-stinger spell as promised.

"It's not just about wind and sand," Reg explained. "You've got to keep the individual grains spinning and swirling, so they act like tiny razors. And remember if you draw them together, you turn them into a wall. I connect the spell to me so when I move my arm, the sandstorm mimics my gestures. I tighten my fist, the sand fuses, and boom. No enemy can stand against that kind of hit."

We were using the miniature battle ring inside the moon module. I mulled over Reg's words. My trigger was to imagine something, and that made it happen. I still wore my silver star necklace, which was a charm against accidental use of magic and stifled the amount of power I could use while it hung around my neck. It scared me to take it off even though it felt like I was wearing a muzzle. Did I want to try the new spell without it? A shudder wracked my body. I left it on.

My eyes remained closed as I turned my attention to the sand at my feet. The mound was made of tiny particles, but I imagined each one to be the size of a boulder, attached a thread of magic rooted in the Earth element, and then shrank them back down again. I was worried the grains might actually grow huge and crush Reg and me, but I guess my magic was getting used to my process. Or I was getting better at separating some thoughts from others.

After I cemented the connections in my mind, I gave it a whirl.

The sand spun around in a small circle in front of me, near the ground. I engaged a few more connections, and the tiny tornado doubled in size. Some sand brushed against my leg, and I pushed as best I could to move it away without shoving too hard and letting it go like I usually did with a spell. Holding onto magic too long drained a magician, but the neat thing about spinning bits of sand was that I used Earth and Air elements until it became self-sustaining.

"Damn fine job!" Reg shouted above the sound of the

tornado, which was already taller than he was. I stopped adding to its height and instead expanded its girth. I was sweating like crazy. Maintaining control and contact with that many moving objects made my brain hurt.

But I loved it.

"Run!" I yelled, laughing when Reg took off at top speed. Then I had a revelation about distance. If Reg ran fast enough and I lost sight of him, what good would the Sand-stinger do?

But what if I attached it to him somehow?

I didn't have much time to think it over because he was almost to the ridge of trees lining the swampy area of the practice ring. I created an imaginary bubble out of solidified Air in my mind, leaving holes between the connections like it was a large net, then I compacted the sand particles. I didn't want to suffocate Reg, I wanted to trap him and the sand together. Once it was done, I shoved the Sand-stinger into the Air sphere, forged a thread of brown and blue transparent aura light, and then basically lassoed it around Reg.

The sand followed him as I released my connection. The only tie to me that remained was the usual trace magic left behind, showing which spell was used and the nature of the magician who cast it.

Reg grunted. I ran in the direction where he had disappeared, climbing a little hill. There he was, surrounded by the Sand-stinger, being shredded by the tiny razors of spinning sand crystals.

Or, he would have been, if he didn't have his shield up. He proved he was definitely an Irregular when I saw that he was laughing and shouting with glee at the spell I had just worked. Normal magicians never took delight in the odd twists of spells. They were too conservative.

And maybe scared.

I felt a give in Reg's shield spell. I was keeping an eye out for that because my magic was stronger than his. Once his shield faltered, I essentially popped the bubble of Air I made and the sand flew everywhere as it dissipated.

Just because I was a tidy person - at least, when it came to magic - I swooped up all the sand and returned it to the mound it had formed before we started.

"You did it!" Reg shouted triumphantly as he ran to my side. "I can't believe you kept it together like that, especially once I was out of sight. You've got to tell me how you made that Air bubble that trapped the sand but didn't snuff me out. We could use this spell as a restraint."

"Sure," I said with a sudden attack of shyness. I had never worked with other magicians the way the other kids did. Most of them connected to at least part of their magic earlier than seventeen. But even when they didn't, children of magicians still learned a lot about the practical side of their family's business.

My parents had been so obsessed with finding a way for me to tap into my magic we never had time. Working on spells, and succeeding, was new and awkward.

"Come on," Reg said. "Let's sit down. See if you can walk me through it. I want to follow your magic."

Reg and I walked to a low wall made of cinder blocks, sitting near enough to grasp hands. The best way to generate a magical connection with another magician was to hold on to them.

I concentrated on our connection and pulled Reg's magic as close to mine as I could. It felt a lot like when I used to play with my birthday balloons. I would try to bring my hands together while the balloon was between them without popping it. If I was careful, I could get my fingers to touch before the air pressure inside shoved my hands back apart.

It was wobbly, but I maintained the contact with Reg, who was helping from his side. Once our connection was stable, I formed another Air bubble.

"Ah," Reg said. "It's a net instead of a solid sphere. Interesting. We've always used a fishbowl shape with a lid we occasionally open so our enemies can breathe, but their spells can't break through. The net you made rebounds magic with the aura spreading between the strands of Air. It seems so simple, but none of us thought of it before. This will be more secure, and we won't have to assign an agent to monitor their breathing."

My own breath came out with a whoosh of relief. I dropped our connection at the same time I let the bubble collapse. It was like juggling three live fish that were trying to squirm out of my hands and back into the water. I could manage, but it was messy. And tiring.

The two of us stood and I giggled when Reg gave me a fist-bump. He waggled his fingers, setting off little starbursts of magical light when he did it. I probably would have thought he was the coolest guy ever when I was seven.

Who was I kidding? I thought he was pretty cool at seventeen.

"I'm starving," I said, ready to end the practice session. "Let's see if there's any food set out for tea."

We strolled through the castle together and into the kitchen, which had the closest sink. We both washed our hands and were chatting when Peter came in.

"What are you guys up to?" he asked. He smiled, and I could feel the usual warmth his Light brought into the room.

"Inventing new ways to torture and imprison our enemies," Reg said. It sounded like he was joking, but he was telling the truth. Irregulars were a tough bunch, and humor kept us from getting overwhelmed by the job. At least, that's what my uncle told me. And I believed it. Even practicing to be an agent was stressful.

"Awesome," Peter said. He handed me a towel so I could dry my hands. "You think you can show me that one?"

"Yes. You use Air, too. Who knew that element would turn out to be useful that way?" I asked.

"Right? I always wondered if I should have tried to bring Fire over with me instead."

Most magicians spent a lot of time wondering if they messed things up because they were so young when they set their magic at ascension. There wasn't anything we could do about how much light and dark we had within us once the Ascension Ceremony took place, and it was no use trying to delay to change the balance. The ceremony had to be performed as soon as possible after the Magician reached adulthood and connected to their magic. If we didn't do it, sometimes the magic went wild, and it would eventually drive us insane. Which occasionally happened.

I shoved that terrifying thought aside. The little spark of an idea about developing elemental magic after the ascension was pushed away too. At least for the moment.

"Well, once we've shown the right people, a new crop of magicians may want to explore Air again," Reg said. They had ignored that element for generations. Many magicians never bothered to develop it because it wasn't as fancy as Fire. I wondered why Peter chose Air. Maybe because he didn't care about flash and glitter. Besides, he would never have used Fire no matter what regrets he said he had. Fire killed his parents, and he witnessed it. Nobody would ascend with an element like that even if it were standard for his family bloodline.

We left the kitchen and headed into the study. Aunt Peony told us earlier that she was going to go old school on tea service, and sure enough, when we entered the room, there was a rickety little tea cart with a fancy porcelain teapot and teacups. Fortunately, she also set out tons of food on a couple of the side tables. The second I smelled the thick slices of medium rare roast beef and horseradish sauce, my mouth watered. I was starving.

"How did it go?" Peony asked. I wandered over to where she sat and planted a kiss on her cheek. I was still getting used to casual displays of affection, but it was worth it when I saw how pleased she was.

"Great," Reg said. "I think we've got a new restraint spell worked out. Lia used it when she was practicing the Sand-stinger. We ought to run all our old standby spells by her. A fresh set of eyes could do a lot of good. Get us out of our creative rut."

Peter rested his hand on his chest, pretending to gasp in shock. "Lia," he said. "Have you been turning the world upside down again?"

"Something like that," I answered breezily. "Now shut up and toss me that jar of marmalade. It's three-citrus, and I bet it'll taste great on my sandwich."

Peony stifled a moan of distress when Peter chucked the jam jar at my head, but I deflected it, and it landed gently - with the lid still firmly attached - on the table. I used a dainty silver spoon to slather some onto my beef sandwich, then snagged a few parsley sprigs from the garnish plate and popped those on there too.

"Good Lord, child, what on earth is that?" Reg asked, sounding horrified.

"Oh, ye of little faith," Peter and I said in unison. We laughed, and I cut my huge sandwich into manageable triangles and gave one to Reg to try. He bravely took a bite and looked shocked. And pleased.

"Ha," I said. "Why doesn't anyone believe in me? I rock."

Peter and Reg snorted, but I let that slide. Reg's contented face and the speed his slice of sandwich disappeared was thanks enough.

CHAPTER EIGHT
I Pick Up a Few Tricks

REG AND TIAN BET on everything, continually passing a gold coin between them. When they tallied who won which bet, it always came out even. They never needed more than the one coin.

They placed wagers on events as well as people. Like when I met Seth and Harris. Apparently, they had a bet going as to which of the brothers I would have a crush on. They passed the coin back and forth because they lost since I wasn't interested in either of them. I was too hung up on Chas for that nonsense.

Besides, I didn't like triangles at all. At least, not love triangles. Sandwich triangles were an entirely different matter, of course.

Tian came out to the beehive fields with me and my aunt to learn parts of the business. She and Reg weren't members of what used to be considered the "ruling class," so they didn't have a large family corporation to work for.

Most magicians were like that, actually, since families like mine had cornered the market a long time ago and shut them out. That left them to seek temporary contracts with the larger clans or compete for service jobs.

Tian had an affinity for Light and was good with her hands. She had the skills to help make wax candles and seals, lip balm and soaps, the trademark of Laurus Commodities. My aunt had offered her a job.

"I wasn't sure I would ever find the man meant for me," Tian said as she unlatched one of the hives. "Reg walked into the tavern where I was working back in Ireland, and the second he caught my eye, it was all over. For him. It took another year and a lot of convincing before I realized he was the love of my life." She was so sweet and practically glowed with goodness, but she was also stubborn.

I giggled. It was funny to think about Reg as a young man chasing after Tian.

"Sometimes it isn't love at first sight," Peony agreed. "Love can creep up on you. Before you know it, an anvil drops on your head, and you realize you've been in love for a long time."

I wondered if she was talking about herself. Our conversation made me realize I didn't know as much about my aunt and uncle as I would like. We had been so busy training for the trials it was difficult to find a moment to sit and talk. The same thing happened with me and my parents, only we never had our chance to get closer after I finally tapped into my magic.

"Well, Reg definitely had to whack me over the head good," Tian said with a wry smile. "But I've never regretted leaving with him. My dad was disappointed I was departing the country, but he understood. The whole area had gone downhill and there wasn't much opportunity anymore."

Once the Center of the Universe had moved to San Francisco, the magicians followed, and a lot of small towns in the old countries died out. It made me sad, especially since we could transport ourselves instantaneously anywhere on the planet. Not everybody needed to relocate. But magicians were such power junkies. Status meant everything to some people. Magical high society moved when the Center shifted.

Big magic corporations like mine had to be close to both the center of the universe and government, so we didn't have a choice. My father, Donovan Rector, created a satellite business when we moved so it wouldn't decimate the villages we left behind. They were doing well, the surrounding area a bustling, healthy economy. I felt a surge of pride. He had done a good thing.

"Do you still see him?" Peony asked. I was glad she brought it up. I didn't want to be the one responsible for finding out Tian's dad passed away the hard way. Like right in the middle of a sunny day, collecting honey and beeswax.

"Oh, he finally followed us here," she said to my relief. "He keeps an eye on the house while Reg is on assignment. Dad babysits, too, when I go with Reg. Best nanny in the world."

I envied Tian's closeness with her family. Then I thought about Peony and Armageddon, and Peter. And Mort. And once my cousins got back that winter from deep undercover work, my family circle would expand again. Maybe I wasn't so alone after all.

My aunt saw the smile on my face, and I caught her and Tian exchanging a look. I wasn't sure what they were up to, but I bet I wasn't thinking about what they thought I was. And surely Peony didn't believe the subject of love caused me to reminisce about Chas. Because that didn't bring a smile to my face. Or hers.

The sun dimmed. Clouds moved in to block the light, casting us in shadow. I latched the cover of the hive I was working on and stood up. The day had lost its glow for me, and I wanted to go back inside.

My aunt placed her hand on my arm, pausing my flight. "Lia, are you okay?" She studied me intently. I think she was reading what I was beginning to think of as my darkness-balance meter. I was sure I showed more dark than light to her seer's eyes.

"If you don't mind, I'd like to go up to my room and brood a while," I said. There was no use trying to hide the plunge my heart had just taken.

My aunt touched my cheek as she nodded. I turned to Tian and begged her pardon, then hightailed it out of there. I hated crying in front of people. I think everyone at Castle Laurus had seen it happen three times over by then. But still. I could maintain a little decorum around Tian and the Irregulars.

That would be a refreshing change.

I stomped up the stairs, then closed and locked my bedroom door. I kicked off my work shoes, tossing myself face down on the bed as memories of Chas flooded my mind and pain gouged a hole in my chest.

Love sucks.

I spent more time with the younger agents. Lucky for me, Seth and Harris turned out to be a lot of fun. They helped pull me out of my funky moods.

"Try to get out of that," Harris said. He was swirling a web of Water, pulling it out of the ground to surround me. We were outside behind the storage rooms wandering around before lunch. There was only so much time I could spend moping in my bedroom. I met up with them near the kitchens on my way downstairs, but just a moment passed before Peony and Reg booted us outdoors. I was an apprentice, a new member of the Irregulars, and still under my probationary period, but Harris and Seth were full agents, and it annoyed them to be ejected from the room along with the kid.

The kid, of course, being me.

But once outside, they agreed to exchange spells. The brothers acted like they were offering me some kind of favor, a treat for the newbie. And that was cool as long as they didn't muss my hair and make baby noises. Even though I had put up with worse in the past. Maybe that's why their condescension didn't bother me. That and I figured guys in their early twenties liked to feel they were way more experienced and powerful than a girl of seventeen.

And they were powerful and experienced, considering they were in the Irregulars and just ended their apprenticeships. But my magic and talents boosted me to an even higher level. Which had potential for a little fun.

And I needed a distraction.

I threw up a standard shield between the Water and me. I really hated getting wet when I was wearing jeans. And I hadn't used my battle hairstyle that morning, so my chestnut hair practically floated around my shoulders, the humidity making it frizz. I didn't think of myself as vain, but I couldn't stand looking like a mess on top of being condescended to.

Instead of trying to find a weakness in the Water mesh swirling around me, tightening and getting closer, I simply bolstered the Dark inside me, tapped into its power, and shoved outward.

The web of Water exploded into millions of drops, soaking the brothers.

"Holy cow, Lia. What the hell did you do?" Seth shouted. His eyes were wide with shock. He was also obviously impressed.

"That was freaking awesome!" Harris added. "You've been holding out on us."

I laughed and casually adjusted my blouse. It had hitched up on me when I tugged my elbows in to keep them from getting knocked about by the Water spell and had exposed my belly button.

"I'm sorry. I guess I pushed a little too hard," I said. Excitement coursed through me. I had just used my magic without a cohesive, clear image of the result I wanted inside my head. I sort of leaned into it and then unleashed the power. Like taking a deep breath and then blowing out as hard as I could. It was an extension, only a slight exaggeration, of what I naturally did. Maybe that meant

I could figure out how to use my magic in such a way I could skip my imagination entirely. Or cut that part off. I especially wanted to avoid plunging the planet into darkness because I had a nightmare or was in a bad mood and forgot to put on my star necklace.

"Are you kidding?" Harris asked. "Seth was helping me control the Water spell with Air. You just blew our magic apart, and nobody but Ged has ever done that before." Harris had a look in his eyes that made my cheeks flush.

Seth must have noticed because he stepped in front of his brother and winked. He was trying to connect with me, point out that there was something we felt together, turn my attention to him. An excellent flirting tactic.

I looked away. As far as I was concerned, I was already taken. "That was a cool Water-net. It's not all that different from the Sand-stinger Reg showed me," I said.

"Really? That's interesting." Harris used Earth and Water elements, so anything that had to do with the ground beneath our feet interested him.

"Actually, Reg also uses Air, and it's a big part. I guess you guys could try that together, but I was wondering." I stopped and studied them. They looked open and engaged, which meant they would probably help me experiment. "I know our light and dark factors are set when we ascend but have you thought about working on your elemental magic? I haven't read a thing about it being impossible to expand element use after ascension, and I've come across a few passages in my historical texts that suggest you might be able to develop them at any time. It won't be easy, but I think anything we can do to enhance our arsenal is worth trying."

Seth and Harris exchanged a knowing glance. I wondered if my earnestness seemed comical to them. I cringed inside when I remembered how hard my classmates used to laugh at me when they felt I was taking things too seriously for them.

"You really think that will work?" Seth asked. He didn't look like he was about to mock me. I should have realized that Irregulars wouldn't make fun of somebody else. No, usually agents were the ones who were laughed at. At least, when they were young. We were all a bit quirky. "I've wished a million times I could toss in one or two more elements when working my spells. I'm not sure if it can be done, but I'm willing to try it."

"Same here," Harris interjected. "Which elements do you use?"

"Me? I brought all four of them with me during my ascension," I explained. I left out I also used Light and Dark. They may be fellow agents, but I didn't have to give away all my secrets. "Otherwise, I'd experiment by myself. But since I already have them, I can't see if any of the techniques would work or not. If you don't mind, I can show you some info I've found. Come up with a routine or program or something. If that's okay."

"Cool," Harris said. "I'm on board. I like partnering up with my brother, but if one of us gets knocked out, or we're separated, we can't work some of our spells. It'd be great to do them on our own."

I nodded. Being able to rely on others was a good thing. But having to rely on them was dangerous.

"Ditto," Seth agreed. "But we don't know how long we'll be here. Can we start this afternoon?"

Their quick agreement surprised me, but I was thrilled they were so eager. Some of their efforts might help me delve deeper into the nature of magic. Then I would be able to get into blood magic and see if there was a way to break a blood oath. Just in case Chas wanted out.

What was I thinking? Of course he did. He must be living in hell ever since he had to go back with his father, Oberon. A man who was the absolute worst of the worst. I really hoped I never had to see that man again. At least, not until I pried Chas out of his clutches.

Pushing that thought away, I turned to answer in the affirmative. I was happy to start immediately. Then Peony stuck her head around the back of the building where we were standing.

"There you are!" she called. "Come on in, we're ready for lunch. Sorry about kicking you out. Reg had some highly sensitive information he needed to go over with us. Since Ged and Mort are out, I'm the one they report to. Scary, isn't it? Letting Flighty Peony run the show?"

I shook my head and gave her a quick hug when I reached her side. "People are stupid," I said, trying to reassure her, but Peony just laughed. I should have known the rumors and obnoxious names didn't hurt her feelings.

"Well, I can't disagree with that," she said. "Sometimes, they really are."

We headed into the castle for lunch. As usual, there was a huge spread, and the guys attacked it like they hadn't eaten in a month. I held back and let them at it. My appetite tended to fly away when I thought about Chas.

After a moment of deep depression, I decided to skip the main meal and made myself a sundae instead. My aunt raised her eyebrows at me, but I shrugged and dug in. Sometimes a girl needed ice cream in her life. And chocolate syrup.

And most especially whipped cream.

We were still eating when Mort showed up. I looked behind him for my uncle, but the doorway was empty.

"What happened?" Peony asked in a tense voice. I wasn't scared until I turned and saw the look on her face.

"It's Armageddon," Mort said. "He's gone."

CHAPTER NINE
I'm Ashamed of Myself

I COULDN'T SLEEP. I was too worried about my uncle. Peony and Mort wouldn't talk about what was going on, and I finally stomped off to my bedroom alone. Too bad Peter was on some stupid errand because I could have used a boost of Light.

My poor pillow would never be the same. I kept smacking it around and plumping it, hoping to get comfortable. I should have tried meditation and knocked myself out with a spell, but I was afraid news would come in the night, and I wouldn't be able to wake up and respond when needed.

"Whatever," I said out loud into my dark bedroom. I tossed my beleaguered pillow on the floor and got back up. I traded my pajama bottoms for sweats and pulled a hoodie on over my baggy t-shirt since the corridors were usually a tad chilly. I headed downstairs. I wasn't hungry but a little chamomile-mint tea would do my nerves wonders. I hoped.

I was passing the arboretum in the center of the castle when I noticed there was a patch of darkness that wasn't quite as deep as the rest on the opposite end from the practice dome. There had to be a light source somewhere in there. Curious, I decided to investigate.

Reaching out with my senses, I stepped into the shadows. There was a small light-crystal in use, made by my own company. Rector Enterprises produced so many light crystals they were almost literally a dime a dozen. Because each crystal was infused with my family's spells, it was easy for me to latch onto their magic and find the location. I carefully stayed on the path to avoid trampling the smaller plants. My ears felt weird. Like they were seeking a sound, any sound, to help guide me through my near-blindness.

Then there it was. A sniffle and cough. My aunt's voice was behind it, muffled and stuffy.

"Aunt Peony?" I called softly. I moved further into the garden, and the deeper I went, the fainter the darkness got until particles of light broke through the shadows. Then shapes. A tree. A bench. A crying woman.

"Oh," I breathed, freezing in place. My aunt heard me, but I wanted to give her a chance to pull herself together before I stepped around the lavender and verbena.

"You can come out," Peony said. I slipped over to the bench and sat down beside her. She took my hand and squeezed. "I came out here to be alone and clear my head, but I'm glad you're here."

I carried a handkerchief that belonged to Chas with me everywhere, so I tugged it out of my pocket and handed it to her. She gave me a watery smile and dabbed her eyes. She blew her nose on a tissue she pulled out of her pocket, and even though I was worried about her and loved her, I was still really glad she didn't use my handkerchief for that.

"Can I help you?" I asked.

Peony patted my cheek and shook her head. "No, sweet. And I don't want you to worry. Armageddon has disappeared before. I've been through this a few times." Her voice hitched, and I knew beyond the shadow of a doubt something else had gone wrong. Mort had never looked that worried or exhausted. And my aunt wasn't acting like she had been through this before.

"I can help, you know." Seers rarely received warnings about those close to them. We had to find another way to reach him. I cleared my throat and strengthened my voice. "I have a lot of power just sitting here inside me, waiting to turn me into a hero."

Peony laughed. My heart lifted. "I know you do," she said. "I promise, if I can figure out what to do, I'll be happy to utilize your strength."

"Good." I smiled and folded the handkerchief into a damp square and stuffed it into my pocket after she handed it back. It was polite to keep a handkerchief once offered and then clean and press it before returning it. But my aunt was the one who bought it for Chas and knew I wouldn't want to lose sight of it. I wasn't ready for that yet.

"Speaking of which, how are your lessons with the other agents going?" Peony asked. I could tell she wanted to distract herself from her worries by focusing on me.

"I've learned a lot. I think I'm ready for the next level,"

I answered. But her seer's ears caught the lie in my words.

"What's wrong?" My aunt leaned closer so she could pat my arm to comfort me. And it worked. I even relaxed enough to blurt out the truth.

"I don't think I'll ever be a full agent. I'm always such a mess inside. How can I make choices for everyone else when I can't figure out how to get my life to work right? How can I protect those I love when they don't stay?" Tears burned in my eyes, but I wouldn't let them fall. I wanted to just sit and talk like an adult. So far, I hadn't figured it out.

Peony gave my shoulder an abrupt shake. "None of that from you, sweetheart. You've just started your journey, and negativity can derail your progress. Don't do that to yourself."

"But I make so many mistakes." The lump in my throat grew larger and cut off the rest of what I wanted to say.

"Nobody comes out of their ascension a fully formed magician. That's why we have our apprenticeship years. And nobody has ever lived their life without loss. There's nothing wrong with you, and you can't blame yourself for somebody else's choices. If Chas's love had a flaw, it was his own and not yours. Eventually, you will see that, and it won't hurt anymore. You'll make it through this and come out stronger on the other end."

I leaned into my aunt, resting my head on her shoulder. She didn't have Light to share the way Peter did, but I still felt the same warmth and care, the same lift in my heart. "I wish I were stronger. I wish I knew what to do."

"You'll figure it out. You will discover your plan, for your personal life, and as an agent. We all have a role to play, my dear, even if you have to climb a mountain of pain to get there. And I'm right here, giving you all the love I've got. You will make it. You can do this."

My aunt spoke as if she were repeating a prophesy, with only truth in her words. But how could I believe them? How do I have faith in myself when the guy I loved found it so easy to walk away? When I could damage and destroy with only a thought?

The love coming from Peony was almost tangible, wrapping around me, breaking through the darkness that always sought to drag me down. The moisture in my eyes dried, and I sat back up. I shouldn't get so upset with Chas. She was right. I would find a way. "Do you really think I belong in the Irregulars?"

"Absolutely. I can see it. When the time comes, you're not going to just do your job. You'll be brilliant." My aunt gave me another hug.

That's when I saw the small pile of tissues and two of my uncle's handkerchiefs. They were damp and crumpled in a heap on the bench behind her. Peony must have been alone for a long time, crying silent tears so she wouldn't worry the rest of us.

"Thanks, Aunt Peony." I wasn't sure what else to say.

"We should head inside," my aunt suggested. She shook herself, lifted her chin, and stood. "I should get some sleep. It was after one in the morning when I came in here, and we may need to get up early. You should consider going to bed as well."

Apprentices were under strict guidelines, but since we did so many spells at night, it was hard to make a rule about bedtimes. Peony would never directly tell me what to do. She respected me too much for that, and I reached my majority on my seventeenth birthday, anyway. She wouldn't send me to bed like a child.

I didn't deserve her respect, though. I wasn't a real adult if it hadn't even occurred to me that my aunt would be so upset. I was too busy thinking about myself. How disgusting. "I will. I'll get my tea and then go back upstairs."

"Okay, sweetheart. You have a good night. We'll talk more about this tomorrow." I could hear the faintest hesitation in her breath and realized she was still holding back tears. I nodded and let her go. If I hugged her for too long, she might cry again, and she wouldn't want that. And I might start crying, myself.

Peony pulled out another light-crystal and handed it to me so I wouldn't be left in the dark when she left. She was thoughtful like that, and it came naturally to her. I sighed. I still had so much to learn.

I tossed the crystal into the air and imagined an invisible box around it, then floated it right above my head. The crystal followed suit in real life, and there it hovered as I walked out, lighting my path without me having to hold it. Instead, I stuffed my hands in my pockets and slouched out of the arboretum as I headed into the kitchens.

The lights were on. So much for getting a little quiet time with my tea. Way too many people were awake.

My annoyance melted away when I saw Peter sitting near the table in the middle of the room, of all things eating a teriyaki beef and sprout sandwich with mustard sauce and grilled onions. I recognized it because I had made it earlier. When I lost my appetite, I wrapped it in a cornucopia to keep it exactly the way it was meant to be eaten, with cold, crunchy sprouts and warm beef.

My mouth watered. I was suddenly ravenous. "Welcome back!" I said brightly. I took a step towards Peter, but he held up a hand, and I stopped.

"Don't even think about it, Rector," he said around a mouthful of sandwich. He swallowed and narrowed his eyes. "This is great, I don't care if I stole it, and you can't take the other half."

A laugh burst out of my mouth. My best friend was incorrigible. I reminded myself I really only wanted a light snack with tea and headed over to the sink. Peter scooted the other half of the sandwich towards me despite what he said, but I shook my head to indicate he could have it.

"Where have you been?" I asked. I didn't know if he could tell me all the details but it was worth a try. I peeled a banana and ate it while I filled the teakettle with water, then set it on the wood-burning stove to heat.

"Assignment," he said oh so helpfully. "Here, scoot." I wasn't sure how he finished the sandwich so quickly, but he nudged me aside and washed up in the sink.

I tossed the banana peel into the trash. "Wow, what a gentleman." Peter only winked at me as he dried his hands. He had no shame. I moved around him to check the temperature of the tea water, but he snagged the sleeve of my hoodie, and I stopped.

"Lia, tonight is one of those nights," he said. I immediately turned and gave him a huge hug.

Tension had stiffened his entire body. It was definitely one of those nights. The ones where he can't talk about what just happened. And tried to act like everything was normal, but it wasn't. I tugged on the darkness that was hovering somewhere near his heart, and after absorbing it, he relaxed and stepped back.

"You shouldn't have done that," he said. His eyebrows moved together with concern. "I'm more than capable of handling that little bit of Dark. But you walked in here already off balance."

Peter's worried gray eyes looked into mine. I turned away and checked the tea kettle as an excuse to break eye contact. He knew me too well, especially since we spent so much time together in the infirmary after the Taines attacked us last spring.

"It's fine," I assured him. "I wanted to brood a little anyway, and too much Light would make it a wasted effort. Mort got back tonight."

"And that's bad? Are he and Ged done with their assignment?"

"No, that's the thing. Mort can't find him. Uncle Ged's missing."

"What the hell? Why didn't anyone tell me? Where's Peony? Is she up?" Peter tossed the dish towel aside and started for the door.

"Wait. Peony's exhausted and already went to bed." I sighed. Now I ruined Peter's night on top of everything else. The extra darkness I had siphoned off him swirled around inside me, pressing against my skin. I had to get rid of it before it affected my mood and I started yelling or

92

something.

I pulled the light-crystal Peony handed me out of my pocket. I had made a few just like it in the ring when I was fighting for my company and required to perform a basic Rector spell. Back when Chas had told me the secret to defeating his family's magic. Which gave me an idea.

Tossing the crystal in the air, unnecessary to work magic but quickly becoming my signature move, I broke the light spell on it and shoved as much Dark into it as I could without making it explode.

The kitchen dimmed around us.

"Whoa, Lia, what a trip." Peter's eyes were locked on the crystal.

"Right? But it worked. I don't feel like screaming at you anymore." I grinned and lowered the crystal to rest on the counter out of the way.

"Well, that's a relief. Your fits suck," he said with a lopsided grin on his face. "So fill me in on the details."

We sat together on the chairs by the stove where my water was steaming. "I don't know much," I admitted. "Mort arrived without Uncle Ged and told us he was missing, and then they made us leave. I came across Aunt Peony on my way downstairs and was going to ask her for more details, but she wasn't up to it."

Peter understood that was code for her crying and didn't press me for more information. "Who else was there when Mort arrived?"

"Oh, Reg and Tian are still here. And Harris and Seth."

"I see," Peter said. There was something in his voice that caught my attention. "Are they still courting the lovely

Lia?"

"Whatever." I smacked his arm. Everyone wanted to pair me off. I tried not to resent it. They meant well. They didn't want me to pine away for Chas for forever, but it hadn't been that long. How many months would it take me to get over being betrayed by the love of my life?

More than a couple.

Peter snorted. He walked to the stove and dropped in the tea bags to steep. "Ged's gone missing before," he said.

"That's what Aunt Peony said. It's more than that. She was hiding something. She's scared, for real. I think something bad happened. I'm going to try to get her to tell me about it tomorrow when she wakes up."

One thing I liked the best about Peter was that I could count on him to take me seriously. My aunt and uncle meant well, but they still thought of me as a kid and tried to protect me from everything. Being attacked and almost killed a few times didn't help, of course, but that wasn't my fault. And plenty of grownups get attacked all the time, too.

"I'll go with you. We can tag-team her until she breaks."

"Sounds like a plan," I said, grinning. The crystal pulsated slightly. It had turned a strange muddy gray color with swirls of black mist moving around, trapped inside.

"Can you do something with that? I can barely see," Peter said as he squinted.

He was right. The kitchen light was having a hard time competing with the darkness emanating from the crystal. What would I call that if I made it into a new product? Dark didn't really glow, so was it an Anti-shine? A Lightsucker?

I was never going to be a good CEO.

Picking up a dish towel, I reached over to drop it on the crystal. The room immediately brightened. "Better?" I asked.

"Totally. Now tell me why you were practically stewing in darkness when you walked in. Was it all because of Ged?"

I sighed. I filled two mugs with tea and handed one to Peter after spooning in a bunch of sugar. He definitely had a sweet tooth. And it gave me time to think before answering him.

"That's what started it. I'm really worried about Uncle Ged, and I couldn't get to sleep. It annoyed me when we got kicked out of the room during Mort's report, too. I know I can help. But when I saw Peony crying in the garden, I realized I never even thought about how she was feeling. I was like a selfish little kid, never looking at or seeing somebody else's pain or point of view." I couldn't bear to tell him I didn't think I would make a good agent. He might think less of me.

Peter sighed and set his mug down. "Quit being so hard on yourself. The Irregulars are new to you. There's no way to know what's normal and what's not. And we see some freaky stuff, so not realizing somebody else is dealing with a bunch of drama happens to us all the time."

"Yeah, but she's my aunt and I'm not three years old."

I rinsed my mug and set it in the sink. Peter set his next to mine, and we wandered out of the kitchen. I headed down the hall aimlessly while he loped along beside me. I could tell he was brooding because there was always a tiny pucker in his lips when he was deep in thought.

"You know you're too hard on yourself, don't you?" he asked. He was studying the wristband he was wearing. It looked like one Chas made for us that helped us see in the dark. I still had mine, too, but it was upstairs in a box I kept hidden under my desk in my workshop.

"No, I'm not," I retorted. "I'm furious at myself, and if you were being honest, you'd admit I was a total selfish jerk. If you're my friend, you'll just say that instead of excusing it." I tried not to allow my self-loathing to leak into my gait, but I couldn't help stomping as we walked.

"If that's the case, then fine. You're a selfish jerk. Better?" Peter grinned at me, and I shook my head, my lips quirking up. I had asked for it.

Everyone was always giving me a pass because I had been an official adult for only a few months, but I was better than that. My whole family created a company that had spent hundreds of years trying to help others. Rectors were raised learning how to problem-solve and find creative new ways to fix issues and see to other people's needs. Yet I didn't even think about my aunt once.

As it turned out, shame was something I wasn't all that great at dealing with. "Not really better after all," I said, losing the tiny smile. "I'm sorry for being so grumpy. And I'm really glad you're back, too. Are you going to be here a while?"

We climbed the stairs to the second floor and paused near the window opposite the top step.

"Yeah, I'm done with my assignment. I need to check in with Mort and Peony tomorrow to see what's next but I should be around for a while."

"Good." I leaned against the wall, fiddling with the curtain tassels in my distraction. "You better get with them early, because Mort said he will head out first thing to keep looking for Uncle Ged. I also wanted to work on something with you. I've been going through some of the oldest spell books I've got, and I think you can bridge your magic so you won't have to draw your spells. I know Uncle Ged was working with you on that, but I found something a little different."

"Sure, I'd love to. I need a break, anyway. If there isn't anything urgent pending, I'll ask if I can take a few weeks off and just laze about with you."

"Ha. I will work you like you've never imagined. You might even pick up a few additional elements, too."

"Really now?" Peter asked. He pulled the curtain fabric out of my hand, probably worried I would accidentally pull the whole thing down. I occasionally had issues with stuff like that.

Laughing, I winked at him. Small crystals lit the halls of the castle, but they were dim. Peter could see the gesture, though, because of his bracelet.

I pushed the rest of the memory about the wristband's origins out of my head. I was too tired to allow myself to go down that path again.

"Yes, really," I replied. "Come on, let's go to bed. I've already been up too late, and I want to get an early start. Besides, you look like you're about to fall over. Didn't you get any sleep while in the field?"

"Not for the last couple of days. All right, give me

another hug. I missed you. I was in a cold, dark place and your hugs are always warm and sunny." Peter pulled me close, and I felt a tremor go through him. I had been too focused on myself when he got back to sense that. I gave him an extra squeeze and a burst of warmth. His face dropped to my shoulder, making his voice sound hollow. "I don't know how you keep your darkness from coming through. But thanks."

I kept my darkness under tight control. Always. Making sure none of it leaked out to harm my best friend in the world was the least I could do. Peter leaned back and patted me on the head. So annoying. I growled at him, and he laughed.

"Night, pipsqueak," he said.

"Night, beanpole," I replied.

Peter made me feel better. At least well enough that I could crawl into bed and actually fall asleep. All I had to do was keep the nightmares away.

CHAPTER TEN
I Get Ready

THREE DAYS LATER, AND still no word from Armageddon. Peony lost weight and had bags under her eyes, and I didn't know what to do about it. Or about anything. There was nothing solid to go on. We didn't even know if there was actually anything wrong. It soon became an unwritten rule that we would proceed as normal until we heard otherwise.

And as much as I wanted to focus on my uncle's disappearance, I had other pressing obligations that were worrying me. Armageddon was supposed to escort me to Rector Enterprises so I could check in. The winner of the trials was prohibited from making any changes to the company for three years after the competition, but it was still mine, and certain ceremonial actions needed to be performed.

Not that I didn't want to go. I spent a lot of time at our headquarters when I was growing up, and it was like a second home. My other home, the manor house in San

Francisco, was far too dangerous for me to live in on my own. As an apprentice, I couldn't anyway. But even a visit was out of the question because of the potential danger. Stopping by my company was at least possible.

"Come on," Seth said, distracting me from my thoughts. He was waiting at the bottom of the staircase I always used. "We've got something to show you."

"Yeah? Like what?" I couldn't help being suspicious. Seth and Harris were a couple of real jokers sometimes. I guess their twenty-five percent darkness was the perfect amount to make them mischievous without the occasional flare of cruelty behind most practical jokes.

"That's for me to know and you to find out, little girl," he responded. Seth liked to think he was sexy because nobody could figure him out, but I thought it was annoying. And he wasn't my type, anyway. Being four years his junior and more than a foot shorter put me at a disadvantage that only hard work and a judicious application of charm and sophistication could conquer. If I wanted to. Which, I didn't.

Instead of going to breakfast, I followed him outside. My stomach grumbled, but I ignored it. I kept up an annoyed, bored look on my face. No need to let on that I was wildly curious. That would only encourage his outrageous behavior. But I did want to know what had gotten Seth up that early.

He led me around the castle until we reached the trees. Not that close to the outer border, but I was still on alert for danger. Just in case.

"Oh, my gosh, Seth. When are we ever going to stop

walking? I'm starving!" I said, cringing at the whine in my voice. There was something about his desire to remind me he was older that made me want to act like a little baby around him. I couldn't seem to help myself.

"There you are!" Harris called. We jumped down a low ridge where a small fire was burning in a clearing ringed in rocks. It really wasn't his fault he was standing right where I had spent the best day of my life with Chas.

Darkness dimmed my eyesight, but I tried to ignore it.

"Hey, Harris. What's up?" I asked. If I heard the brittle edge to my voice, so could they. Maybe they would chalk it up to me being crabby in the mornings and not because my heart felt like it had just been squashed.

"We've been working on expanding our elemental magic, as you insisted, Madam Taskmaster. Look what we figured out." Harris cleared his throat. He was actually nervous. I focused as hard as I could on him to stop thinking about what a good kisser Chas was. And butterflies. I didn't want to think about the butterflies Chas had summoned, turning the entire area into a vision of gossamer beauty. It almost killed me to remember.

Harris lifted his hand, and a layer of dirt rose in response. He flicked his fingers and dropped the soil on top of the fire, effectively snuffing it out. He then scooped up a cup he had on the ground next to him and poured water onto the mound to make sure it was fully extinguished.

"Check this out," Seth said, grinning proudly as he pointed to Harris. As if I weren't already looking.

Harris snapped his fingers, and the mud he had made burst into flames. There wasn't any wood for fuel. The water itself was burning.

"Whoa, cool!" I said. "That's awesome! Okay, do it again and show me how."

The two of them laughed. Harris kicked some more dirt onto the fire snuff it again and shook his head.

"It's Seth's turn. You can try to trace that."

I was dying to know how they did it. Not only had Harris used the element of Fire, which he hadn't developed enough to claim at his Ascension Ceremony, but he also caused the opposite element, Water, to generate flames. That was such a trip.

Seth picked up a stone and pointed to another small fire at the edge of the clearing. I could sense it was burning wood as any standard issue fire did. He then tossed the stone towards the fire, where it hovered above the flames. He made a fist and it sprayed water, snuffing them out.

"Wow!" I shouted.

Seth grinned at me and winked. "Did you catch it?" he asked.

"All I sensed was Fire." My forehead wrinkled. "How is that possible? Are you cloaking the Water somehow?"

"Nope. We finally worked it out last night. We can use the elements we selected during our Ascension Ceremony to connect to the other elements. Once we got it to work, we noticed that we couldn't see a signature trace for the new element. So we used Fire to make Water, and nobody can trace the Water."

"That's amazing. Seriously, you guys rocked it." I gave credit where credit was due. It was a fantastic accomplishment. "Okay, tell me how. I need to know."

They laughed again.

"Whatever you say, pipsqueak. Do you mean now, or after we eat?" Seth cocked his head to the side and gave me his quirky, mysterious smile.

Oh, yeah. Food. I was about to tell him to show me when my stomach growled. "How about after?" I suggested.

"Sounds like a plan. Let's go inside before everyone thinks you've been kidnapped and they send out the guards."

I snorted. They probably would, too.

Somebody knocked on my bedroom door. I glanced at the clock on my dresser and knew my aunt had arrived to hustle me along.

"Come in," I called. I was standing inside my closet near the mirror, trying to tug my dress zipper up all the way. I heard her shuffle closer. "Can you help me? This thing is driving me nuts."

"Sure," Peter said as he walked up behind me. I jumped. Wow. I read that completely wrong. I couldn't sense his magic at all, or Peony's, but I assumed she was the one who entered my bedroom. I shook my head slightly to reset my train of thought.

I met Peter's eyes in the mirror as he rested his hand on the small of my back to hold the dress in place. As he tugged the zipper, the warmth emanating from his fingers trailed all the way up until the zipper stopped at my neck. I guess guys weren't totally worthless in the dressing room after all.

Peter smiled as he stepped away, and I turned to face him.

"Thanks. I thought you were Aunt Peony. I was hoping she'd help me pick out shoes. I want everything to be perfect when I go to Rector Enterprises. It's funny, but I can't seem to make any decisions. I didn't even choose this dress. Aunt Peony helped me decide weeks ago, but I just got a whole new batch of shoes shipped here from my house. Now I'm starting to wonder if the ones we picked out earlier are too plain or something." I was babbling. I felt awkward, maybe slightly shy, which was so weird, because it was just Peter. It wasn't like Chas had come back to me and I was awestruck by his gallantry and bravery and dedication.

Peter nudged my arm, and I blinked.

"Earth to Lia. Snap out if it." Peter walked over to the white velvet bench in the center of my closet, more properly called the dressing chamber, and plopped down. He leaned back on one elbow and stretched his legs out, crossing his ankles.

"What are you doing?" I asked.

"Don't be ridiculous. If you're going to agonize over shoes, I'm going to get comfortable. Peony has done this a thousand times, and she takes forever. I can help, though. Go on, grab the top picks and I'll tell you which ones rock it."

I burst out laughing. "Are you kidding me?"

"Nope. I've got style and class, Ms. Rector, and I can prove it. But get a move on because Peony sent me up here to get you to hurry."

Shrugging, I opened the shoe closet, which I thought was hilarious since it was a closet inside my closet. I wasn't sure anyone else would think it was as funny as I did. When

I told Mort about it, he just stared at me like I was crazy.

I was wearing a power suit. Well, power dress. At least, that's what I called it. Within the variegated brown fabric, golden threads were woven throughout glittering and glimmering, and surging with protective magic. I had a pair of low-heeled nude pumps picked out. But now that I had so many more gorgeous shoes to choose from, I was second-guessing my choice. I was at a total loss.

I grabbed three of my favorites and held them out for Peter.

"Oh, heck no Rector. What's up with all the brown and nudes? You're supposed to make a lasting impression, but does it really need to say you're boring and stodgy and can't wait until you're sixty to prove it?"

"What?" I tried to say more, but I was laughing too hard.

"No, no, no. Here, sit." Peter jumped up and placed his hands on my shoulders, turning me around and pushing gently until I was seated on the bench. His behavior bemused me enough to follow along. "Let me handle this. At least your closet has potential."

Peter skimmed the shelves, each lined with light-crystals. Another Rector specialty - closet lighting for the rich and famous. My mother used to laugh when my father grumbled about it, but it helped to pay the bills and made us enough profit that we could match each crystal sold with light and heat-source crystals to donate to the poorer countries around the globe.

"Not bad, Lia. I take it back. You're not stodgy. You're just trying too hard to impress the people who are trying to impress you. They all watched the competition and know what you can do. No need to worry. Ah, here we go." Peter turned to face me, but his hands were hidden.

"What?" I asked again. I guess I wasn't all that eloquent after all.

"Close your eyes and don't peek. I'll put them on so you can get the full effect when you look in the mirror."

My mouth quirked up. Peter was acting silly. But it was distracting me from my nervousness which I was sure was the point. "All right, fine. But hurry in case I need to do more searching if they're lame."

Peter made a face at me, and I closed my eyes, holding out my foot. His hands really were quite warm.

A short while later I had my heels on and stood. They were likely the ones with four-inch heels and if he thought I wanted to tour my company wearing those stilts, he had another thing coming.

Peter positioned me in front of the mirror, and I opened my eyes.

There I was, just like normal. The tight bun in my hair was for the office environment I was about to visit, with a couple of battle braids on one side to denote my status as a working apprentice and agent. My hazel brown eyes glittered with amusement. Peony continually encouraged me to wear browns and golds, and I did it to humor her, but it was funny to see myself wearing it all the time. In the end, I didn't care what I had on, as long as I still looked like myself in there somewhere.

My gaze slipped down to my feet, and I chuckled. It shocked me that my legs looked killer. Four inches of heel and three little straps in varying shades of gold practically glittering on my feet made a huge difference.

"Okay," I said. "That's not half bad. But I'm going on the obligatory official tour, and my feet will kill me by the end of the day." I laughed as the image of me hobbling around while trying to look dignified and capable crossed my mind.

"Wow. You have access to almost infinite power, and you haven't figured out how to walk on Air yet?" Peter asked. That shut me up. Huh. I never thought of that. "Ha! I knew it. You need serious help."

"Fine. Whatever. I don't have time to change them anyway," I said. I wasn't going to admit he had fabulous taste and make his head grow any fatter than it was.

"Sure, sure. Now come on, we've got to meet Peony downstairs for the security briefing."

We couldn't wait any longer for me to take my introductory tour of the company even though I basically grew up there. I used to run through the corridors and hide from the apprentices who all could do something I couldn't figure out how to do myself. Magic, magic, everywhere. But not for me.

The two of us walked carefully while I gripped onto Peter's arm. He steadied me while I kept playing with the Air until I worked out a way to negotiate the action of walking while simultaneously taking pressure off my feet. Not easy. I preferred the way Peter practically flew through the Air, but it would look too juvenile and like I was incapable of walking like an adult. Some capable CEO I was.

Fortunately, by the time we reached the bottom of the

stairs, I finally figured out the knack of it and was ready to walk all day in six-inch stilettos if needed. Not that I owned any shoes that insane. But I was that comfortable.

"It's okay," Peter teased. He was still holding my arm in case I slipped, and gave me a gentle squeeze. "You can just owe me one."

I huffed some air out of my mouth to indicate my disgust at his bragging and then entered the study where my aunt was waiting.

"My dear, you look gorgeous!" Peony rushed to my side. She wore a cherry-red dress with black heels and matching black buttons marching down the front like she was fresh out of some movie made in 1940.

"Nobody will notice me with you around. You're so beautiful," I said, hurrying forward to give her a hug. Ever since I came to live with her and Armageddon, I was a tactile junkie. I held everyone's hands and hugged them every chance I got. My parents loved me, but they were more formal and anyway, I spent a lot of time in different boarding schools. Touch was a new and wonderful way of expressing myself and I had seventeen years of being a solitary little girl to make up for.

"As if anyone will care about an old married woman with somebody as fresh and lovely as you standing beside me. Besides, this is your moment to shine. Speaking of which, I love your shoes."

Peter raised an eyebrow and gave me a look.

"Fine," I said. "I admit it. You've got good taste. Happy now?"

"Definitely." Peter looked around. "Where's everybody

else?"

"Harris and Seth went to check the protection spells on the limo again," Peony answered.

"The limo? Oh my gosh, that's awesome," I said. "I thought we'd have to take Uncle Ged's carriage again. You're not old at all, Aunt Peony, but Uncle Ged is ancient."

She laughed. "My dear, Ged is an old coot. He just hasn't gotten enough gray hairs yet. It's misleading. Besides, I love the limo and never get the chance to take it anywhere." Peony grabbed my hand and tugged me towards the cabinets lining the walls. "Come on, let's find some interesting things to stuff in your pockets."

She opened the doors that hid the Scatter-bursts and Fog-blinders. I took five of each.

The absolute best thing about the fancy dresses created by magicians was they had pockets, and the pockets were deep. Almost bottomless since they expanded inside to hold anything yet remained hidden from the outside.

I didn't really need mechanical spells anymore, but in our line of work, we never knew what would happen. Anyone could use mechanicals, even a mundane, if one was nearby and willing to help. Most ran when they saw a magician was about to have a showdown. Not that I blamed them. It was terrifying to be in the presence of magic with no way to protect yourself.

Mechanicals also couldn't be traced the way spells could be. I popped a couple of Shields into my pockets, too. And some Flash-bangs. I might need time to get away.

"Ready?" Peony asked. Her blue eyes met mine. Something was there, buried inside. I wondered for a moment if she saw something I couldn't. It was entirely possible she did. My aunt was a powerful seer, but seers couldn't reveal their visions until the time came. Whenever that was.

"As ready as I can be," I said. "Let's do this thing."

CHAPTER ELEVEN
Field Trip

PEONY SLIPPED HER ARM through mine as we walked out of the study together. It was just the two of us. I had been so preoccupied I didn't even notice Peter had left while I chose which spells to bring with me. We headed down the hall to the foyer to meet the guys.

Harris and Seth waited in the foyer, leaning against a column right inside the front door of the castle. They were dressed up like Peter had been, and I nodded in appreciation. Nothing brought out the handsome in a guy like a nice suit.

"Wow, Lia. You sure clean up well," Harris said. Seth stayed silent but tried his smoldering look on me again.

My lips twisted with amusement. "Thanks. I bet it isn't nearly as shocking as you two looking presentable for once."

Peony laughed.

"We're ready to go when you are," Peter said as he joined

us. He held his arm out with a formal bow to my aunt, which she accepted. That left me with the brat brothers, but they were surprisingly gracious and escorted me like the gentlemen they were.

I slid into the limo, sitting next to my aunt and Peter, facing forward. Seth and Harris positioned themselves on the seat across from us.

"Are you nervous?" Peony asked. I was, but I didn't want to say that out loud in front of everyone. My various schools had trained me for various social interactions. But this would be new for me. Even though I had known the officers and employees at Rector Enterprises my entire life, becoming CEO at seventeen hadn't been a part of the plan. Ever.

"Maybe a little nervous," I admitted begrudgingly.

"I'd think there was something wrong if you weren't. Focus on the fact they want to see you, are happy for you, and have faith in you. You've got three years as a figurehead to prepare. No big deal, right?"

"Right," I agreed hollowly. I didn't think it would affect me that way, but I was missing my parents more than ever. They spent tons of time on the road, traveling the world and trying to do good for a lot of people. They had also been seeking a way for me to ascend into my magic on my seventeenth birthday. And I was beginning to wonder about that. It only mattered that I ascend on my exact birthday if one special law came into effect because my parents had died. Which they did.

But why did they think that?

Did they know they were going to die?

And why didn't they spend more time with me if they thought they wouldn't be around for long?

A tear leaked out of my left eye. For some reason, I was glad it was on the side where Peter sat. Probably because I suspected he would find a way to discretely wipe it away for me so nobody else would notice. Which he did.

I cleared my throat and smoothed imaginary wrinkles in my skirt. The driver called back, indicating we were about to transport the rest of the journey using the transition spell. I closed my eyes and braced myself, shrinking into the seat.

The world tilted inside my head. It was like suffering from the worst case of car-sickness ever. Right when I was about to throw up, we were there.

Blinking rapidly, I heaved several deep breaths to shake off the effects. Nobody else seemed as bothered by the transition spell. Or maybe they were just better at hiding it.

My gaze drifted to the window, and in the distance stood Rector Enterprises.

When I was little, I loved visiting my father's company. It looked more like a castle than our manor house did, which was basically a rectangular box made of brick. I thought castles were cool. It didn't occur to me back then to marvel at the amount of magic it must have taken to move the group of buildings from the United Kingdom to the hills south of San Francisco in the seventies. When my father was young. Before he had even met my mother.

I had been too young to comprehend the nature of magic on my many visits. But now I had finally ascended and was old enough to understand. I bet every magical family who worked for Rector Enterprises was needed to shift the bulk of a rectory, stables, and a later-period regency mansion from their original resting place to California.

The main building came into view from where it had been hidden by the gentle slope of the nearest hill, grass already brown from the dry summer. A sigh escaped despite bracing myself for the sight. My father had it built years after the move to California. Although he used solid gray cement blocks to match the color of the other buildings, the newer facility was still an eyesore.

Sure, it was huge and modern, innovative and industrial. An acre-sized building with entire walls made of mirrored glass. But it also looked like a giant cement box with weird things sticking out everywhere - satellite dishes and solar panels, a helicopter landing pad and odd cement angles created for decorative purposes.

There was nothing about it that held the charm of the old country. I caught myself once again wondering what on earth my father had been thinking when he approved the design.

With a snort, I fell back on counting my blessings, grateful it didn't have those weird cut-out circles and pod chairs like other buildings from the seventies. Or worse, those terrible green, yellow, and orange accent colors. Oh, my gosh. Or shag carpet.

Nobody said anything, but Seth and Harris both bit back a smile. They were used to seeing companies and magician housing compounds of questionable taste. By comparison, Rector Enterprises really wasn't that bad. At least the colors on the outside of the buildings matched. If the main facility weren't surrounded by so many picturesque buildings, it would have been impressive and intimidating.

That's what I kept telling myself anyway.

The limo pulled up to the gate, and we stepped out of the car while security looked us over and prowled around under the vehicle. The guards were even more thorough than the ones at Castle Laurus, where my uncle had placed so many protection spells it was practically impregnable. But Rector Enterprises had way more strangers coming and going than the castle. When they were done, the sergeant on duty shook my hand and welcomed me back.

Everyone climbed back into the limo and drove to the main building. We entered through the massive front doors, giant sheets of crystalline glass that sparkled and shone. I wondered if the others could tell they were so bright because of their foundation of Dark. None of them look puzzled, or like they realized something might be odd about the spells. I bet Armageddon would have noticed. He could sense the darkness in me in a way nobody else could, and the building spells were no different.

"Ms. Rector, it's wonderful to see you," Caeli Cael said as we entered. Like many Rector employees, she chose to wear the traditional clothing of her culture during ceremonial occasions. That meant she greeted us for my official tour wearing an ice-blue kimono. She wore modern make-up, though. I made a mental note to ask her the trick she used to draw attention to her stunning, dark brown eyes. I used to always ask her for advice. She had grown up working with my father like most of our employees had done and was like an aunt. Her name meant "Starry

Heavens," and she was probably the nicest lady I had ever met. It was wonderful that she was the one who greeted us.

"Thank you. I'm so happy you're here," I returned with warmth in my voice. Caeli used to slip me cookies and tell me I was pretty. My parents had been focused on my education and always said being smart was more important than being pretty. They were right, but I felt being both was better. They thought I was too cheeky and rarely gave me compliments. Somehow, in my mind, being without magic made me think the sight of me was unbearable. Caeli helped me feel that I wasn't the ugly duckling I feared I was.

We shook hands. She was almost all light. I was really not surprised by that.

My little entourage followed along as Caeli took us on a tour of the facility. While I was familiar with every nook and cranny in the place, this was the first time I was responsible for everyone around me. It gave the occasion a sense of gravity I had never felt before.

Things went well. I was also thrilled that I could keep up a constant stream of Air to pad my feet. Not only was I probably more graceful than ever before, but I wasn't even remotely tired by the time the tour was done.

We stopped and had a chat with the men and women in the cafeteria. We sat and talked for quite a while, enough that it was tea time before we left and we shared a light meal. It was an excellent tour, and a nice visit, but I regretted staying so long the moment a guard arrived. He spoke quietly to Caeli as I was clearing my spot at the table. The hairs rose on the back of my neck. I turned slowly, narrowing my eyes at him.

Something was going on. I wish I hadn't eaten that piece of cake with my tea because it roiled around in my stomach in reaction to the tension.

Caeli strode over to where I stood, the empty plate still in my hands. She took it and set it on the table.

"I'm afraid we have visitors," she said. I raised an eyebrow. Our security team wasn't letting just anybody through the gate anymore. Too many unknown enemies.

Peony slid over to stand beside me. I could feel her magic radiating off her as if a ball of fire surrounded her. In fact, red was shooting through her golden aura and it added to the image. "Who is it?"

I guess I should have asked that, but dread had turned the cake into a brick and I was wondering if it was going to make its way back up my throat instead.

"The Council has sent an envoy to inspect the facility," Caeli replied.

Usually, that wouldn't be cause for alarm. Not at Rector Enterprises, anyway. The Council was allowed to send members to any company to inspect working conditions for the employees, a practice that dated back to the late 1350s. After the infamous magician Yersinia Pestis set off the darkest spell ever created and the black plague decimated almost sixty percent of Europe's population.

Workers became important because there were fewer of them. Instead of the terrible bondage of a serf, they became free agents and could negotiate for the first time. Many magical families sought to bind them using wicked, corrupt deals.

The Rectors never had serfs. In fact, the family was large enough back then that we did all the work ourselves. It kept our products in high demand and it was easier to keep our secrets without outsiders to contend with. I thought about Yersinia - and all the people she killed - and shuddered. It was so confusing when something so awful could also be that helpful.

Pushing the thoughts about her out of my head, I concentrated on the present. An inspection by the Council - specifically the division called the Council of Families - meant that at least one of the prominent clans would arrive in my lobby shortly. And I didn't need to be a seer like my aunt to know who it would be.

"The Taines are here, aren't they?" I asked. Anyone with ears could hear the happiness had leached out of my voice.

Peter, who had been sitting across the room with Harris and Seth and chatting up a couple of cute interns, was suddenly by my side. Our arms were touching, warmth and Light emanating from him and into me. The cake in my stomach even lightened and I thought I might make it unscathed out of the nightmare where I had to face Oberon again.

Then Caeli spoke again. "Oberon Taine has arrived with his sons."

Chas. He came to me!

I jerked my eyes to the monitor hanging on the wall. A camera in the lobby broadcast to the different departments and break rooms. Sure enough, Oberon had entered the facility, and behind him stood his sons Adler, Barrett, Keaton, and Titus. I held my breath, waiting, then in walked Chas.

Everything went dark except for him. After several seconds of intense scrutiny, studying every plane and curve of his face, noticing again the stunning combination of golden brown skin and eyes that matched exactly, my vision cleared. I realized Clarissa was also there, hanging all over Chas like the tramp she was. His Promised.

Once again the cake churned in my stomach and vomiting became a very real threat.

"Come on," Peony said. We turned and hurried out the door. Once we were out of sight, we ran up the stairs leading to the promenade to look down into the lobby. I touched the glass, which lined the balcony, and it darkened. We could observe everyone there but they could no longer see us.

"He's brought all his sons," Seth said. "And a cousin. I'm glad it's not Francine. She always makes everything worse. I wonder why they included Clarissa? She isn't known for her skills in battle." He was assessing the group below but didn't know our history. Seth and Harris must have been on Mars when it all went down. I was on the front page of every newspaper, sobbing my heart out on the floor of the arena as I watched Chas betray me. I guess my humiliated grief was poignant or something.

"She doesn't have any useful skills," Harris responded. "Except maybe -"

"Come on," Peter interrupted. "We need to get going. Lia, let's head to the executive president's office so you can greet them." He tugged my hand, hustling me along behind him. I doubt anyone noticed that my feet weren't moving as quickly as the rest of me. I vaguely realized this felt similar to when Peter took me for a ride on Air. A good memory that helped center me for what came next.

I entered my father's office under my own power, dropping Peter's hand as I walked over the threshold. Then I realigned my thinking. It wasn't my father's office. It was mine.

Looking around, I decided what belongings of his I wanted to store away, and in a split second, I tapped into the magic inside me to transport the clutter into an empty shed on the Laurus property. I could keep it there until I was ready to sort through it, including the essential papers about projects my father was working on before he died.

I pictured my aunt's personal workshop, a set of rooms decorated with class and taste. I used that as a pattern as I leaned into my magic hard and created office furniture from thin Air. Nobody had been allowed into the office after my father's death several months prior, so I bolstered my power by using all the dust hiding along the edges of the room. But the element of Dark, all that darkness pouring into me once I saw Chas walk in with Clarissa on his arm, was the real power.

Once finished, I was weak, but giddy, more light than dark at that moment.

"Amazing," Seth said. The way he looked at me made me uncomfortable. He and his brother had powerful magic, too. They looked at Armageddon that way sometimes. I bet if they knew what a mess I had made of everything in my life, they wouldn't be in awe of me. They would probably wonder who I stole all my furniture from.

My gaze slid to Peter to check out his reaction. He looked like he thought Seth and Harris were hilarious and maybe they were. I felt a little better.

Shaking off my discomfort, I looked around, satisfied with the results. My father's office was now cleared of his modern furniture and filled with delicately carved antiques. Or my magical version created with Earth and Dark.

I had created several wide, sturdy chairs, which I gestured for my friends and aunt to use. I fashioned them out of a light-colored wood with large scrolled arms and pleasing smoky-sage leather cushioned seats. I grouped four in front of my desk, offset to my right so when I sat, I could speak to all of them without craning my neck.

A huge desk now dominated the room, decorated with carvings that matched the scrolls on the arms and backs of the chairs. Although I had just created it, the wood looked like it had been well-loved and aged with dignity. I included a blotter and quill set with sealing wax on the desktop. Magicians still used those ancient tools for official contracts. I left out the Blood-capture quills and bottles, though. Maybe I would have to write a blood oath in the future, but there was no way I would give the components of that particular spell a place in my office where I would have to look at them all day.

They reminded me too much of Chas.

Off in a corner, I created a matching table, lovely tea cart, wet bar, and built-in bookshelves where I could meet with others on joint projects. I kept my father's books and only changed the shelves to wood from the modern metal and glass.

That left the smaller, rickety chairs. The wooden legs and backs were carved too, but thinner and the cushions were also pretty scrawny. I stifled a giggle. The Taines wouldn't find anything comfortable about their visit to my office.

"I adore the silver claws on the bottom of the chair legs," Peony said. "I'm really impressed, my dear. I would love to sit with you and have you recreate some for me once we're back to the castle. I like my antiques, but certain pieces get heavy use, and I don't want to damage anything with historical value. These are wonderful and I wouldn't have to worry when Ged gets too enthusiastic when he's presenting me with a new spell." Her fingers skimmed over the silky texture of the arms on her chair.

Her praise filled me with warmth, which helped fight off the darkness threatening to overbalance me again. I was having a hard time maintaining control and kept slipping back into self-doubt. Chas and Clarissa were the focus of my humiliation and pain, but Oberon was the author. He also witnessed the failed Ascension Ceremony. I had fainted in front of everyone, one of my more cringe-worthy moments. And now he was here.

All the worst Taines would be in my office shortly. I cleared my throat and looked around the room again. Something was missing. Empty. Cold.

With a snap, I snatched several of my favorite paintings from Peter's workshop and materialized them on the walls of my new office. Much better. Peter's face lit up, and he smiled his special smile that showed his slightly crooked tooth. I couldn't hide my answering grin. That would teach him for stealing my sandwich without asking permission first.

I stood behind my desk, taking in the results. Not bad. Seth and Harris watched me with admiring eyes. Embarrassed, I focused on Peony instead, who still glowed with pride.

A moment passed. Silence reigned. Then the Taines entered my office. Almost all the people I loved and hated together in one room. Great.

"Ms. Rector, Ms. Laurus," Oberon Taine said as he nodded at my aunt and me. His close-cropped pale blond hair reflected the light emanating from the light-crystals lining the ceiling. I noticed he didn't tack on the customary "nice to see you again." Not like any of us would believe him if he did.

"Oberon," I responded. It was all I could do to remain civil and keep my lip from curling in disgust. "I see you've brought your family. Please, have a seat."

I gestured to the empty chairs on my left and took thinly veiled pleasure in watching them hesitate. The chairs wouldn't collapse, but the Taines didn't know that.

Oberon's oldest sons glared at me, but when I allowed myself a quick glance, Chas wasn't looking at me. The fact he didn't sit would have made me feel better about my trick with the chairs if he hadn't positioned himself to stand right behind Clarissa.

"What can I do for you?" I asked. I wanted to avoid pleasantries if possible. Being polite took too long.

"As per the 1358 Accord, we are here to inspect your premises and interview your workers," Oberon sneered back. Formalities out of the way, he continued with a bite in his tone. "Send for your floor manager, and we will get started."

Right on cue, my floor manager walked through the door, dressed in a smart suit of navy pinstripe, all business with her up-swept red hair interspersed with traditional Scottish battle braids. Iuvo must have headed upstairs as soon as she found out they had entered the building. I wanted to make Oberon's demands seem hasty, as if he were the one who didn't know how things worked. Iuvo's immediate arrival made Oberon look impatient and rude. I knew we scored a hit when his nostrils flared.

"You sent for me, madam?" Iuvo asked. She acted like there weren't seven enemies in the room, her moss green eyes focused solely on me. Perfect.

"Yes, thank you for being so prompt. Oberon has stopped by for an inspection. Will you please escort him to the workshops?" I smiled at Iuvo and kept my face carefully turned away from Oberon. I was trying hard not to sneer at him. I didn't want to look as ugly as he did when he acted superior.

Iuvo nodded. Oberon wasn't happy I used his first name when speaking to my floor manager, but once I did, he had no choice but to follow my lead and interact on a less-formal basis.

"Please come with me, Oberon," Iuvo said, her tone unflappable. She had known me since I was three when she first came to work in the central office in the San Francisco area. She had worked for my family her entire life and would perform her job without a flaw. Any mistake she made was cause for a Petition of Redress by the Taines. Nobody wanted to waste time or money on fighting it, especially a professional like her.

Oberon rose and stalked out the door. His oldest sons trailed behind, but Clarissa stayed in her seat with Chas hovering behind her as if he couldn't tear himself away. He still hadn't met my eyes, and it was pissing me off. I wasn't the one who had done anything wrong. Not even close.

"I think I'll tag along," Harris said. He must have taken a hint from my aunt. She was prohibited from going on the tour with Oberon, but Harris and Seth weren't related and could make sure the Taines didn't get handsy with our products or try to set up our employees or leave some nasty spells behind.

Seth and Harris headed out the door together. Peony eyed Peter, and the two of them leaned closer to hold a whispered conversation.

And the entire time I was standing there like an idiot.

"I need to make a few purchases while I'm here," Peony said. She rose, and Peter stood with her. He hesitated, waiting to see if I wanted him to stay. I glanced at Chas, but he was no help. If he wanted to talk, he would give me some kind of sign. Or maybe suggest Clarissa go with my aunt to the store. We gave him plenty of chances. But he did nothing.

"Tell them to put it on my account," I said. I nodded at Peter, glancing back at his chair, showing I wanted him to stay with me. He caught on with no confusion. Neither of us could read minds like Mort, but we still had a connection that worked much the same way. I didn't want to be outnumbered, and Peter always helped me remain calm. I needed him.

Then I turned towards the source of the tension in the room. The one that wasn't me, anyway.

Before I could say anything, Clarissa spoke in that stupid gorgeous voice of hers. "Interesting office," she said.

She ran her finger along the side of the chair near her leg since the rickety chairs didn't have arms. I wanted them to feel like they might fall off. I considered using magic to rock it a tiny bit to knock her off-balance but decided I was above that.

Chas made a noncommittal sound of agreement. A pained grunt, maybe.

Clarissa sneered as she slid her hand into the pocket of the battle vest Chas was wearing and pulled out a handkerchief I recognized. It matched the one I had been carrying around with me ever since he had given it to me.

Then she pretended to wipe dust off her finger, her stupid pert nose wrinkled. "Your staff hasn't done a good job."

What a little snit. There wasn't any dust because I used it all when I worked my spells to create the office furniture. "I'll be sure to tell them how you feel about them," I offered, oh so helpfully. "In fact, I can call them in here if you wish to address them directly."

She should avoid pulling her teeth back that way. It wasn't anywhere near a smile and made her look old. I happily made a mental note so I could cause that look again some time.

"No, no. I would never do such a thing. You may do it

since they seem to know you so well."

It was my turn to grit my teeth. She was right. I was friends with all our staff, both at my company and at home. Some magicians considered that a low-class trait, but not my family. We knew our employees deserved more respect than Clarissa was giving them. As an insult, it lacked credibility. So why did it sting?

I meant what I said when I offered to allow her to talk to them. The staff had bloodlines going back centuries longer than hers and would have no trouble making sure she felt every drop as they put her in her place.

"Of course they do," I said. "Anyone with any knowledge about running a business knows they are only as strong as their lowest ranked employees. Not that the class system exists here. We have far too many nobles on staff to waste our time on false ranking. I know you wouldn't understand, but the major clans prefer to be informal around each other."

Double-whammy. She wasn't nobility, not a part of the old families in any way, and I just told her she never would be. And I got in a good dig about her lack of business sense. Ha.

Chas's head jerked up, but he didn't meet my eyes. Instead, he made a small gesture, patting Clarissa's shoulder gently. Like he was comforting her.

Hey, she started it.

"Would you care to look around?" Peter suggested. "We can check out some of the public areas if all the dust bothers you. We don't want you to be uncomfortable."

He told that lie really well. I couldn't even tell he hated

127

her almost as much as I did, which I knew for a fact he did.

"No, I'll stay here. I'm perfect just as I am."

Oh, please. I rolled my eyes because at that point, nobody was looking at me anymore. Wait. Surely Peter wasn't checking to see if she was as perfect as she said. Right?

My phone buzzed. I pulled it out of my pocket, careful not to accidentally set off the mechanical spells I had stuffed in there. Goodness knows I didn't want the Wizz-bangs to hit the Shields, causing sparks and smoke to shoot out of my dress. How humiliating.

More humiliating than usual.

I cleared the notification, ignoring the email I had just received. I could read it later. I was too upset to pay proper attention, anyway.

What bothered me the most was Chas had his chance. He could have encouraged Clarissa to go for her stupid walk with Peter, and then we could have been alone. But he didn't do it.

The overabundance of Light I felt earlier finally disappeared, and once again I had as much darkness inside of me as I ever did. So, thanks to Chas, I was back to my struggles with the Dark. What a guy.

Suddenly, I was furious. I thought he cared about me. He said he loved me. He said he didn't want to make the oath and leave me, but there he was, all manly and protective of Clarissa. Months of worry turned to anger and pain. What a coward for not looking at me.

Peter noticed the change in my mood. The room may have dimmed a little, or maybe he recognized the look on my face. He backed up a step where Chas wouldn't be able to catch the movement out of the corner of his eyes and shook his head at me.

No, Lia, don't do it.

Whatever. I raised my hand, but before I could do or say anything, Oberon walked back into the room.

"I've seen everything I needed to see," he told me.

I lowered my hand. I honestly wasn't sure what I was about to do, anyway. All I knew was I could feel shadows leaking out of my eyes. Like tears, only more painful.

"I bet you have," I said. I didn't extend my hand for the usual handshake among nobles. I hated that stupid courtesy, and I couldn't handle touching his nasty, Taine-tainted hand. A glance at the monitor in the corner showed me his sons and Iuvo were in the lobby.

"I will send a report to the Council with my concerns." Oberon's lip curled. "You don't have a father, young lady, so let me give you a word of advice. Watch your back. Especially when you can no longer hide on your uncle's land. Come along, Chas. Time to go."

Oberon turned his back on me and walked off. He was taunting me. Chas was so firmly in his father's control that he didn't even try for one moment alone with me even when Oberon wasn't in the room.

As Chas leaped to follow his orders, my fury boiled over. I latched onto the first thought that popped into my head. Oberon turned his back to disrespect me, to show me he believed I was too weak to harm him. The corner of my mouth lifted as an idea came to mind.

I snapped my fingers.

It was like a spell went off, even though I didn't use

any magic. Oberon spun around with his hands in the air, clutching a shield-crystal, and yes, he actually activated it.

"Something wrong, Oberon? Do you need anything else?" I nonchalantly leaned against the edge of my desk. He was afraid of me. I beat him in the competition for Rector Enterprises and even though his emotional warfare was admittedly getting to me, he was still scared of my magic.

Good.

I gave him a big, fat, smug smile. He dropped the shield-crystal back into his pocket and acted like he hadn't activated it. "No. We're done."

"Oh, well. In that case, please have a nice afternoon." I extended my hand to shake his after all. Touching his slimy aura was worth what I did next.

There was no way to deactivate the shield-crystal he set off. Not that quickly. He couldn't pretend it wasn't there when it stopped our hands from touching, either.

But even though it was the best shield on the market, it also happened to be one of mine. Rector Enterprises always made the best.

I grasped Oberon's hand and shook. By rights, I shouldn't have been able to reach through the shield like it didn't exist, but I did it anyway. I broke his spell without hesitation, without a ripple of magic to indicate it took any effort at all. And gave him a little zap.

Check and mate, buddy.

Oberon walked out without another word. Chas followed as if he didn't have a care in the world. As if I wasn't even in the room. That would have gotten to me except I saw how tight his lips were. The anger drained out of me.

Chas sacrificed everything to save me. I tried to remember our separation was painful for him, too, even if he wasn't acting like it. His dad probably pre-planned the entire meeting. Knowing Oberon, he had controlled Chas by threatening to harm to somebody Chas cared about.

I watched as Chas ushered Clarissa out the door. I felt sorry for him. He had to be hurting, too. He had to.

But did he really need to rest his hand on the small of her back like that?

CHAPTER TWELVE
I Want to Know Why

"WHAT DID HE DO?" I asked Seth and Harris. It didn't matter who answered me once we climbed back into the limo as long as I got the scoop.

I sat between my aunt and Peter again. I felt sorry for them. They were getting the brunt of the magic I couldn't stop from leaking. It was like they were sitting next to a live wire that randomly buzzed them.

Zap. The two of them winced. I struggled to reign myself in.

"He didn't go very far," Seth said. "He seemed really interested in the confidential areas, but Iuvo kept him out. She called the employees to us for questioning. He even tried to peek through where the door cracked open. What a busy-body." He shook his head in disgust.

"I wonder why he cares? He can't do that type of magic." I looked at Peony. She had relaxed once I finally stopped my leaks.

Zap.

Well, I was trying. At least I was maintaining control for longer periods.

"I want to know why he came. Why now? What's he up to?" Peony patted my arm, and I smiled weakly in response. I don't think it fooled anyone, though.

"This is the first time Lia's been off castle grounds since the trials," Peter pointed out. "Oberon has probably been waiting for her to leave the boundaries so he could follow her trace. His tour was just an excuse to get at her. And be annoying."

"And show off his control over Chas," Peony added. "I'm sorry, honey, I know that was difficult. It was hard for me, too." My aunt sighed. She and my uncle had taken Chas in when he was fourteen, and they cared about him like he was their own son. Armageddon had saved him from the nightmare of the Taine household, but Chas returned on my behalf.

Supposedly on my behalf.

Even though I sensed sadness in his aura, I also saw a connection between Chas and Clarissa that existed outside the Promise spell for their future marriage. The kind of link that was only forged if he was fine with being promised to her, not fighting it. A bolt of pain wracked through me, but I kept it from zapping my aunt or Peter. I leaned into my aunt's side for comfort and to comfort her. She had to be missing her foster son.

"I wish Oberon would stop being so useful to the Council. Then he could go away," I said. The Council really had no business working with assassins. It was sick. And

133

the Taines were a blight on the planet, even outside those services.

If the Council ever decided to quit using the Taines, they would dispose of them. The whole clan, from Oberon down. I should have felt at least a little guilty about my desire for their destruction, but the darkness inside me only gave a satisfied lurch.

"So what's up with you and Chas?" Harris asked flat out. "There was some serious tension in that room. And a faded trace between you two."

I groaned. I really hated talking about it. "He's an ex. I swear, haven't either of you done a search on me yet? It's all over the Internet." I shifted in my seat, annoyed that I had to explain. How out of touch did a person have to be to miss all the press generated by the competition? It wasn't like people battled to the death to control a magical corporation every day.

"Ah. Well, we've been on the other side of the world for a while. News doesn't travel out into the desert."

"Ha," I said, disgruntled. "Maybe. We used to date. Sort of. But then he got stupid and made an oath with his father. In blood."

Harris let out a low whistle. "That sounds serious. What did he sign?"

I stared up at the roof of the limo and said nothing. I really couldn't deal with it.

"He reinstated the Promised marriage to Clarissa and swore to remain in his father's service for life," Peter explained, coming to my rescue. I closed my eyes and tried not to zap him again by accident. Or on purpose.

There was a brief silence.

"It was to save Lia's life," Peony said. I could tell she didn't want anyone to think ill of Chas. At that moment, I didn't care if they did or not. It was too hard to feel at all.

"Well, that sucks," Seth said. Something about his voice struck me as funny, and I laughed. I looked at him and Harris, grinning like a fool. They really were a lot of fun to be around.

"Totally." I dropped my gaze, smoothing a wrinkle in my skirt. "But I'm trying to get over it," I added.

Peony and Peter looked surprised. I didn't blame them, since I continually ranted about Chas over the last several months, insisting I was on a lifelong quest to free him.

But how he looked, how he acted, the trace between them made me realize Chas didn't want to be saved. At least, not from Clarissa. Sure, he felt terrible about having to leave at the time he did it, and he still hated his father. But after months of separation, Chas was finally near me and he kept putting his hands all over Clarissa.

He didn't look at me because it made him sad. And under his sadness was guilt. And under the guilt was…

Relief.

What a jerk.

Drizzle had blanketed the castle grounds with shiny drops of water, shining like miniature rainbows. Glowing orbs of light coated everything. What a beautiful welcome home. We had transported right outside the gates. After a thorough check, the guards allowed us back onto the grounds. I loved how Castle Laurus looked in the distance.

Grand beams of sunlight burst through the dissipating clouds, highlighting the set of windows on the west side where my bedroom and workshop were located. It filled me with a sense of belonging.

"Do you want some tea?" Peony asked.

Exhaustion sapped my will, but I wanted to spend time with somebody who always, always made me feel confident about myself. And loved. "I would adore some tea. I'm going to change out of these clothes, and I'll meet you in the kitchen," I said.

"How about my private study? It can be just the two of us."

"Perfect," I agreed.

We slid out of the limo while one of the outriders, a woman named Aureum Videte, or Golden Spy, held the door open. She did side jobs for my uncle as well as a standard security rotation. I really admired her. She gave me a smile and a wink. It was nice that so many people at Castle Laurus supported me. I was feeling needy.

Peter gave my arm a squeeze and then took off with Harris and Seth. Knowing them, they were headed to the pool for an evening swim. On a typical day, I would have joined them, but I needed some cozy time.

I ran upstairs to change. I forgot I had the mechanicals in my pockets, so I tossed them into a tray I had set out on the hutch near my bed. I tugged on my ratty pair of teal plaid pajama bottoms and a gray t-shirt with the name of one of my old schools emblazoned across the front. I zipped my hoodie as I hustled back down the stairs. I left my hair alone, not wanting to deal with brushing it out.

The bun was a little tight, but I ignored the discomfort.

My aunt had a beautiful, welcoming study. She had furnished her office with meticulous care, creating a place of beauty that I copied at Rector Enterprises. Her desk was a delicate antique from the 1700s. She also had groupings of chairs for visitors, but none of them were uncomfortable or rickety like the ones I created especially for the Taines.

Her meeting area had a table and chairs that glowed with magic and furniture polish, an embroidery hoop to the side near the bookshelves, and tea cart. I was happy I had matched the right wood tones at my Rector office. My magic was only as good as my imagination. Turns out it was a bonus that I spent years of my life bored out of my mind, whiling away countless hours daydreaming as my parents dragged me from place to place. A required skill when the only way to perform magic was to visualize it first.

"This has been quite a day, hasn't it?" Peony asked. "I'm surprised at how tired I am. All I did was shop while that disgusting man and his sons poked around in another part of the building."

I flopped down on the sage colored upholstered settee near the door to her workshop. "I'm glad it's over." I considered talking to her about Chas and what happened, but I was afraid I would get too emotional. And I wasn't sure how I felt about it yet. I pushed those thoughts away for later. "And I'm glad Seth and Harris were there."

"Oh, me too. I wanted to ask," Peony said, but then hesitated. I looked up from where I was studying my feet, which I had slipped into hot pink fuzzy slippers before coming downstairs. "What do you think about them?"

"The Irresistible Andersson Brothers?" I grinned, picturing Seth's smoldering looks and Harris's straightforward smiles. "What's not to like? Dark, mysterious Seth and bright, charming Harris. Once they stopped acting like I was a little kid, they became downright bearable. Why?"

"Just wondering," she said with a small smile on her lips. She looked away and poured our tea.

Oh. That. My aunt was matchmaking a mere couple of hours after I declared that I was trying to get over Chas.

"They're cute, Aunt Peony, but I'm not interested. Besides, they're troublemakers. They would be a bad influence on me," I added primly.

Peony laughed. I was glad I amused her but also a little annoyed because I meant it. Ever since Reg and Tian began taking bets on which brother I would fall for, it was frustrating to talk to any of the adults. And irritating how right they all thought they were.

"Where's Mort?" I asked. I regretted using his absence as a distraction because the veil in her eyes dropped and I could see that she was sad again. Still sad, I guess, except out in the open thanks to my careless change of subject.

"He went to speak with the Council, then he'll search for a trace leading to Ged."

"Why don't you let me go, too? I bet I could find one. Peter and I have been practicing, and I'm getting pretty good at following traces. Plus, we're family. You know I should be able to find him better than almost anyone else."

"No, absolutely not. Armageddon would have a fit if you left the castle boundaries again. He'll probably be upset we went on your tour today, but it couldn't be helped."

"Finding him is more important than my company," I said. "If I left to visit Rector Enterprises, I should be able to leave for him."

Peony's eyes softened. She set her teacup down and moved over to sit beside me so she could give me a hug. She gave the very best hugs.

"It isn't that dire," she said.

"That you know of," I replied. I didn't want to hurt her by saying it out loud, but my uncle's disappearance could be really, really bad. He may be the strongest magician in centuries, but that didn't mean he was invincible.

"I haven't dreamed about him," she said. "If he were in desperate trouble, he would reach out to me. And he hasn't. There's probably something happening that requires a delicate hand and extra precautions that are keeping him from us."

I had to trust that Peony knew what she was talking about. She had been an Irregular for almost as long as Armageddon. But her statement sounded like a lie to my ears, and I suspected there was more going on than we realized.

"I can do a Blood-of-my-blood spell," I said. "I've read up on that. I don't think it will leave a trace and I don't need to leave the castle to do it."

"Absolutely not," Peony said. She stood up and took our teacups over to the cart. "Those haven't been used in decades. They can connect you to him and then what happens if he's trying to keep his presence a secret? An experienced magic user would see the connection. Even if they weren't sure what it was, they would grow suspicious."

That's when I realized my aunt thought he was in real danger. The kind of danger that meant my spell could get him killed. She knew her statement about it being a delicate matter was a lie once she said it. It happened that way sometimes, with seers. I was starting to wonder if I had some premonition magic myself. Seers can usually tell when somebody is lying, even when that person believed they were telling the truth, which fooled other magical methods for detecting lies. But I could hear a lie, too.

"Okay, I won't," I said truthfully. For the moment. "But I really want to help. I'm not a magic neuter anymore."

Peony's shoulders relaxed. She stopped fiddling with the teacups and turned back. "I know, sweetheart. I just don't think now is the time for that."

I nodded my agreement. If she thought Armageddon was in mortal danger, she would move heaven and earth to find him. All I wanted was to make sure I wasn't left out when that happened.

"Well, then. I'll look in my books and see if there is anything else that might work," I suggested.

"Sounds good. Will you do me a favor? Can you keep this to yourself for now?"

I nodded. She meant that she didn't want me to speculate and rope the guys into helping me figure out how to help without her permission. She knew me too well. That was exactly what I was going to do.

Later.

I headed for the door. There wasn't much time left until supper, so I figured I could swing by the pool and get the guys to wrap it up so they wouldn't be late. Despite everything, I was hungry.

"Lia?" my aunt called. I turned and looked at her. "Sweetheart, I need to hear it."

I sighed. Yes, she definitely knew me too well. "I'll keep it to myself for now," I promised. I didn't put a time limit on it, and she didn't ask. Neither one of us wanted to box me in. Just in case.

Darkness embraced me as I walked down the hall.

CHAPTER THIRTEEN
Breach

ONLY TWO MORE DAYS passed when it happened.

Like I told my aunt, I had been combing through the books that lined my workshop. Besides the Blood-of-my-blood spell, I didn't find anything useful. It soon became an obsession, and I carried most of the ancient tomes with me in my backpack. It was annoying that when I had a flash of insight, I had to drop everything and run upstairs to get the book I needed. I was lugging around pretty much my entire library, although, looking at my backpack, nobody could tell.

Back when the first expansion spell was created for containers like bags, satchels, and pockets, they had only figured out the size and shape differentials. They couldn't figure out the weight. It was great they could fit as much as they wanted into a small space, but it quickly became too heavy to carry and wasn't remotely practical. My uncle's family invented the weightless spell. The Laurus clan then formed a partnership with the Weavers, and they both still made a ton of money from it. Good thing, too, because the upkeep of castles was brutal.

"Give it a rest," Harris called. He was tossing little rocks into the pond. Then he would lift the rock in the air and set it on fire. Air and Fire weren't even his elements, but he was using them regularly. It was so cool we could expand elements that way. And the Air and Fire elements he used were totally untraceable.

Amazing.

"All right, all right. Give me a sec," I said. I stuffed my notepapers into the open book to keep my place and then shoved them into my backpack. "What's so urgent that you can't wait five more minutes, anyway?"

"Are you kidding?" he asked, laughing. "Lia, you told me to wait five minutes over an hour ago!"

Oh, wow. Oops. "Sorry, man. There, see? I'm done. You have my undivided attention. Tell me what you need."

"Er, I don't actually need anything. I'm bored."

I would have been annoyed, but Harris really was charming. "What are you, ten?" I asked, not wanting to give him the wrong idea. "You should have said something - or left." Fortunately, he knew me well enough to recognize my teasing tone.

"Whatever, lady. I'm the guest here. You're totally supposed to cater to me."

I snickered in spite of myself and walked down the slope until I stood next to him, looking up into his eyes. "So what do you want to do?"

"Uh," Harris started. And then stopped. A light flush

spread across his cheeks. He obviously had no idea. I huffed with impatience, but before he was forced to think of something to say, Seth showed up.

"Hey, Peony asked me to come get you. She just got word that Vir Fortis is coming."

I was sure plenty of people felt like a visit from the Mayor of San Francisco was a big deal. But even though I sort of liked him, his personality rubbed me the wrong way. And it was so hard not to laugh every time somebody said his name. It meant "strong man" or "hero," which clashed with his short, rotund form and bald head.

"Fabulous," I said sarcastically. "Well, Harris, there you go. The mayor is a lot of things, but he's not boring."

We hurried back to the castle. Once again, I had to change clothes. It was so annoying. I even grouped together entire outfits and stashed them in my hutch, so I didn't have to spend so much time going in and out of my dressing chamber just to change out of the formal meeting clothes I loathed.

I pulled on a cute skirt in black and buttoned a white blouse over it. I added a formal battle vest in the traditional black and dark blue pattern, indicating my status as an Irregular. Remembering Peter's advice, I chose a pair of strappy, four-inch heels.

I groaned, knowing I couldn't leave my hair down. Fortunately, the mayor would be tied up in security a little longer, so I used a silver clip to sweep my hair up on either side, causing the chestnut locks to cascade down my back in waves. I wore my silver star necklace, as always, and I popped in some silver hoops before dabbing on some tinted lip gloss. I looked in the mirror in my closet to make sure I was presentable. It hummed with magic, but as usual, I didn't have time to investigate why.

A short while later, I joined my aunt and Harris in the entryway.

"Seth's still trying to find his shoe," he said, excusing his brother's tardiness.

I giggled. "Really? Exactly how does one lose a shoe, I wonder?"

"You got me. I bet he'll steal my extra pair of dress shoes so he can come down. We've heard all about the mayor, and Seth can't wait to meet him."

I groaned. The Andersson brothers thought they were hilarious, but I wasn't in the mood for their antics while talking to an important connection. The more political relationships I had, the better. I needed the good graces of the major players in the magical corporate world if I wanted to continue to run a successful business.

Oh, no. This was it. I sounded like I was forty, worrying about my connections. Great.

Sure enough, Seth came down a short time later. He must have borrowed his brother's shoes because he moved like a man with pinched toes. Peter arrived right behind him.

Vir Fortis acted protective and fatherly towards me, and I think somewhere inside his head, he thought of me as his protégé. Which was silly because he barely even remembered I existed until my parents died and I humiliated myself publicly with him standing right next to me. Not my finest moment. But he was the one who announced my win at the trials, which I guess linked us and made him feel partially responsible for my victory.

Whatever. Maybe that meant that he thought Rector Enterprises would continue to be an influential and successful company and he wanted to suck up. The more people who believed that, the more likely it would happen.

Man, I hated acting like such a plastic.

Aureum Videte must have been on guard duty again because she walked through the front door. Dressed in the Laurus family uniform and looking terribly official, her black hair had been styled into neat cornrow braids with threads of gold woven down the length of one, honoring her Golden Spy name. Her dark brown skin almost glowed with strength and vitality. The mayor would eat that up.

"He's coming up the walk," Aureum warned us. "We've got our guys lined up every few feet as an honor guard."

My mouth quirked up at the corner when Vir Fortis entered the castle. His chest was sticking out so far with pride there was a real chance he might burst.

"Potentia, my dear woman, how are you?" he boomed. He greeted my aunt first, which was proper etiquette since she was the lady of the castle and the wife of my guardian. I winced when he continued. "How are things running without your precious husband? I've been worried. I wanted you to know if you need anything, anything at all, you can call on me. You are not alone or helpless. Our families have always watched out for one another, and I don't want you to feel left out in the cold."

Ha. As if Vir Fortis could handle even one-tenth of the magic my aunt could.

Peony stiffened. The mayor was holding her hand in a formal gesture, but I could tell she wanted to yank it away. I could almost feel the annoyance rolling off her.

"You're too kind, Mayor. I thank you for the offer, but I'm sure a man of your stature is too busy to worry about me. I have my niece, and she is all the support I need. Lia, come and say hi to the mayor."

I stepped forward. I didn't blame my aunt for parading me around as a distraction. I had a feeling she was having a hard time not smacking him.

"Mirabilia, how lovely you look," Vir Fortis said. I almost groaned out loud. I hated my formal name. He could have used my magician's name, and out of respect should have, but he wanted to remind us he had known me my entire life and he was a close enough family ally he could take a few personal liberties here and there.

I extended my hand, and he finally let go of my aunt. Lucky her - his damp palm was disgusting. She stepped out of reach, and when I glanced at her, she winked at me.

"Mayor Fortis, it's wonderful to see you again. Won't you join us the sitting room?" I tugged gently and led him to the formal visitation room. Back in the day - say, the eighteenth century - the sitting room was used to greet and spend time with reigning royalty, nobles, and the magical elite. The best part of owning a centuries-old castle was that it never failed to inflate the ego of the self-important visitors when they thought their rear ends were sitting in the same chair as other, more royal rear ends. A stroked ego always helped with negotiations.

Not like we were negotiating anything. Yet.

"Certainly, my dear." Vir Fortis turned towards my aunt and indicated with a nod of his head that he wouldn't need to formally meet our male companions. The guys shifted to the sides of the room and leaned casually against the walls and against the backs of the furniture. I could feel a slight hum of magic as they shielded themselves from the mayor's sight. He wasn't strong enough to notice they were still there, giving them a chance to practice their covert observation skills and stave off boredom. Although I couldn't imagine how watching the mayor yap his head off could be any fun.

Peony and I sat together on the love seat. The two of us sought close proximity, knowing we might need moral support, and it kept us away from the mayor's damp palms.

"Tea?" my aunt asked. At his nod, she poured for him, and then passed me the teacup and saucer. I leaned closer to his chair and handed him the cup. "What can we do for you this afternoon, Mayor Fortis?"

Vir Fortis took a sip of his tea and then sat back like he had all day to spend in our parlor. "You always did make the best tea, Potentia. Thank you. I've come to check on you. Your circumstances have me concerned, and I wanted to ensure you knew you had an ally in these troubling times." Wow, he sure was laying it on thick. "I was sharing my concern with a dear, close friend of mine, and she suggested I visit to help relieve your mind. You know Tenere Gladium, always one to keep an eye on things and look out for the welfare of others."

A nasty shock crawled through my body. Tenere was the head of the Council of Families. She was typically feeling concerned about something, sure, but usually, it was more about power and corruption and less about feelings and tears.

Which caused me to wonder about the mayor's intentions. Since he name-dropped one of the highest-ranked members of magical society, at least politically, he obviously meant business.

"We're managing," my aunt replied vaguely. Caution was always the best choice when you had no idea what a person's motives were.

"And how about this lovely girl's training? Is she able to keep up with her apprenticeship duties despite her master being gone?"

And there it was. He was here to check on me, not make a few pointed and offensive inquiries into how well my aunt was doing. The real question was, did the head of the Council of Families suggest that line of questioning? Was Tenere worried I would go crazy and destroy the world because my uncle was missing in action?

"Lia's progressing beyond our expectations," Peony answered, her tone even and calm. "I'm proud of my niece, as is my husband. There is no gap in her training. As a member of the Irregulars, she has been complying with the strict guidelines and rules. There are several fellow agents on site with us. They are more than enough of a help. You may reassure Tenere we're fine."

Vir Fortis nodded absently as he sipped his tea. He wasn't as outgoing when there wasn't anyone to perform for. Seth grinned at me. At least, not an audience he could see.

"Good. Now, young lady, how have you been? Have your guardians been treating you well?"

Although it was a typical question, even the faintest hint that my uncle or aunt could harm me in any way made me furious. "I'm as well as can be. Aunt Peony and Uncle Ged are the best of relations. I'm grateful for their care and guidance."

The benefit of learning manners was that there were tons of phrases I could fall back on when I wasn't sure what to say. My annoyance would have left me speechless otherwise.

"Indeed." The mayor glanced around the room one more time, his gaze skipping right over the guys as he stood. My aunt and I followed suit. "Thank you, ladies, for such a pleasant visit. I'm very busy, and I'm afraid I can't stay any longer. I will let the Council know you're doing well."

He looked at me sternly. I blinked up at him, widening my eyes just the slightest bit, trying to look innocent and helpless. I mean, sure, I could juggle hundreds of crystals in the air and shatter fire, but that didn't mean I was any match for a big strong man such as himself. I threw my entire being into conveying what I hoped was the right message. *Ignore me. I'm too weak to matter.*

Vir Fortis shifted his gaze away, and I watched as his eyes again skimmed over Peter and Seth, who were leaning against the bookshelves. They were still essentially invisible to the mayor. Not a bad trick. I didn't even know it was possible to hide from a magician that way.

Peony slipped her arm through the mayor's, and they walked out together. I followed as meekly as I could. I caught Peter's look and had to bite my tongue when I saw he was trying not to laugh. Maybe the mayor bought my innocent act, but Peter knew better.

When we reached the door, Vir Fortis once again bowed over my aunt's hand and took his leave.

I wrinkled my nose.

"Don't say it," my aunt warned.

"Fine," I said. "I promise not to mention that smarmy kiss on your hand ever again if you tell me why he acts so weird around you." The mayor was a pompous blowhard, but I had never seen him so distracted and awkward.

Peony sighed. "He courted me before I met your uncle. Or, tried to. I wasn't the least bit interested."

"Oh, man. That's so gross. So while he was here spying for the Council and making sure I wasn't plotting to overthrow them with my evil cohorts, he was also hitting on you?" My voice was shaking.

"That seems to be the case."

I wanted to scream, and laugh, but the look on my aunt's face kept me quiet. Mostly. I did accidentally let out a squeak.

"Exactly," she said. Peony turned and gestured to the guys, who were still hanging back. "You better get her out of her before I decide she isn't too old for a spanking."

Peter cracked up. My aunt had raised him, and he knew she was kidding. I think.

Harris reached me first, so it was his hand that grabbed mine and dragged me down the hall.

"Where are we going?" I asked.

"Not sure yet, but something tells me we can't get there

151

soon enough to satisfy your aunt. Imagine, Vir Fortis was her beau. What wouldn't you do to keep that information out of the tabloids?"

I snorted. He pulled me closer to the back stairs, and I used an extra bit of Air to steady my feet as he led the way.

"I'd die," I said.

"Exactly. Now go get a more practical outfit, and we'll meet the others in the glade on the south side of the property. I'm sure Peony will be grateful if we gave her a chance to live that down."

Laughing as I made my way into my bedroom, I closed the door for privacy. I pulled out one of the outfits in my hutch and changed quickly. I shuddered, thinking about having to change into a dress and corset every time company came like women used to do in the old days.

I tugged on my purple and yellow plaid sneakers and headed back down the stairs. Not that I was really concerned I would bother Peony, or worried that she would lose her temper. I just wanted to give her time alone in the castle. Or as alone as she could get.

Under the hilarity and awkwardness, beneath the rejection and anger she felt at the thinly veiled threat on my life by the Council, my aunt was in pain. And the best thing I could do for her was give her a minute to find her equilibrium. And if she couldn't do it, I would be there. There were magical methods to help somebody achieve inner peace even if it meant I would go back under the dark.

It would be worth it. I loved her that much.

We were standing right outside when the sirens went off. Loud and terrifying, they were the sound of a perimeter

152

breach in a place that had never been breached.

"Run!" Peter shouted. We spun around together and headed straight for the castle at top speed. I had been taking part in safety drills for months and knew its solid walls, infused with magic, were the best defense we had. Peter slammed the doors, and I almost ran into Harris as the four of us jostled in the foyer.

"Where's Peony?" I shouted, my breath hitching as an imaginary knife stabbed me in the side. Too much running, too soon after we ate our picnic lunch.

"She's with Reg and Tian," Seth called. He was right on my heels, taking the stairs two at a time, heading to the guest chambers down the hall from my room.

I burst into my bedroom just as a small explosion rocked the castle door on its hinges. That meant the enemy had to be close. I couldn't believe it. How was it even possible that somebody was attacking Castle Laurus? How did they get through the defenses and onto my uncle's land in the first place?

My backpack leaned against an upholstered chair positioned against the wall near my workshop. I snatched it up as I strode over to my hutch. I shoved the mechanicals I had forgotten about after my trip to Rector Enterprises into the sack and then scooped up some clothes. I didn't have a lot of time, so I grabbed without looking too hard.

The door to my workshop was open, and something about that set off alarm bells in my head. I pulled the iron key out of my wooden trinket box and shut the door, turning it in the centuries-old lock. I dropped it into my backpack then crouched into a fighting stance when I heard pounding feet headed my way. I straightened again when I saw the guys as they raced into my bedroom.

"Let's go, let's go, let's go!" Harris chanted, rushing us towards my closet. I was completely weirded out to see the three of them in my room. The drills were created to get us upstairs and then we were supposed to rendezvous, but I never remembered the next step. My feet seemed to know, though, and I finally recognized the memory charm when my mind cleared.

My closet was the way out, and my mirror was a door.

It was funny how memory spells worked. Magicians hid their escape routes so their enemies could never find them, and the best way for the secret to stay hidden was for us to also forget about them. Especially important for our guests to forget. But when the knowledge was needed, we knew what we had to do and where to go. No wonder my mirror hummed with magic, and I never investigated it. Memory spells protected themselves.

Another loud explosion shook my bedroom door. Seth picked up my backpack from where I dropped it in surprise and gave me a shove towards the closet where Peter was already hiding.

Hiding? No, not hiding. Performing a spell.

Peter said a few words as he stood in front of the mirror in my closet, then fogged it up near the corner with his warm breath. He drew two small marks in the condensation and the entire thing went black. The normally reflective surface turned into a door.

There was no time to ask him questions. What he did, how he did it, none of those things mattered at that moment. We needed to go. Peter jumped to the side, switching positions with Harris and Seth, who had been hovering around me. People running and shouting in the corridor outside my bedchamber drew our attention.

The door burst open as three men in dark brown with ski masks covering their faces forced their way in. Time slowed to a crawl as I took in several things at once.

In the hallway behind the men, Reg was launching spells for all he was worth, although there wasn't any dust or sand around to use. He must have been pulling magic straight from his inner core, which could burn him out. A method only used in the direst of circumstances.

Cold chills ran through me when I realized the object on the ground at his feet was his wife Tian, lying motionless. Instinct took over, and I launched a Shield at the men, shoving them back into the corridor. I chased after them, desperate to save Reg and Tian, but Peter's hand clasped my shoulder and yanked me away. He slammed the door and dragged me back towards the mirror.

"Seal the door," he ordered. He had nothing to write with and couldn't do it himself. I was horrified at what I had just seen, wanted to help, not run. But the compulsion of the memory spell overwhelmed me again. I closed my eyes and imagined a cinder block wall instead of my bedroom door. My eyes snapped open, and there it was, blocking the way.

Peter grabbed my hand and ran with me back into my closet. Harris and Seth were gone, already escaped through the portal. They were the advance guard, the more experienced agents, and wherever we ended up, they would be the ones who sprang any traps.

Peter shoved me through the mirror. A split second later, he followed. We plunged into the darkness together.

CHAPTER FOURTEEN
Blood and Lead

WE WERE STILL ON Armageddon's land. I had assumed we would be somewhere far away, maybe in a desert halfway around the world, but no. Instead, we appeared in the woods near Castle Laurus above an old redwood tree.

I spotted Seth and Harris on my way down, already standing guard. Their stances active and alert but relaxed, which meant no enemies were nearby. Yet. I almost hit the ground before I realized that would be a terrible thing and threw my arms out to break our fall. A giant waft of Air flew up and cushioned us only a foot off away from disaster.

Oof. I should have spaced the particles further apart for a softer landing.

"Great catch," Peter said. He looked like he would throw up, swallowing hard several times. Come to think of it, my stomach felt pretty rocky, too.

"Thanks," I said. "Sorry about the landing."

"It's all good." Peter helped me to my feet. My backpack

had fallen during our descent, and he lifted it from the dirt, shaking off the dust. He slung it over his other shoulder, the one he wasn't already using to carry his.

"Come on," Seth said, jogging to meet us. "There's an Air tunnel leading out. We need to get there quick, it will close up again in five minutes. Permanently. We must be on the other side before it does."

We took off, Seth in the lead and Harris trailing behind to watch our backs. As the junior members of the Irregulars, Peter and I maintained our position between them. Our location was especially important while we were in the field because the way we triggered our magic caused a built-in hesitation. Peter because he had to draw to work magic, and me because I had to picture spells in my head first. More direct agents would always have to surround magicians like us. Another reason to wonder if I was really cut out to be a real agent.

I had no trouble keeping up with the pace, grateful I was outside when the attack came, and I had my tennis shoes on instead of a stupid formal outfit. Remembering it was easier to tour Rector Enterprises in heels when I used Air, I stirred up the dirt at our feet and grasped some in my hand. I used it to anchor my spell, but then turned it into the Air element the new way I had been practicing with Seth and Harris. The spell I created lifted and pushed us all forward faster, yet would leave no trace for our enemy to follow.

It looked like we were about to go over the cliff, but we didn't. Instead, there was an opening in the sky to plunge through, and we did. Right after Harris entered the portal, it snapped shut behind us.

"I don't know why, but I was kind of expecting a slide," I admitted.

We stood clustered together on an Air-bridge. The portal had moved us from Laurus land to another location. A small town loomed in the distance, the four of us higher than the buildings in the distance. High enough to be out of the way of tall buildings, and low enough not to run into any helicopters or airplanes or stuff like that.

"Right?" Peter said, grinning at me. Thankfully, nobody was afraid of heights. Taking a deep breath, I pushed away my anxiety and took my backpack from him, slinging it over my shoulder.

"That was a smooth move, Lia," Seth said. "I'm glad you shoved us forward. It'll leave a trace, but we should be okay now that the portal has closed."

I relaxed my clenched hand and let the dirt I had been clutching sprinkle onto the Air-bridge below our feet. It outlined our path for a short distance. One tiny rock tumbled over the edge, disappearing as it fell towards the ground.

"Not a chance," I said. "I used Earth to work the Air spell and brought it with me."

Harris whistled. "I didn't think of that. It's untraceable if you commune elements," he explained to Peter, who wasn't there when we discovered that little trick. Man, I had been so busy that I hadn't even had time to tell my closest friend about it.

Peter looked impressed. "That's something I need to learn. When we have time. For now, does anyone know what the next stage is? I don't have any other recovered memories to fall back on." He shifted his weight. He didn't go near where the dirt fell off the edge of the path in the air, but my nerves jangled anyway. What if he slipped? What if there was another time limit and the Air-bridge spell ended while we were still there?

"Oh," I said when a memory block suddenly lifted. "That's why I thought there should be a slide. It's because there is one. Come on, we're supposed to go this way." I edged forward and then sat down carefully. "Race you to the bottom!" I shouted, then pushed off.

It was a pretty cool slide. I sensed my uncle's magic in it, and I guess he was getting bored by that time in the escape route plans because the bridge turned into a tube and we spun around and around, like a water slide would, if there were any water. A wild and fun slide that looped us upside down at least three times.

To be fair, Armageddon had to contend with the ebb and flow of magic in the space between where the portal started and where it ended. Swirls and movement of power in an ever-changing magical landscape existed everywhere and nowhere, even in thin air, five stories above the ground. It probably needed most of the loops.

We came to a halt at the end of a side street. I recognized the place from a series of pictures my uncle had shown me during our escape drills, although I never had the chance to go there in person since I was basically locked up on his property twenty-four hours a day.

We were in Leavenworth. Not the prison in the middle of America, the other one. The town closest to

Armageddon's land in the Pacific Northwest.

"Where do we go from here?" I asked. All three of the guys looked tousled, but poor Peter looked almost green.

"There's a safe-house here in town. I know we haven't read you into all our backup plans and escape routes, Lia, but from this point on, we wouldn't need an implanted memory block. This is our normal spy stuff," Peter said.

"Oh, hilarious," I said as I slugged Peter's arm. I told him a while back I was convinced my uncle was a spy when I was a little girl. I never saw him but heard the rumors. That was silly, of course. Armageddon was so much more. But Peter thought it was funny and always joked about us being spies.

Harris and Seth took off in opposite directions to check our surroundings. There wasn't anyone on the street where the slide ended. We had landed in an unpopulated area surrounded by warehouses. My uncle likely chose that as a landing place so we didn't have to worry about attracting attention when we appeared out of nowhere.

Peter stayed close until we reached the main street, a handful of cars passing us by. Harris and Seth joined us, shaking their heads.

Nobody waiting to ambush us.

Peter tugged a memo notepad out of his pocket and flipped it open. He detached a tiny pencil and drew a few quick marks, four lines in a box. "I'm using the Earth left on Lia's hands to generate a You-didn't-see-me. We should be able to make it to the safe-house unnoticed."

Spells like that took very little magic and would be difficult to trace. Especially if I washed off the Earth element once we got where we were going.

We walked silently along the street until we entered the downtown area. People were milling around, going about their day, cars driving up and down the streets. A few young men lounged on a bench talking and joking. Two women with strollers crossed the street to reach the park. Typical activities in a small town.

Peter took the lead. He lived nearby and had visited many times. It was always better to utilize the agent with the best contacts in the area. We headed to a corner coffee shop. A hole-in-the-wall that smelled fantastic, with dark, private corners and cast-iron decorations on creamy beige walls. Almost as if we had walked into a sepia-tone picture. Except with lots of ivy.

I watched as one woman at the counter collected her drink while she checked out Harris. He smiled at her, but before she responded, her eyes glazed and she turned to put a tip in the jar. She forgot we were there thanks to Peter's spell.

We made our way to the back of the shop where a faux fireplace decorated the wall. I almost didn't notice the hum coming from the bricks, but once I did, I realized it was another portal, like the mirror in my closet.

"This way," Peter said. "Come on up."

He placed his palm against the wall, threads of light bursting out, engulfing his hand. After a short pause, a transparent gray shadow floated out and surrounded us. It was a Shadow-veil and would block us from sight. Nobody else would notice when the faux fireplace became a very real door.

Peter entered first. He quickly climbed the stairs spiraling up two more floors until we were on the third floor. The number three was powerful and often used in magic. The triangle, the Trinity, the triquetra. The only odd thing happening at the moment was that the coffee shop was in a one-story building.

Knowing Armageddon, I guess not that strange after all.

Harris and Seth brought up the rear, the brick fireplace closing behind us, sealing us in. When we reached the top of the stairs, we crowded together on a cramped landing and Peter knocked seven times, then after a pause, three more.

The door opened, and a goddess smiled upon us.

"Kamini," Peter said warmly. "What an unexpected pleasure." He leaned forward and gathered a tall, gorgeous woman into his arms and hugged her tight.

My left eyebrow raised all on its own.

"Peter! Come in. Who are your friends?" she asked. Kamini stepped aside and let us pass, then closed the door behind us.

While Peter handled the introductions, I eyeballed her. She had long, lustrous black hair and these deep, soulful brown eyes full of mystery and allure and all the things guys fell all over themselves for when women like that entered a room.

Kamini shook my hand firmly. Her magic came from Fire and Air. Her light side outweighed her darkness ninety percent to ten, so I was positive all those hidden depths were an illusion. No way somebody that good could be that interesting.

I totally wasn't jealous, either. It was just the truth.

Seth was all over her like a fool, too. It was really embarrassing for him. I only hoped I didn't look as appalled as Kamini did when he kissed her cheeks in greeting. It was a perfectly acceptable gesture of courtesy, but nobody did it anymore. Expect old guys, reprobates, and the occasional quirky charmer.

Seth thought he was a quirky charmer, but I knew better. He was definitely a reprobate.

I looked away and took in the safe-house. We stood in the main area of a typical apartment, complete with a little living room, a small kitchen, and a dinky table and chairs crammed into the corner. A massive TV was mounted on the wall, four or five gaming consoles with multiple controllers strewn about nearby. I assumed staying in a safe-house meant you had to lie low and lying low got boring pretty quickly. Even with outdoor privileges like I had at Castle Laurus, it was a drag, but it had to be worse being stuffed into a sardine can with no windows.

Kamini was done enchanting the guys, so she finally turned back to me. "I'm so sorry. You'll want to wash up. I'll show you to the bathroom."

I could have found it myself considering how tiny the place was, but I followed her anyway to look friendly. I stuffed my hands into my pockets. Earth-users always sported dirty fingernails or stained jackets, and magicians understood that. But I was at a disadvantage. There she was, all sweet and ultra light inside, so there was no way she was making me feel that way on purpose. Apparently,

164

my awkwardness was entirely on me - I couldn't resent her for acting superior because she wasn't acting. She genuinely wanted me to be comfortable. Which made me resent her even more.

Oh my gosh, what a nightmare.

I decided to do the only thing I could do. I would overflow with sappy kindness. "Thank you, Kamini. You are so sweet to concern yourself over me. It's been a difficult afternoon, and as silly as this sounds, a small convenience is a huge comfort." What was I saying? I couldn't believe it. I was babbling like a lunatic.

Kamini beamed in response and then held the bathroom door open for me. It was a tight space, and I had to sort of push my way around her. I brushed up against her and accidentally knocked her off balance. Not like it did her any harm. She gracefully righted herself and gave me another comforting smile.

I pondered creating a huge rock to hide under. How mortifying. I was such an ox.

She finally left when I shut the door, not bothering to look up and smile at her again. She had smiled so many times, I could never catch up to that, much less surpass her.

I turned to the sink and washed my hands. A glance in the mirror forced a groan from my lips. There was a smear of dirt on my cheek, a black fleck - probably pepper from my lunch - jammed in my teeth, and my hair was sticking out everywhere from the crazy escape Air-slide. Thanks so much, Armageddon.

If it wasn't his stupid Air-slide, it was his genes that did me in. His hair stuck up all the time, too. Except nobody ever said anything because they were too scared of him.

Too bad I wasn't that intimidating. Or tall. I could have gotten away with more if I had a more imposing presence.

While my internal tantrum ran its course, I washed up, creating a toothbrush and toothpaste using the dirt on my face as the magic source before I cleaned that, too, and then scrubbed my teeth until they sparkled.

I still had my backpack with me, so I took extra time to change. I used the dust and sweat on my dirty clothes to generate cleansing magic and cleaned them on the spot. Nobody ever wrote about things like that in the ancient tomes I had been studying, but I thought it was cool to clean clothing using its own dirt. Maybe I would write my own tome someday and teach future generations all about the magic of hygiene. It could be a companion to the massive codex my aunt created for healing magic.

Get a grip, Lia.

Since Kamini was so beautiful and wore a summer dress, I skipped my casual clothing so I wouldn't look like a slob compared to her. Instead, I put on my Irregulars uniform. I had no idea what was coming next and decided that I could get away with wearing it without looking like I was trying to show off.

The battle vest fit close enough to highlight my curves and chest. Kamini looked like a model. She was a thin, willowy beauty. I would never top that so I enhanced my other assets.

I brushed out my hair and took the time to braid it on one side, looping the dangling end around so it twisted into a ponytail. Eyeballing my reflection, I decided I was

166

presentable enough to join the others.

The guys were squashed together on the couches when I came back into the room. Everything was so cramped, and they were over six feet tall.

"We should contact Peony," Seth was saying. "She may need us to return and help fight." He looked frustrated. The memory charm had directed our feet along the path my uncle created for us, following the directive to get out and get away. It had to be hard on a warrior like Seth to leave the battle behind the way he did. The way they all did.

Because of me.

Armageddon wanted me out of there, protected from my enemies. He made me the priority, but that left my aunt and anyone else in the household vulnerable. And sure, it was his job to play guardian until I reached my final majority. On my twenty-first birthday when my apprenticeship contract ended, I would be an entirely free adult magician. But not yet. I understood.

I felt so guilty, though. "We should contact her at once," I agreed. "I want to help."

Peter was sitting beside Kamini. Of course. But to my relief, he looked concerned and caring like normal instead of star-struck by her beauty. "You know you can't do that," he said. "We have to stay away until Peony communicates with us." Peter stood, and I shifted my weight to lean farther from him, feeling like I needed to distance myself from him despite the tiny apartment. He usually supported me.

"Protocol dictates we wait for contact, not initiate it,"

Harris said with regret. "We must be patient. Peony and Reg are formidable agents. They'll be okay."

I sighed. There was a chair crammed in a corner near the TV. It was the only available place to sit, so I crossed the room and plopped down. "Fine. Let's just stay here and do nothing while my family and home are being destroyed."

Peter and Kamini exchanged a glance. How annoying.

"None of us like this either," Peter replied. "But you'll find that once you've been on assignment a few times the most difficult part of the job is to hold off and judge the right timing."

My eyes narrowed. The darkness inside me expanded. Was my best friend, my champion, my hero, scolding me like a child? And what did that smug Kamini think of me as he did?

I opened my mouth to answer, but I was interrupted by a snapping sound outside indicating something had just transported to the safe-house.

Peter strode over to the door and pulled it open. He should have checked for enemies before doing so, but an envelope lay on the floor instead of an ambush. I guess I would let it pass. No need to embarrass him in front of the others by pointing out his flaws the way he did to me.

"It's from Peony," Peter said as he unsealed the envelope. His eyes rapidly scanned the pages. "Ah. She said the attackers are gone from the castle and the land, but she's concerned they are still nearby. She suggests we make ourselves comfortable and wait a while."

I stifled a groan. Stay in the safe-house with Kamini? Heck no.

"What about Tian?" I asked. The image of her lying at Reg's feet haunted me.

"She's injured, but will be fine. Peony is nursing her until she can be safely moved. She's called in more guards and the other agents but wants us to wait on another message."

Ha. I wasn't going to wait. And those instructions didn't sit well with the others, either. They would probably go along with me if I came up with a plan.

"How did they get in?" Seth asked. "Ged has that place on lockdown. Nobody, magic or mundane, can break through those defenses."

He was right. What happened to all the magic Armageddon had woven into his land over the years? And the walls of Castle Laurus were steeped in enough protective magic they would rise and attack a foe if needed.

Except when they didn't.

"Could be a Drain-flow spell," Harris suggested. "They could tap into the link to his land and use it to pull down the defenses."

"No way," Peter said. He stuffed Peony's message into his pocket. "He's too good for that. He wouldn't let that happen."

"Unless he's hurt and can't defend himself," I said. I finally realized what had been bothering me the whole time ever since my uncle disappeared. No matter how finicky his assignment, how dangerous his circumstances, he would protect his home, first. He was always connected to his family and wouldn't leave us open to attack.

That he left us vulnerable meant he couldn't protect us

anymore.

"Maybe not," Peter said. "It could be any number of things."

I jumped to my feet, unable to sit still while I was so agitated. "It could be, but I doubt it. It's not like he'd be tricked into breaking home-and-hearth magic. You know it. Something has to be wrong. And if we can't go home, we should spend our free time looking for him. I don't feel a prohibition spell against it, do you?"

"No, I don't." Seth stood and walked over to me. "Lia's right. We can't sit here doing nothing when Armageddon might be in trouble. We all owe him way too much to hang around playing video games and napping."

I was glad Seth was on my side. He was the bossier of the Andersson brothers, and sure enough, Harris came to stand by us to support his brother. Not like he was reluctant. I felt nothing but concern and purpose coming from him.

The three of us turned as one to look at Peter.

He shrugged. "Fine by me. You all act like I'm your dad or something. I've wanted to help Ged since Mort reported he was missing."

The corner of my mouth quirked. That was why he was my best friend.

"Well, then," Kamini said. All eyes focused on her. I wish she stayed out of it. This was Irregular business, she wasn't powerful enough to be an agent. "It looks like you guys have a new plan. What will you do first?"

I swear she was looking at me. Maybe she thought I would have no idea, and it would make her look smarter and more mature if I was clueless, even if she was almost all light inside and was supposed to be above such tricks. Maybe she was working that ten percent of darkness for all it was worth.

"I know exactly what I'll do," I said with conviction. "I've been developing a Blood-of-my-blood spell, and I'm going to find him."

Peter's eyebrow rose. "How will you keep them from tracing the spell back to you?"

"Easy. I'll piggyback it with lead. Just like I altered Earth magic to use Air."

I admit, it felt great to be the recipient of three admiring looks from my team. And one confused look from my newly discovered rival.

"Brilliant!" Harris said. "Let's do it."

Lead was basically the opposite of blood. It was inert, dense, heavy, dead. Blood teamed with life. It was vital and important and created some of the most powerful magic in existence. Lead was lowly, reviled, and poisoned anything it touched. Practically worthless - and ignored by magicians. Only alchemists tried to use it. There wasn't anything else less like blood.

Harris and Seth shoved the furniture back. Peter and Kamini stood to the side while I stepped into the center of the room. I sat with my legs folded into a lotus position and used the extra darkness that had been building up inside me to create a circle of seven creamy-brown beeswax candles around met. I snapped my fingers as I imagined them on fire just because I thought it would look cool when they lit.

Showtime.

I closed my eyes and sucked in a cleansing breath, meditating to clear the built-up emotional turmoil. I was focused, fully aware I was about to try something nobody had ever done before. I also had to push away the excitement that came with working magic, difficult magic, new magic. It felt good to be a part of the world my inability to tap into my magic had kept me from for so long.

On a whim, I removed the silver star necklace from around my neck. It was about time for me to practice magic without it. I wished my uncle was there to see, to comfort me, to guide me. But he wasn't. Instead, I was doing this to find him. I needed access to every bit of my power.

When I was ready, I leaned into the spell and heaved.

CHAPTER FIFTEEN
Contact

THE FLOODGATES OPENED. AIR rushed around me like I was drowning in it, my perception of reality and the elements mixed and confused. Blood magic was powerful. Tapping into it the way I did, warping it through the lead to suit my needs, using it to be the opposite of what it was intended to be, flipped my world upside-down.

I think. I could have been right-side up and the entire rest of the world upside-down for all I knew.

When the colors settled and I could breathe again, I found myself locked in a box. At least, it felt that way. There was pressure on all sides of me, and blackness blinded me. I wished, for the first time, that I had brought the bracelet Chas made that enabled me to see in the dark. I had hidden it away so the sight of it wouldn't hurt me. I shouldn't have been such a baby. Useful tools should never be scorned because of their source. I wouldn't make that mistake again.

I could hear, though. Something was moving near me,

making a strange popping sound infused with a distinct liquid noise. It wasn't like anything I had ever heard before, and my ears struggled to identify the source. After another few seconds of trying to make sense of it, all I could determine was the noise was coming from behind me.

My body remained motionless despite my efforts to turn around. I tried to raise my arm to see if I was near anything, but I couldn't.

But the smell. I smelled that before in my locker. Rotten eggs.

Except no, not quite the same as eggs. I sifted through my school memories, not all that pleasant a task, and came across a fleeting thought about my chemistry exams. They were the most brutal finals we took. Not only was chemistry difficult because we had to learn mundane as well as magical formulas, it was closely related to alchemy. And since I couldn't access my magic at the time, people called me an alchemist a lot. It was especially painful because even if I had nothing against alchemists personally, everybody knew they were a total joke.

Well, everyone except me. Not anymore. Not now that I realized lead was much more powerful than I was taught. And alchemists used it all the time.

Oh. I had been making gunpowder. We learned how to do that in seventh grade, crazy as that sounds. It was one of the ways teachers showed magical neuters like me the basic steps to mixing spells. You had to be exact, or there were very real consequences, just like with magic. Skills also useful for the workers in the warehouses and back rooms of businesses all over the globe, building up stock for the magicians doing the real work.

For some people, learning support skills was humiliating. I didn't mind, but I was scared I would end up one of those magicless workers, turning Chemistry into the worst class I ever had to take. I was so preoccupied with the idea everyone must be laughing at me that I dropped an ingredient all over the floor. Sulfur. Which smelled like rotten eggs.

The stench of sulfur filled the air as I sat in that strange box.

My skin was tacky and damp. And it was warm, much too warm, warm enough I was parched and really, really needed a drink. I would make myself one out of the surrounding Air, using the humidity in my favor, but the box encased me, separating my magic from everything else, including the elements. There was nothing left to connect me to the world.

It wasn't until somebody kicked me in the back, knocking me to the ground, that I understood I had been sitting in a chair. Connections and events flooded my mind. The reason I couldn't see anything was because I was blindfolded. The box was really a skin-tight shield. It kept me frozen in place, and I had been working on a way to get out. I must escape and face my attacker, stop him from hurting my family.

Hurting Peony, my wife.

The darkness shattered when I realized I was merged with Armageddon's mind, thinking his thoughts, using his senses.

He could see light around the bottom edge of the

blindfold, a pulsating glow throbbed in the distance, in the direction of the heat. I needed to communicate with him, but something tugged at me, hard, jerking me away. I shouted his name.

Armageddon.

He was a quick thinker. Despite how confusing it must have been to hear my voice ricocheting against his skull, my uncle instantly responded. In the seconds before I disappeared from his mind, my brain expanded with a torrent of information.

Then he was gone.

"Lia? Can you hear me? Lia?"

My brain slowly embraced reality. Peter sounded worried. He was holding my hand. The candles surrounding me had been extinguished. Wax pooled by my face.

"Why am I on the floor?" I asked as I sat up. My cheek was itching from the carpet fiber. I would have to wash again because who knew how many feet had tracked in goodness knows what while skulking in and out of the safe-house? My elemental senses identified several types of dirt and vegetative particles. Ha. Kamini must not be big on vacuuming, the slob.

The silent insult made me feel better. My good humor tilted the balance of light inside me, finally outweighing the dark like it was supposed to.

Peter helped me to my feet and kept me steady, his warm hand wrapped firmly around my upper arm.

"Man, it was so freaky," Harris said. "You lifted into the air, spun in a circle, and then hovered like you were sitting in an invisible chair. Then out of nowhere you dropped to the side and slammed into the ground. How's your face?" He sounded worried but also impressed. I was coming to recognize that tone from the people around me.

"My jaw hurts," I said, surprised as the pain descended on me. "And my cheek. Shoulder. Elbow. Wow, that must have been some fall."

"No kidding," Peter said. "Can you remember what happened? You were in a trance."

I ticked off the events in my head, processing my experience. I sat on the carpet. I created the candles. I invoked blood magic using lead.

Shocking. Alchemists knew more than we realized. I made a mental note to research their methods. They weren't well-respected in the magic world. Yet not only could I use lead to create untraceable blood magic, I also learned that lead amplified magic beyond anything I could have imagined. Alchemists must use it to strengthen their magic, too.

My face twitched. I didn't like my attitude about alchemists, same as any other judgmental magician, was limiting and unfair. Lead was awesome. Why did we mock somebody for using it? It was unkind and blinded us to magical realities.

I pushed away that uncomfortable thought and then concentrated on what had happened next when I visited my uncle's head.

As if they had been waiting for me, memories exploded behind my eyes. Landing in the dark box, the slow return of my senses, realizing I merged with my uncle when I thought of Peony as my wife instead of my aunt. Because of the amplified blood magic.

Then more memories, other thoughts that weren't mine. Cupping Peony's cheek before turning to leave. Looking down on the lavender bush that was usually taller than I was but Armageddon towered over, then the bright red of the roses. Stepping into my uncle's carriage. Except in my newly acquired memories, it was my carriage since I was thinking from his point of view. Then having a fleeting thought about protecting my niece Lia, me, myself, herself, the sweet girl my uncle loved more than she would ever know.

But I did know because I felt it. And I loved him and my aunt just as fiercely.

A tear escaped. Peter dried it, cupping my cheek the way my uncle had cupped my aunt's, gazing down at me with concern. Fingers touching a sore spot below my eye, probably a bruise.

Then I jerked away from Peter as the memories of nights later, weeks later, an ambush flooded my vision. My magic, no, Armageddon's magic, being frozen, cut off, separated somehow. A box, a shield, a skin-tight trap. And a voice echoing in my memory, a man's voice, telling me he had taken me, that soon it would happen, that he would kill me when the time came.

Not me. My uncle. Armageddon was the one who was going to die.

And then more tears fell, my tears, Lia's tears. Peter grasped my arm, refusing to let go, me being grateful he wouldn't.

A vision. My uncle, trapped. Lost. Fire pulsating in the distance. The smell of rotten eggs. And a structure, a small tower, glimpsed before the blindfold was tied over my Armageddon's eyes.

"He's at a volcano," I said. "I'm not sure how, but I was a part of him, and he saw it."

"Did you recognize anything? Do you know where it is?" Seth asked. The guys were standing close, too close, but at that moment I welcomed it. Their proximity comforted me.

"No, I haven't. But Uncle Ged has. He's been there before with his sons when they were little. It was Mount Lassen."

"And it's active?" Harris asked. His forehead wrinkled, magic humming in the air around him. Stress and anger, worry and resignation. Protection.

"Looked like it. Smelled like it, too," I said, wrinkling my nose.

"Okay, then," Peter said. "Now we know where we're going." He led me to the couch where I flopped down. He reached forward and tugged my little star necklace out of my vest pocket and fastened it around my neck. Good idea.

Kamini was in the corner watching us. "I can give you provisions, of course," she said. "Will you stay the night before leaving?"

I guess being in the clan who ran safe-houses for the government would make a person able to roll with quickly changing events. Good for her. I was having a hard time keeping up with what had just happened, myself.

Heaving a sigh, I rested my head against the back of

the couch. I was exhausted, but I also wanted to hit the road and save my uncle. We had to avoid magical means of transportation. Traveling to California would be quite a drive.

"We should stay," Peter said.

"We should leave," Seth argued. "We have no idea how much trouble he's in or if we'll get there in time."

Nobody asked what would happen if we didn't get there in time. We already knew what he meant.

"He'll be okay for a while longer," I said. I cringed inside knowing my uncle was dying of thirst, truly desperate for water, and hurt. I also knew from the memories Armageddon implanted in my brain there was a routine, and the man who held my uncle against his will was done for the night. He wanted to keep my uncle alive for a while, so one of the guards would eventually give him something to drink.

The age-old struggle went on inside me. Should I or shouldn't I?

I needed to get to Armageddon, and fast. Nobody knew why the enemy had taken my uncle prisoner instead of killing him right away. There was no way to tell when the ax would fall. But I couldn't face what was coming, whatever that was, unless I was fit. Well-rested. Ready. Sharp.

Same with my teammates.

That was it, too. I realized in that instant the love I felt, however real, however profound, was blanketed over with a steel-core of practicality, logic, and odds. It was a balance I knew well. The Rectors had always been torn between light and dark. We knew how to utilize all sides. I had learned realism at my father's knee. A lesson I could never forget because it made me who I was, flowing in the Rector bloodline. And if we were going to win, we needed to be at our best.

Armageddon would survive if we didn't leave right away. And we needed to be prepared.

Easy.

"We need to stay," I declared with confidence. I kept my eyes closed for a split second, afraid of what I would see on their faces. Then, never the coward, I looked at each of them. "We need to. We don't have to be here long, okay?" I studied Seth. He was struggling, but there was something in my words that made him realize I was right. Much in the same way I could tell when somebody was lying, I guess I could now show others when I was telling the truth. Or make them think I was. The wisdom of my choice was debatable, but they wouldn't sense that from me.

The tension left Seth's shoulders. Harris also relaxed, and that's when I realized he was as upset as Seth had been.

"Fine. But we only need a few hours, right? We can leave in the night." Seth raised an eyebrow at me, waiting to see if I would fight his suggestion. Which I wasn't interested in doing. "It's better to travel in the cover of darkness, anyway."

"Exactly," I agreed. "Let's go to sleep. Where do we sack out, Kamini?"

The lovely lady smiled stiffly and led us down the hall. Her aura indicated she was using magic as she moved. The hall was expanding - the entire safe-house was expanding - as we walked. No wonder things were so cramped. Kamini and her family must manipulate the space between dimensions to create the safe-house. That's why she had escorted me to the bathroom. She was creating it as we walked.

Man, I was such a jerk. She was doing crazy good magic.

There were two bedrooms. Kamini wanted to separate us, but I told her we would take the room on the left and dragged the guys in behind me. She gave Peter a quick hug, and he thanked her for her help. Once we were inside, though, I used Air to generate enough energy to expand the bedroom and add another cot to the three that were already there. I got a horrible feeling when I thought about us being separated, so I followed my intuition. It hadn't failed me yet.

"How long do you want to sleep?" I asked Seth. I felt like he needed me to defer some of the planning to him. He wasn't a total egotistical jerk, but he was used to being in charge on most of his missions, Harris being the more easygoing brother. The two of them had joined the Irregulars at the same time even though Seth was a year younger, so they held the same relative rank. Seth was a powerful magician and seasoned agent. He deserved respect.

"Let's do three hours," he suggested. "That will give us time to meditate."

I nodded my agreement. Meditation would stretch our sleep time, and we would be as refreshed as if we had slept all night.

Seth and Harris slid my Air-barrier aside and took off, jockeying for position to see who could hit the bathroom first. Once we had our plan settled, I guess that meant they could compartmentalize the journey ahead and spend some time acting like idiots.

"How are you doing?" Peter asked, a look of concern still on his face.

"I'm better. I need sleep like you wouldn't believe," I said over my shoulder as I prepped my cot. I tossed my backpack underneath and then pulled the sleeping bag open. There weren't any windows, but it was cool inside the room, and I had an urge to snuggle down and hide. I sat down and kicked off my shoes.

"Yeah, but something is bothering you. Come on, scoot over." Peter squeezed beside me on the cot. It wasn't all that comfortable, but it felt nice to lean into him and skim a bit of his Light to buoy my spirits. Guilt about my decision jabbed at my heart. I didn't want Armageddon to hurt anymore.

Sometimes I hated the balance within.

"He's in pain," I whispered, my lips barely moving. Either Seth or Harris would be out in the hall waiting for his turn at the bathroom and might overhear me. I shook my head, rattled by my swirling thoughts. My brain was scattered all over the place.

"I know," Peter murmured back. "But you're right. We need to be in good shape if we're going up against somebody who could get a drop on Ged. A good night's sleep is the least we can do to give ourselves a fighting chance."

I rested my cheek on Peter's shoulder. He was so warm

and comforting. For one minute, all I wanted was to feel like I was going in the right direction when I made my first hard decision in the field. And Peter always made things feel right.

"It's mean," I said. "To leave my uncle where he is even three hours longer is flat out cruel."

It was a good thing Peter had so much Light. He had enough to share with me even when I started to go under the Dark. And if that happened, all the logic and sense in the world couldn't stop me from losing control.

I admit I also felt better because Peter was hanging out with me instead of Kamini. Oh, yeah. I was a jerk.

"Right is right. It's never easy to make decisions while on assignment, but we all have to do it. It's an advantage to have as much darkness as you do, actually."

"Wow, thanks man," I said. I tried to sit up, but the cot was tilting under Peter's weight, and I didn't manage to even stop touching him, much less pull away completely.

"Look, it's not easy for anyone. But you have to admit, you lean into your darkness more than the light when you're following logic instead of emotion. Imagine what it's like for the rest of us when we're trying to do what's right, and we have barely any Dark to steady us."

"But who says following your heart isn't right? That light isn't my strength? I mean, that's kind of depressing, Peter."

He reached out, wrapping me in his arms. I could feel his body shaking and realized he was laughing. I couldn't help grinning into his chest.

"Whatever, Rector. Skim off a bit more Light so I won't

have to worry about you slipping into darkness while we sleep."

I nodded, my forehead banging against his chin. It was easier to soak in more of his Light when we were both happy. I was more open to it when I wasn't a gloomy jerk.

That made sense, considering how hard the darkness seemed to fight to keep me off balance.

Only a minute or two had passed before Peter stood up. My batteries were charged enough to avoid the crazier nightmares. I hoped. But that didn't stop me from missing his warmth and peace.

Peter climbed into his cot. He had changed into sweats earlier while I was stewing in my jealousy and looked tired. He might have given me too much Light. I narrowed my eyes, studying him carefully, but then shrugged. He was always hard for me to read.

Seth came back first. "I'm hitting the sack. Nobody participate in any pillow talk, okay?" He let out a huge yawn. "I need to sleep bad. Today has been enough to drain anyone."

"Tell me about it," I responded. Seth mussed my hair as he passed by, making me scowl. I was sick of people messing with my hair and acting condescending, but whatever. I would touch the awesomeness that was my hair, too, if I were him. I yawned again. I slipped into the sleeping bag and punched my pillow a few times to plump it up. My lids were drooping when Harris walked in and made his way to his cot. I felt better at once, the four of us together again. I hadn't even realized I was that tense until I finally relaxed.

I used a little of the darkness inside me to close the door

and seal it. It tipped my balance a smidgen more towards the Light, and I smiled again as I fell asleep.

CHAPTER SIXTEEN
Dreamland

THE VEIL OF SLEEP shifted into unconscious reality, and I was in the suffocating, damp dark once more. It wasn't entirely black, but the color of true darkness, which was blue, deep blue, and the shapes and shadows were the black things.

I looked around, bemused. I had been on a roller coaster in my dreams, or a water slide, when I was ejected and tossed into a world of uncomfortable semi-reality.

Coming towards me was a shape outlined in transparent gold. When I realized who it was, I wondered if I was still dreaming after all.

"Mother?" I called.

She smiled at me. She looked so much happier than most of the times I saw her while I was growing up. That made me sad, and the dark blue of the night surrounding me grew darker, and the shadows I always had to struggle against closed in.

"Lia." Her smile faded. I reached out for her, but no matter how many steps I took, I wasn't any closer. "You can't trust him."

I sighed. I believed her. She obviously felt compelled to warn me, but I already knew I couldn't trust Chas. He made that perfectly clear when he stopped by Rector Enterprises with the new love of his life. I wondered if that had been another ploy of his father's and decided it probably was. But Chas didn't need to put his hands all over Clarissa, and that told me all I needed to know. He was okay with his choice to leave me. He had moved on.

My mother shook her head. I was about to ask her what she wanted since the guardian angel thing was still new and I wasn't a natural at figuring that stuff out, but something else interrupted my train of thought. Heat I could see as well as feel, causing the air itself to waiver. Pulsing, glowing, encroaching molten rock.

Magma.

That's when I realized Armageddon was reaching out to me, breaking through the vision of my mother. I turned away from her warning and took off in the direction where I sensed my uncle.

"Uncle Ged? Can you hear me?" I yelled as I ran. My feet were moving too slowly, just like in any standard-issue nightmare. But it was a vision, not a dream. My previous spell had left a connection between us, but I was afraid I wouldn't reach him in time, regardless. I had already prolonged his captivity so we could build our strength before the fight. I didn't want him to wait a second longer than necessary if I could help it. Even in my sleep.

Of course, I tripped. How could I not? That's classic Nightmare 101.

Dried cinders on the ground scraped my hands. It hurt, but I pushed myself up and ran again, ignoring the pain. Thankfully, I was wearing the Irregulars uniform I had changed into that night and not some stupid prom dress or worse, naked. Nightmares sucked that way.

I climbed over a ridge near the heat and pulsating light, almost falling over the edge of a cliff. It wasn't a steep ledge or a far drop, but I would have gotten hurt if I hadn't checked myself.

Below me, I saw the outline of a man sitting in a chair. He was bound with a skin-tight magical shield and rope and had a hood over his face. Armageddon, alone.

No, not alone. Right behind him was another man. I couldn't hear what he was saying, but I could tell from his movements that he was shouting. Then he lashed out and kicked my uncle, knocking him and the chair over.

I had heard of lucid dreaming. We had even studied the technique in school. It meant I was aware that I was asleep, that I was dreaming again, that I was visualizing what it must have looked like when I inhabited my uncle's head, and someone knocked us to the ground. And since I was dreaming my memories, I could control my dream reality.

Suddenly, I wasn't on the cliff anymore. I was near my uncle and running. I was going to reach him. I was going to stop that man from hurting him.

Close, so close, when the stranger looked up. His eyes narrowed, and he raised his fist as if he wanted to hit me, even though he was too far away to reach me. Before I could duck, although I wasn't sure what I was trying to dodge, a hand grabbed my arm and yanked me backward.

I glimpsed my mother before the darkness faded and I was in the safe-house, awake.

"Damn it!" I shouted.

Like lightning, all three of the guys were on their feet, their backs to each other, facing out to confront the danger. They surrounded me, the object of their protection because of my shout. I felt bad for waking them up, but I was also impressed by their speed and agility. And that they were ready and willing to protect me.

How sweet.

"Er, guys? Sorry about that. I was about to contact Uncle Ged when I was yanked away by my mother."

That would have sounded crazy to anyone who wasn't an Irregular. Even ordinary magicians weren't used to dream-walking or contacting the guardian spirits of their ancestors directly.

The tension left the room. Seth groaned and flopped back down on his cot. Harris stretched and cricked his neck, rubbing a sore spot. Peter stood motionless, still on guard, as he studied me.

"Did you see anything useful?"

I was so glad he was there to keep me on track. And help me avoid feeling like an idiot for needlessly waking everyone out of their meditative sleep.

"Now that you mention it, I did see the guy's face. The one who was kicking Uncle Ged." I cringed, still pissed off. Nobody treated my family that way.

"Do you think you can describe him?"

190

My eyebrow rose. Interesting. I probably could, actually. "You want to sketch him for me?" I asked.

Peter nodded in confirmation.

Harris collapsed onto his cot. It was only about five minutes before we had set our internal clocks to wake us, but we were under the compulsion to finish our meditative sleep. Harris fell back into a deep sleep as fast as Seth had just done. I shook off my compulsion. I slept enough for one night.

I walked over to Peter's side as he dug around in his backpack. He pulled out a sketchpad and pencil. We sat together on his cot, my body tilting towards his.

"Tell me everything you can about him, and I'll try to follow your description."

I thought it over. I didn't know how to talk about what the man looked like. I wished Peter had been with me, then he could have seen for himself.

Huh. Maybe he could, anyway.

Closing my eyes, I concentrated for a moment. I cleared away all thoughts except the stranger. He was tall, probably as tall as Peter. He had wavy black hair and a scar on his cheek. I set that image in my mind and then reached out to take Peter's hand. He was such a good sport that he rolled with it, linking his fingers with mine without hesitation. I tugged on the Light inside me that I had skimmed from him earlier in the night. Even though it had blended with my Light, I could still feel the connection to him inside it.

I slipped the memory of the stranger into the shard of Light the way I put magic in a crystal and then gently pushed it to Peter. I squeezed his hand and released the breath I didn't realize I had been holding.

He grunted. "Wow. That's the first time that's happened. Cool." In a few short minutes, the stranger's face took shape on the tablet Peter held. He was incredibly talented. And fast.

"That's him." My lip curled in disgust. "That's the freak who's been torturing my uncle."

"Good job. We'll show Seth and Harris when they wake. I felt the extra push you gave them. How much longer will they be asleep?"

"Only an extra twenty. I owed them for waking them up for no reason."

Peter nodded. He put the sketchpad back and sat up, this time leaning into me so our arms and legs touched. He was warm, like always.

"Do you need some of the Light back?" he asked.

I wondered then how it must feel for him to reduce the Light he held inside when he gave it to me. I couldn't tell what kind of light-to-dark ratio he had, which was frustrating and forced me to obsess over whether I took too much and would turn him towards the dark. But it dawned on me at that moment that it had to be taking a toll on him to give me Light so often.

"No." I didn't want any more. Ever. I was being selfish and never even thought of him. Some friend I was.

"Are you lying?" he asked. Peter's eyes twinkled at me, and I shifted my gaze. I couldn't help it, the corners of my lips lifted, but I smashed them together, trying not to smile like a guilty toddler.

"Maybe. Does it hurt you when I take your Light?"

"Oh, no. Is that what you think?" Peter slid his arm around my shoulders and gave me a squeeze. I sat rigidly, not believing him.

"Yes. I don't want to harm you, too. I never even bothered to ask." Guilt flooded me, but then it eased, and the weight inside me lessened. Peter was giving me some of his Light despite myself. Impressive. Nobody else had been able to get around my natural shield unless I wanted them to.

"I told you, it doesn't bother me. Keeping you sassy isn't a hardship in the least."

I let out a weak laugh. Fine then. I couldn't sense a lie in him, so I accepted his offer without further comment. Within moments, I was smiling my gratitude.

"So, how are we getting out of here, anyway?" I asked. We had arrived at the safe-house using my uncle's magic escape route, but now that we had another destination in mind and couldn't risk taking magical transport directly there, I was at a loss about what to do next.

"Kamini will get us a car. Travel arrangements are handled by the safe-house staff, and she's great at her job." The tone in his voice changed, and I jerked to my feet before he could realize how much I had stiffened at the sound of her name.

"Then what?" I shifted the sleeping bag, rolled it up, then placed it at the foot of the cot.

"Then we'll hit the local airport and commandeer one of the planes to take us where we're going. We have a few on hand in case of emergency since this town has an airstrip."

It figured. The Irregulars had assets and contacts all

over the world. Why not in a tiny town in the middle of Washington state? Of course, it was the closest town to my uncle's property, so it made sense to have access nearby.

Harris and Seth's meditation ended. They were instantly alert like before, but this time there was no alarm in their movements.

"You guys ready to go?" I asked.

Seth tightened his lips before he turned and stretched. Harris ignored me completely. He always tried that, but it never worked out for him.

I picked up a piece of scrap paper Peter dropped while he was drawing the man I saw in my nightmare. It had a few pencil marks on it, like the papers Peter used to work magic usually did, but there wasn't anything important on it. I crumpled it up and then tossed it into the air.

The paper burst into flames, white smoke filling the surrounding space in an enclosed sphere I had made of thickened Air. Then the lack of oxygen caused by my air-tight shield snuffed the fire.

A small butterfly remained.

With a thought, I popped the little bubble I made. Tiny black bits of burned paper floated to the floor as the smoke dissipated. The butterfly fluttered over to Harris and landed on his shoulder.

The look on his face must have meant that I caught his attention after all.

"Almost ready?" I asked jauntily.

"Come on Lia," Harris said. He stood frozen, still trying to focus on the butterfly slowly opening and closing its wings. "Seriously?"

Seth burst out laughing. "Dude, Lia doesn't like to be ignored. You know that. Consider yourself lucky she didn't make a roach to climb up your leg or have the chair kick you like last time. Besides, that was a sweet little trick. Learn to do it, and you'll never have trouble getting a date."

Groaning, I shook my head in exasperation. Sure, it was totally histrionic for me to turn paper into a butterfly, but it looked impressive, and Harris wouldn't be able to ignore me. I didn't expect them to consider it a good way to pick up girls. Men were so absurd.

Peter slugged me on the arm. I shrugged and winked at him. I imagined the butterfly back where I got it from somewhere halfway around the world in a field of flowers, and it disappeared.

"Let's get a move on," Peter said. "We'll catch you up on a few things in the car."

The Andersson brothers nodded their acknowledgment and finished packing. They had small bags, the kind you hung on your belt. They were compact, but like other magical carry-alls, they could hold anything that could be squeezed through the opening. They used it as a jump-bag like the rest of the Irregulars. I had one, too, but since I hadn't been out in the field before, I didn't have it on me when everything went down at the castle. It was in my workshop. Thankfully, I had thought to stuff my backpack with clothes when I had the chance so I had something to wear.

I unsealed the door, and we headed back down the hall. It was narrow and cramped, worse than before. We probably strained Kamini's magic. I sucked in a breath, drawing in the surrounding Air, and used it to lean into the magic that created the bedrooms and corridor in between dimensions. Everything firmed up, expanded and brightened like the apartment was waking up and stretching. Kamini would be able to sense somebody was giving her magic a boost, but I didn't want to embarrass her or think I didn't respect the job she did by making a big deal out of helping her. I cloaked my identity so she wouldn't know who it was and hid the trace from her. Some magicians could be super touchy.

"You guys heading out?" she asked when we reached the living room.

Peter took the lead. He was obviously the one she addressed. Harris and Seth shuffled their feet so they would remain with me, all of us aligned slightly behind Peter. It planted the subconscious idea that Peter was in charge and would speak for the group. Rank and position were critical in the magical world, and we all played along. Technically, Seth and Harris were higher ranked agents, then Peter, and I didn't rate at all because I wasn't officially sanctioned to go on a mission yet. But outsiders like Kamini wouldn't know that. Irregulars were a group apart, and it wasn't her business.

"Yes. Thank you so much for your hospitality." Peter shook her hand. She looked up at him like he was the hero of the universe. I stifled a giggle. She didn't seem so smooth when she was mooning after him. The few hours of sleep helped reset my equilibrium, and I relaxed. Peter was a great guy, and I didn't blame Kamini for liking him. If they ended up dating, I would see her more often, and her unfortunate phrasing when we met was no reason for me to hold a grudge forever.

"You're always welcome here, you know," she said prettily. I stared hard at the ceiling.

"I do," Peter replied. "I'll make sure the Council knows your family is always prepared for any circumstance."

"Thank you, that means so much to me." She paused and smiled sweetly. "I've got the car keys here. It's downstairs in front of the coffee shop and all gassed up, ready to go. Unless you'd like to stay for an early breakfast?"

I didn't want to be rude, but time was wasting. Fortunately, before I had to say something to interrupt the dumbest flirtation I had ever seen, Peter cut her off.

"We'll have to take a rain check. Thanks for your help." He took the keys from her hand and gave her a side hug. I could tell she wanted it to be more, but we were in a hurry.

We headed downstairs and made our way through the coffee shop. Kamini released the spell on the door, and we stepped out into the pre-dawn, ready for the next leg of our trip.

CHAPTER SEVENTEEN
A Younger Me

A PICKUP TRUCK WAITED by the curb. Faded gray and older than my uncle, but large inside and would run well and safely even though there weren't any seatbelts. That kind of thing happened in old cars sometimes. Our carriages didn't have them either. Since all or most of the occupants of the vehicles were magicians, somebody was sure to keep the passengers from harm. I hated feeling like I was about to fall out of the seat at any moment, so I always wore a seatbelt when one was available. But the truck would blend into the back road areas where we would be driving and was probably the best choice.

I kept listing all the good things about the stupid pickup in my mind. It was better than admitting I was a spoiled brat because I actually thought for just one moment a limo would be waiting for us. A brief flash of disappointment and anger had even burned through me.

"Shotgun!" Seth shouted. Harris had already swiped

the keys and would drive. I climbed into backseat and sat next to Peter. I didn't have my license yet, so I couldn't offer to help.

We headed out-of-town driving southeast towards Cashmere where the airstrip was located. The airport was tiny, but that's all we needed. I was glad Harris was driving so fast. I wanted to save my uncle, and we couldn't get there soon enough for my peace of mind.

"So what was up this morning, anyway?" Seth asked.

"I saw our target." I explained my nightmare in detail. Peter showed him the sketch, but neither Seth nor Harris recognized the man.

"Once we get to the airport, we'll have the caretaker make copies and send them out to our contacts in Northern California. Maybe somebody will recognize him," Peter said.

"Better have them send it wide," Seth suggested. "That guy might be a stranger to the area, but he has to have lived somewhere."

Peter and I nodded in agreement. Going international was a good idea.

"Tell me more about pushing your memory into Peter's head," Harris said. "Sounds handy."

I laughed. Harris was always calling my little discoveries handy. It made me feel good, useful too, but I also felt a tiny bit annoyed. They were simple things. Obvious. What on earth had they been doing with their time if not experimenting with their magic? Why did so many magicians take their power for granted?

"It really helped. I wasn't sure where to begin - I've

never had to describe somebody to an artist before. Then I remembered how my uncle pushed those memories into my head when I was linked to him during the Blood-of-my-blood spell. I used a bit of Peter's Light to hold the memory. Like I do with crystals to make them radiate light. Then I pushed it into his head."

"Interesting," Seth murmured. He was sitting with his arm hanging over the back of his seat, turned partially our way. He gave Peter an odd look, but before I could ask what that was all about, he continued. "Do you think you could try that with me? I'd love to see how that works."

I had to hand it to them. Even if they seemed somewhat lazy about inventing spells and coming up with new ideas, they wanted to learn everything they could once they found out about it.

"Sure. Let me skim some of your Light," I said. I reached out in my mind and imagined myself tugging a tiny sliver of the Light Seth had inside him. He grunted but said nothing, waiting patiently.

I integrated it into the rest of my magic, and my balance lightened infinitesimally. I wove it into myself until it was as much a part of me as it had been a part of Seth although I could still feel where his influence was and it was easy to keep track and isolate it.

"You got it okay?" Seth asked.

I nodded. I thought about what to send him and remembered how he looked when he and his brother were performing magic together. There was something both intimidating and inspiring about it, and for as long as I lived, I would always think of them that way. I froze that vision in my head - the brothers standing side by side, surrounded by bursts of light. I let my feelings of pride and admiration for them leak into the memory and then set it in the Light, just like I did before with Peter.

Interesting enough, I could feel Seth's connection to Harris in the Light I had skimmed. There was a link between the two of them that ran deeper than an ordinary partnership. Almost symbiotic. It was probably part of the reason they were Irregulars. I shelved that thought so I could discuss the nuanced nature of magic with my aunt and uncle about it someday when things finally went back to normal. Or what passed as normal for us.

I used the link between brothers to send the memory not only to Seth but also to Harris.

"Whoa," Harris said. He kept driving steadily, but shook his head. "Is that your memory? How did I see that, too?"

Seth sighed, a bemused smile on his face. "Lia, that's awesome. Is that how you really see us?" He looked at me in such a way that I squirmed. Maybe I put a little too much admiration into that memory. I didn't want them to get the wrong idea.

"Yeah, you guys are a trip. See how it worked, though? It was like I filled your Light the way I would a crystal and then put a trace on who it came from and sent it back. You have something that links you to your brother, too, so I used it to send it to him as well."

Harris let out a low whistle. "Man, that's top secret stuff about my brother and me, you know."

I didn't. But I figured it out on my own so nobody

needed to know I learned one of their classified secrets. "I won't tell, I promise. Now, do you want to send me a memory?"

Seth nodded, his mouth quirked into a crooked smile. He glanced at his brother, and Harris gave him a nod. After a short pause, I felt Seth tugging on the Light inside me.

I couldn't help it, and it wasn't my intention, but my shields went up and I kind of thrust Seth away.

"Ouch! What the hell, Rector?"

"Sorry! I didn't mean to Give me a sec, let me relax, and you can try again." I cringed. What I had done was as rude as could be. I tried to settle down. My entire body was trembling, and it occurred to me that I was on the verge of a panic attack. Again.

Peter slid his hand over the seat until it rested on mine. The Light inside him practically leaped out and surrounded me, filling me with positive energy and calm. My breathing, which had sped up without me realizing it, slowed and the pounding of my heart grew quieter.

I took a deep breath, then blew it out. "Okay, I'm ready. Just go slow."

Seth nodded. He closed his eyes, and I felt the lightest of pressures in the center of my chest as he leaned into the magic inside me. The shield was still up, but I concentrated with fierce determination and practically tore out a chunk of Light and shoved it at Seth. His magic surrounded it, and like when I was learning to throw fireballs, I released the connection the Light had with me.

"Dang, girl, chill. You're going to kill me with all that giddy happiness," Seth said.

I thought he was joking until I saw the grin on his face. Okay. I may have sent him more Light than I originally intended. "Um, you're welcome?" I shook my head, not sure how to respond.

"It's hard to decide what memory to share, isn't it?" he mused. "Oh, I got one."

I felt pressure again, and reaching out, identified the crystalline shard of Light with my trace waiting for me. I scooped it up and brought it home through my natural shield.

Instantly, I was in Seth's memory. Before me was the old dorm building from a school I had attended in Switzerland for a semester. My parents sent me there because they had a top-notch magic development program and they hoped it would help me. Harris was standing next to me, and we had been laughing about a prank we pulled on our cousins.

Their cousins, I reminded myself. I was seeing through Seth's eyes, so Harris was standing next to Seth, and they were the ones who had pulled the prank, not me.

The door of the dorm flew open, and a younger version of me ran out. I was a mess. Somebody had pulled a prank of their own and drenched me in red paint. An older girl, shortly before her ascension and who had accessed her magic before she was even thirteen, liked to lob paint balls at the students who couldn't fight back. The cream of magical society attended that school. People like me, those without magic, were always the lowest on the totem pole. My family name had bought me entrance into any academy or social club on the planet, but it couldn't make anyone be nice. Until I could prove I was one of them, I was a target just like anyone else.

Jennifer. That was her name. The memory that played before my eyes reminded me of that. A stray thought of my own overlapped the memory from Seth. I was surprised that I had forgotten the incident had ever happened. At the time, I thought I would never get over it. My frustration and pain were very real, and the way our class-system worked didn't help magical neuters like me. But I did forget it, and I forgot about Jennifer until I saw her through Seth's eyes as she chased me out of the dorm with globs of paint swirling in the air around her, ready to throw. I watched as I slipped and fell to my knees, adding to my humiliation. She raised her hand to launch another volley of paint, but instead of soaking me, she froze.

I never knew why she didn't keep going. It had been vitally important to me that nobody would see me cry and the younger me ran away. But now I had a new perspective. Seth's memory showed me why she stopped tormenting me.

It was Seth and Harris. They worked together to throw a magical shield of Air and dust around her, nearly invisible but strong. They tied her arms to her side with a spell and the swirling paint globs she had magically levitated brushed the inside of the standard fishbowl shaped Air-sphere they had used to trap her. It forced her to let the paint drop when the spell tightened. Then she realized it would get all over her if she continued to levitate the paint.

Harris and Seth squeezed the sphere tighter, and paint got on her, anyway. She was staring at the Andersson brothers in horror, and I could feel by the movement of his face that Seth smirked back at her. My own face lit with a grin, taking pleasure as I took part in the memory of stopping a bully. Seth and Harris were seniors. I had been in the eighth grade. Jennifer was a junior, and they knew she didn't want to rock the boat too much with a couple of well-placed, good-looking guys.

The part of me that was still me giggled out loud in the truck. Of course Seth knew he was attractive. He teemed with confidence. It was one of the things I admired about him and was maybe a little jealous. I wasn't sure if I would ever feel that way about myself, not after all the mistakes I had made.

The memory ended when Seth snapped off the spell, and Jennifer ran inside the dorm, leaving red paint footprints.

"I didn't know you had seen me before," I said, fully myself again and back in the truck. The memory was still there, a new memory that formed by my viewing Seth's, the same way I remembered television shows or movies I had watched. The Light that carried the memory was already spent, burned into nothingness once it played out.

"We weren't sure who Jennifer was chasing, so we asked around. We wanted to let you know she wouldn't do that to you again, but you left school by then."

"Wow. You're awesome. Why didn't you tell me?"

"Honestly? Neither of us remembered." Seth chuckled. "We had no idea we had seen you before until you tripped on the path in the Air on the escape route Ged made for us. It looked so familiar that I kept thinking about why. I meditated on it for Recall, and there you were. Gosh, you were so cute when you were young." Recall was a useful spell that helped magicians remember things they had heard or seen only once and had forgotten. It was used a lot by our police forces, and the Irregulars were associated with them in a round-about way. Agents used Recall all the time.

"Yeah, yeah. I used to be so cute, what happened?" I finished the joke for him.

"No way. You're gorgeous. Your uncle made us promise to stay away, but if he didn't, we'd be acting like fools trying to get you to date one of us."

Well, then. That was definitely interesting news. I felt a flash of annoyance at my uncle's interference, but I couldn't keep the grin off my face. It's not every day a girl gets a compliment like that. "Ah, sure. Thanks. Now tell me, did the memory I sent you fade with the Light?" I had assumed it did, but I wanted to change the subject and take the attention off myself.

"No, it's still here. Did mine fade?" Seth's forehead wrinkled. "Interesting. We should figure out why," he suggested.

I nodded my agreement. Although I brought it up as a distraction, experimenting with magic was becoming a hobby of mine. I loved to see what we could do, and the Andersson brothers were fun to work with. But even more important, they were willing participants.

"Your memory of the man from your nightmare is still here, too," Peter said quietly. I frowned. I didn't think about that when I sent it to Peter. I had no idea it would stick around so clearly. I showed Harris and Seth a great memory, and all I did was send my best friend the face of an enemy. Guilt filled me.

"Let me think of something else, and we'll try it again. I'll send you a good one this time," I promised. Peter huffed a laugh and told me not to worry about it, but I did.

I spent the next several minutes of our trip trying to decide which memory to send him. Even though I had only known him for six months, we had a million shared experiences. I saw him every day, and he had been there for me when I needed him the most.

Peter fighting the Taines. Peter soothing me when I was lost in darkness. Peter helping me find the trigger to my magic. Peter holding my hand in the infirmary when we were both injured. Peter filling me with Light.

The question was, how did I limit the good memories to only one?

"We're almost there," Seth said, interrupting my train of thought. The truck slowed, and Harris turned off at our exit.

I glanced out the window. There was nothing but swirling gray shadows. Harris slammed on the brakes. At that moment, a Shadow-veil had dropped over the pickup, and the ground shook.

Somebody was waiting for us.

CHAPTER EIGHTEEN
Ambush

"GET DOWN!" SETH SHOUTED. I dove forward, cramming myself between the seat in front of me and the one I had been sitting on. The truck swung around as it skidded sideways.

At least, I thought it was sideways. Peter had hurtled over to my side of the truck to protect my head and shoulders and I couldn't see.

"It won't stop," Harris yelled as the pickup gave a sickening lurch. "Hang onto something, we're going over!"

That didn't sound good.

The truck tilted onto its side. Everything slowed to a terrifying crawl, which should have given me time to react, but I didn't. I couldn't.

I slammed into the door, my shoulder taking most of the impact, although my head slammed into the window as the truck's passenger side hit the ground. Peter tried to brace himself, but he fell on top of me anyway, smashing my face against the back of the seat. His shoulder knocked the wind out of me, and I couldn't take a breath, my lungs jerking frantically.

The pickup continued to roll, and we were upside down, the four of us tumbling together against the ceiling, crashing into each other, my backpack slamming into Seth's ribs.

White smoke filled the truck as the vehicle stopped rolling, then it slid sideways as my chest continued jerking. I still couldn't breathe.

The guys slumped where they landed. Peter crushing me convinced me whatever that smoke was, it had knocked them out. I drew Air from the edges of the truck at once, creating a small sphere around my head. When the jerking of my diaphragm stopped, I could suck in a breath of clean air.

With another crash, the pickup lurched, and way too late, I finally reacted and braced the four of us to keep our bodies from crashing into each other again. The veil of shadows disappeared just in time to show me we were sinking. I had a vague thought about crossing a river on the way into town when we were attacked. Icy water poured into the truck through the vents, and I slapped up a spell, blocking it as best I could.

I sorted more clean air out of the smoke and created a sphere of breathable air for each of my unconscious friends. Then I braced myself against the seat. I made sure the door was unlocked and then heaved, trying to force it open. Thoughts of dragging the guys to safety filled my head.

The door didn't budge. I frantically reviewed my

memories of all the movies I had seen where vehicles sank to the bottom of a lake with screaming passengers inside. I could only remember that the water had to be over the entire vehicle to get out. Something about the pressure equalizing.

Oh. Yeah. The inside of their vehicles were always filled with water, too. Wow. I thought that was for dramatic effect, but now I knew I was never getting out unless I let the water in.

I had a wild thought about magically busting out one of the windows, but in a flash of insight, I realized our attackers expected to knock us unconscious and then drown us. It was safer to pretend they were successful since it would have been impossible to drown a group of magicians who were awake. They would be on the lookout to see if any of us maintained consciousness. A muffled explosion of magic would be a dead giveaway.

Somebody had to be waiting along the banks of the river to see if we floated to the surface or not. When the shadows above us renewed and then grew even darker, it occurred to me they would want to make sure there was a cloak spell surrounding the area so there would be no witnesses.

That meant we were being watched. Better to remain in the truck as water filled the cab.

I thickened the Air-spheres, pulling more oxygen from the water leaking into the vents. I cleared my mind, then solidified my magic with a firm image of what I wanted the spheres to do. A few seconds later, I allowed the cold water to pour into the vehicle, my new Air-spheres pulling oxygen in and pushing carbon dioxide out, my version of scuba gear. The rest of the smoke and air left the cab, bubbling to the surface. The magicians waiting above would expect that.

They would also be watching for smaller air bubbles. I created a balloon out of thickened water molecules and enhanced it to become the opposite element. Like I did when I used Fire to create Water magic. Except this time, I made my balloon irresistible to pure Air. Whenever one of us expelled a breath, the resulting bubbles raced to the balloon instead of the surface.

My entire body shook. It could have been the stress, and fear, but I was also going into shock. I needed to get three unconscious guys out of the submerged truck unnoticed by enemies unknown and oh yeah, we were all under water.

Sometimes my life had way too much drama.

The cab of the pickup was finally full of water. I grabbed my backpack and looped it over my shoulders, then placed my hands on the door. I wasn't sure how much strength I needed, so I pulled power from the Water around us and heaved the door all the way open.

It was dark at the bottom of the river. But my mind continued to supply answers, instinct or adrenaline or training rising to my need. I remembered that Peter still had the bracelet Chas made him. I slipped it off his wrist and tied it onto mine so I could see in the dark.

I swam out and turned to deal with the guys bobbing inside the vehicle. Tugging Peter's arm, I floated him out the door fairly easily. I imagined a magical tether spell, using it to tie him to the frame of the door so he wouldn't float to the surface. Then did the same with the Andersson brothers.

By the time I was done, it was really crowded by the truck door. I swam back in and looked around to make sure we left nothing behind. Seth and Harris had their bags tied to their belts. Peter had a backpack, too, and I yanked it out from where it was jammed under the seat where he had been sitting. When I swam to his side, I slipped it onto his shoulders and then clipped the straps around his waist so it wouldn't come off. I could barely make the clip work since my hands were shaking so hard by then. Warmth seeped into me when I touched Peter's arm and before I could stop myself, I pulled some of his Light into me, warming myself, and the tremors gentled.

It wasn't on purpose. It was probably survival instinct. But I still felt terrible, like I was taking advantage of him while he slept.

Creepy.

I reached out to the Earth below and basically magnetized the four of us. At least, our feet. We slowly sank until we looked like a group of weird plants growing on the bottom of the river. Worried about what shock could do to the guys, not to mention the effects of what was in that white smoke - and despite my reservations - I tugged more of Peter's Light and used it to alter the crystals in my backpack. I usually had a few on me because they were the bread and butter of Rector Enterprises, and one of our more critical alterations had been to change them so they could radiate heat for the poor in colder regions.

But I only had three. Great. Since the guys were

unconscious, they needed more protection than I did. I slipped a crystal into a pocket in their battle vests and zipped them up so the crystals wouldn't fall out in the water. I would have to take my chances and hope swim-walking would be enough activity to keep me warm. But just in case, I wrapped my arms around Peter and soaked in more of his Light, which he had always freely given me and apparently still did, even while passed out. I didn't want to, but I was trying not to freeze to death.

I instantly felt better. The warmth soon radiated throughout my entire body, and my mind cleared. I hadn't realized my thoughts had been getting so fuzzy.

Sending a thought of supplication to my guardians - or as I thought of it, crying out to my mother and father for help - I took the path of least resistance and followed the current downstream.

It was both harder than I hoped it would be, and easier than I thought it would be. The guys were deadweight, but the water buoyed them up enough to be manageable. The spell I cast to keep our feet pointed down stopped them from flopping around me too much, but it was like trying to herd a bunch of wayward cats.

I was afraid to let the current take us and used the force of the Water to create a counterbalance so we could move with the flow but not be at its mercy.

It was so surreal. I wasn't sure how long we were down there before I felt a jerk on my magical tether. I turned back to see what was happening, and Peter's eyes were open. He wouldn't be able to see in the dark, and even though he could breathe, he probably thought he was trapped in a drowning nightmare.

Reaching back, I grabbed his hand. I think he knew it was me because he didn't fight, he just held on tight. Then I squeezed his shoulder to reassure him. I guided his other hand to my waist, and he left it there as I hoped. I didn't need the contact, but I thought he wouldn't worry so much if he knew exactly where I was.

I slid the bracelet I stole from Peter off my wrist. I loosened the slipknots and then slipped it around both our wrists.

My vision dimmed since the magic was meant for one person, but it worked well enough to tell where we were. I had no idea what Peter would think was going on, but I brought my finger to my lips, miming a shushing motion and pointing to the surface, shaking my head "no." Then for good measure, I ran my finger over my throat in a slicing motion to indicate floating to the surface would mean a bloody death. If we were lucky. I mean, whoever attacked us obviously wasn't messing around.

A thought popped into the back of my mind. Maybe the reason my parents couldn't save themselves from their car accident was because they had been rendered unconscious, too. I planted a mental reminder to look into it later when I had a moment.

Peter gripped my hand, and I turned away to lead on. The counterbalance spell kicked back in, and we slowly followed the current. I caught a nod from Peter out the corner of my eye as he worked out my spells. It was a little easier to pull Seth and Harris once Peter was awake and actively helping me keep them steady. I think he woke up earlier than they did because he was the first one I created the air filter for.

We had swum quite a distance when the current got rougher, and a massive pile of rocks rose in front of us. There was no going around it, but I couldn't tell if it was safe to float to the surface yet. I imagined the rocks getting softer in my mind, and they became squishy, like gelatin.

I pushed through, and the guys followed, my personal parade of wet magicians.

It took forever to make it to the other side, and I couldn't see at all the entire time. Seeing inside a gelatinous rock wasn't exactly what the bracelet was designed for.

Once we were all back out in open water, I let the water sweep us along again. In no time a sandbar reared up in front of us, the current buoying us to the surface. There was no reason for our enemy to place a lookout on the other side of the rocks. At least, I hoped not. I was too tired and cold to keep it up any longer.

I dropped the breathing-sphere spell when we hit the air and shook my head, trying to shift my hair out of my eyes. Peter slipped the bracelet we had been sharing off and stuffed it into his pocket, breaking our connection. I mopped my face, attempting to dry it somehow with my wet sleeve.

"What happened?" Peter's breath came out in small pants. He dragged Harris further up the bank and left him next to Seth.

"After the truck rolled into the river, they hit us with a spell that knocked everyone out."

"How did you stay conscious?" he asked.

It suddenly hit me I was supposed to stand back to back with Peter and keep an eye out for enemies. Peter joined me in guard duty, shifting into position as if we had done it a thousand times. Which we sort of had since we practiced at Castle Laurus all the time.

"You knocked the air out of my lungs when you landed on my diaphragm," I said over my shoulder. "I couldn't breathe at all. It scared me to death, but it gave me time to pull clean air over and keep the smoke out for when I could breathe again. I did the same for you guys, but you were already passed out by then."

"Thanks, Lia. You saved our lives, you know."

I basked in the warmth of his approval for a few seconds. A girl really likes to be appreciated sometimes. Then I shivered again and got busy. "No problem, my friend. Hold on a sec, I'll take care of this," meaning our soaking wet clothing. With only a flicker of a thought, I yanked every bit of water out of our clothes and shoes and in a split second, we were dry again.

"Nice!" Peter said.

The fact the Andersson brothers were still unconscious was worrying me, but then I noticed their breathing pattern change, indicating they were about to wake.

The humidity had tweaked the tips of Peter's short hair. The sun brought out the red highlights hidden in the brown, reminding me of the day I first met him, and how handsome I thought he was before Chas distracted me.

"I'm glad you're still alive," I blurted out. My trembling was getting worse despite the warmth of the day.

There weren't any enemies on the horizon. Something

in my voice must have convinced Peter I needed him more than a lookout because he spun back around, took two giant steps, and scooped me into his arms.

"Why, thank you, Rector. I'm thrilled to be alive, too. Come on, give a guy a hug. Time to celebrate life or something," he said.

I smiled against his chest where I had buried my face. I could feel his chin on the top of my head moving gently back and forth. I loved that he was still keeping an eye out for danger. It made me feel safe.

"I took some of your Light," I confessed in a muffled voice. "I'm sorry. I couldn't stop shivering, and it practically leaped at me."

Peter's laugh had always been infectious, but it was entirely different when I was close enough to hear it rumbling in his chest. I didn't want to laugh too, though. I wanted to snuggle into it even closer.

"My Light's your Light, Lia. Here, have as much as you want," he said. More of his Light sank in bone-deep, right where I needed it. It was almost like being healed.

I groaned and selfishly let him continue. Then I worried I would drain him like some weird magical vampire. I pushed away. The shaking had stopped, and for the moment, that was enough.

"Thanks," I said. I grinned at Peter, a side-effect of feeling all that Light roiling around inside me. Sometimes I wondered how Peter kept his feet on the ground considering how much Light he must have. Maybe used a spell like the one I used underwater.

Finally, Seth and Harris shifted, and they opened their

eyes one after the other. Since they were connected the way they were, the white smoke sleep spell was probably amplified between the two. When it wore off enough to loosen its grip on them, they woke together. That theory seemed to make the most sense, anyway.

"Wake up, sleepyheads," I joked.

Harris pushed himself up on his elbow and looked around. Seth groaned and continued to lie on his back, staring up at the sky.

"Damn my knee hurts," Harris said.

It wasn't until he said something that my own injuries clamored for attention, especially the shoulder I had been babying under water, the one I landed on when the pickup flipped over.

"What on earth happened?" Seth asked. "Why am I so wet?"

"Oh, sorry," I said. I repeated the same spell-call for the water in Harris and Seth's clothing. "After the truck rolled and the white smoke knocked everyone out, we hit the water and went under."

Seth sat up with a jerk. "Are you serious? How did we get out of that one?"

Peter grinned and pointed at me. "The mighty heroics of the youngling," he said.

"Ha, funny," I said. Their admiring looks were embarrassing me again. "Peter weighs about a thousand pounds, and when he landed on me in the rollover, he temporarily killed my ability to breathe. Good thing, too, otherwise we'd have all been out when we sank."

Harris let out a low whistle.

Seth stood up cautiously, checking for injuries. "That's insane," he said. "What did you do when we went under? How did we end up on this luxurious stretch of dirt?"

"Ah. Well, I created an underwater breathing helmet thing out of Air and Water for each of us and then hooked you guys to a tether and swam out along the bottom."

"Oh, is that all?" Seth asked sarcastically. The look on his face made my cheeks warm, and I shyly looked down at the ground. "You lugged three grown men as deadweight across the bottom of a rushing river? How did you stop us from floating up into enemy arms?"

"I used the Earth as a magnet, and it attracted your feet. I made it weak so it would keep you down but not tangle you up in the stuff on the bottom of the riverbed." I was distressed to see the weeds, rocks, and growth at the time. It looked like a death-trap, but nobody got tangled up, so I put it out of my mind.

"Excellent," Harris said.

Seth studied me a moment and then took the few steps over to where I stood and squeezed my shoulder. "Good job, Rector. I'd take you in the field anytime."

I looked back up at him and grinned. "I'll hold you to that," I promised. The hardest part of getting a spot on a team was finding somebody willing to lug around the newbie. It looked like I wouldn't have any trouble with that after all.

"I haven't seen anyone patrolling the area," Peter called out from where he had positioned himself, once again playing lookout. "Let's get back onto solid land and see if we can acquire another vehicle. We need to get out of here before they send scouts looking downriver for our bodies. We're visible from this position. If they think to check."

"Yeah. And maybe get something to eat," Harris added. "Whatever they used to knock us out makes me want to puke. I need to eat something solid before I hurl."

I let out a snort of laughter. Harris was all stomach.

We trudged across the water on the north side of the sandbar where the river was at its thinnest. Harris solidified the surface so we could walk on it instead of getting wet. Not like I couldn't dry us off again, but the shaking had come back, and I wanted to avoid draining my energy any more than I already had. It also worried me I might be coming down sick.

As if I needed that on top of everything else.

It looked like my stint as the one in charge was over. I was relieved. Dragging three unconscious bodies along the bottom of the river was exhausting, and I didn't want to think anymore. I shivered as we walked up to the edge of Highway 2. Seth flagged down a beat-up SUV with mud coating the sides.

Hitchhiking was easy when you were a magician. Set off a Come-hither spell, and then a Nothing-to-see-here so the mundane humans didn't pay attention to their passengers. Since we were on the run, we would take the precaution of making our driver forget he had ever picked us up, much less remember he took a detour north and over the border into Idaho as Seth suggested.

"You sure you want to skip Wenatchee?" Peter asked. "They've got an airport, too."

"Yeah. I'm pretty sure it was the Taines who attacked

us," Seth said. "Mort and Ged told us they've been monitoring the nearby towns in case we passed through. They haven't been in this area for weeks. Or so we thought. If they were in Cashmere, I don't want to find out they're still in Wenatchee, too."

"Sucks," Peter said. He shifted deeper into the torn fabric on the back seat of the SUV. The two of us were in the rear, crammed in near some old car parts and dirty red shop rags. Seth and Harris occupied the middle two seats, which were a little better but covered in animal fur, probably a white dog with really long hair.

I sneezed.

Peter looked at me with concern, and I shrugged. My throat felt funny and my ears clicked when I yawned. I was sick, and there wasn't a thing I could do about it.

"Yeah. Frank here will take us where we need to go next," Harris said. Frank, the man who picked us up off the side of the road, ignored the four of us as if we weren't in the car. Seth said he was good with memory spells, and I could tell he wasn't exaggerating. Frank wasn't woozy or confused like most people under a spell that shut down their memory center. Mort told me it felt like blacking out after drinking too much, but I had to take his word for it. Rectors were too close to the edge of darkness to lose control like that. Ever.

We had to find other ways to be the life of the party, I guess.

I sneezed again, and sure enough, Peter pulled out a handkerchief and handed it over. I dug around in my backpack for some tissues to blow my nose because it was too gross to do that in a snowy-white fluff of pretty fabric like Peter's handkerchief. I used it to dab my watering eyes, instead.

"Are you sick, or is it allergies?" Peter murmured close to my ear. I leaned closer, my heavy head dropping onto his shoulder.

"I think I'm sick," I whispered. The other two heard me anyway if the groan Harris let out was any sign. Seth punched him on the arm and shook his head. He was probably telling his brother to shut up since I saved their lives and deserved to be babied and coddled. At least, that was my hope.

Peter slipped his arm around me, and I closed my eyes, exhausted. The best thing about traveling with the three of them, besides the fact that Peter was always willing to be my personal heater and pillow, was there were enough powerful magicians to remain on alert so I could relax. Not that it was all that likely the Taines would guess we were in a beat-up old SUV driven by a guy named Frank.

"Take a nap, Rector," Seth ordered quietly. "We'll be in the car for a while. Maybe some rest will help."

"Thanks," I mumbled. I slipped my arm around Peter's waist and clung to his shirt. I hated being sick. It always made me feel like I would slip and fall, even when I was sitting down. Peter tightened his grip. I think he remembered that from when we were in the infirmary. We had both been injured, not ill, and we talked a lot since there wasn't much to do. It was one of the thousand things that came up as we fought to stave off boredom. I was glad he remembered or else I would worry he would think I was trying to get fresh with him.

Nah. Peter knew better than that.

I sank down into sleep, relieved to let go.

CHAPTER NINETEEN
Armageddon Gets Real

I WAS WALKING IN the river again, dark water all around and three unconscious bodies tethered behind me. I didn't know if I would ever make it out.

My body felt bad, too. Like my head was stuffed full of cotton, and the Earth wanted its power back and was dragging every bit of energy I had into the ground as payment.

"You look terrible," Armageddon said. I saw him then, appearing beside me in a chair. "I would love to hear the story behind why we're underwater, but I'm not sure we have much time. I want to make certain we get to the important stuff first."

"Uncle Ged!" I shouted. The water disappeared, and I ran to his side. Magma glowed red in the background. The sky was overcast, and a bit of the murkiness from the river remained. I coughed.

How crappy was it that I couldn't stop being sick for

one minute, even in a dream?

"Hey there, Mirabilia," he said in a weary voice, using my full name. I was embarrassed by what it meant, had been my whole life. My uncle had used it once or twice, and it was okay because he believed it. He really did think I was "wonderful."

That was the best part about family. At least, my family. They thought I was great, even when I wasn't.

I tugged on the ropes that kept him lashed to the chair, but couldn't loosen them or cut them with the pocket knife I had on me at all times, along with a few crystals blanks, just in case.

"I can't get you out," I said, frustrated.

"Skip it, I'm fine where I am. We need to talk. I can feel you traveling in our sleep. You're going the long way," he said with a wry smile.

"Someone ambushed us. We're driving north and east through Idaho and Montana for just a little while, and then we'll come to you through Nevada. It'll take twice as long." I didn't apologize, but there was regret in my voice.

"Don't worry about me. I'm fine for a couple more days. He's waiting for something. I overheard the guards discussing it. Hopefully, that means you'll have time to heal from your cold before you arrive. Fighting is difficult when you're sick."

"I'm worried about you, though," I said. I rested my hand on his shoulder, not sure how to hug him while he was tied to a chair and secretly afraid there was a way to pass germs to him in a dream. Especially since it wasn't entirely a dream. The Blood-of-my-blood spell linked the users in ways that always surprised a magician. It was never the same, always as unique as the people using the spell were. It would be just my luck I could make him sick.

"I can't figure this man out," Armageddon said. "I haven't yet discovered his motives, except to make me pay for something he thinks I did. He may have been young when it happened because I don't recognize him as an adult. And I'm unable to use any of my magic around him."

"What? How is that even possible?" A bolt of fear lanced through me. My uncle had immeasurable power. How could he be trapped like that? What was blocking his magic?

"I don't know. Yet. When you arrive, be prepared for physical combat. There are three men who help him guard me, maybe more. Bring as many agents as you can who know how to fight dirty. My kidnapper knocked me flat before I knew what happened." My uncle looked embarrassed of all things.

"When I wake up, I'll tell the guys. Peter and the Andersson brothers are with me."

"Ah, my escape route probably kicked in. Wait. Was the castle attacked? Where's Peony? Why isn't she with you?"

"She's fine, don't worry," I said, reassuring him as best I could. "The four of us got away while Aunt Peony and the others stayed behind. There were at least three of them. We aren't sure how they broke through the protective spells, though."

"The leader could have negated them. I don't know how he does it. Were the rest of them fighting with magic?" he asked.

"Yes, they were lobbing spells all over the place."

"I see. He must have left by then." Armageddon paused for a brief moment, working out the problem in is head. "That's a proximity issue. Or he has another limitation to his strength to negate magic. I'd love to find out what spell he's using. There was a short time earlier where my power felt like it was trickling back, but things were still hazy from all the drugs he'd given me. I believe that's when my captor was at the castle, breaking the home-and-hearth magic. That may weaken me, but it doesn't stop me from using magic. Try to draw him away again, and I can save myself."

My blood ran cold when he mentioned drugs, but I nodded to indicate I was focused on his directions. It was a good idea, but I had no clue how to go about doing that.

"What does this guy want from you?" I asked.

"No idea. I've been trying to talk to him, but he doesn't seem interested in conversation."

He didn't say it, but if the enemy wasn't talking to my uncle, that meant he spent the bulk of the time hurting him. The hand resting on my uncle's shoulder tightened. I loved him and despair over the thought of him helpless held me in its grip and wouldn't let go. The decisions I made had prolonged his pain and the danger he was in, and I wished I could fix it.

"I'm going to kill him," I blurted. And the thing was, I felt like I could. I already set aside the love and care I had for my uncle to give us the best chance to battle our enemy, and now I realized the darkness within me really was enough to allow me to snuff a human life. An evil, foolish magician who took my family. At least while I was this angry.

"It may come to that," Armageddon agreed. "But let's take this one step at a time. I'd rather arrest him. And we should be able to. He can be bound with rope just as easily as I can. I'm embarrassed to say he got a jump on me because I rely too heavily on my magic now. I must book a few sessions with Mort to remind me of the tricks I learned as a boy before I became the mighty magician I am today."

My uncle was trying to relieve tension by cracking jokes, but it didn't work as well as it usually did considering he was tied up, cuts and bruises covering his face. It also made it hard to laugh when my guardian and mentor didn't even bat an eyelash when I said I would kill somebody because he believed me.

And it was okay.

Being an Irregular was so weird.

So was the fact that I meant it.

"I have my books in my backpack. I can probably find something that will help."

"Well, that's interesting. Why are you lugging those things around? Not that I'm not grateful."

"I've been experimenting with the guys and it was more convenient that way. I also wanted to see if I could free Peter from having to draw to do his best work," I explained.

"Excellent line of study. Have you discovered anything useful?" he asked. There we were, my uncle tied to a chair, sitting along the edge of an active river made of molten rock, and he still had that bright spark of interest in his eyes.

"I think so. I saw a few things that might help. I've also

been working with Seth and Harris a lot. We found a way for them to use the other elements by connecting through the ones they didn't connect to when they ascended." Magicians had been stuck in the narrow limits set at their ascension for as long as our recorded history existed. Despite the circumstances, my uncle wanted to go into the details so he could forget about his situation for a while.

"Good job, Lia!" he said. "Write me a report so I can read it when I get back. I want to share it with the other agents." Despite their flexibility and additional powers, most of the Irregulars were limited by their elements just like any other magician. It was thrilling that my research could help keep them safe. It felt wonderful, like when I provided charity to the poor. Altruism was the price we paid, gladly, to offset the work we did in the dark. Maybe helping my fellow agents could balance the shady things I would do while in service to the Irregulars.

"Is there anything else we should know?" I asked. We needed to get back to business because I had no idea how long the dream would last now that my strength was ebbing away. I sneezed. "Has he given you any hints about his identity at all?"

"Nothing. I'm afraid you'll come in blind. And as a relative and known associate, he could have done his research and figured out your weaknesses. Be on the lookout for that if he tries another attack. It will put you at the disadvantage. Fortunately, his focus seems to be riveted on me and he may not recognize you. Stay back as long as you can behind the experienced agents. I'll keep working on him when his magic weakens enough for me to slip into his head." Armageddon always tried to give as much information as possible about our assignments before we went out into the field, and I could see how frustrated he was. And that he didn't like me being out in the field. But now he knew Castle Laurus was no longer safe.

"It's fine. We'll figure this one out. Hang on, okay?" I didn't want to get mushy, but I was freaked out by the scene in front of me and what I saw in my previous dream when he was being brutalized.

"I will." My uncle's head jerked to the side. "He's coming. Go. Run. We don't know what will happen to our connection when he gets near, or if he can sense you. He must not be forewarned."

I gave his shoulder another squeeze and then with one last intense look, I hurried into the shadows in the distance.

And not a moment too soon. The enemy called my uncle's name, and the darkness melted into a puddle. The dream crashed around me as I jolted awake.

I had answers, but I was also left with questions. Like how did our enemy stop our magic from working? What did he want?

Helpless numbness had touched me as the dream dissolved. I recognized the feeling. It was how I had felt my entire life until I finally connected to my magic.

There was no way I would let anyone put me back in that position again.

I turned to where Peter sat by my side, my loyal friend. "I just had another dream about my uncle. We've got work to do." It would have sounded more impressive, I was sure, if I hadn't sneezed again.

CHAPTER TWENTY
We're In For a Long Haul

"GOOD OLD FRANK," HARRIS said as we climbed out of the SUV. "I'm going to miss him. He was great company."

I would have rolled my eyes more dramatically at him, but I was too stuffy and run-down to put in the required effort.

We were at a used car lot in Missoula, Montana. Seth and Harris would pay for the car since they had the funds all Irregulars get while out on assignment in the pouches tied to their belts. Peter and I were standing outside with our backs against the wall of the main office. It was well-kept, much to our relief. That meant the quality of the vehicles they sold was likely pretty good.

Peter scratched a mark in the dirt at our feet and cloaked us from view just in case the Taines or any other random enemy was lurking nearby. I dabbed my nose, quietly babying myself.

"Got it," Seth said a short while later. I had to hand

it to the magical world - spells made the excruciating business of working on a deal so much quicker since we could tamper with the mundanes. That seemed sketchy to me, but it was accepted practice while on a special mission for the Council and had its benefits. Armageddon insisted his agents pay a fair price if we used those spells.

Technically, anything an Irregular did was a special assignment for the Council. That was a tricky provision my uncle had worked into our contracts when he took over the elite fighting force.

I wasn't sure what color it used to be, but the nondescript vehicle they bought was a faded reddish orange with blotches of that gray stuff I saw on beaten up old cars all the time. It was a dinky little thing, too.

"Will we all fit?" I blurted. I was tired of being crammed into back seats, and that thing looked like we would need a shoehorn to wedge us all inside.

"Oh, ye of little faith," Harris said, laughing. "Seth and I used opposite elements to expand the interior without leaving a trace."

A pang shot through me. I had forgotten to tell my uncle about that aspect. Untraceable magic would be an incredible advantage.

I grunted in acknowledgment. I was getting crabby and found myself not really caring what the guys did to the vehicle. I flat out didn't want to get back into a car, and we were still in for a really, really long haul across several states before reaching my uncle.

"Wow, somebody woke up on the wrong side of the bed," Seth teased. I wasn't in the mood, but I felt a small, begrudging smile raise the corners of my lips, anyway.

"Maybe," I said. Then sneezed again. I wanted to cry. What a lame thing to happen on my first mission.

We piled in. I looked around, relieved Harris hadn't been exaggerating. They designed the spell to make the inside exactly like the limo at home. The one Peony and I liked to use. It had a huge back seat. Two of them, since one faced the rear of the car.

On one seat sat a blanket and a giant box of tissues. I turned my face away, not wanting them to see the tears filling my eyes when I realized they really were going to pamper me after all.

My head felt like it was filled with lead and my eyelids drooped. I was so tired I didn't remember dozing. I wasn't sure how long I had been out, but when I woke up, Peter and Harris were deep in conversation while Seth drove.

"I don't like using mundanes that way," Peter was saying. "I usually stick with magic users when I develop a contact. It doesn't seem right to force something on them when they have no choice. They can get hurt, too."

"Yeah, I shy away from them myself," Harris answered. "Seth was more open to it, but we once had to use a vendor in a park for help, and he ended up getting burned pretty bad. It's sick to do that to somebody so helpless compared to us."

I sat up and ran my fingers through my hair. Apparently, I had untwisted my braids for comfort while I slept. It was probably sticking out everywhere.

The guys were talking about contacts, people who could help us while we were out on missions. There was a lot of debate in the upper class about whether we should use mundanes. They were fully aware of what we did. Although they couldn't get away from us fast enough when we used spells in front of them. Plus, magicians usually took over everything since we had such an advantage over mundanes.

A few of our Elders suggested pulling back to keep from overwhelming them with our powers. But in the end, the Council decided we had just as much a right to success based on our talents as they did, even if our talent was magic. Magicians had all the advantages and had been in charge of every great civilization all the way back to the Egyptians, and before, although that time was shrouded in mystery.

My parents were in a society that pushed for mundane rights. Once the three-year-long holding pattern ended at Rector Enterprises and all my contracts expired, I was going to renegotiate them to ensure my parents and their contribution would be remembered. Charity and good works were the Rector Family's penance for having so much darkness within. It was such a part of who we were, our altruism was almost a blood oath.

"I've had little contact with mundanes," Peter admitted. He was so friendly and outgoing I tended to forget that he was a Makenna, and they had tons of enemies. Although Peter's clan had died out, their old enemies and allies still sought after him. My uncle thought they would want to use him to lead an uprising. That was one of the reasons my aunt and uncle had adopted Peter, besides the fact that Armageddon was the agent Peter's parents attacked, their

234

backfired spell killing them. Adopting Peter was for his, and our protection - and a way for Armageddon to make amends.

Too bad that meant Peter was home-schooled until he ascended. Then he could attend college, but the students were magicians. That was the only way to work around our strange apprenticeship schedules. He also didn't get out much unless he was on assignment. Peter was almost exclusively in the company of magicians.

I had several interactions with mundanes and thought they were ingenious. I was creative with my magic, but I couldn't imagine inventing the things they came up with without it. But it was a respect I had from afar.

"You aren't missing much. Although Seth and I used to go out on our liberty weekends at school and pick up mundane girls. They like a magician better than a guy with an accent. We had both."

I laughed. They turned, finally noticing I was awake.

"Wow, it's getting deep in here," I teased. My nose was so stuffy I sounded weird. And my throat hurt. "Are you going to list off all your best features for us next?"

"Hush. You know we're prime examples of magical manliness. We're true-blue chick magnets," Seth called back. He seemed at once both far away and very, very close. Expanding the inside of the car had some freaky side-effects.

"True," I freely admitted. My mother once told me during one of our rare mother-daughter talks that no matter how confident other people acted, they could still be hurt. They might be under more pressure than I understood and I should always keep that in mind. And I had no desire to be mean.

Besides, they were attractive, smart, and funny. And all of us knew how magic was a draw for mundanes if we stayed too long in their vicinity. When they weren't running away in fear, we were so appealing to them that it was a little embarrassing.

"How are you feeling?" Peter asked.

I was miserable, that was how I was feeling. "Okay, I guess," I said. I wanted them to think I was tough, regardless of my earlier need to be coddled. "I'll be fine when the time comes to confront our enemy."

My reward was the look of approval on Peter's face. "We'll be stopping soon to get food and stretch our legs. You could check out the medicine aisle while we're there," he suggested.

I bit back a groan. I missed my aunt, who was a phenomenal healer and had a ton of herbs on hand. Instead, I was stuck with mundane medications, which always made me feel hollow inside. It was better than constant sneezing, though. That would throw off my aim.

Seth pulled off the road and parked near the main store in a travel center. It was the kind of place that had a bunch of restaurants all around, with showers in the bathrooms. I purchased a token and locked myself inside one of the stalls and cranked up the hot water.

Ah, bliss. The steam helped clear my stuffy nose, and I felt more human by the time I was done. I went all the way and washed my hair, too, using the shampoo in the tiny travel bag I bought along with the bottle of liquid goo they called medication. I arranged my hair with the brush I had zippered into the small pouch on my backpack by braiding it into two braids, one on each side of my head. I looked like a pioneer girl, but I didn't feel up to plaiting the usual battle-braids.

I tugged on a pair of dark gray yoga pants and a black t-shirt. Despite the warm weather, I slipped on a hoodie and then tossed all my dirty clothes into a plastic shopping bag, stuffing them into my backpack before skulking out the door.

"Hey, there you are," Peter said. "I was wondering if you got sucked down the drain or something."

"Ha." I scowled.

"Come on, grumpy, let's get you some food. Then we're going down the road a short way so we can commune with nature while we eat."

I perked up. I always felt better when I had the chance to surround myself with the elements and soak them in for a while. Maybe it would also help me feel less awful.

After a quick glance around, I walked over to one of those refrigerated areas where they stocked salads and fruit cups and other cold foods. I ignored the sandwiches completely. They were always so bland and never had anything interesting on them, not even sprouts for a little crunch. Just mushy chicken salad. Or tuna salad, which scared me. Who bought fish at a gas station?

Not me.

"Look around," Peter said, grinning. I was sure he knew what I was thinking by the look on my face. I wished we could try out the cute diner across the way, but my insistence on taking a shower had used up a chunk of time.

"They've got tons of different things in there. Even a rack with fancy bread. I bet you can come up with something interesting if you tried."

I sucked in a determined breath and then narrowed my eyes, studying the layout. I glanced over at the bread and nodded to myself. "Stand back," I told Peter. "This is no place for amateurs."

He laughed and got out of my way. After a moment's pause, I decided to go old-school and gathered a few ripe bananas, a tray of bacon and rubbery eggs, honey-wheat bread, and creamy peanut butter from down the aisle. I grabbed a beat-up red grocery basket and tossed in several other items, forming an idea for our next meal. It felt appropriate that I was roughing it while out on a mission, but Peter was right. There was no need to give up my creativity and eat a sketchy egg-salad with no horseradish or onions or dill pickles or celery-salt like some kind of barbarian.

I almost crowed in delight when I spotted several containers of yogurt with berries. I grabbed those, too, and then snapped up a bag of salt and vinegar chips and four bottles of peach sweet tea.

There was one nasty moment when it came time to pay, and I realized I only had my card. I never carried cash, but obviously, I couldn't use it, or else everyone could trace me that way. Sure, magicians used magical methods to find people, but they weren't above tapping phones or tracking credit card purchases. Whatever worked.

Peter slipped beside me and tossed down a couple of twenties. I looked up at him and smiled sheepishly. Of course, he was prepared.

"Don't worry about it," he said on our way out. "You don't have your pouch yet. We've got a bunch of cash in them. Seth and Harris shared theirs."

I let it drop, but I wanted to wail about my rookie mistake. I hated how being sick turned me into a worse baby than normal. Good thing he saved me from myself.

"You guys ready?" Seth asked. He and Harris were lounging against the car near the gas pumps.

"Yeah, we're done. Let's go." Peter took the groceries from me and held the door open. I climbed in and hurriedly scooted over. He hopped in and set the bags down by our feet. Seth drove back to the highway a little too fast, knocking me sideways into the window where I hit my sore shoulder.

"Ouch," I mumbled. Peter and I exchanged a knowing glance as we chuckled. Seth was turning out to be a speed demon.

It didn't take long to get to the scenic-view rest stop (with no bathrooms!). There was another car already there, but the people were dozing inside with the windows rolled down. We grabbed the plastic grocery sacks and headed out along a path that had a sign indicating there was a picnic area a short distance away.

There were a few tables, and the view was okay. There wasn't a stream nearby, but Earth and Air would cover all of us, and we could make do using other methods.

I emptied the bags onto a table. Seth and Harris watched me warily. They bought their own lunch, two of those gummy sandwiches, but they weren't tearing into them. I didn't blame them. With a scornful huff, I tossed a pack of veggies and dip their way.

"Here, keep yourselves occupied while I make some real food," I ordered. They gratefully threw their junk sandwiches down on the table and wandered off to refresh their Air and Earth elements while crunching on some carrots. I shooed Peter away, too, so he could soak in the sunlight. His main elements were Air and Light, so it was the perfect spot for him to recharge. I wasn't sure how depleted he was, but I wasn't taking any chances.

I tore off the plastic covering the breakfast tray and pulled out the bacon. It was a tad underdone, but that worked for me. I knocked off bits of cold egg and looked around to make certain there were still no mundanes nearby. Knowing about magic and watching its casual use were two different things. I didn't want to cause a scene.

Since it was just us in the clearing, I pulled out one of the crystal blanks Peter had tucked away in his backpack. He showed me all the different pockets and his hidden stashes of crystals and spells just in case we ended up on the bottom of a river again with only me conscious. Which I feared could actually happen, knowing my luck.

I used the darkness I always seemed to have in abundance to alter the crystal into a heat source. Then I finished cooking the bacon until it was crispy and smelled fantastic. Spreading peanut butter on slices of honey-wheat bread, I added the bacon to one side and sliced up the bananas for the other. After pressing them together, I carefully toasted the bread.

The eggs went into the garbage bin and I dumped the berries into the empty container. I trashed the yogurt, cringing at the waste, but it was all runny, and I was afraid it was bad. Besides, I only wanted the berries, anyway.

It was a simple meal, but filling and tasty. I definitely rose to Peter's challenge.

"Hey!" I called out. "Come on over and eat."

The guys obviously hadn't been too far because they heard me and trotted over to the picnic table in record time.

"Thanks, Lia," Harris said. He bit into the sandwich and looked surprised. He kept chewing and then stuffed more into his mouth right away, so I assumed he liked it.

"How cute," Seth said. "You cut them into little triangles." But he shut up too once he began to eat.

I loved an appreciative audience.

The berries I served as-is, and the salt from the chips plus the peach tea helped cut through all that peanut butter. It was a nice meal. And when we were done, Peter cleaned up the garbage, which I thought was awesome.

My only disappointment was that it was hard to taste anything. My nose wasn't stuffy thanks to the medication, but somewhere inside my head, I was still clogged up. I couldn't smell well and my food wasn't as interesting as normal.

"Hey," Peter said. He sat down beside me on the bench. "I know you need recharging yourself. Let's go over there by that tree."

I looked over to where Peter indicated and perked up. It was perfect for me. If I lay on the ground, I could commune with Earth, and the dappled shadows from the leaves would allow me to recharge my Dark and Light sources. The breeze would take care of Air. There wasn't any Fire or Water, but I could bring a water bottle with me. Water users always insisted on clean, fresh water from natural sources, but any water would do. I had a lighter in my backpack, and there was a BBQ grill not too far from the tree where we could start a small fire.

"Looks good, thanks," I said. Peter helped me up and pulled me along behind him. I was simply too run-down to be my normal self. Once we were near the tree, I picked a dappled patch of grass and flopped down.

"I'll build a fire," Peter said, chuckling. He had never seen me ill before, so I guess he thought my misery was funny or something.

My lids drooped as I soaked in the world around me. I needed all the elements, even the darkness. I did feel healthier, especially when I could tap into the fire Peter started.

"Thank you so much," I murmured. Peter came back to where I lay prone on the grass and sat close to me. He stayed outside the shadows as he continued to refresh his Light element.

"Feeling better?" he asked.

"Definitely." And I was. My face still felt like it was plugged up somehow, but the weakness in my bones was leeching into the ground as the Earth element inside me recharged. I sucked in a giant breath of Air and held it for a moment and then exhaled with a whoosh. "What do you think is happening at the castle right now?" I asked. I missed my beautiful bedroom with the huge, soft bed. And infirmary. Peony could have fixed my cold for me.

"I'm sure they're analyzing the defenses," Peter responded after a short pause. "I bet Mort is back so he can help."

"I thought Uncle Ged's defenses were fool-proof," I said. A twinge of pain distracted me as the memory of Chas showing me the castle defenses popped unwelcome into my mind.

"So did we. Well, as fool-proof as anything can be in the magic world."

I nodded absently, yawning as my body felt as if it were sinking down, rooting into the soil below me. A breeze played across the skin on my arms after I tugged up the sleeves of my hoodie, and it connected with the Air element within. Exposed skin always helped the process. So did meditation, but I wanted to stay alert while outdoors, the same as the guys did. Meditation was awesome, and we could recharge quicker, but it left us vulnerable.

"It scared me when I saw Tian on the floor," I admitted. I was the only girl in the Irregulars, besides my aunt, and sometimes I felt like I had to prove that I wasn't emotionally weaker than the rest of them just because I was at a disadvantage physically. Not that Mort wasn't teaching me to kick butt. But Peter was my best friend, and he wouldn't judge me.

"I was, too," he replied. "We haven't lost anyone since Ged took over the Irregulars. I hope I never find out what it's like to lose a fellow agent."

"Definitely," I agreed. "Especially now." I was referring to the fact that my uncle was being held prisoner by a

243

psycho who liked to beat him. I suddenly felt vulnerable, exposed, and tugged my sleeves back down and curled onto my side, an arm tucked under my cheek so I wouldn't be lying face down in the grass. I glanced at Peter, who was sitting with his back against the tree. He must have finished communing with the Light.

"I wonder how they got through, though," Peter idly speculated. He picked up a few blades of grass and drew a small mark in the dirt to help them float the short distance between us to tickle my cheek. I huffed out a weak laugh and rubbed them away with my sleeve.

"They started on the border around the backside," I said. "That's where we got hit by the Taines." I shivered despite the warm afternoon. Peter and I both were injured in the attack last spring. Even though it was a pretty spot and we walked there often, the thought of it in the context of another attack reminded me of the dread I initially felt right after I was healed. It had taken me a month to be comfortable going there again.

"We strayed over the border that time. The Taines didn't break through, so I don't think there's a weak spot or anything."

That was true. The thought made me feel better. "So they had to get through the redirect spell that would have turned their feet to the main gate, and then the border spell that sets off the alarms and triggers the first round of our offenses."

"What bothers me is that the spells amp up every layer they go through, the closer they get to the castle. How did they survive the spells embedded in the castle walls? They're lethal." Peter scowled and threw a grass blade.

I thought about the day I went up on the ramparts with Chas. We had just completed a security drill. My uncle suggested that Chas show me around while the protection spells were active. For the first time, instead of being sad when I remembered how close Chas had stood, or how I loved it when he slid his arms around me, I was annoyed. At myself. I was so guy crazy at the time that I didn't remember the details of his explanation.

I cringed. I guess I was over Chas enough to realize what a fool I had been. Lovely.

"The alarms eventually went off, though."

"True," Peter said. "There were people still in that area when the others reached the ground floor of the castle. They must have set it off somehow."

An idea struck me, and I bolted upright, turning towards Peter. "What if the person who broke through the spell was too far to cover the men trailing behind? Uncle Ged thought there was a proximity issue."

"I see what you mean. So there was probably somebody walking through, stopping the spells from triggering, but it didn't break the spells. And when he got far enough away, the others were no longer protected and set them off."

I put a hand to my temple. My head was spinning, doubtless because I sat up too fast. "Exactly," I said. I shifted forward and squeezed my eyes shut. Peter must have moved silently because I was surprised when when he slid his hands around my arms, bracing me. I leaned against him. He cradled me against his chest until the spinning stopped. "Wow, that was fun."

I scooted down again until I was on the ground. It gave me a sense of solidity, took away the weakness.

"Are you sure you're okay to keep going?" Peter asked. I could hear the concern in his voice. I was reminded again of our time in the infirmary. He had sounded like that when he first saw me with all my injuries.

"Yeah, I'm fine. I think the congestion is throwing off my balance. So as long as I'm lying flat, we're good."

Peter laughed. He waited quietly as I regained my equilibrium. I soaked in more of the elements, trying to use the excess to somehow heal myself. It must have worked because I felt better.

"Have you had enough?" he asked. "If there was such a thing as element gluttony, I think I'd have to accuse you of such."

The corner of my mouth quirked up, the way it usually did around him. "Maybe," I said casually. I felt full inside. It made me sleepy and wired at the same time. I tilted onto my back and raised my arms above my head and stretched. My shirt tugged up, exposing my belly button. "You tell me." I guided Peter's hand to my stomach. As warm as my skin was, his hand was warmer.

"You feel like you've had enough sunlight," he said. "The other elements are replenished, too. You ready to leave?"

I groaned at the sound of his voice. It was brisk, like he had decided it was time to get down to business. And honestly, it really was. I heaved a deep sigh. "Okay, okay. Let's get Seth and Harris. Time's wasting."

Peter stood up and then held out his hand. I took it and

cautiously climbed to my feet so I wouldn't get lightheaded again. Peter let go and picked up my water bottle, which had gone warm, and extinguished the fire. Fire safety was important to Peter since his parents had died in a fire of their own making while fighting my uncle. Makennas were traditionally big Fire users, but his element turned towards Light instead, which was adjacent to Fire and what most magicians considered the element of good. The only family that had ever used Light for evil works was the Taines, and that was a secret only they knew. And me.

Thanks, Chas. I suspected he regretted telling me once he turned his back on me and ran into Clarissa's arms. The only person outside the Taine clan to know their weakness wasn't the love of his life. I bet that felt weird. And maybe a little scary.

I followed Peter to the car. Harris was leaning against the trunk, looking bored. Seth was chatting up some mundane girl with what my mother always called "large assets." I rolled my eyes so hard I wondered if he heard them ricochet against my skull because he glanced over at me sheepishly and then wrapped up the conversation. Apparently, it was a signature move of his to rest his hand briefly on a girl's arm, because that's what he did. She gave one of those light, lilting laughs that were so fake but guys seemed to fall for every time.

Instead of turning towards the car, Seth headed my way.

"You look a little better. Less death-like and more wax statue," he said.

"Wow," I said, but then cracked up. "Thanks. At least

247

that's progress."

"Too right. Come on, I'll walk with you." Seth held his arm out with his elbow crooked, and I linked my arm with his. His Light wasn't as strong as Peter's was, not really an element he used at all, but the connection still warmed me inside. I loved having friends and colleagues I could trust and show my affection for without restraint. My parents were so distant and formal I never got enough hugs. I had to make up for it somehow.

It also helped me walk faster than I would have on my own although Seth slowed his pace for me. I really was dragging.

He escorted me to the car. Peter was already inside and had put the pillow and blanket back on the seat for me. Ah, bliss.

"Lia and I had an idea about the attack on the castle," Peter said once the Andersson brothers were inside and we drove off. Peter explained our earlier conversation. He rested his hand on my head, making me feel safe and warm. It was pleasant enough that I dozed off again.

CHAPTER TWENTY-ONE
Craters of the Moon

I WAS STILL TIRED when I woke. I couldn't shake the feeling I had seen my mother again, but didn't remember anything about the dream.

"Hey there, sleepy-head," Peter said. He was sketching in his notepad but set it aside when I sat up.

"Where are we?" I asked. The braids in my hair probably looked like shucked corn-cobs - all wispy and messy. I loosened them and quickly ran my fingers through my hair, trying to coax it into waves instead of doing its own thing. The second I was done, I twisted it all together and looped it into a bun. Good thing the messy hair bun was in style. Or so I told myself.

"Arco. We're back in Idaho." He smiled as he watched me fiddle with my hair. Peter was lucky he kept his hair so short, otherwise that slight wave that always made the longer bits stick out on the ends would be a nightmare.

"That's only a few hours down the way," I said. No

wonder I was still tired. I hadn't gotten all that much sleep after all.

"Yeah, but Ged said he can hold out a few days, and we need to stock up on mechanicals since our direct magic won't work when we get there."

That made sense. "But why Arco? We could have gotten a few more miles down the road before stopping again."

"Ah, looks like somebody doesn't remember her foundation classes," Peter teased.

I stared at him blankly. Foundation classes were the first classes on magic offered in school. They told us the what, where, and why of how things worked. Even Alchemists took those classes.

Why would I need to remember Arco? We never studied that town. In fact, the only geography we studied were national parks, monuments, and landmarks, since magicians in government moved to keep our most critical magical places safe from human progress.

Oh. "Craters of the Moon," I said. There was a national monument and preserve close to Arco.

"Bingo. And you aren't even fully awake. Good job." Peter grinned at my sour look. "We're going to swing by Craters of the Moon and work up some mechanicals there. Nobody can distinguish our trace where so many other magic spells have been created."

"Clever," I admitted begrudgingly. Peter only laughed at my bad mood and handed me a bottle of apple juice.

I took it, still scowling, but I was secretly pleased. How thoughtful.

"We're picking up a few supplies before heading out

there," Peter said, explaining why we were in a parking lot. "Seth bought the juice, by the way. They left me behind to act as lookout while you played Sleeping Beauty."

I snorted. Sure. I had been sleeping in the car for hours. My hair was a disaster, and I could tell from my reflection in the window that the seat had left marks on my face from where my cheek had been pressed into the grooves in the upholstery. Hardly a beauty.

My eye caught a movement outside. Harris and Seth were back. I rubbed the sleep out of my eyes and wondered if I should take another dose of the cold medicine. I was feeling better and decided against it.

"You guys ready?" Seth asked as he slid into the passenger seat. Apparently, it was Harris's turn to drive. He glanced my way and bit back a smile.

Great.

"We're good," Peter said after I nodded.

Harris was, fortunately, a more conscientious driver than Seth, and my head didn't bang against the seat when he took off.

"I need more crystal blanks," I said. "I used the last of my light-crystals keeping us warm under water." I shivered. It had been a long, cold walk while I was the only one awake. It surprised me I didn't have nightmares about it, but then realized all of my efforts to contact Armageddon, and likely my mother playing guardian, kept me from reliving those events in my sleep.

"No problem. There's always a friendly stationed at national parks and preserves. They'll have plenty of blanks on hand."

I sighed. I learned that in school, too. I hated how slow and stupid being sick made me feel.

"Want something to eat?" Seth called back. "We bought one of those soup cup things."

"Sure," I said. I wasn't particularly hungry. I never was when I was ill, but I needed to keep up my strength. We had already delayed rescuing my uncle in the name of becoming stronger and more prepared, and my illness had wiped out all the benefits from that.

"I knew you were sick, but now I think you must be dying," Peter said as he took the soup from Seth.

I looked down at it and wrinkled my nose. Beef stew with carrots. I hated cooked carrots.

"It's fine," I murmured. "With no sense of smell, I can't taste a thing, anyway." I still picked out the carrots, though. Peter held out an empty grocery sack for me without comment, and I tossed them inside.

The drive to Craters of the Moon went smoothly. I wasn't expected to keep an eye out like the others, which was good, because I dozed off again. Peter touched my arm gently to wake me when we arrived.

This time I had slept with my cheek against the window in hopes it would help all the lines left on my skin from the seat fade. I was about to meet the minor magician who was stationed at the preserve and was getting sick of being embarrassed because I looked like a wreck.

The need for a quick stretch overwhelmed me as I stepped out of the car. I glanced around as I shook out my arms. The land around was stark but beautiful. The rock formations seemed like they went on forever.

"Hello, there," a stranger called as he walked towards us. "I'm Luč Nguyen. Welcome to Craters of the Moon."

I studied him, memorizing his features in case I ever ran into him again. He was one of the friendlies, magicians posted throughout the world who had a contract with my uncle to help the Irregulars when needed. He was of average height, with dark brown hair and eyes. He was nearly bursting out of his uniform shirt and khaki shorts, muscles well-defined probably because he had to hike everywhere.

When I shook his hand, I could tell he was eighty-five percent light inside and tapped into Earth element magic, which meant he must love his job at the vast park.

"It's nice to meet you," I said. Out of nowhere, the reason Luč had introduced himself by his real name instead of his magician name made my stomach roil violently. Lower-class magicians were considered crass and over-reaching to use their magician name as if they were at the same level as magicians such as myself and my family. How awful the elite must seem to the rest of the world. No wonder we had so many enemies.

"I'm Lia," I said. I couldn't handle the thought of introducing myself by my magician name. I wasn't more important than Luč was. I didn't mind following the rules of society when I was smack dab in the middle of it, but it was obscene to pull rank in a place where the man knew more than I did about the area in his charge. Running the park was a huge responsibility, and if things were fair, he would have as much respect as the mayor of San Francisco.

Luč's eyes crinkled when he smiled. There was something about him I really liked, and despite my inner turmoil, I couldn't help smiling back.

"Come on, I'll show you the map we've got posted and tell you where the best places are," he said. We followed him into a small building. There was a giant map on the wall, breaking down the different areas of the park.

Peter winked at me. I could sense approval behind his eyes although I wasn't sure what I had done. But as long as I was finally doing something right, I would take it.

We studied the map while Luč explained the various formations and discussed the diverse types of earth and minerals in the preserve. We decided that we should go to the Monoliths because it had the best elements for our purposes.

"I've got a load of blank crystals in the storage room," Luč offered. I lit up when he unlocked the door, and I saw multiple cases in stacks containing the clear crystals I loved to use the most. The logo for Rector Enterprises was stamped on the sides of the boxes, and I filed that away in my memory. I would have to ask Iuvo, the floor manager, to send a cornucopia to Luč as a thank-you for helping us. It wasn't required since he was a contractor for the Irregulars, but I bet he would love to have a light-weight, renewable food source while out on the trail. Giving him one in gratitude for his services seemed like the right thing to do.

A fleeting thought about Kamini flashed through my mind. Should I have sent her something in repayment for her efforts? Peter crossed my line of sight as he moved deeper into the storage room. Nah. She was his friend. Let him take care of it.

Seth and Harris grabbed a handful of crystals and dropped them into their pouches. Peter took a few and then held my backpack for me while I shoved two entire boxes inside. I never wanted to be without plenty of blanks again, not since I had gotten so sick because I didn't have a sufficient number of crystals to stay warm underwater.

"Are you sure you have enough?" Peter asked, eyes glittering with humor.

"Har har," I said. "I have no idea what we'll need, but I want to be prepared. Besides, these were provided by Rector Enterprises. I can replace them."

"And they are covered in dust. They must have been pining away for some sweet magician to come along and make their existence have meaning."

Really? I wasn't sure when Peter decided to talk like a romance novel, but it was ridiculous.

The drive to the Monoliths was impressive, to say the least. Seth was driving again, and in addition to being stuffy and hollow from the cold, I was getting car sick. But I still caught glimpses of the austere beauty all around us.

Definitely a great place to commune with Earth and Air. The surrounding rocks were rugged, broken, harsh. Two exceptionally large stones were beside a walking trail that stood apart as if they were the ruins of an ancient, massive gate leading into Rome. And they sort of were. Except they were a magical entry to a vast well of power.

There wasn't anyone there, so we hustled through the standing rocks and came out into a magic upwelling hidden from sight.

I looked around, impressed by the sheer beauty

surrounding us and the spell that protected magicians from the mundane hikers. We were still outside and the blue sky stretched on for miles. There was a wavering translucent wall on all sides that assured no mundane would ever know we were there. In fact, I was positive only a magician as strong as Armageddon could see where we were.

"Wow," Seth said eloquently.

"Yeah," his brother responded.

I shared an amused smile with Peter while Harris checked out the view. Then we sat in the four stations of the compass to do the basic cleansing and preparedness spells. Peter was facing me. He was in the South, the station of Movement, leaving me in the position of North and Destiny, since the Rectors worked best where they could see their foes. It was the leader's place, to sit in the north like that, but nobody seemed to mind.

Seth was wild and did well when he sat in the East where magicians reached our Turning Point. Hopefully, he could envision a portent while there because we could use a head's up. I was getting tired of being surprised all the time.

Harris was in the Western quadrant of our spell compass, the area of Self. All our visions would filter to him. Magic left an impression, and something useful may pop up. He was more tranquil than his brother and was the obvious choice for calmer work.

"Here, take these," I said. I handed them five crystals each. "Keep the blanks you pocketed for later. We'll use these so you can have backups." The pressure behind my nose made my voice sound funny, but I pushed through my annoyance and focused on the task at hand.

After a little discussion, we shifted our seats slightly to align with true north. We eventually settled on which spells we thought would be the most useful. Nets, Shift-sliders, Flash-bangs, and even some real bombs with explosive force. I had a short, heated conversation with Seth, the result of which had the two of us turning a few crystals into storage containers, like a small glass vial except with fractals and much sturdier, filled with pepper spray.

Yeah, the kind police use. We were concerned that if there was nothing but magic inside, and our enemy somehow negated indirect magic, too, then we would be in a lot of trouble without something entirely non-magical on hand. I also dragged out one of my favorite books from my workshop library and flipped through its contents.

"I think we should try to make some spells like Peter's bracelet," I suggested, kicking myself again for leaving mine behind. It wasn't until I caught Peter studying me that I realized I said that without thinking about Chas at all, or how he had been the one who had them made for us as gifts.

I wasn't sure how to feel about that. But I decided it might be a good thing.

And that was a kind of scary. I mean, who gets over the love of their life? Nobody. So if I got over Chas, then it might not have been the epic love I thought it was.

Which was maybe a little sad.

What if I was just a romantic idiot and didn't know myself at all? Would I ever meet my one true love if I was so blind? The movement of Peter's hand snapped me out of it. His eyes met mine, and I gave him a small smile. He really was as good looking as - if not more than - the Andersson brothers. Without the huge ego.

"Hey, earth to Lia. You were saying?" The way Peter looked at me when he tried to get my attention was off. That's when I realized I must have spaced out for a lot longer than I thought. Oops.

"Oh, sorry. Yeah. We should make trinkets to see in the dark since we don't know when we'll arrive. And I like the idea Seth had of zapping the enemy. We can probably trap lightning or something inside a crystal. Maybe tune it so it won't zap us but get anyone else."

"Totally. We need to disguise the trinkets, though. Even an alchemist would recognize the purpose of Peter's bracelet and try to rip it off." Seth jerked his chin in Peter's direction as if the rest of us might not be sure who he was talking about. In response, Peter's eyes crinkled the way they usually did before he smiled.

I studied Seth for a moment. He really was a good-looking guy, even if he was twenty-one and too old for me. According to my aunt, anyway. He shifted his shaggy dark hair out of his face from where the breeze had blown it, and a slight sparkle caught my attention.

"What about an earring?" I asked. Seth had pierced his ear, and there was a small, glittering diamond on the post. I snorted with amusement. Typical Seth.

"Oh, cool," Seth said. "That's a great idea. We can use gold posts. I bought a bunch a couple of weeks ago for my dress-down days and forgot they were in my bag. I saw them when I was storing the extra crystals." He rummaged around in his pouch until he found the little card with the earrings and handed them to me.

Only Seth would have different earrings for different days. I could have made the earrings myself, maybe drawn gold from the earth, but using what we had was easier. Plus, they were shaped like Celtic knots and were pretty cool looking.

I removed the silver star necklace from around my neck and handed it to Peter since I wasn't sure if it would hinder me if I left it in my pocket. Giving somebody the ability to see in the dark wasn't exactly a simple spell, and I didn't want to have to contend with my star's capacity to hold me back.

At least adhering magic to gold was beyond easy, which was why magicians used it a lot. It was also why alchemists always tried to scrounge or even create more since they had very little power. They could fill a golden vessel a portion at a time without losing any of the magic previously contained there. Like filling a cup with rain a little bit every day, until it was full. The resulting liquid was all still water.

In fact, I had seen amazing and well-crafted spells performed by the alchemist students at school. Better than the spells some of the elite magicians created. Like lobbing paint balls at eighth graders.

Shame jolted through my body. Why did I think alchemists were unworthy just because their magic was weaker than mine? I knew what it was like to be unfairly targeted, yet I didn't question the status quo. I even laughed with Mort about how becoming an alchemist if I never connected with my magic would have been too low for me.

I was the worst person ever.

A popping noise from one of Seth's spells jerked me out of my reverie. Pushing my revelation aside for some serious thought later, I closed my eyes and took a deep breath, drawing in Air. I filled myself with power straight from the sun. I needed the Light, which had always leaked out of me faster than Dark.

The shadows our bodies cast on the ground rushed towards me as I tapped into the power of darkness. I didn't need to open my eyes to see that our shadows had disappeared because I could feel it. But I also heard Harris gasp in surprise. I grinned.

Holding the gold earrings in my hand, I tightened my focus, then imagined them glowing briefly for a split second with the light of a thousand suns. Most people didn't have to be as visual as I did, but I needed to push in the magic somehow and vision was my method.

"Wow, Lia, give a guy a warning next time," Seth said. "I don't think my eyes will ever be the same."

I looked around and saw that all three of the guys were rubbing watery eyes.

"Oh, no. I'm so sorry," I said. "I'll try not to let my magic be discernible to other people again." I cringed when I realized that I should have cloaked my spell. That was standard procedure and being out in the field made it even more important to keep spells hidden from prying eyes.

"It's fine," Peter said, as always, trying to reassure me. "That was a tidy bit of magic there. And watching you suck all the darkness from the world is such a trip."

I laughed. "Thanks. Come on, let's try them out. I used the shadows to bind with the Light inside the gold. The spell should be self-perpetuating and last, well, forever I guess."

They each got one earring, and I kept the matched set with the golden triquetras, the Irish trinity knots, for myself. The design in the center was made of silver, and not only did I like the design, but the combination of the two metals gave me the ability to add in a couple of extra spells I wanted to experiment with later. Plus, I had the feeling that Seth didn't really care about them since they came with the packet. But the triquetra was a part of my family crest, and it felt right to use them.

It was still daytime so we couldn't test them yet. I added a binding spell so the earrings would only work for one owner, and the posts needed to be worn for a few hours for the spell to settle in and become permanent, anyway.

"Thanks," Harris said. He fiddled with the earring and finally got it in. "Do you think it brings out my eyes?" He batted his eyelashes at me.

A puff of air bursting through my lips was my only answer.

"Come on, let's finish the weapons. I'm going to make a bunch of Flash-bangs and Smash-forces," Seth said. He punched his brother on the arm.

"Great idea," Peter said. "We may need to flatten somebody along the way."

We all ended up making Flash-bangs, mechanicals that set off a flash of blinding light as a distraction before smashing a person to the ground. I was good at making them since I had a hefty blend of Light and Dark in my magic, but Seth made some really nasty ones. I suspected his mischievous personality had a lot to do with it. I also made a few Smash-forces, which did the same thing without the blinding light for a more covert attack.

Eventually we had enough mechanicals - I hoped - and dusted ourselves off, ready for a break before we drove south again. Seth and Harris decided they wanted to go for a hike, but I still felt so bad that all I wanted was to sit and soak in the last of the sunlight instead of climbing all over the place. The Andersson brothers would see some amazing sights, but I was so tired I didn't care at the moment.

Peter stayed with me. We were in a protected zone and the brothers could go off without us. I felt bad because he probably wanted to prowl around and check things out. He took a lot of walks and explored the area surrounding Castle Laurus when he was growing up and loved nature. But we were on assignment and that meant we stayed in pairs.

"Don't worry about it," he said.

Peter must have known what I was thinking. I looked up from the bench where I had collapsed. It was outside the magical field of the Monoliths and intended for tourists. The view was gorgeous.

"If you give me a minute, I'll shake this off and we can go check out the rocks," I lied. There was no way I would feel up to it, but I wanted to be fair and decided I could trudge along with Peter so he could explore and enjoy himself.

"Are you kidding? You're as pale as a ghost." He sat on the bench next to me and gazed out at miles of landscape that indeed looked like they were craters on the moon.

"Besides, Peony and Ged brought me and their sons here when I was a kid. So I'm good. Now come on. You can doze if you want to."

Peter slipped his arm around me and tugged me closer. I dropped my head on his shoulder, relieved he wasn't annoyed. A nap sounded wonderful, and I didn't have to feel guilty after all.

"Thanks," I mumbled. My eyelids were already glued shut.

"No problem, Lia. I've got your back. Now hush, I'm trying to meditate."

I wanted him to see the weak smile that was my response to the bossy tone he used when he was letting me off the hook, but I was too tired to lift my head. I was sure he could feel the curve of my lips against his neck where my face was nestled, and I decided that was good enough.

Peter shifted slightly and pulled me tighter against him, securely holding me to his side.

My last thought before sleep overtook me was that I really hoped I wouldn't drool.

CHAPTER TWENTY-TWO
I Almost Destroy the World

I MUST HAVE FINALLY gotten over the hump because when Peter shook me awake, I felt better.

My nose was still stuffy, but I was relieved to see I didn't leave a wet spot on Peter's shirt. There was a limit to what a person will put up with, and I was wary of reaching my it with my best friend.

Harris and Seth were back, so we walked to the car and headed out. It seemed a little rude, but I was glad we didn't stop to say goodbye to Luč Nguyen. I was feeling antsy about how long we had stayed, and any further interaction would have eaten up precious time.

"Hang on to your hats, ladies and gentlemen," Seth said. Since he was driving that didn't bode well for our safety.

With a screech of tires, Seth took off and recommenced our long-haul trip. Peter handed me a bottle of water courtesy of a small drinking gourd built into the side of the car. It was a luxury product made by Rector Enterprises, and I wondered where the guys snagged one while they were updating the interior with their spells. The gourds worked like a fancy cooler, but the elites liked them, and my company sold enough to fund more of our charitable projects. Maybe the Anderssons were so wealthy their sons had them on hand.

A fleeting thought about my parents came to mind. They had always been so committed to helping others. Sometimes my former schoolmates made nasty comments behind my back - ensuring I heard them, of course - slandering the motives of the family who owned one of the largest corporations in the world. They said it was all about the money, and a good image helped make more allies, but it had been my experience that it had the opposite effect. We earned more enemies because of our good deeds than anything else we did, including vanquishing evil magicians. I huffed quietly to myself, thinking about what that said about us as people.

Nothing very nice, that was for sure.

"We should keep going. No more picnics," Harris declared from the front passenger seat.

"Agreed," Peter replied. "Except for quick pit stops, we need to make up time. I don't want to leave Ged with that psycho for any longer."

Sighing, I began to peel an orange. Maybe a dose of vitamin C would help clear up the lingering effects of my stint underwater. I paused long enough to blow my nose, and Peter finished peeling the orange and even pulled it apart into segments for me, laying them on a napkin I had taken from the last gas station we visited.

"We'll shoot for Reno," Seth decided. "It's just over eight hours from here, but we can trade off when we're tired." He let out a yawn. "I'm good for at least half the trip. There's a safe-house there, and then we'll head to the volcano after we sleep."

Traditionally, magicians struck at midnight, a powerful time for magic. Even for those who used Light, as long as the moon was out. Reflected sunlight from that heavenly body was enough. Since the Irregulars didn't exactly follow tradition and our current foe dampened or blocked magic anyway, we would show up for battle whenever we got there. That meant maybe noon. Maybe twilight. Maybe at three the next morning. The point was, we would take the enemy down at a time of our choosing, not his.

"Why do you think he's at Mount Lassen?" Harris asked. "It's isolated, sure, but not exactly devoid of people."

"There are plenty of places to hide, and if he uses Fire, Lassen is a great spot to tap. Fire and Earth users have been visiting the area a lot over the last few years, so it's an active volcano again," Peter answered.

Ever since the Center of the Universe had moved to San Francisco, more and more magicians had poured into the region over the following decades. That concentrated the magic, and the old power centers were reawakening.

"Oh, hey, check out that sack over there," Harris called back.

I looked down at my feet, and sure enough, there was a tattered plastic grocery bag with fine dust coating. I reached out to pick it up and grunted when it wouldn't budge.

Seth and Harris laughed. "Sorry, Rector, we enforced it and expanded it inside, but we were too pooped from all the other spells to turn it weightless." Seth eyed me in the rear-view mirror and grinned cheekily.

I huffed, but before I could cast a spell to make the bag easier to lift, Peter reached out and hefted it onto the seat between us. He didn't make a sound, but the muscles on his arms bunched from the effort and my eyebrow lifted. Impressive.

Peter untied the handles, which were knotted together to keep the bag closed, and we peered inside.

"How beautiful," I breathed. It was filled with blue volcanic rock. Which looked like an Earth-user's version of Water frozen in time all rippled and shining dully in the light of the car.

"We thought you'd like that. There's a lot at the preserve. Harris went crazy when he saw it, and we figured you would want some, too," Seth explained.

Rocks would be useless for Seth and Peter, neither of whom used the Earth element. Unless they wanted to try our new backward way of using the opposite element. Before I could say anything, Harris started to babble.

"Look, we could really juice those things up for the coming battle. Kind of fight fire with fire, you see? We can make some sweet Soothers with that in case there's any active lava in the area or magma in the caves. Then we could fill several with water like you do with your company's water-crystals, except use them to douse any fireworks headed our way. I wasn't sure how much to get so we shoveled a barrel load in there. We took turns carrying it but after a while, it grew too heavy for us, and we wouldn't have even gotten it out of the park if I couldn't manipulate the land around it to carry it out and tilt it into the car. That was easier than the weightless spell."

The rest of us grinned. Harris was acting like a little boy on Christmas morning.

"Sounds good," I answered in a muffled voice. I yanked a tissue out of the box near me and blew my nose again.

"We can spell them the next time we make a pit stop. We should be able to do the whole load in ten minutes, tops, as long as we touch the ground."

Harris was right. We could create loads of awesome mechanicals pretty quickly if we had a plan and used our bodies as a conduit for the magic of Earth. I probably wouldn't even have to think too much about it, either. Imagining things might be the trigger that sparked my magic, but I wanted to expand my abilities, so I didn't have to stop and envision every tiny little thing. The same way Peter wanted to perform magic without always having to write it out like a line-drawing, or imagine a picture he drew in his head.

We were quick thinkers, but nobody thinks as quickly as magical instinct.

I scrunched down into the upholstery and rested the back of my neck on the seat. My nose was both stuffy and running, and I was sick of being sick. I really did feel better, but there was a lingering exhaustion that kept draining me. Like gravity took my power into Earth instead of Earth giving magic the way it was supposed to.

"Are you doing all right?" Peter asked. He leaned over

the bag of blue volcanic rock between us and studied me intently, eyes narrowed.

"Yeah, I'm fine. I'm tired of being sick, you know? I feel better, but I'm worried about what will happen when we meet the enemy, and I sneeze or something and give away our position."

"We could always shift everything one more night," he suggested. Peter looked concerned, and I could tell that was the last thing he wanted to do.

"No way. Uncle Ged needs us, and I'm not leaving him there. I was there, Peter, and he hurts. He hurts bad."

Peter slipped his hand around mine and squeezed. A flood of comfort filled me along with his Light, and I sighed. A slight cough escaped, but I ignored it.

I stayed awake the entire four and a half hours to Elko in Nevada, and I was more than ready to get out and use the facilities when we arrived. Thank goodness we needed to fuel up again or else I would have had to beg them to stop before my bladder burst.

There was an empty field not too far down the street from the gas station, and Seth drove us there when we were done gassing up. Peter chose to walk the short distance and got there at the same time.

"Let's do this thing," Harris said. The corners of my mouth rose into a matching smile. There was something so appealing about him when he was excited like that.

Peter and Seth hung back while Harris and I used Earth to shift the bag of volcanic rocks into the center of the field. Seth threw his hands up, and I felt the blanketing effect of a Nothing-to-see-here spell. It didn't look like there was anyone around, but as agents, we could never be too careful.

Harris poured the volcanic rocks onto the ground and shifted them into three groups while I slipped my silver star necklace off again and handed it to Peter, who tucked it into his pocket. Harris and I took a few minutes to center ourselves and stood near each pile with our hands clasped over them, much like the custom of magician brides and grooms holding hands over a pool of Water and a candle of Light. It was a great way to increase joint magic. Even mundanes had the habit of standing over things like that in their ceremonies although it didn't do them a lot of good without magic behind the ancient gesture.

We spelled the first pile into Soothers. When any of us threw them, a force of magic would burst out and smother whatever was nearby, the way a blanket covered a fire. It was like a universal antidote. If wicked magic were a poison, anyway. Which it sort of was.

When we moved on to the second group, I took the lead and used the Rector-patented method of making water-crystals. Except using the volcanic rocks rather than the usual crystals gave me a headache. I connected the blue color and swirls of the rock with the Water magic inside me, and they finally melded together into an explosive Water-powered grenade without further balking.

I tossed in a small sparkle for the heck of it. I think the part of me that took after my uncle made me do it. He made our escape route into a twisty slide. I made our volcanic grenades into glitter bombs.

Just because I could.

The third pile, mostly shards and lumps that gathered at the bottom of the bag, took longer. I ended up reaching out and yanking a little magic out of both Peter and Seth to add to ours and created something special. Like the wobbly air net Reg helped me create. All any of us had to do was toss a handful of the pebbles and dust at our target, and it would bind him.

We split the mechanicals evenly when I was done, despite my sneezing fit. I stuffed my volcanic rocks into my backpack, annoyed I didn't think to buy a leather pouch to attach to my belt to hold them. I would have to create it using magic, probably during the second half of our drive.

Seth pulled out a ball and threw it at Harris's head. Harris thrust out his hand and caught it before it caved in his skull.

"Cool," I said. I sounded bored and unimpressed like any other elite socialite, but thought it was fantastic.

"You think so?" Harris asked. The tone in his voice warned Seth, who took off running across the field at top speed. Harris turned on his heel and launched the ball at him, who leaped unnaturally high to catch it above his head.

Those two were freaks.

"Let them work off some steam," Peter said. "We'll cram back into the car soon enough. Want to stretch your legs?"

"Sure. I'm not totally exhausted. Yet." I smiled at Peter, and he took my hand, placing it in the crook of his elbow as we strolled around the perimeter of the field.

"Tell me more about the area where Ged's located,"

Peter suggested. "The more we know about that place, the better."

I thought about my dream, tapping back into the power that linked me to my uncle and allowed me to see out of his eyes, to form memories in my own mind.

"Well, it was dark of course. I couldn't see the ceiling, but he was in a massive cave. He was tied to a chair and covered in some kind of hood. I think it was magic, but fabric brushed his skin, too, so maybe it was a real bag. There's a deep, deep pit nearby glowing red from the magma. Uncle Ged's really close to it. I could feel the heat, and he's thirsty a lot because it's making him sweat."

I felt a twinge of pain and guilt at the thought of him there, alone, waiting for a rescue that was taking too long. I shoved my feelings aside and concentrated on the image of the location in my mind. I wanted to know it like the back of my hand by the time I got there. I set it firmly into my head so I would be familiar with every inch of enemy territory.

"Lia!" Seth shouted in the distance. Peter and I turned towards his voice.

I gasped. In front of us, maybe ten yards from the road, was a vast pit forming out of nothing, filled with a dark, pulsating heat. Red and orange, a moving shell of black, and glowing yellow.

Lava.

Exactly like I had pictured in my mind.

My hand fluttered near my collar, but my star necklace was missing. How did I not remember to put it back on?

A strangled cry broke through my terror-frozen lips.

Peter yanked on my arm, keeping me from slipping over the edge of the chasm. The heat felt like it was baking the bones inside me, but I shoved that thought aside, terrified I would somehow actually do it and kill myself since I didn't have the silver star around my neck protecting me from the accidental use of my magic.

Peter finally stopped dragging me behind him once we were back on the street, just within Seth's spell, which still hid us from view. There was no way the locals wouldn't notice a pit of lava randomly showing up one day.

"Here," Peter said. He sounded mad, and I shamefully took the necklace he thrust at me and clasped it around my neck. What kind of fool forgot to put on the only thing keeping them from destroying the world?

The kind of fool named Lia.

"Thanks," I said. My voice shook almost as hard as my hands.

Back in control of my magic, I narrowed my eyes at the field, superimposing how it looked before we got there over the view of the newly created pit of doom. Thankfully, I still had the power of Peter's Light bolstering me. The anger and frustration I felt towards myself brought the darkness surging up, and that was never helpful when I was trying to gain back my confidence. Not like there was a whole lot of that to go around. Not with the constant string of disasters I caused every time I let my guard down.

As soon as I could reach my center, look within, and pull the strength of my magic out, I blanketed the field in front of me with the image in my mind, calm and normal. And there it was. Plain, boring. No sign of lava or anything remotely dangerous.

Unless I considered the fact I was still there.

Which probably counted.

What a nightmare.

I could feel myself slipping under the dark, but Peter gripped my shoulder and gave me a shake. "That was my fault, not yours," he said.

"No, wearing that necklace is my duty," I shot back. I sounded crabby as well as stuffy.

"True, but I'm your partner and I was holding it for you," he pointed out. "I forgot to give it back."

Maybe he was mad at himself and not me. It was my responsibility, but Peter taking part of the burden still made me feel better. Maybe I could balance out the darkness after all.

"Well, okay. It's totally your fault then," I said.

Peter huffed out an exasperated laugh and tugged me to him, giving me a hug. He did that thing where he rested his hand on my head, gently stroking my hair, and I felt his Light flow through me. I heaved a huge sigh against him and closed my eyes. I squeezed my arms around him, still shaken by what I had done.

Seth and Harris reached our side. "You guys okay?" Harris asked.

"Yeah," I said. I didn't want to turn and face them. I was so embarrassed.

"Good," Seth said. "That was some seriously freaky crap there, Rector. But so awesome. I can't wait until Halloween. Can you imagine the kinds of horrors we can set up for the neighborhood kids to get through before they earn their candy?"

I burst out laughing. It was the most random thing to say, but it tickled my funny bone. I pushed away from Peter and turned to study the Andersson brothers. They both looked impressed, not angry. My shoulders slumped in relief.

No harm, no foul, I guess.

"Come on," Harris said. "Let's get back on the road. We need to be on our way and I think we have enough weapons." We walked back to the car slowly, enjoying the last few minutes of freedom before getting back into the car. It really didn't matter how roomy it was. We were all sick of it.

It dawned on me that Peter might still be mad at me when he sat across from me instead of next to me. I sighed and turned to the side, stretching out on the back seat, staring up at the ceiling.

I admit it. I was moping. But I deserved a moment to wallow in self-pity. Because of a stray thought, I had almost destroyed the world.

Well, okay, not the entire world maybe, but I could have definitely screwed up the local area. And since I had infinitely more magic available to me besides the amount I had already used by the time Seth shouted his warning, it could have been the whole world next.

Right when I thought I would end up losing the benefit of Peter's Light, he reached out and touched my cheek. It wasn't until then I realized I was crying.

What a baby.

"Let it go," Peter whispered. "It was my fault. And

you're too sick to be doing all these spells. It's too much. Try to sleep. You might see Armageddon again and then you can make sure he's still okay."

A sigh escaped my lips, but it sounded more like a sob. It had been a rough day.

Then things really did get worse. Once I fell asleep, my mother was waiting for me. She held out her hand, and when I reached for it, instead of grabbing hold, she used magic to throw me away.

I landed, crashing right into my uncle, who was still hooded and tied to that infernal chair. "Lia," he said through dry, cracked lips. "There's something I need you to see."

And just like that, he threw me away, too.

CHAPTER TWENTY-THREE
The Best Day Ever

MY BODY WAS HURTLED right into the enemy, who had been standing guard nearby.

It felt kind of slimy. And kind of good. I decided not to examine that too closely and instead concentrated on what was happening.

At that moment, I was inside the head of a little boy, sitting in the back seat of a car, holding onto his new puppy.

"Happy birthday, David," my mom said.

Well, not my mother. His mom. David's. Except she looked just like my mother to my eyes, probably because I was looking at her from David's perspective. Looking at her with the love a boy had for his mother. The same love I had for mine.

Part of me slipped, and I became less aware of who I was.

If I pulled back enough to remember I was Lia, the woman was a stranger. But she had the same look in her eyes that my mother always did when she looked at me. It really hit me exactly how much my mother had loved me even if it had been from a distance.

"Thank you, Mommy!" I said. Since I was a little boy, my voice was high. Higher than the voice I used, me, Lia Rector. My real voice was alto. But this boy was a pure, sweet soprano. "Thank you, too, Daddy."

I turned and looked at my daddy, who was driving the car. He was the tallest man in the world. He told me so himself, at least a hundred times. I wasn't sure if I believed him at first, but he was taller than all the other dads of the kids in my class so it had to be true.

No. Not in my class. Not in Lia's class. It was David's father who was taller than the other dads.

Internally, I wanted to cry, if I could cry with somebody else's eyes, surrounded as I was by the luminous ache of David's hero-worship and love. I saw my father instead of his. Donovan Rector, who was dead, and I had yet to see in my dreams. Donovan, the last CEO of Rector Enterprises, the man who spent his final day on earth trying to help me connect to my magic. A thing he always did. For me.

Suddenly, I wanted my father so badly I wondered if the boy David's eyes glistened with the tears I tried to shed and could not.

I had less control over myself than when I merged with Armageddon's mind through the Blood-of-my-blood spell. It hurt more, too as I struggled to maintain a sense of individuality and remember who I was. Lia Rector. Praelia Nox. Armageddon's ward. All the parts of who I was couldn't hold out against the self that was David, a little boy who had just gotten a puppy for his birthday.

Our eyes strayed to the small animal lying on the seat beside him. He thought the puppy was really cute.

So did I.

That's when my natural shield crumbled. Our thoughts the same, the merge complete. Except for a vague sense I was still myself in there somewhere, I became David and the agony I was causing myself by fighting to remain Lia ceased.

"It's the best present I ever got," I chirped in my soprano voice.

"I'm glad you like him. Do you know what you want to call him? I bet you can think of a really clever name," my mommy said. She smiled at me again, and I felt so good. She was the prettiest mom in the world. Lots of kids were jealous because their moms were mean, but mine wasn't. She was nice.

I knew exactly what I wanted to name my puppy. He was black, with brown parts on his face, but to me, he looked like a shadow, and that's what he wanted me to call him. I could tell.

"His name is Shadow. Shadow Racer," I said. "I'm going to teach him how to run really fast."

"What a wonderful name," Mommy said. "Shadow Racer."

"Good choice, son," Daddy said. He was still driving, but he slowed the car down, and I could see the smile on his face when he turned to look over his shoulder to make sure there weren't any cars in the way that would make us crash. He pulled into a parking lot near a store with shiny lights that hurt my eyes.

"You two stay here," he said. "I'll grab the drinks and pay for the gas."

He disappeared into the store. I forgot to ask my dad to buy Shadow something to drink.

"Mommy, do puppies drink milk?" I asked. I was scared that Shadow wouldn't get enough to eat or drink and then he would get sick.

"Not this one," she said. She was twisted all around with her back to the window so she could look at me and held out her hand. She stretched just far enough to pat the puppy where he sat. Her eyes crinkled at the edges like they always did when she told me she loved me. They were dark brown, just like Shadow's. Her hair was as black as his was, too, but had shiny silver strands in it. I had the same color hair, and I imagined myself running in front of Shadow, showing him how to race, all the kids jealous because I matched my puppy.

Somewhere inside, the person who was still Lia smiled at the thought. Lia also used to like pretending that there was a connection between herself and her toys if they looked alike. She wasn't lucky like David, though. She never owned a puppy.

"Will Daddy remember to get Shadow some water?" I asked.

"I know he will. I can see him through the window, and he just bought a small bowl to hold the water."

My daddy always took care of everything. I leaned over and tried to snuggle my puppy, but my seatbelt got in the way. Since we weren't driving, I unclicked it and bent over, carefully laying my head next to Shadow Racer, my hair blending into the fur near his belly.

I touched the puppy's side, feeling it get bigger and smaller with each breath he took. He was so soft.

"I had a good day," I whispered. "Mommy and Daddy took me to the zoo, and we had cotton candy and ice cream, and we ate lunch, and I asked for macaroni and cheese at the lunch place and Mommy said it cost too much but Daddy told her it was my birthday, so I got birthday macaroni and cheese at the zoo, anyway. Then we had a piece of cake and Mommy said not to eat too much or else I'd throw up because of too many sweets, but I ate the whole thing, and I didn't get sick at all. Then they stopped by the store on the way out of the city, and they picked you up and gave you to me, and this is the best day ever."

My mom's hand rested on my head and lightly scrunched my hair. I didn't shake her off. I hated when people patted my hair, but since I had such a good day, I let her.

Besides, it felt nice.

My eyelids closed slowly, and it was hard to open them again. I wanted to look at Shadow and see his belly rising and falling and count how many times he took a breath in a minute but I couldn't because I was sleepy and it was warm in the car, and my mommy was playing with my hair.

I probably would have fallen asleep if the monsters didn't shatter the windows with a roar. It felt hot, and all the air got sucked out of the car, and I couldn't breathe for what felt like forever.

Then I screamed. A piece of glass cut my cheek, and I was scared because Mommy was screaming, too, and I had never heard her scream before. She had never been scared before. She was the one I ran to when I had my nightmares, and she always looked at me and told me it was okay because she wouldn't let any of the bad things I saw in my sleep ever happen for real. She said she was really good at killing monsters.

But that's not what happened. Mommy screamed and threw my daddy's jacket over me, and everything went dark. I tried to tug it off, but the car was shaking, and I wasn't sure what to do. The puppy was squirming, so I held onto to him, sliding my hands around his belly to keep him still.

Shadow Racer kept trying to wiggle away. I pulled him up against my chest. Mommy stopped screaming. She made another sound, a horrible sound, and then it was quiet in the car.

I peeked out from under the jacket. The puppy wanted to get away, but I wouldn't let him. I took him with me when I climbed into the front seat even though there was broken glass everywhere.

There wasn't any glass where my mommy had been sitting. I knelt in her spot by the door and stuck my head out the window, trying to see where she went.

Before I could call out, the sound of her name froze in my mouth. She was on the ground, on her side. Her legs were bent, and her arms were above her head, and even though I didn't know what the word really meant, I knew she was dead.

Gone.

Just like the wicked witch in the story. She died, too. Mommy told me only the bad guys died, but she was on the grass, and she didn't move, and I had never seen anybody real die before, but that was what happened.

I tried to call her name again, but I couldn't do it. I turned to scream for my daddy instead, but when I looked his way, the store wasn't there anymore. There were a lot of broken things on the ground, and smoke came out, but the store was gone.

My mouth was open, but I couldn't make a sound.

A crunching noise came from the darkness on the other side of the junk pile where the store used to be. Footsteps in gravel. The bad guys were coming! I slid into the back seat again and pulled the jacket back over my head the way Mommy wanted it to be. It was really big and heavy. My daddy wore it when it got cold and he needed to work outside, and my mommy borrowed it from him.

"Come out!" I heard a man yell. He had a scary voice, and when he shouted, thunder boomed and shook the car.

I didn't want to. He scared me. I stayed where I was. The jacket slipped when the car started to shake, knocked around by the wind and rain that was suddenly hitting the car.

"You can't stop me!" It was a woman who said that, but not my mommy. My mommy was still lying on the ground.

"There you are," the bad man said. He sounded happy, and the thunder boomed right over the car, making my ears pop.

Then it was quiet. I waited a really long time, Shadow Racer pushing against me. I thought maybe he was scared because his heart was beating really fast.

I heard crunching outside again, the sound of the bad man's footsteps. I held Shadow tightly and scrunched my eyes closed, and then the footsteps moved away from the car. After a few minutes, I slipped out from under the jacket and looked over the edge of the window again.

Mommy was gone!

I put Shadow down on the floor and then got up on my knees so I could lean out the door, but no matter where I looked, all I could see was garbage and broken glass and bricks and the broken sign that used to be on the store. But she wasn't there anymore.

What was I supposed to do? I thought and thought about how to find her. Maybe I could be a detective! The big bad man scared me, but I watched the Mighty Magicians on TV before breakfast, and they Always Use Their Heads. The magicians went looking for the ice cream machine when somebody stole it from their park, and it left marks on the ground when it was dragged away, and they followed the drag marks.

There were marks on the ground that looked just the same. I would follow the drag marks, too.

I took one last look at my puppy. He was watching me and wagging his tail. He was a good boy. I picked him up and put him in the big side pocket of my daddy's jacket and zipped it until only his head peeped out so he could see. I pulled the jacket on and opened the car door.

The fabric got stuck under my knee, and I tripped and

284

fell on the ground, cutting my chin. I started to cry. It hurt, and I was really scared. But nobody came to help me. That made me cry harder, but then Shadow Racer yapped at me, and I stopped. He was right. I had to find my mommy.

The drag marks were hard to follow because the parking lot was made of gravel and sometimes the marks disappeared. They led away from the blacktop and the gas pumps, and I followed where they led.

The marks disappeared again, but I wasn't worried anymore. I could see Mommy lying on the ground in the distance, on the grass behind where the store had been. My daddy was next to her. They both were on their backs with their hands at their sides. I thought somebody was supposed to make their arms cross over their chests. When people died in the book about the witch, their arms were crossed but my parents looked like they were sleeping.

I looked around, but nobody else was there. I ran over to where my parents were and knelt down between them.

Maybe they were still alive!

I patted my mommy's cheek, but she didn't wake up. I touched her shoulder, and then I shook her, but she still didn't wake. I turned to my daddy and tried the same thing, but he just lay there, eyes closed, not moving. I put my head on his chest, but I couldn't hear his heartbeat. I turned back to my mommy, but I didn't know what to do. I reached out to shake her again, but I couldn't move my arm. It was frozen. My whole body was frozen.

In the distance, where the deep darkness was hiding things behind the junk pile, I heard the bad man coming.

I got up and ran. There was a dumpster behind a

wooden gate not too far away, and I raced for it so I could hide before the bad man saw me and killed me too.

The big door that usually hid the dumpster was open, and I closed it behind me. It was stinky in there, but I didn't care. I couldn't let the bad man get me, too.

"Did you find anyone else?" I heard a stranger call.

"No, this is it," the bad man answered. "I'll call it in. Thanks for coming, Mort."

He sounded angry. I lowered myself to the ground and slid quietly over to the space under the door of the dumpster and peeked out. Shadow wiggled in my pocket, but he stayed quiet.

There were two men. I wasn't sure who the bad man was, so I studied them both. The Mighty Magicians Always Paid Attention to Details so they would never get a spell wrong, and I paid attention, too. I wanted to tell the police about the bad man, so I needed to know what he looked like.

"No, let me report it. You keep an eye out just in case they come back before we've cleared the site," the stranger said. His was the different voice, the one the bad man called Mort. I couldn't see him very well, but I didn't care, because he wasn't the one who hurt my parents. I turned and studied the bad man closely.

Inside me, the person who still called herself Lia wept in horror.

"I doubt it. They're cowards. And they know they can't stand against the 'Mighty Magician Armageddon,'" he said. "They're too afraid to stick around. Not after that explosion."

286

He wasn't a Mighty Magician. They were the good guys, and Armageddon was a bad man. I studied him as hard as I could, memorizing every line in his face, the shape of his eyes, how long his hair was, everything. I concentrated so hard, my eyes hurt. But I would never forget.

I almost screamed when I saw Mort wave his hand over my parents and they disappeared. But I kept quiet. I had to wipe my face on the sleeve of my daddy's jacket, though, because it was hard to see while I was crying.

Mort disappeared, too.

All that was left was Shadow Racer and me. And Armageddon.

I wasn't sure if I should try to fight him, but then I decided that I would. I stood up and pushed the giant wooden dumpster door open, but when I stepped out, he was gone.

It was an empty field. There was no store, no gas pumps, no car, nothing. There wasn't anything there except Shadow and me and my daddy's big jacket.

I spun around, and the dumpster, there only a second before, was gone too.

"No!" I yelled. "Don't go! I want to fight you!"

It didn't matter that I was only six. I didn't know how to use magic yet, but I was going to hurt the bad man, anyway. I was a good guy and good guys always win. But he was gone. Everything was gone. And when I turned to look, the parking lot was not only gone, it had small weeds poking up around it as if the store had never been there.

I opened my mouth to shout my challenge again, but instead, I screamed. Shadow Racer whimpered as I dropped to my knees. I couldn't seem to stand. My cheek was pressing into the dirt, and the puppy was squirming in the pocket between me and the ground. I was screaming and screaming, and I wasn't ever going to stop.

But then my puppy licked my face, startling me. I thought he was safe in my pocket, but he wasn't, he was standing by me, licking my tears.

What if he got away?

What if the bad man came back and killed him?

I shut my mouth. I didn't want the bad man to hear me and come back. I wanted to get Shadow Racer and keep him safe. My mommy and daddy gave him to me. I couldn't lose him, too.

I rolled over and pushed myself up. Shadow yapped at me, and I held my hand out to him.

"Here, Shadow. Come here, boy," I called. He came close enough for me to grab. I put him back into the pocket in my daddy's jacket and then turned around.

Nothing looked familiar. I wasn't sure what direction to go to get home.

My daddy always told me if I got lost, not to walk away. He said to hug a tree and wait for somebody to come and find me. He said if I ever got lost, they would use a Finder spell and those didn't work if I kept walking.

My parents weren't there anymore, but my grandma was waiting for me. I was going to see her for my birthday dinner. If I didn't get there soon, she would be worried and come looking.

I spotted the shape of a tree in the distance. I walked a long time to get there, but I made it. Even with my daddy's jacket on, I couldn't stop shaking. My feet didn't work right anymore. I kept tripping. I wanted to lie down and never get back up again, just like my mommy and daddy. Maybe they would come and get me then.

Shadow Racer yapped once. I patted him and then looked up and there it was. The tree. It had a smooth, white, papery bark. I leaned forward and hugged it.

The leaves rustled as I cried. I wanted my parents back. I wanted my grandma to find me.

I wanted to catch the bad man.

But nothing happened. So I hugged the tree, hard, but my body kept shaking. Then the tears stopped, but I still held on, trembling and weak and scared.

And then finally, finally, my grandma used her spell so she could find me.

She arrived in a ball of golden light. The Novato family was mostly light inside. I didn't understand what that meant, but my daddy said it all the time, and he said we could use it to go anywhere, whenever we wanted to.

And Grandma wanted to come get me.

"David, baby, there you are. Come here, honey," she said.

I couldn't make my arms let go of the tree. She walked over to me, pulled my arms open, and then turned me so I could wrap them around her, instead.

She was warm. She smelled like chocolate and peppermint. I closed my eyes and took a deep breath. "I want to go home," I said.

"Where are your parents?" she asked.

I started crying again. She held me tight and let me.

Finally, I could talk again. "The bad man killed them," I said.

Grandma gasped, gripping me tighter. "No!" She sounded scared.

But I wasn't scared anymore. I was mad. I would find the bad man. I would always remember what he looked like. I would never forget his name. Someday when I was bigger, I would get him.

"He killed them," I said. "Armageddon came and took them away."

CHAPTER TWENTY-FOUR
We're All Tired of Driving

WAKING UP FROM THAT vision wasn't easy. It felt like I was drowning and just as I was about to break the surface and breathe again, I realized there was another three feet of water above my head. My breath whooshed out in a furious stream, and before I inhaled water, I saw a golden light burst through the darkness and somebody dragged me to the surface.

Hacking, I sucked in air between sobs. My body was shaking, and I hurt all over. Somebody thrust a handkerchief into my hand, and I used it to mop my eyes while a fierce warmth flowed through me and my vision finally cleared.

"Are you all right?" Peter asked. He was sitting across from me in the back of that infernal car, his head ducked down so he could look me in the eye. His hands were on my upper arms, and they were the source of the warmth and light.

I nodded but didn't speak, still struggling for breath

and trying to control my tears. I was scared. I was confused. And I was choking on it.

"Everything good back there?" Seth called. His hair was sticking up on one side where he had been leaning his head against the window, sleeping while Harris was driving the second half of our journey into Reno.

"I'm fine," I croaked. I picked up the water bottle Peter handed me and gratefully nodded at him as I took rapid sips. I wanted to wet my throat without choking, or worse, cramping my stomach and heaving it back up again.

"Did you see Ged?" Peter asked. He looked worried and kept his hands on me. I greedily took what he offered. There were too many shadows clinging to me, and his Light chased them away.

"Only for a second. He wanted me to see something else instead." I stopped. I blew my nose on a tissue as an excuse to avoid talking while I tried to sort out my feelings about what I saw.

"How did he look?"

"Not great. But he seemed stronger than the last time I saw him." I thought back to my dream and something odd occurred to me. "In fact, he was able to use a spell to grab me and propel me into our enemy. I didn't think about it then, but he couldn't have done that before."

"Maybe he's figured out a way to reach his magic through that nullifying field," Peter guessed.

"I don't know. I didn't have time to think because he shoved me right into the guy and suddenly I was him." I shuddered, remembering that slimy-yet-good feeling.

"Did you pick up anything that could help us?" Seth

perked up.

"Yeah, his name is David Novato. I think he's around your age, maybe a little older. It was hard to tell, though." My eyebrows drew together in concentration as I struggled to remember anything else that might be useful. "His parents died on his sixth birthday."

Birthdays carried a lot of significance in the magician world. Destroying somebody's family on a day like that would guarantee the trauma would be the worst, and unforgettable. Almost like a spell had been worked into his blood and it would never leave. My uncle would never have done that to an innocent child.

Except he did.

And I couldn't figure that out. Why did he do it? And why didn't he look for little David, the way he looked for Peter?

"That's rough," Peter said. He leaned back and handed me more tissues. I smiled my thanks as I pulled myself together.

"Yeah. He was so happy, too. Such a cute little kid to turn into such a monster later in life." I scowled. I wouldn't allow sympathy to creep in and make me weak. I pushed Peter's Light aside and tapped into my Dark. I needed to think clearly, rationally, emotionlessly.

"What happened?" Harris asked. He was still driving. It was dark outside the windows of the car, and besides the occasional light flashing by, I mostly just saw my reflection.

"The kid spent his birthday at the zoo with his parents, and they stopped for gas and snacks on the way home. They parked in the gravel. It was this tiny podunk place with only two pumps. There was a sign that said they had to pay in advance." It was all so confusing for poor David, and I was trying to sort through the shock and agony he felt to find a useful memory. "Mort and Uncle Ged were there."

Maybe there was something in my voice. Peter grew still and looked at me steadily. "What did they do?" he asked.

Tension rose in the air like a thick cloud, and I wished I could tell what he was thinking. I reached out to him with everything I held inside me, but I was blocked by the shield he had thrown up around himself. Just like the times he came back from an assignment, and he couldn't tell me about it. I wasn't sure he even realized he had done it.

"I think Uncle Ged was the one who killed his parents," I murmured through numb lips. It was only a small lie. There was no doubt in my mind that was what had happened, but it seemed like I was somehow betraying my uncle by saying so in such bold terms.

Peter grunted, his brow furrowed. Now he was the one who couldn't reconcile the events with what he knew. "You think kidnapping Ged is revenge?" he asked.

I nodded. That had to be what my uncle needed me to know. That this guy, David Novato, wanted vengeance. And he was doing a good job, too. At least until we showed up. Then he would regret every blow.

"Well, that must have been a barrel of laughs," Seth said. He tugged something out of his pocket and tossed it at me. "Here, you probably need this more than I do."

I caught it and looked down. Chocolate. I shook my

head at him but couldn't keep the grin off of my face. "Yeah, maybe I do. Thanks." I tore off the wrapper and popped a piece into my mouth. Heaven. Closing my eyes, I sank back against the seat, sighing loudly. The guys laughed at me, but I didn't mind. Calories always helped after a bad vision, and everyone knew chocolate was the universal symbol of bliss.

I should examine my dream, but there would be nothing there for me except pain and confusion. I sighed again and broke off another piece of chocolate. Peeking over the seat in front of me, I made sure Seth and Harris weren't looking, and then slipped it to Peter. I didn't mind sharing with him, but if I offered any to the other guys, I would never see it again.

He winked at me and then shifted his weight so he was leaning against the window. It looked uncomfortable, and I frowned at him.

"What?" he murmured.

"You'll get a crick in your neck," I whispered back. Seth had dozed off again and I didn't want to bother him. He had done most of the driving, and I wanted to let him sleep.

Peter shrugged. "I don't have a pillow."

"Don't be stupid," I said and patted the seat next to me. He let out a huff of air that sounded a lot like a laugh and slid across the way. He slouched back, and I leaned against him. Once I was comfortably situated with my head on his chest near his shoulder, he tilted his head so it would rest on mine.

We often sat like that when I was having a hard time

right after Chas left me. It was comforting for the both of us, although I had forgotten until that moment that Chas was a like a brother to him and Peter had been hurting, too.

I was so selfish. A small jolt of acid burned through me at that thought, but my contact with Peter kept it from turning into darkness.

"Does it ever drain you when you do that?" I asked. I didn't need to explain what I meant because he knew me that well by then.

"No. It doesn't drain me at all. I've been thinking about that lately," he said. His words were slow and fuzzy. "I wonder if something is happening between us that's like your work with the opposite elements. I don't try it, the Light just seems to flow into all the parts of you that need it. And it squeezes some of your Dark out and into me. It's like an exchange, except somewhere between you and me, your Dark turns into Light. We're basically recharging each other."

"That's crazy," I said. My head bumped his chin when I sat up, and he groaned. "Magic transference doesn't work that way."

"I know. Man, Lia, can't you let me sleep?" Peter rubbed his hand down his face and guilt flooded me. Poor guy. I had been sleeping a lot for days. He must be exhausted since he had to watch my back that whole time.

"Sorry," I said and slouched into his side. It made him grunt, and I smiled into the crook of his neck.

"Brat," he said. "Come on, let me doze a minute. We'll be there soon and I need to be alert when we get there."

I wanted to say more but bit my tongue for his sake. I

felt guilty even though it wasn't my fault I had been so sick. I blew my nose one last time before settling back down.

Despite the nightmare I just had, I still wanted sleep. I closed my eyes and concentrated on Peter's Light, which surrounded me like a cocoon, and relaxed. He was so warm, and comfortable, and I no longer had to worry about draining him. I guess things weren't so bad after all.

"We're here," Harris called out. My eyes popped open, and I sat up, stretching.

"Where's here?" I asked. I glanced at the clock, and even though it wasn't quite midnight, it felt like we had been driving for a week. "Can we get out?"

"Yeah, we're good. The safe-house has a security perimeter shield spell, and we're already inside it." Harris opened the door and slid out. I followed as quickly as I could and was overcome by the need to stretch again. I reached my arms up to the sky and arched my back, groaning. It felt so good.

I looked around curiously. We were in the suburbs, and when I squinted my eyes, I could see the transparent light-blue honeycomb that indicated a protection spell surrounding the two-story house, the lawn, and the driveway where we parked. I could make out houses of the same general size and shape down the block. It was kind of a boring neighborhood.

"So, the safe-house is in a house?" I asked dumbly.

Seth snorted. "Yeah. Most of them are. You were just spoiled because the first one you ever saw was in a coffee shop. I admit that was really cool." He popped the trunk

297

and dragged out a small bag. I didn't know when he even got it, but I shrugged and turned back to the car. Peter had climbed out, so I leaned in to grab my backpack and closed the door behind me.

"I'm starving," I said.

"A girl after my own heart," Seth teased. "Let's go find something to eat inside before I faint from hunger. Maybe if we're lucky, one of your food cornucopias will be there."

I walked up the sidewalk next to Seth, feeling proud. Rector Enterprises supplied food, drink, and energy to most of the safe-houses all over the world. That way, bringing in supplies wouldn't tip anyone off that more people were staying there than usual.

A comment I had overheard once, long ago, popped into my head. My father had been talking about a safe-house that some magicians wanted to set up in a shoebox, and he kept trying to tell the poor guys it didn't matter how large it was inside - if nobody could get through the opening, it wouldn't work.

The memory brought a smile to my face. That is until the safe-house door opened, and Kamini was standing on the other side.

CHAPTER TWENTY-FIVE
I Didn't See That One Coming

THE DUMBEST DESCRIPTION I have ever heard was when some woman had "sparkling eyes." Ha. And yet there Kamini stood, her eyes shining and happy to see us, and when Peter stepped forward to say hello in a thrilled voice, they sparkled.

Why was she even there?

"I used a transfer spell to get to Las Vegas," Kamini explained when she noticed our surprised expressions. "And then drove here to Reno to meet you."

"Well, it's good to see you," Peter said. He gave her a side hug but left his arm around her for longer than necessary, and she took the opportunity to lean into him like she wanted to stay there forever.

"I thought a familiar face would be nice," she said modestly, grinning.

"How sweet," I said. I thought I had done a good job pretending I meant it, but the look Seth and Harris exchanged made me wonder. "Aren't you afraid they might have followed your trace to Vegas and then tailed your car?"

Somebody had to ask the logical questions. None of the guys acted like they were going to as we shuffled our way into an open, airy living room.

"Oh, no." Kamini looked so gracious and sweet I didn't expect what came next. "I know you're still an inexperienced apprentice so that might seem like a good question, but my family has a network for that. I drove in seven separate vehicles with three different disguises. Other family members tailed me for an hour after each stop to change cars to make sure nobody was following. It's standard operating procedure. Your uncle helped set it up."

Slam. How embarrassing - for me. So now I was a petulant, ignorant fool. I sighed. "That's great," I said through tight lips. Kamini was genuinely so nice there was no way to snipe at her for calling me inexperienced without looking like an idiot. Especially since it was true.

She smiled and offered to show me to the restroom so I could pull myself together. I skulked off behind her. My hair probably looked like a wreck, and I was sure I had something gross jammed in my teeth again because I couldn't catch a break.

I wanted to hide as long as I could in the little half bathroom downstairs. It was cramped, but the mirror was large, and I could see myself down to my knees if I leaned back.

And of course, I was a rumpled mess.

I gave up on trying to outdo Kamini. Besides, that crack about being an inexperienced apprentice made me embarrassed to put my uniform on, so I changed into a pair of navy yoga pants and a blue shirt with white stripes. It had a v-neck, so a little cleavage showed, my only attempt at competing. I blew my nose for the five-hundredth time. It was still stuffy, but otherwise, I felt human again. Maybe only a bit tired. I bushed my hair into a ponytail high on my head, then spun it around and around, looping it back on itself until it became a bun. I used a bright yellow scrunchy to keep it in place.

Whatever. I refused to put on any makeup and look like I was trying to challenge Kamini's undeniable beauty. Besides, there wasn't anyone there I wanted to impress.

Really.

"Feeling better?" Kamini asked, surprising me. She was waiting outside in the hall when I opened the door.

"Yeah, I'm great." I pushed by her and went back into the living room. The guys were finishing sandwiches Kamini must have provided for them. So much for a big meal. My stomach clenched, no longer hungry anyway. Seth raised an eyebrow when I hurried over to the love seat and sat beside him. I didn't look Peter's way. I wasn't sure why, but I was annoyed at him. I didn't even care that meant Kamini had a choice and could sit next to him or by herself in a chair.

I knew it. She chose the spot next to Peter on the couch. Of course.

"We've got laundry facilities if you need them," Kamini offered.

"That won't be necessary," I said. "I'll take care of our clothes if you guys want to give them to me. I can get them clean in no time." If I could dry off my clothes in an instant by pulling the water out by magic, there was no reason I couldn't get rid of any foreign matter from the clothing just as quickly. And it would give me something to do in the other room so I didn't have to participate in the conversation. The mood I was in didn't bode well for our peace of mind or casual social discourse.

I felt a stab of desire to knock Kamini out of the way and sit next to Peter. His Light would help me battle the darkness inside me that was making me a gloomy wretch.

Instead, I leaned into Seth when he gave me a quick hug of thanks before he stood up to yank his clothes out of his pouch. I needed the comfort. But like a typical guy, he couldn't wait to dump laundry on the only female on the team.

Maybe that was unfair since I offered, but I didn't care. I was crabby, and as long as I stewed silently, I decided I could be as unfair as I wanted.

Harris handed me his clothes next. My arms were full, so I headed over to where Kamini had indicated the laundry room was located so I could spread out and work my magic. I left the door cracked open so I could hear the conversation, but not take an active part. I didn't have enough control over myself.

My hand snaked up, and I touched my necklace delicately, reassuring myself that it was still there. I had a sudden, overwhelming fear I might have left it off again and one of my stray thoughts would obliterate my friends.

"How was your trip?" Kamini asked.

"It went well. We were ambushed near the airport,

though." Harris sounded all tough and casual about it. I glared at the shirt in my hands, then gave it a vigorous shake.

"How scary!" Kamini exclaimed. "Were any of you injured? Do you need anything?"

"No, we all made it out okay," Seth said. He sounded fierce and manly, too. I wanted to gag. The two of them had been unconscious. All they did was have me drag their sleeping bodies back to dry land. Big deal.

"Thanks to Lia," Peter said. I froze. Had he heard me? Did I say that out loud? "She was the real hero of the hour. Not many people can say they saved their entire team on the first day of their first assignment."

I grinned as I laid out the jeans and uniforms the guys handed over. His compliment washed over me like a shot of Light straight from the source. Peter was the best friend a girl could have. The darkness even let up a little. He must have noticed Kamini dissed me earlier and wanted to put her in her place for attacking his best friend.

"True," Seth said. I could picture the dark, mysterious look on his face, trying to charm the only girl in the room. "She was a real trooper."

Okay, that wasn't as good as Peter's compliment, but it was enough to allow me to refocus and whisk all the dirt, sweat, and blood out of Seth's clothes. In a second, they were clean and fresh.

Oh, yeah. I was good.

"I'm glad to hear it," Kamini said. "It seems like such a dangerous assignment for somebody who doesn't know what they're doing."

Wow. She sounded so nice and sweet and concerned while she dissed me like that.

"Lia's the type of person who will always help. Despite coming into her magic only recently, in every circumstance, she has found a way to win," Peter said. I could barely hear him, but there might have been a little anger in his voice.

Kamini must have thought so, too, because she changed the subject. "Well, I'm glad you made it here in one piece. Do you know how long you'll be staying?"

"At least one night. We haven't decided yet," Harris said. He may have liked Kamini, but he wouldn't let her in on our plans, and it was pushy of her to ask. It wasn't her place.

Heaving a sigh, I closed the laundry room door so I couldn't hear anymore. If my internal voice was going to lead me down a path that turned into a class war, I didn't want to follow. I already felt guilty enough about how I dismissed alchemists like everyone else did. I didn't need to act like support staff were beneath me, too.

I finished cleaning Harris and Seth's clothes, then spent extra time folding them carefully. I needed to force myself into a better frame of mind. I mulled over Peter's comments and it helped brighten my mood. I had that sense of his lightness again and it buoyed me up inside. By the time I was ready to join them again, I could act chipper and engaging.

My mother once told me that the best way to get back at the girls who hogged all the attention because of their looks was to steal the attention away with my winning personality. She said people remembered how you made them feel better than how you looked, so their positive memories of me would last longer.

It sounded like decent advice. Besides, there was no way I could outshine the goddess of beauty with no makeup on.

There was an awkward pause when I walked back into the room. "Here you go," I said, honey dripping from my voice as I handed Harris his clothes. He smiled his thanks and put them away.

Seth held out his arms, and I gave him a flirtatious half-smile when I passed him his clothing. His eyebrows raised, but I kept it up, catching his eye and making sure it looked like we were sharing a moment, an understanding about something that nobody else knew. I was laying it on a little thick since we weren't exactly flirting buddies, but I saw him shrug before he stuffed his clean clothes back into his pouch and lightly rested his hand on my arm while he said his thanks.

Oh, yeah. That was a good move. My skin felt warm where he touched it. If I had a crush on him, I would probably have swooned or something.

"No problem, guys. It was nothing." I sat next to Seth, and he left his arm by his side so it touched mine. His leg also pressed against me. I normally enjoyed casual contact with others, but I had a brief sense of uncertainty about it. Did I go too far?

Maybe. But the contact also gave me the confidence to look at Peter and Kamini.

She had her legs curled up beside her on the couch, bringing her body closer to Peter. He wasn't touching her, but I bet his nose was filled with her stupid perfume.

I shook off a wave of annoyance. What was wrong with me? Peter deserved to be happy. If Kamini would make him happy then so be it. In fact, I would even help.

That's why when Kamini offered to show us around, I told her I was too tired and would rather stay behind. It was easy enough to get Seth to stay, too, just by pressing myself a little more firmly into his side. He shifted, then slid his arm onto the back of the love seat, right behind me.

Harris raised an eyebrow. Then he got a glint in his eye. "Yeah, I think we're all mostly wiped out. Why don't you show Peter where our rooms are? We'll head up there when we're ready to go to bed."

Peter shrugged and followed a beaming Kamini out of the room.

"Isn't it weird how driving for hours and hours can tire you out?" I said. "I was sitting and dozing all day long, and yet all I want to do is sit around more."

Seth chuckled. I leaned my head back, genuinely tired, forgetting that his arm was there. I ended up resting my neck on his arm as if I were trying to snuggle into him.

Oops.

He shifted slightly and suddenly the entire right side of my body pressing against him. Now there's a guy who had moves.

"That is funny," Seth murmured. I closed my eyes because I didn't want to look at him. I kept accidentally hitting on him and was afraid of what I would see.

"It is weird," Harris said, his voice also quiet. Maybe he was helping pave the way for his brother.

Oh my gosh, what had I gotten myself into?

Then an image flitted through my mind, and I saw the younger me again through Seth's eyes, a part of the memory he had sent when we were experimenting in the truck. Seth and Harris helped keep me safe when I was in eighth grade even though I didn't know it. They were both kind-hearted and couldn't stand bullies. And they were good looking, too. If I was going to flirt with somebody, there were worse people.

Although I probably should have chosen Harris since he was the fairer of the two and didn't look as much like Chas. I cringed and my eyes popped open. How shocking. I hadn't even thought about Chas the entire time I was accidentally throwing myself at another guy.

That was progress, I guess. I shoved the thought of my ex-boyfriend out of my head and looked down. I noticed a thread was coming loose near the outside seam on Seth's jeans. I reached down and tugged on it absently, wondering if I should try to cut it off before it unraveled more.

"I think I'll wash up," Harris said. He beat a hasty retreat, heading down the hall towards the half bathroom I had used earlier, leaving Seth and me alone. Even though some of my flirting with him was unintentional, I still felt a thrill of excitement go up my back.

"How are you feeling?" Seth asked. He peered down into my face, which really wasn't all that far from his. His lips looked firm, and I wondered how they would feel if he stole a kiss despite my uncle making him promise to stay away from me.

"I'm better. Still a little stuffy, but otherwise I've recovered."

"That's good," Seth said absently. I realized his fingers were playing with a bit of hair that was sticking out of my sloppy bun. My mouth opened to respond, but I wasn't sure what to say. I hesitated a second too long because my partially open lips were all the invitation he needed.

Wow. He really knew how to kiss. I could feel it all the way down to my toes. I shifted and before I knew it, I was kissing him for all I was worth, his arms wrapped around my back, plastering me against him. The emptiness that had been hurting me since Chas left was suddenly filled. It was wonderful to feel whole again, wanted again.

I could have stayed that way for hours. He was that good. But my nose was still stuffy and after a few more seconds, I realized I would have to pull back to take a breath or else I would suffocate. I recalled my hands from where they were clasped around Seth's neck and slid them down his chest to help me back away.

Man, he felt so good, though. He was really fit.

I pushed against his firm chest just a bit and Seth broke off the kiss. I gasped in some oxygen and made a small noise when all the air whooshed back out. I guess that was enough to convince him I was enjoying his attention because he leaned forward again and kissed me until I was cross-eyed.

My body melted into him, and before I became desperate for air again, he pulled away on his own and then slid his lips across my jaw and over to my ear. I shuddered when his teeth gently bit my earlobe. Electricity shot through me when his warm breath caressed me. "I've wanted to do this since the second I saw you," he murmured.

I groaned. How things had gotten so complicated so fast was beyond me. But my body seemed to crave something he offered. It shivered on its own and snuggled closer.

That was all the invitation he needed because he gripped the back of my hair to hold me steady and worked his way back to my mouth.

And yeah. I liked it. I liked it a lot. I tried to press myself even closer. And I could tell he liked it too because he answered my movements with a groan of his own.

I didn't know what would happen next, but whatever it would be was interrupted by Harris clearing his throat.

"Sorry, guys. Ah, Peter's been calling us. I think we need to go upstairs."

I pressed my face into the crook of Seth's neck so I wouldn't have to show my burning cheeks to Harris. Oh man, how embarrassing. I listened until his footsteps went all the way up the stairs, and then Seth and I were alone again.

"Well, as much as I'm enjoying myself, duty calls. Come on." Seth grinned at me. I smiled back, deciding to brazen it out. We slipped off the couch. He leaned closer.

I stood frozen, wondering what he would do, worried and excited he might kiss me one last time, but he didn't. He tugged the stupid yellow scrunchy out of my hair and handed it to me. My bun must have fallen down while we were making out.

With a sigh, I looped my hair back into order as best I could without the help of a mirror. By the time we hit the upstairs loft, I probably looked downright normal.

Not that I was. There surely wasn't anything normal

about accidentally falling into some kind of relationship with a guy you only vaguely noticed before. And I knew it was a relationship because no matter how fast and loose Seth acted, no guy would have told a girl how much he wanted her unless he was positive he already had her.

Oh, well. I would think about that later. At the moment, I was too freaked out to decide what I really wanted, anyway.

Kamini showed us to our rooms. I doubted my magnanimous gesture of sending the two off together did either of them any good because Kamini's lips didn't look as swollen as mine felt. That or Peter wasn't a good kisser.

Something inside me rejected that thought as soon as it occurred. No way. I knew it as well as I knew my own name that Peter would be amazing to kiss.

And that left me wondering why I was thinking about kissing him right after I just kissed Seth.

Man, I really was tired.

CHAPTER TWENTY-SIX
I Find a Letter

I TOSSED AND TURNED all night. Even though it might be too soon to get into a relationship with somebody new, it was too late to avoid thinking about it because I was pretty much already in one.

Besides, Seth was gorgeous, and a good kisser. Those were his upsides.

On the downside, he was four years older than me, and my uncle was probably going to kill him.

But since I jumped into it all hot and heavy, how would I step back and just drop it? That wouldn't be fair or very nice. Not that it mattered. I was under no obligation to move forward if I didn't want to. But strangely enough, I did. So I would. Even if it was unexpected.

I punched my pillow a few more times and shoved those thoughts out of my head. I really, really needed sleep. I was going after my uncle soon, and I had to be strong. I did my best work when I was well-rested.

Sighing loudly, I took three big breaths and then forced my thought patterns into a meditative direction. It was a trick magicians learned while still in school. It helped on tough test days. The teachers wanted us to learn the knack because every working magician was occasionally faced with a disturbing situation and we needed enough sleep to stay on our toes.

The only drawback to meditative sleep was that sometimes I woke up so abruptly at the implanted time that it startled me. Like I was waking from a nightmare but couldn't remember what it was. It wasn't exactly comforting and seemed stupid that a sleep technique meant to promote inner peace left me feeling so freaked out.

Or, it could be that Seth and his amazing kisses were too much for my subconscious to figure out for me.

I got up and trudged to the shower. I had been thrilled to see that my assigned bedroom had a private bathroom. I was spoiled by my chambers at Castle Laurus and the rickety little half-bath downstairs just hadn't cut it.

And I couldn't imagine accidentally meeting someone in the hallway on my way to a shared bathroom. The horror.

Was getting together with him really so bad, though? Seth was hot, and he was smart, and he liked me. He bought me apple juice when I was sick. He told me he had wanted to kiss me since we met. Another thrill of excitement shot through me at that thought. Surely I wouldn't feel that way if I didn't like him, too?

And I wasn't taken or anything. I accepted that Chas and I were over somewhere on the road to save my uncle. It was time I moved on. And I felt so whole when

Seth kissed me. He made the emptiness go away.

The image of how it looked when Chas rested his hand on Clarissa's waist flashed across my mind, causing my lips to draw into a scowl as I gritted my teeth. I definitely didn't owe him my loyalty. I scrubbed my hair a little too hard, angry at that memory the most.

After I rinsed off, I tugged my clothes out of the depths of my backpack and laid them out along the counter. I kept my towel wrapped around my body while I spent a few minutes cleaning them the way I cleaned Harris and Seth's clothes the night before, except I swiped the natural strawberry scent in my shampoo and wove it into the fabric. By the time finished, there was a faint fresh scent of strawberries and sunshine, since I used Light to magic it in. Maybe, if the whole Irregulars thing didn't work out, or Rector Enterprises failed, I could go into the laundry business.

Lightning fast clean and a signature scent of summer.

I snorted as I folded my clothing, gently pushing the pile into my backpack. I tugged on a pair of threadbare jeans that hugged my hips and showed off my belly button when I raised my arms and my t-shirt hitched up. It was a gray athletic shirt with a logo faded into illegibility on the front, leftover from one of my various high schools. I didn't even remember the name anymore, but it didn't matter. It was soft and pliable and comfortable. It also made me look killer. Kamini might have Peter's attention, but I noticed Seth had been checking her out, too, and for better or worse, he was mine.

And I would make sure she knew it.

I used my tinted lip balm. It tasted like raspberry and highlighted my lips just enough to draw attention to them. I didn't need any mascara because my lashes were naturally long and black (thank you, mother) and I skipped the eyeshadow. No need to look like I was trying - it would ruin the artless effect I wanted to pull off.

Then I plaited two small braids starting at my temples and tied them together behind my head to keep my long hair out of my face, like a headband. I could always put in my battle braids later - if I needed to. I had read in countless magazines that men loved natural, touchable hair, and I would use that to my advantage.

I slipped on white socks with my pink and white polka-dot tennis shoes. They were somewhat feminine, and I had learned during my many interactions with Harris and his brother that Seth thought girls should look like girls.

That probably meant he was a chauvinist at heart. I didn't mind catering to him to attract his eye, but he better get used to that being the only girly thing about me. Not to mention, I was a stronger magician than he was. He needed to deal with that up front, too.

And that was that.

I made sure I packed all of my toiletries back into the carry sack and headed out. I was finally ready to face the day.

Nobody was downstairs. I snorted. They were all still asleep. Of course. I mean, I was looking really cute, and I only saw people when I looked like a disaster.

I shuffled off to the living room where we talked the night before and set my backpack down. I dug around until

I found some of the magic books I had been dragging with me and decided it was as good a time as any to crack the code to allow me to weave indirect magic into my direct magic spells. It sounded crazy, but the enemy we were about to face could kill the magic around him. I wanted to confront David Novato with all the power in my arsenal. There was no way I would let that man beat me. It was time he realized that kidnapping my uncle was the biggest mistake of his life. Because Armageddon's ward was going to take him down.

As soon as I figured out how.

It took two solid hours, but I did it. I finally found a method to piggyback indirect magic into my spells as long as I had the ingredients available. The key was to crush the herbs and elements in my hand while I was forming my direct magic spells. As a bonus, I even discovered a new method of amplifying meditative sleep so we wouldn't have to stop and rest overnight anymore.

Satisfied, I stood up and stretched, trying to work out the kinks in my neck and back from hunching over the ancient books for such a long time. I closed my eyes and took a deep breath, reaching up towards the ceiling. Although I hadn't heard a sound, I knew when Seth entered the room. I could feel it.

My shirt had popped up a little from the waistband of my pants as I stretched. I smiled and opened my eyes, catching Seth's gaze as I tugged his hands towards me to slide them around my exposed midsection. It was nerve-wracking being so bold, but I wanted to show that I was still interested in him and that his touch was welcome.

"Good morning," Seth purred.

"I didn't hear you come downstairs," I said as I lowered my arms, my soft shirt sliding over Seth's hands, hiding them from view. He tugged me towards him and looked down into my face for a long moment. I couldn't keep the corners of my lips from moving upwards. It felt wonderful to have somebody find me that interesting again. I missed being the focus of somebody's attention and my breath caught in my throat in response to the look in Seth's eyes.

"I'll show you how to silence your steps," he offered. Before I could ask for more details, he leaned forward and kissed me gently. Slowly. It was so different from the urgency the night before, but as a slow burn started in my stomach, I decided I liked it even better.

When we pulled apart, Seth had tangled his hands in my hair. He didn't let go.

"Hi," I said, like an idiot. Something about the way he was staring at me made my heart pound even harder than his kiss did.

One side of his mouth quirked up. "Hey," he replied. Then he leaned towards me, and this time, I met him halfway. I was eager to feel his warm lips on mine again, and one tiny part of me wanted to avoid talking. I didn't know what to say, and a kiss was a good distraction.

Only seconds later, I heard somebody clear their throat. Seth and I broke apart. I turned to see Peter and Harris on the stairs, staring down at us. Harris looked exasperated, and Peter looked...

I wasn't sure how Peter looked, actually. He turned to run back upstairs too quickly for me to tell. He held out

316

his hand when he reached the last step, and Kamini was suddenly there, carrying a bundle of clothing. Peter took it from her, and that was when I realized she had taken care of his laundry for him.

Whatever.

Seth slipped his hands off my waist, which made me feel cold and lonely. Irritated that Kamini could throw me off my game like that, I plastered a friendly smile on my face and followed him over to the love seat where a few of my books still sat piled up where I had discarded them.

"Is anyone hungry?" Kamini asked brightly as she glided gracefully down the stairs. "I can make French Toast and omelets if you'd like."

"That would be great," Harris said. He seemed to be the only person in the room not preoccupied with something.

We sat around looking awkward while Kamini bustled off into the kitchen. Peter stuffed his clothes into his backpack and flopped onto the recliner.

"We should get closer to the volcano tonight and see if we can gather some intel before going in," Peter said, launching right into making plans. I relaxed although I didn't realize I had been so tense until then.

"Yeah, this guy's been on a nocturnal schedule. We should hit him during the day. He'll be tired," Seth said. He put his arm around the back of the love seat again. I didn't lean against him, but I was glad. The more we interacted, the less uncertain I would feel about it.

I just didn't want to make everyone else feel uncomfortable. At least, that was probably why I felt so weird about it all. And I didn't want to think too deeply about how I was feeling. Because I had more important things to think about. Like saving my uncle.

The darkness that was always with me crept closer to the surface, and my racing heart settled. Who knew my dark side could counteract my anxiety attacks?

"That's what I thought. We'll go in tomorrow. I think Ged's waited long enough," Peter replied. "Lia, if it's okay with you, I'd like to do another session without your necklace. The sooner you get used to monitoring your stray thoughts, the better."

He didn't mention the mistake I made before, but turning the park into a lava pit was still fresh on my mind. I never wanted something like that to happen again. The darkness inside me expanded a little, and it was enough to tip my near-balance into the negative.

"Sounds good." I jumped up, trying to distract myself from the feelings of resentment and annoyance rising. None of the guys deserved to be the target of my internal upheaval. "Why don't we head into the loft while Kamini makes breakfast? We can do some work before we eat."

I always worked better on an empty stomach, and Peter readily agreed. I knew he remembered that about me. Peter remembered everything about me. That's what made him such a great friend.

We headed upstairs while Seth and Harris bickered and teased each other. It was a little annoying, but it also reminded me of how they convinced a bully to leave me alone when I was barely fourteen, so in the end, their behavior caused me to smile.

"So, what's up with you and Seth?" Peter asked. "I

didn't know the two of you were dating." The loft was mostly unfurnished, but there were a couple of chairs, and his battle vest was laying across one of them. He shifted it out of the way, and I could tell by the streak of dirt on one side that Kamini hadn't cleaned it for him.

"It's kind of new," I answered, acting casual. I had no idea how I really felt about it, much less how to talk about it. I held out my hand for the vest, and Peter handed it over. We both sat instead of getting to work. I listened for a moment to the muffled sounds of furniture rattling and realized that Seth and his brother were likely wrestling.

Honestly, you would think they were a couple of children the way they acted at times.

"I guess so," Peter said. He had a laugh in his voice, and when I looked over at him, he was smiling. "I'm glad you're moving on."

I didn't know why, but his comment annoyed me.

It was probably the darkness roiling inside me. I should have asked Peter for some of his Light for balance, but I stubbornly refused. I didn't want help from somebody so eternally cheerful. It got to be annoying.

I shook his vest. "This needs to be cleaned, too," I said.

"Yeah, I forgot to hand that over last night. Too tired, I guess. I can take care of it. I don't need the house honey to do it for me."

It was strange that Peter used that term. It wasn't very nice, and I narrowed my eyes at him, trying to decide whether he was making a dig at me. I was sure he noticed I didn't like Kamini much, so maybe he meant her.

"No, let me," I said. "I did all the other ones, anyway.

319

Besides, you can't call on all the elements the way I can."

Peter looked surprised. I think my annoyance and frustration showed. He probably thought I was mocking his magical abilities.

Guilt poured through me, bringing more darkness with it. I could tell I was on edge, but my annoyance kept me from speaking up. Besides, I didn't want Peter to know I needed him that much. It made me feel weak that I couldn't handle my magic on my own. Especially since I had been preparing to balance my dark half my entire life. If I couldn't do it, I had no business being in charge of Rector Enterprises, and all of my enemies were right about me.

Peter stood. "True, you probably would have an easier time than me. Why don't you take care of that while I check out my bedroom? I think I left my pencil box behind."

Peter hurried down the hallway, and my shoulders slumped. I was a terrible person. And mean.

Really, really mean.

I slid onto my knees and spread Peter's vest on the floor. One pocket crackled when I smoothed the fabric, trying to get it to lay flat. I could clean it even if there were something in there, but my mind was already muddled, and I was concerned I would accidentally remove the ink on the page along with the dirt on the vest in case it was important.

I unzipped the pocket and slipped a folded piece of paper out. I assumed it was a drawing. Peter may need to make marks to perform magic, but he was also an artist and sketched little drawings here and there on every random corner that was blank. He didn't even notice he did that, but it was a part of who he was.

I looked to see if there was anything drawn on the page or if I could toss it in the trash when a word caught my eye.

Why was my name on Peter's papers?

It took a second to realize it wasn't his writing. It was familiar, and I studied the loops until I remembered it was my aunt's handwriting.

I wasn't holding sketch paper. I was holding Peony's letter from when she told us not to return to the castle. The thing was, I didn't remember my name being mentioned when Peter read it to us. Just that we shouldn't come back because of the danger.

My name seemed to take on a life of its own, and my curiosity got the better of me. Since Peter shared the letter with us already, it wasn't like I was doing anything wrong while reviewing it.

Right?

Besides, if my name was on it, I should read it. Irregulars were supposed to gather information in any way possible, and this was directly about me. Jerking my head in a decisive nod, I unfolded the rest of the pages and skimmed the first part since I remembered it well.

I was halfway down the other side of the page when I saw my name again. I had to read it three times before the beating of my heart stopped distracting me from the meaning of the words.

"Peter, don't read this next part to Lia," I said under my breath. My aunt had written a secret to Peter, and I couldn't unsee it. I murmured the words out loud as I read them. "I don't want her to know how badly Tian was hurt. She's too fragile right now and already takes too much onto herself. Stay positive and keep her distracted. Don't let her out of your sight and make sure you keep the darkness at bay. She's clever and powerful, but it's still too dangerous to return. I prefer you to remain at the safe-house, but if you decide to leave, find a way to protect her. If you find Ged and there is danger, she doesn't have the experience she needs to temper her power. If she loses control and Ged gets hurt, I'm not sure what she'll do."

There was more, but I couldn't read it. My hands were shaking the pages, and the pounding of my heart was making it impossible to focus my eyes, my vision jerking with every thump.

Fury filled me. I beat the top magical families to win my company back, and this was what they thought of me? That I was an out-of-control child? Talking about me behind my back, planning to keep me out of the fight?

A jolt of pain shot through me. The pounding in my head grew stronger as a pattern emerged.

Peter giving me his Light. His insistence on working on my control. Me confiding that I wasn't sure I would ever be an Irregular. Him sticking to me like glue, taking care of me. Me losing control without my necklace.

Humiliation burned through me. Maybe they were right. Maybe I was a pathetic loser who screwed everything up. I tossed the letter aside and almost ripped the sturdy fabric of Peter's battle vest with the violence of my magic. It was clean all right, but rumpled because I couldn't control myself.

I jumped to my feet. I could feel the darkness surround me like an aura and my anger turned cold.

"Hey, what's going on?" Peter asked. I hadn't heard him when he walked back into the loft, and I spun around.

"Oh, nothing. Everything is great. Here, take this," I said. I made a gesture without thinking about it first. The vest flew up from the floor, slamming into Peter's chest. One of the zippers caught against his arm and scratched him.

The sight of his injury pushed me over the edge.

"Lia-" Peter started to say, but I cut him off.

"Don't even try it! I saw the letter Aunt Peony sent you. You guys think I'm worthless."

"What? No! That isn't what she meant."

"Oh, right. I forgot. I'm just a ticking time bomb ready to go off and screw everything up. I'm so glad you're around to play babysitter to the inexperienced apprentice." I didn't care that it wasn't Peony who had said that. Kamini's comment still stung, and I wanted to hurt Peter as much as she had hurt me.

"Lia, calm down," he said firmly.

Oh, sure. That was literally the last thing he should have said. "Screw you, Peter!" I shouted. I pushed the chair over and kicked it out of my way, storming towards the stairs. "I'm not a dog, don't try to get me to heel. You're not my boss or my king. You're not even my friend so stop pretending. How dare you?" To my humiliation, scalding tears filled my eyes. "How dare you pretend to care about me? You're a freaking babysitter. You didn't need to act like you were my friend. I'm fine on my own. I don't need you.

I don't need Chas. I don't even need my parents. So go to hell!"

I whirled around and took the stairs two at a time. When I reached the floor below, Harris and Seth stood frozen, staring at me in shock.

Well, great. Now they would think I was a big baby, too. Seth would wonder what he saw in me and go after some prettier, older girl, just like Chas had with Clarissa. Or Peter with perfect Kamini.

Screw the Andersson brothers, too. I didn't need them. I was more powerful than they were put together.

Gathering Air in my hand, I yanked my backpack to me from across the room. I made another gesture and stuffed the books I had been studying that morning inside before slipping the straps over my shoulders.

Peter reached the ground floor and held his hand out as if to stop me. "Lia, wait a second," he said. He sounded so calm. Like a psychiatrist talking to his patient while they were having a psychotic break.

I wasn't, though. I had come to a standstill inside. I was angry, but not about to lose control. Not like before, in the field of birds. I would never do something like that again, and Peter would have known that if he were a real friend. "Just back off, Peter. Stay away from me."

Kamini chose that moment to enter the room. She had on a cute little white apron edged in lace like some housewife from the 1950s. They had a lot of pictures of women like that pinned to the walls in the guy's dorms at school.

A sneer contorted my face. What a tramp.

"Is everything okay out here?" she asked.

"It's fine, we're just hashing things out," Peter said. He was still calm, and all I wanted at that moment was for him to be as mad as I was.

Then it hit me. He wasn't upset because he didn't care. I wasn't his best friend - I was his job. I was such an idiot for not realizing that before. Peony had probably asked him to baby me since the day I got to the castle.

Betrayal flooded through me like acid. I almost fell, the darkness came upon me so fast. Instead, I glared at Kamini and then at Peter. I totally ignored Seth and Harris. They were just visitors. My anger wasn't for them.

It was for Peter.

An image formed in my mind. Peter, in pain. Peter, with sparks of fire attacking him like a swarm of locusts. Peter, sorry.

My necklace was the only thing that saved him. And at that moment, I wasn't sure if I was relieved or angry that it did.

More darkness came, and then cold. My vision blurred, and I wondered if I was about to faint. I reached out and ripped some of Peter's Light from inside him, despite knowing taking something that had always been freely given had to hurt.

But now I knew he gave as if to a child, an out-of-control monster who needed a keeper. And I didn't want that. I wanted to prove I could balance myself on my own. That I was strong enough to take what I wanted, from anyone.

Even the one who lied to me.

I pulled more of Peter's Light so I wouldn't fall. The

darkness receded slightly as I walked away. Peter was on his knees, gasping. Seth and Harris were running towards him, not sure why he was on the ground, but trained to help their fallen comrade. Good. He could wallow in his weakness for a while and know I didn't need him or anyone else to be my magical nanny.

I strode to the front door and then paused. I turned back to face them.

Kamini was staring at Peter in horror. Harris and Seth were on either side of him, grasping his arms, helping him to his feet, checking him over, searching the room, trying to identify the source of his sudden weakness and pain.

Peter was looking at me. I saw him open his mouth, probably to try to stop me. But he said nothing. He was frozen. Maybe he finally realized that I knew he didn't care about me after all. Maybe he was scared.

Reaching up, I clasped my necklace. I tugged on the chain, breaking it, and threw it at him. I didn't even need to use my magic for the star to hit him hard enough to cut him right below his eye.

There was enough of his Light inside me to realize what I had just done was wrong, terribly wrong, but also enough darkness I felt satisfaction instead of sorrow.

I twirled around and stormed out the door, slamming it behind me.

With a parting thought, I imagined the doors and windows melting away, double-thick cinder blocks in their place. With a shield made of thorns. I infused the spell with the burden of the Dark inside me since I had so much. It would take them a long time to break out of there.

Even so, I ran. Urgency filled me with the need to get away as fast as I could.

I didn't need a keeper. I didn't need Peter to protect me from myself no matter what Peony said. The darkness cleared out all my self-doubt, and my mind steadied. I would save Armageddon by myself. In fact, I was the only one who could.

My feet moved faster than humanly possible. I wasn't even aware of how I did it, but I was near the highway before my thoughts settled enough to accept that I needed help to get across the state border and closer to the volcano simmering in Lassen Park. With barely a thought, I burned the trace attached to my magic, turning it into cinders and ash, which blew away on the wind. There was no way they could track me.

A semi-truck stopped at the light before heading onto the highway. It was going my way.

I stepped forward so the driver could see me, and I stuck out my thumb. He did a double-take and then looked me over. I could almost feel his interest as if he shouted it, the mundane attraction to magic working in my favor. I smiled up at him, eyes glittering.

A sharp burst of air whined against my ears as his brakes settled and he undid his seatbelt. He slid across the seat until he was on the passenger side and opened the door, looking down.

"Where you headed?" he asked.

I studied him. He wasn't as young as the rest of my team, probably in his mid-thirties, but the difference in our ages didn't seem to bother him. I held his gaze for a moment, the same way I had with Seth.

"I need to get to California," I said. "Are you traveling west?"

"Sure am. Come on up," he said. He leaned over and held out his hand to help me climb on board.

I took it.

CHAPTER TWENTY-SEVEN
Armageddon's Mistake

I HATED HOW THE truck driver kept staring at me. Mundane humans felt a compulsion, an overwhelming attraction towards magicians. They couldn't help it, so I didn't blame him for that part. But I wished he would keep an eye on the road. Sometimes it narrowed into a sharp turn, and I didn't want him to drive into a ditch because my magic was such a distraction.

"What's a pretty girl like you doing traveling alone?" he asked. "Do you need me to call anybody for you?"

"No, thank you. I just want to get to California. I'm short on cash so taking a bus was out of the question."

I wasn't certain if that was a reasonable cover story or not. I was chagrined to realize that I had no idea how to interact in mundane society. All that training and schooling, and I still wasn't prepared to act like a normal girl.

Funny how that happened without me even noticing.

"Well, lucky for you, that's exactly where I'm going. It

looks like it might rain," he added. The semi-truck driver squinted as he stared out his window. "I can't remember the last time it rained this time of year, but it's pretty cloudy."

I sighed. I was more like my uncle than I realized. I was certain the storm clouds were there to match my mood. "Yeah, thanks. I really appreciate you helping me out."

He seemed like the type who needed positive affirmation, and sure enough, he stopped squinting at the sky and turned to look at me again, a smile on his face. It was hard, but I tried to be patient since it wasn't his fault magicians were so compelling.

"No problem. Hey, you want a drink or something? I got some water and soda at the last stop. I have a mini-fridge behind your seat if you need anything."

"I'm fine. Actually, I'm a little tired. Would it be terribly rude if I rested for a bit?" I asked sweetly. Since he was looking at me again, I tilted my head a tad and peered up at him with a side-glance. Chas told me I looked cute when I did that, and I wasn't above using it to my advantage now that I knew it gave me one. It certainly helped things develop between Seth and me.

Not like that's what I wanted to happen with the truck driver. Ew. I just wanted to butter him up a bit.

"Oh, you take a nap if you need to, honey. I'll wake you up when we're ready to stop."

I maintained eye contact a moment longer. It was a straight stretch of road anyway, and I wasn't scared we would crash or anything. Then I looked away and took a deep breath, holding it several seconds before letting it out. I stretched to further relax. I was still boiling with anger inside, but I needed to refresh myself and decided a meditative sleep would help me prepare for my upcoming confrontation. I didn't have a moment to spare, and since I left so early, I would be confronting David Novato at night when he was at his peak strength.

Of course, I would be my strongest then, too. So he was the one who needed to worry, not me.

I took another deep breath and released it with a sigh. The truck driver was watching me out of the corner of his eye, but I let it slide. It had to be tough to be in close proximity to a magician. Especially since I didn't know how to dampen the effect I had on mundanes yet.

"Oh, wow. I'm so rude," I said. "We haven't introduced ourselves. I'm Lia."

"Nice to meet you, Lia," he said. He looked amused. Maybe my manners seemed antiquated to him. I wasn't sure. "I'm Ray."

"Nice to meet you, too, Ray," I said.

He reached out his hand, and I shook it solemnly. Something about that made him chuckle, and he squeezed a little too hard. Some men didn't know their own strength.

I slid my hand onto the seat next to me and leaned backward. I scrunched down and laid my head back. I wasn't convinced I could sleep like that, especially since my head kept sliding.

"Aw, you look miserable. Why don't you slip on back and use the bench seat? You'll be more comfortable."

I twisted to look behind me and studied the space. There was a nice setup back there, with a recliner chair, small galley and a tiny fridge, and along the back was a plush bench seat that had a blanket and pillow on it, used as a bed. No wonder truck drivers slept in their cabs at night.

"Oh, I'm not sure I should. That's your personal space," I said. There was something about it that made me feel uncomfortable, and I again wondered about the usual interactions between mundanes and magicians. I didn't want to be rude, especially since he was nice enough to drive me to where I wanted to go.

"What a sweetheart you are," he purred. "You look exhausted, and that's what it's for. Go ahead, I washed the blanket this morning and everything."

It worried me I would offend him if I didn't take him up on his hospitality. There were certain social norms and expectations in the magical world, and I could only assume they were similar for mundanes. My aunt always offered a room for guests to use when they came for a visit even if only for a few hours. There was always a bed and seating area and a bathroom. This was like a smaller, trucker version of her hospitality.

"Well, if you really don't mind, I think I will. Thank you again, Ray." I slipped out of my seatbelt and carefully took a few steps. The truck swayed as it went around a curve and I had to grip Ray's shoulder to keep myself upright, but he just chuckled and kept driving.

I finally stumbled far enough to sink down onto the makeshift bed. It was soft and felt wonderful under my hand. I slipped off my sneakers and stretched out. The swaying of the truck made me nervous, so I shifted closer to the back of the vehicle and braced myself, my back jammed into the corner to stabilize my body against the movement. It was a little awkward, so I propped my arms behind my neck to ease the pressure on my head.

Good enough.

I sucked in a meditative breath and snuggled my backside into the cushions firmly, making sure I was secure. And I was. Being a truck driver didn't seem like a half bad life.

"Yeah, you get some rest. I'll wake you when it's time," Ray said.

That was the last thing I heard before the darkness of sleep overtook me.

"It's almost time," David Novato said. A wave of sadness shuddered through me as the memory of the little boy he had been came to mind. The contrast to what he had looked like as a young child was stark. He was hollow now.

That was my thought, not Armageddon's, even though I could tell I was channeled inside my uncle's mind again. "You don't have to do this," Armageddon said. His weariness drained some of my strength. He was so sad. "It's not too late. You have done nothing yet that can't be redeemed."

Our enemy laughed. I felt my uncle despair. It was like he was grieving. He also felt guilty.

I gave Armageddon a mental burst of love. I didn't blame him for what had happened that long ago night, and I didn't think he should blame himself, either.

"Oh, sure, sure. I smashed your castle in and kidnapped you, and it'll be all good if I walk away now? What do you take me for?" David sneered.

"I don't care about that. I understand what it must have been like. If only I knew you were there, I would have helped you."

I winced when David backhanded my uncle. His face throbbed with pain, and his lip was both numb and in agony, and I felt every bit as if it happened to me.

"Too late, old man. You lost your chance to help me the day you killed my parents."

David Novato hit my uncle again, knocking his chair over backward, closer to the pit where the magma pulsed far below. I was terrified, but he wasn't. He seemed to feel something that annoyed me.

Acceptance.

Some of my darkness was being used to connect the two of us. Another part of it was being siphoned off while my body meditated back in the semi-truck. But there was still enough Dark inside me to keep me angry, and I turned my anger at Peter towards a new target.

Armageddon.

He winced. Not from the pain, but in response to my rage. I was mad, truly furious, that he was willing to let this man brutalize him, maybe even finish the task he set for himself to kill my uncle, all in the name of revenge. And Armageddon waited patiently? At peace about it?

No way. Not on my watch.

Not sure what else to do, I flooded my uncle's mind with images of my aunt, sitting with his best friend Mort. Both worried and searching for him. Peony looked sad, but she also had a longing in her eyes that was always there when he was gone.

It was about time Armageddon saw it. The rest of us had to pay the price for their frequent separations, and he should remember who he was fighting for. How dare he give in? How could he turn his back on his family, his friends? How dare he forget how much I needed him?

More guilt flooded my uncle, but this time it was directed properly. He felt ashamed of himself for wallowing in his past and not fighting harder against David. There were times he probably could have gotten in a few blows, and he never did.

Finally. My uncle could be such a fool.

More of my anger dissipated when I felt Armageddon reach deep inside himself where his source of magic lived, and he reconnected. Wrapped it around himself. Let it crackle through every vein and synapse in his body.

Wow. It was like trying to drink from a fire hose. Overwhelming. But it was his strength, his magic, and he reigned it into a focused burst.

Even though David could negate magic, it worked. My uncle's bonds snapped, and he flipped over backward, landing on his feet.

He tried to throw a pure magic spell similar to a Smash-force, but it was like his magic hit a brick wall and splintered, fading away. By the second time he tried to use his magic externally and let it go, it was gone.

Armageddon and I had the same thought at the same time. David Novato didn't stop magic. He disrupted the link between the magician and the outside world. It felt almost the same as when I couldn't tap into my magic, and I was walking around as a magical neuter.

I hated that feeling.

"Tricky," David said. "But I'll subdue you soon enough. You're helpless without your magic."

He was disgusted. But also wrong. Armageddon could fight with his fists, too. He chose not to.

I felt the darkness creep back. Dark always came so quickly to me. It was annoying, but in this case, understandable. My uncle was acting like an idiot and I wanted to smack him.

"David, please. I don't want to hurt you."

"You should have thought of that before you killed my parents!" he shouted. I quaked inside my uncle, terrified for his safety given the raw fury that overwhelmed the man I knew as the boy David. Who got a puppy for his birthday and called him Shadow Racer.

There was no grace or guile in what followed. One moment David was shouting, the next he launched himself at my uncle and tackled him. Armageddon's head slammed into the cinders, and the ringing in his ears was so loud I wondered if I could have heard it even if I wasn't somewhere inside his skull.

"You took my father away," he shouted, smashing his fist into my uncle's face. I screamed inside his head, but Armageddon remained silent.

"You took my mother away," David yelled louder. Slam went his fist.

Silence from my uncle.

Weeping helplessly, I tried to disconnect. Maybe I could snap out of our connection and back into myself. It didn't matter if I was detected. Whoever ambushed us, forcing our vehicle underwater, could trace my magic if I transferred to my uncle's side. But I didn't care. All I cared about was saving the life of a man I loved as much as my father.

"You took everything and left me alone with him!" David shouted. Slam.

Silence.

My internal whimper.

"You let him take me away! My parents kept me hidden from him, but you left me without protection. My grandmother couldn't hide me the way they did. The only Novato to go dark in a thousand years, and you left me at his mercy. Now you're at my mercy, and soon you'll join my parents in death."

Armageddon lost consciousness when David hit him again. And I was glad, too, because that released me from the spell. It shoved me back into my body, knocking me out of the meditative sleep, away from the angry man beating my uncle.

I was back in the semi-truck. It was parked, and Ray had left his seat. I was no longer the unwilling victim of the brutal assault on my uncle.

Instead, I was the unwilling victim of the assault on myself.

CHAPTER TWENTY-EIGHT
Mundane Smash

THERE WAS A WARM hand resting on my bellybutton. For a split second, I thought it was Seth. I had, after all, invited him to do that very thing that morning. But I was in the back of a semi-truck, and Seth was nowhere near me.

I certainly hadn't given anyone else permission to touch me.

My eyes snapped open. Ray was hovering over me. He was looking at me intently, his hand pressing into my stomach.

"What are you doing?" I demanded. My voice sounded too loud in the semi's cabin, but he was freaking me out.

"Aw, sweetheart, you can't blame a guy for taking what's offered," he replied. He had a fuzzy burr in his speech like he was talking to a simpleton or a puppy or something.

"Get your hand off me," I snapped. I tried to push myself up, but he didn't budge, and his hand kept me pinned. Before I could even think about it, my hands

338

wrapped around his wrist and tugged hard.

He stayed put. In fact, he pressed his hand into my stomach harder as he leaned forward. Ray brought his other hand up and gripped my shoulder.

"Don't tell me you didn't want this." Ray squeezed "You know you wore that shirt to get attention. Well, it worked."

I wore my outfit because it was comfortable and I knew Seth would think I looked cute in it. It had nothing to do with Ray. I didn't even know him or that I would meet him. His comments completely floored me, and the confusion made me hesitate. But then the advice my mother gave me when I went away to school flooded my mind. About how people would say anything to justify their actions. How they would use anything as an excuse to take what they wanted and make it about them. But it wasn't about him. It was about what I wanted.

And what I wanted was for Ray to stop.

I jerked my fist up and tried to hit him in the nose, or gouge his eyes, but his arm was blocking my right hand, and I wasn't as quick or coordinated with my left. I had always thought I could fight off a would-be attacker especially now I had learned combat skills from Mort.

Nobody ever talked about what would happen if you were already pinned down before you even knew you were in trouble.

Nobody ever told me that gravity was not my friend.

I heaved, trying to use my momentum to leverage myself away from him. Ray's body leaned over mine, his weight pushing me back down. He had a strange look on his face, but he wasn't really looking at me. It was like I wasn't even a person to him.

"No!" I shouted at him. "Get off me!"

I struggled, but he shifted again, and there didn't seem to be anywhere I could move that wasn't covered by him. I shrieked, panicking, and he grunted, grabbing my wrist as I tried to hit him again.

I thought about how badly I wanted him off of me, and since I was a magician and not a mundane human girl, it worked. His body flew up into the roof of the truck and then slammed down to the floor with a grunt.

"What the hell?" he mumbled. It dazed him, but I wasn't sure how hurt he was because I didn't stick around long enough to see.

I jerked my body in between the front seats and grabbed my backpack and shoes from the passenger side. It took me three tries because my hands were shaking so badly, but I finally managed to open the door. I jammed my feet into my shoes, the backs of the sneakers collapsing since I hadn't untied them, and then jumped down. I used magic to soften the landing so I wouldn't hurt myself. The last thing I needed was a sprained ankle or to break my leg, but I couldn't handle being inside the truck for a moment longer.

The semi was parked behind some bushes at the edge of an empty field. I could detect traces of pavement and the faded lines of an abandoned parking lot. There weren't any buildings around, so I wasn't sure why anyone would need to park there, but I could see the highway in the distance. I wasted another precious moment jamming my finger into the back of my shoes and worked them up over my heels properly. I couldn't get very far if I ended up barefoot.

I started jogging.

Behind me, the truck door slammed. I picked up the pace without looking back. I wasn't sure what Ray would do, and I wanted to get beyond where he could see my feet blurring with a speed spell.

I didn't know why I cared. It wasn't like I would be breaking some kind of law or anything. But I was used to being discreet, and I didn't want Ray to know any more about me than I had already let slip.

The semi-truck roared to life, and my body jerked, causing me to stumble. Then I launched into a full-out run. I had to slow down as I went over the ridge at the end of the lot so I wouldn't trip. It lowered me beyond Ray's line-of-sight. With a flicker of a thought, the distance between me and the highway disappeared.

Except I wasn't on Highway 395. The sign said it was Highway 70. I gulped. I had no idea where that was. I memorized the route we decided to take, but this wasn't on it. I could hear the semi-truck getting closer. I took a deep breath, closed my eyes, and searched for a trace. I had burned it to ash when I took off, but once I fell asleep, I left another trace since I forgot to set the block pattern in my mind.

It was careless, but I was glad for the mistake that would help me. The light-trail told me we drove to the abandoned lot from the east. I had no other frame of reference, so I decided to go back the way we came until I got to a place I recognized. The drive to Lassen from Reno was supposed to be less than three hours, and it wasn't that late in the day. Even if we had gone on a detour, it shouldn't add that much time to my trip.

Not like running was anywhere near as fast as driving a car.

I settled into a jog, following the trace I left behind while I was asleep. I gathered my connection to the elements around me and was about to set a veil spell so Ray wouldn't be able to see me when the semi-truck drove back into view.

He hit the gas, racing in my direction.

I ran, using my magic, but it didn't really matter. The semi was faster than I was and he caught up with me before I even got all the way up the on-ramp. The window was down, and Ray was shouting at me. I couldn't understand what he was saying, but he didn't sound happy.

He pulled the truck past me and then stopped. I heard the rush of air that came with the brakes, and the door popped open. I stayed where I was, not wanting to run into him.

I guess Ray hit his head against the roof of the semi extra hard because blood slowly dripped down from his hair onto his forehead.

"Get over here," he shouted. He must have thought I was crazy because no sane person would willingly walk into that mess.

I shook my head no. I wasn't sure what I should do. Using magic against a mundane was wrong. In case of emergency, like when we were running from our enemies and used Frank as a getaway driver, or pushing Ray off of me was acceptable, but to use something against a mundane that they could never withstand was wrong. Even evil magicians rarely messed with mundanes. Of course, it was probably less moral compass and more because it was boring for them or something equally creepy.

"I don't know why you're so angry," he wheedled. "You know you want me."

I was flabbergasted. What on earth gave him that idea? What part of "no" did that man not understand? "Leave me alone," I said. I took a step back to see what he would do.

Like the predator he was, he took several steps closer. I edged lower down the on-ramp, and he continued to follow.

"Come on, get back in the truck. I won't hurt you."

I snorted. The guy really did think I was crazy. Or stupid. Anger washed through me, and the shaking in my hands and chest ceased. "You can't hurt me," I said truthfully. "But I can hurt you. And I will if you come any closer." He would take that as a challenge, but there wasn't anything else for me to say. I wasn't getting back into that semi-truck with him.

Ray strode towards me. He looked mad.

Not that I cared.

I threw my backpack to the side and charged straight at him. When I got there, I slammed into Ray and then swiped his feet out from under him.

He fell onto the pavement with a thud and a roar. It worked better than a Smash-force. And was infinitely more satisfying. I filed that information away for later use in the practice ring. I would call that move a Mundane-smash, in Ray's honor.

I stepped on his arm, pinning him to the ground. I looked him in the eye to make sure I had his attention. "No means no, you freak," I said. And then with all my strength, I slammed my fist into his face, knocking him out.

Leaving him in the dirt, I scooped up my backpack, slinging it over my shoulders as I trudged back up the on-ramp. Once I got near the highway, I began to run again, settling into a pace enhanced by my magic.

It was a little like flying.

That made me think of Peter, and my heart lurched at his betrayal. But it also reminded me of how I had used my magic to lift myself off my high-heels when we went to visit Rector Enterprises. Using the same method, I wove that technique into the magic speeding my feet, making my journey a lot faster.

I shoved all thoughts of betrayal out of my head and continued to travel, for hours, until I got back to Highway 395. Since my trace was located to my right, I turned left and began the last leg of my trip on foot.

Now that I had calmed down, I realized transferring straight to my uncle would cause any number of my enemies to find me. The Taines had been keeping watch for me, and so had others. I couldn't afford the delay. I suspected the ambush forcing us underwater was because of the Taines, but there was still a chance the attackers were connected to David Novato instead, and I didn't want to warn him of my arrival.

Magic came to my aide as I continued to run. David declaring he would end Armageddon's life "soon" weighed on me, but I would have to trust I would arrive before the worst happened. Magic was, after all, about perfect timing. Magicians didn't have control over everything, and often an unknown element would divert events in an unpredictable way.

My feet barely hit the ground as I sped towards the confrontation that would save my uncle. I would be exhausted by the time I got there, but elemental rejuvenation would have to be good enough because there was no way I would try hitchhiking again. Ever.

CHAPTER TWENTY-NINE
Confrontation

RUNNING WAS NO JOKE. Especially when you were hauling yourself over hundreds of miles to confront the ultimate magical enemy wearing cute pink and white polka-dot tennis shoes. I was just glad I packed extra deodorant in my backpack.

I couldn't settle my swirling thoughts enough to plan my final confrontation. I was so angry and hurt. And confused. But one thing was sure - I would take out David no matter what.

It was evening before I arrived at Lassen Volcanic National Park. I missed my chance to buy myself something to eat at the store, but I shrugged it off and made a beeline for the bathrooms. The time for building strength through food and rest was over. I locked myself in by shielding the main door so nobody could enter as I stripped down. I pulled water from the sink tap and used it to wash, just like a shower, pouring it over myself with magic. I even washed my hair since it was easier to style it into battle braids when it was wet and slick from a leave-in conditioner. It made it possible to tuck it into a tight, low bun to keep it out of the way.

My shoes and the bottom of my pant were covered in dirt and sand. I popped them into an extra plastic grocery sack leftover from our road trip and tucked them into my backpack, swapping them for my Irregulars uniform, battle vest, and boots.

The mechanicals I had made with the guys went into my various pockets. Spells I had to use close-up like shields and nets, Flash-bangs and the crystals containing pepper spray, were on my left since that was my weakest side and I would be slower to access them. I kept the active stuff on my right so I could rapidly throw out the Smash-forces, Shift-sliders, lightning, and bombs. I had been practicing to tug and toss, the way old-time cowboys would pull their guns and shoot in one fluid motion.

After a moment's hesitation, I tugged the little packets of herbs I made when I was still at Castle Laurus out of a side pouch on my backpack. Most of them were for creating smoke or flashes of light as a diversion, but I was going to implement the idea I had at the safe-house and include lead. Grabbing a small chunk, I forced it to crumble into bits and charged them with magic before adding them to the herb bags.

I wasn't sure if David Novato used blood magic or not, but if he did, I wanted some pure lead available to negate it. I tucked two pieces the size of ping-pong balls into one of my pockets.

A thought occurred to me right before I dropped the shields and the Trace-burn spell. My teammates weren't stupid. They would know where I was headed and didn't need to follow my trace to find me. There was no way I had left them behind, at least, not for long. Groaning, I slipped my backpack over my shoulders. I was so used to hiding from an enemy, it never dawned on me that my friends wouldn't require the same detection spells.

Not that I thought of them as my friends at that moment. But still, they knew me, and that was all any of the Irregulars needed.

As I stepped out of the small bathroom, I felt a little better when I remembered I had other genuine enemies out there who were looking for me. My efforts to burn my trace weren't in vain. I snorted. My mind was a mess.

Preparing myself for meditation, I shook my hands violently, then my arms, and rolled my head before slipping behind a tree and crouching to touch the soil. I pulled out a water bottle and twisted off the cap for access. The sun was hovering just above the western horizon, turning the sky into a riot of colors I would have loved to watch under better circumstances. A narrow patch of pure yellow sunlight beamed onto the ground nearby, and I reached out my other hand to capture some of it in my palm. I sucked in the element of Air while pulling magic from the Earth. Shadows from the tree enhanced the strength of my Dark. I could tell by my mood that there was no real need to amplify that aspect of myself, but I did it anyway. I needed every advantage.

Although it was difficult to do in my awkward position,

I closed my eyes and forced myself into a meditative trance using the new spell I discovered in the safe-house. I timed it for only seven minute. That power number would allow me to magnify the effects of the restorative sleep exponentially. I would emerge as if I had slept for seven times seven times seven, or seven cubed, stacking in the power of three. Basically, it was like sleeping for almost six hours.

That would have to be enough.

When I snapped out of the trance, I stood and stretched. My left foot had fallen asleep, and I spent several awkward moments holding onto the tree so I wouldn't fall over. Once the pins and needles dissipated, I headed towards the magical hot spot between Lassen Peak and Chaos Creek.

Lassen Volcanic National Park was one of the major preserves the Council set up for our use. Sure, mundanes liked to visit, and the indigenous peoples definitely had a prior claim, but their shamans were kind enough to form a treaty. Decades before magicians moved to the west coast, the Council decided they needed to act before the best places all over the world were decimated. Without the permission of the natives wherever we went, the magic wouldn't have worked as well and the preserves wouldn't have been worth the effort we spent to convince the government not to mow them down for a random business. Like strip mining.

I swear, mundanes had no clue how to take care of the planet.

Jogging to work out the rest of my leg cramps, I headed for the place where my spell had indicated David Novato was holding my uncle. There was a permanent spell around the entire area so the mundanes wouldn't see what magicians were doing in the area. David had taken advantage of that to hide his crimes.

Of course, there was no masking the results of the concentration of magic with a veil spell. There had been earthquake swarms and increased volcanic activity since magicians moved into the area, especially over the last decade or so. But they felt our presence as far back as the early 1900s when the U.S. Geological Survey built their first volcano observatory.

Apparently, our activities worried them a lot. Not that I blamed them. Magic was dangerous. It caused all sorts of unintended consequences. They even named an area Bumpass Hell after a mundane man who nearly had his legs burned off in boiling mud from an Earth user's activities before being forced to drag himself for miles to get help.

That had to suck so bad.

I was getting close to the spot where my enemy had been holed up. There was a residual memory from my uncle that told me they would be maybe half a mile beyond the other side of the rocks blocking my path, inside of a massive rocky overhang not marked on any mundane map. I dropped my backpack into a small depression and scooped rubble over the top so it wouldn't be easy to find. I set a charm to hide it in case the worst happened even if David could negate that if he won.

Not that I planned on losing.

I took a deep breath, and just as evening turned fully into night, I stepped into the clearing.

My team was waiting for me on the other side.

"And there she is," Seth said. Anger dripped from his

voice like sharp spikes falling from his lips. He wasn't happy with me. Not that I blamed him. I ditched Seth at the same time I stormed out.

Peter wouldn't look at me. He was busy playing watch guard, but I could tell by the set of his shoulders he was forcing himself to stay turned away.

Which was fine. I didn't want to see his betrayer's face, anyway.

"Well?" Harris asked. He tried to control it, but he was just as angry as Seth. The brothers stood together, a united front against the kid who threw a fit. With my luck, their link probably amplified their emotions. "What the hell, Rector?"

The way I figured it, I had two choices. I could either throw myself on their mercy or brazen it out. And since Peter was in the wrong, I chose the latter. "Fine," I said. "I shouldn't have taken off like that. But whatever, we're all here, we have an enemy not even a mile away, and the time has come to save my uncle. We can talk about it later."

"I don't think so," Harris argued. He had always been so lighthearted, it was a shock to see him so angry. "We're not going anywhere until we fix this mess. Explain yourself."

My mouth opened, but I couldn't think of anything to say. The problem with anger was it burned hot and bright, but also fast. I had been simmering for almost a full day, and I found I could no longer sustain it to such a high degree. Not against my team, anyway.

"Start at the beginning," Seth suggested. There was a bite in his tone, too.

"I'm sorry," I said. That seemed like the best thing to

say, and it was the truth. Remorse flooded me the second I saw them, and I was trying to pretend it hadn't. But I had an important battle in my near future and shouldn't waste all my energy acting as if I did nothing wrong. "I should never have left in the middle of a mission. I can't explain how hard it is to fight off so much darkness. I know it's not an excuse, but I struggle against it all the time. I saw something awful, and it overwhelmed me. It was unfair to take it out on you, and I'll understand if you report me. It was a mistake to ditch you guys." The tears hit me out of nowhere. How humiliating. I wanted to brazen my way through our awkward reunion, but instead, I was about to cry in front of my fellow agents.

The upside was that Seth's anger crumbled, and he set aside the crystals he had been holding so he could rush to my side. "I get it," he said. "We all do. We've seen what the Dark can do. We know you struggle with it. Man, you get so irritable. You think we don't notice? Harris and I forgive you, all right? It's all good. Okay? We were just worried about you. Agents shouldn't split up in the field. Not if they can help it. Especially if one of them is on their first mission like you." Seth ducked his head so he could look into my eyes. I wasn't sure what he was trying to see, but it was almost impossible for me to maintain eye contact.

Everything that had happened since I found that stupid letter in Peter's vest pocket crashed down on me. The anger, the pain. Kamini. Abandoning my team. The connection with my uncle, his agony and despair. Running away from the semi-truck in an empty field. It was all too much.

"I really am sorry," I mumbled. I looked around Seth's

shoulder, and sure enough, Harris didn't seem angry anymore, either. Peter was out of my line of sight. He would throw off my elemental near-balance I had just spent so much effort trying to achieve, anyway. I had an iron core of resentment about what he did. The kind I could build on when I confronted David Novato. So I left it alone.

"We don't have time to get into it, but we're good for now. We've got bigger fish to fry." Seth patted my shoulder. He trotted off to help Peter keep watch while Harris dusted off one of the larger rocks before offering me a seat. I flopped down.

"We'll talk more about this when we get back to the castle. I think we can skip the formal reprimands. Just this once. Don't let it happen again." Man. Harris could be tough. But he was doing me a favor by not reporting me.

"Okay, deal. And thanks."

Harris gave an abrupt nod, ready to get down to business. "Seth and Peter will team up on this one," he said as he sat beside me. "Seth wanted to stick by you, but his Air and Fire elements make him stronger the closer we are to the magma. There won't be much water on hand to use, but Lassen is huge for Earth users like me."

So Harris was assigned to me. Of course. I was the junior agent, inexperienced, and he would have the most accessible power out of all of them.

Besides me. I mean, I had already faced down an arena full of enemies by myself. And I used all the elements. But whatever. Protocol and rules. Fine.

It was a struggle, but I finally wiped the scowl off my face. My treatment had been more than fair, and there really was no time for me to let the darkness rule me, especially when I was facing an enemy. Even if the Rectors used Dark to conquer evil magicians. Our secret weapon. But not helpful if I allowed it to overbalance me while trying to plan. I had to keep my equilibrium.

"How does it look?" I asked. It was strange switching gears. I was all set to face down David and his henchmen alone. Then to have a reckoning with the guys after I succeeded. Instead, I was once again a member of a team, and definitely not the leader. Funny how odd that made me feel. I didn't mind working as a part of a group, but facing down multiple enemies wasn't new for me. I fought the largest number of them single-handedly among the four of us. I could have taken the lead.

Then again, I still had to rely on my silver star necklace like a baby with a security blanket. Well, if the security blanket were made of magic that had grown stronger as the centuries passed. Nothing but the best for a disaster like me.

The anger slipped, and my confidence disappeared with it.

"There are at least five men on a guard rotation," Harris said, interrupting my swirling thoughts. Shaking my head, I focused on the matter at hand. It was too important. I couldn't zone out at a crucial moment while keeping track of all my failures. "We aren't sure how many are near your uncle since we can't get any closer without tipping them off. We'll fight in pairs to take out the guards, then we'll face David Novato together."

The plan was pretty standard, used when we couldn't

determine who lay in wait. With a flash of insight, I offered what helpful information I could. Maybe I was a better agent than I thought. "Uncle Ged talked about David's magic having a limit. It can't extend out for forever, and there would be no way the veil spell would work if it did. So we can probably take on the guards magically."

Harris grinned. "That's a great piece of news. That must be why they could use magic against us at Castle Laurus." He rubbed his bottom lip as he thought it over. "That will save on the mechanicals we made until we get closer to Ged."

"When are we going in?" A pebble bounced away, skittering down the slight slope, launched by my boot. I hadn't even realized I was tapping my feet.

"Pretty much right now," Harris said, standing abruptly. "We already worked out most of the details while we were at Craters of the Moon. The rest we'll have to improvise. Ready?"

Gulping, I stood and brushed off my pants. Harris had streaks of light brown dirt on the back of his, too, and I drew the Earth away with a slight thought. No need to embarrass him. Not like he would even care. We were all about to get dirty. It was funny how magical fights usually turned into brawls. So much for our society being sophisticated and proper.

"As ready as I'll ever be," I quipped. My mind kept waffling between nerves and confidence, but waiting around wasn't going to change that. Besides, if I concentrated on the battle ahead, I wouldn't have to think about how worried I was about my judgment. Armageddon said he had faith in me, but the truth was, I still wasn't sure if I was the right person for the job. Irregulars were a force of their own and made judgment calls every day. And my judgment was considerably lacking if my earlier tantrum was any clue. I had known that for, well, forever.

Harris caught Seth's attention. Maybe they were telepathic. I saw no outward sign that Harris did anything, yet Seth turned and trotted our way as if he had received a signal.

"When Peter gets back from the edge, let him know it's time," Harris said. I squinted my eyes and could just make out the slight trace Peter had left behind when he rounded the tip of the rocky hill that blocked our enemies from view. The guards should have been patrolling the side we were on, too, but so far they hadn't. Sloppy.

Seth gripped my shoulders. I wanted to back away from the intensity in his eyes, but I held still. To my surprise, he leaned down and gave me a quick, fierce kiss. "Take care of yourself," he said before running to his position.

I guess I shouldn't have been thrown off. Guys always kissed their girlfriends before running off into battle. Especially when the girlfriend was going into battle, too. It was lucky. All I needed to do was remember that we were together now and things like that would eventually stop shocking me.

Peter and Seth paired up at the north edge of the hill. Harris and I were already positioned at the southern end, nearest to where my uncle had been tied to his chair. I slipped the small posts into my ears so seeing in the dark would be easier. The sun was long gone, and although an orange glow radiated over the top of the rocky hillside separating us from David Novato and Armageddon, there would be enough shadows in the night to make fighting difficult. And any edge we had over our adversary, the better.

I held onto a couple of nets and Shift-sliders. The whole point was to capture and incapacitate the guards so they couldn't warn David we were coming. Harris and I stood back to back, a few feet apart, standard formation when keeping an eye out for the enemy because we couldn't predict whether they would come around the bend near us.

The sound of a scuffle came from the north, but I didn't turn to look. It was my job to keep watch in my sector and rely on my partner to tell me if Peter and Seth needed our help since he was facing their way. I had been training for months, but keeping my back turned to the enemy was so much harder than I imagined it would be despite trusting Harris with my life. He would let me know if I had to break formation and come to their aid.

If we weren't otherwise occupied. Two men dressed in brown, just like the men who had attacked Castle Laurus, slipped into view. I didn't think we would be available anytime soon.

"Evening, gentlemen," I drawled. The sound of Harris shifting behind me to face the same way assured me that my partner was on his toes. Seth and Peter would have to take care of themselves now that we were engaged.

"Who are you?" the shorter man demanded. His hair was black and long, braided into a fat ponytail down his back. I personally never let my hair hang down like that.

Someone could grab it and use it against me in a fight.

Harris cleared his throat. "Agents of the Council. Please come with me - you're wanted for questioning."

Every magician knew and dreaded those words. They meant all hell was about to break loose if they were uncooperative. But that didn't seem to matter to Shorty. "Well, what do you know? Somebody finally showed up. What do you think about that, Bruce?" He nudged the other guard in the gut, doubling his partner over, the man's shiny bald head dipping so close to the craggy rock face it nicked his skin. What an idiot.

And here I had been worried about the unknown. In this case, it looked like we lucked out.

"Quit it," Bruce hissed.

A chuckle slipped from between my lips. Harris nudged me, considerably gentler than the short guy had done to Bruce, but enough that I stopped laughing. He was right. I was in danger of underestimating my enemy. Even stupid magicians could perform some nasty spells.

"Will you cooperate?" Harris asked. Obviously, they wouldn't, but he had to check. It made everything that happened after easier to report to the Council. They loved their paperwork, but none of us wanted to get dragged before them to explain why we attacked before giving the fools several chances to comply.

Bruce's answer was to dive at Harris's knees. We took that to mean "no" and stepped aside at once. I threw my net spell straight at him, and Bruce stumbled, his feet tangled in firm Air.

Shorty was a real gentleman - he pounced on me. Of

course. It was weird how they didn't try any spells, but since they worked with a magician who could disrupt magic, maybe it made sense after all. I was prepared for the attack, though. My uncle was right about how my enemies would get physical due to my perceived weakness. So annoying.

Harris was occupied with subduing Bruce, who was struggling against the Air net. Shorty was taller than me, so he must have felt super manly attacking a short girl. He loomed over me, raising his fist, but I didn't wait for him to strike. Instead, I shifted my body, dancing away from him, forcing him to spin around to keep up with me. Using his momentum as I grabbed his ponytail, I made him regret not using proper battle braids.

"What the hell?" Shorty roared. I used his weight to drag him down, slamming the back of his skull into the ground, punching his jaw with my left fist. I put all of my weight behind it so it would work. I was tired of how puny my strength was on that side. It worked a little too well, and I scrambled away as he spit out a wad of blood and teeth.

"You really should tie your hair up before a battle," I suggested. "It's dead easy to use against you." I hopped over his swiping kick, simple enough to do since he was still flat in the dirt and cinders and couldn't lift his leg very high.

In fact, his combat skills were so lame, I suspected he was a mundane. Every magical family had access to public magician schools, and basic fighting was part of the curriculum. This guy was too ham-handed to have had any formal training. Mort was by far a better teacher than any I had ever had before, so a normal fighter didn't stand a chance against me. Besides, guys were taught proper hairstyles in class just in case they grew their hair out, and Shorty had no clue. And there was no way a magician would have been taken down that quickly even if he were used to not having magic around David Novato. Some things were instinctual.

A part of me - a very small part - felt sorry for him. But then he rolled over and lunged at me. I couldn't just let him beat me. I wasn't using magic, either. So it was a fair fight.

He almost tripped me. Pity made me slow, but I wasn't stupid. Mort's training kicked in, and I aimed for his temple, knocking him out.

Harris had incapacitated Bruce. He slipped a few zip ties out of his belt pouch, and we tied them up. It was kind of a letdown our first confrontation wrapped up so quickly, but then I shook it off. They were the first line of defense, which meant more experienced fighters still waited around the corner.

No wonder nobody recognized David. We never asked the mundanes about him. He had probably made a few local friends to augment his protection. Too bad for him he chose such weak fighters. Not that I was complaining. I had the battle to wage ahead of me and fighting them was like a warm-up exercise.

A shout rang out in the distance. Harris and I took off north, running to join Peter and Seth, who were in a battle that looked ten times harder than what we had just experienced. Flashes of light and a pulsating aura surrounded them, indicating magic in use.

There were four enemy combatants, also dressed in

brown, but they had the typical pocketed vests and close haircuts. Male magicians almost always had short hair. Not only was it tougher to use against them in a fight, but it kept loose hairs from being harvested to create targeted spells. Besides, cropped hair looked good in a boardroom. Magical corporations dominated the business world, and they were conservative enough to prefer it.

"Down!" Peter shouted. Seth ducked as Peter hurtled a Flash-bang right between two of the men standing behind Seth. I jerked my head away so it wouldn't blind me, then ran to Peter. Another magician leaped around the piles of rocks nearest to him, leaving him with three against one.

I threw a crystal filled with pepper spray at the newcomer. He screamed, hands batting at his face, trying to ease the burning. I slammed the side of his head with a roundhouse kick and he dropped.

Turning to help Peter with the other magicians, I was instead yanked off my feet from behind, unexpected and shocking. At last glance, only allies were at my back.

Sure enough, it was Seth. He tossed me to the side as a huge rock came crashing down. One of our enemies was an Earth user and had no trouble killing us with his power.

Not that it would have been murder. The laws were quite clear. When magicians battled, everything was fair. At least, if they were working for the Council. And the worst part about that was pretty much every magician worked for them somehow. Especially the dark magicians who did their dirty deeds. Funny how that worked.

Harris took on the Earth user, the two of them battling it out, the enemy throwing spells, Harris launching Flash-bangs and Shift-sliders again and again. Peter was holding his own, Seth was busy with the two other men in brown, and that left me.

A small corridor opened between the raging magic and the wall of cinders.

I didn't know how he knew, but he did. "Lia, stay behind us!" Peter roared.

Hardly.

Without another look at him or the Andersson brothers, I slipped through, taking only one knock on my shoulder from a shield of all things. Then I was on the other side. No more rocks, no more guards, no more magic. Just me.

And the man I came to destroy.

CHAPTER THIRTY
Justum Venerit

MY UNCLE WAS STILL tied to the chair. His head was lolling to one side, bleeding from the scalp.

"Who are you?" David Novato asked. Armageddon was right. He didn't recognize me. At least, not yet.

He sounded surprised and suspicious, but he had a nice voice, which really upset me. There shouldn't be anything appealing about my enemy.

"Praelia Nox," I answered. Using my magician's name told him that not only was I capable of challenging him, but I was there to confront him. Not by accident. I wasn't some lost hiker who slipped by the guards. Not when my name meant Battles the Night.

"Well little one, you chose the wrong battle. I'm Justum Venerit, and it's time."

I didn't have to ask what he meant by that. I knew. His name meant "justice arrives," and I had experienced his little boy's memories with grief-stricken agony. David

Novato was ready for vengeance.

Everything fell into place. Why David waited so long to finish the task he had set for himself, why my uncle was alive. Timing was crucial for magicians. Minutes it took to cast a spell, numbered dates on calendars, special holidays, anniversaries. David waited to complete the circle and give himself the most power. His birthday, the same day his parents were killed.

Justice arrives.

At least, that's what he thought. But who decided what was just? Somebody at the top. Somebody who was sanctioned by the Council. Somebody who had been groomed and trained their entire life to do what was right. David Novato didn't mete out justice.

I did.

The world around me slowed to a crawl. The moment had arrived, and I was both shocked and pleased to realize that all my worries, the doubt I had been carrying with me, vanished as if they never existed. Justice arrives.

Brought by me.

My fists clenched as I launched myself at him, the same way I saw him tackle my uncle while I was inside Armageddon's mind. David would never expect a small girl like me to hurtle herself at a big guy like him. But speed helped me leverage my slight weight against him, and I knocked him off his feet.

The thunk his head made when it hit the ground was remarkably satisfying.

My magic was building, but the second I came near him, it was worthless. There was no way to let it out. I tried to use a spell, interested to see if my trigger - imagining a thing as if it were real and then it would happen - might give me an edge. I was disappointed when nothing happened but rolled with it. I was prepared. From that point on, I would always be. My destiny was as an agent with the Irregulars, and I wholly embraced it the moment I spotted David Novato in the flesh. I had a job to do, and I was born to do it.

I leaped up and tried to stomp David's face, but he flipped out of my way and landed on his feet, facing me.

His bloody lips spit out a filthy word.

"Tut tut, David. You kiss your mommy with that mouth?" I taunted him. I knew somewhere inside him, a jolt of fury and pain went through his body, and I hoped it would throw him off his game. That was why I brought up his mother to begin with.

He stopped circling and launched himself at me.

I expected that. He should have realized that I was familiar with his fighting techniques because my first blow was pulled straight from the David Novato book of physical plays. I could tell what he would do the instant he shifted his shoulders.

Hesitating to allow him to get close, I twirled away so he didn't have enough time to react. I couldn't use Air or the Earth to enhance my leap, but I still caught plenty of natural air to clear his lurching form as he dove towards where I had been standing a split second before.

I shifted my weight with the spin I added to my movements and smashed my fist down onto his temple as hard as I could.

We both fell. I had been lucky so far, but he would figure out a way to slam his fist into me the way I had done to him. I rolled when I hit the cinders to put distance between us before standing.

"Who the hell are you?" David growled. He spit blood on the ground.

"Are you hard of hearing? I told you, I'm Praelia Nox. Surely you recognize my name. And I know you recognize my uniform. I'm here to fetch Armageddon."

David let out a bark of laughter, but there was no humor in it. "This is his last night," he said. "Not even you can stop that. The time has come for him to pay the final price for what he did. I have him trapped. I broke his home-and-hearth magic. There is nothing more he can do to stop me. You're so young, and alone. My quarrel is not with you, and you may leave unharmed if you do so now."

It was my turn to laugh. When did he get all noble? "Like you have a choice. An attack on an Irregular is an attack on us all. I'm the one who doles out justice, not you. I won't leave without him. If you're left bleeding in the dirt when I do it, so be it," I said. Except I was easier to understand because I wasn't speaking with a fat lip.

The only answer I received was David charging me again. I was too close to the magma to keep my uncle from getting knocked in. I dove to my left.

At that moment, my biggest cause of regret was that I hadn't spent enough time working on my left-handed skills. I was too slow. That's how David got his hands on me. He latched onto my right arm and swung me around, using the momentum of my body to slam me into the

366

ground.

He didn't let go, though. He held on and sprained my wrist, jarring my elbow and shoulder in the process.

Darkness rose inside me with a fury. I wasn't wearing my star necklace. There were no inhibitors in place to stop my thoughts from killing the man I faced. Except for his own magic, which rendered mine worthless.

My face was down, and I was eating dried cinders. It was agony to move but I finally managed to smash my left hand against the pocket that held a Flash-bang. It went off, the power from the mechanical spell knocking me aside, hard, and David couldn't maintain his grip.

I continued the spin from the blast and unzipped one of the smaller chest pockets. I hadn't counted on my entire right side being out of action, no longer able to access most of the weapons I brought with me.

My hand found an herb bag, which I threw at David's feet. A cloud of smoke engulfed him. I was bemused to notice the lead I had added had a strange effect. Not only was he shrouded in a blinding fog, but there were also small bursts of lightning that zapped him hard enough he yelped. Lead pulling the power of Fire out of wet mist.

I scrambled for a new approach. My earlier fury after leaving my team behind kept me from forming my own strategy outside of relentless fighting until my enemy went down. And that wasn't really a plan.

All that preparation on our trip, and the only actual plan I had included three other people. Two agents busy fighting remarkably powerful guards alongside a guy I was so angry with that I left them all behind in the middle of a mission.

It had been a foolish, dangerous thing to do. And maybe I should have stayed by their side until we subdued the guards even if that risked allowing David to escape or kill Armageddon while we were busy. But it was too late to change things, and I needed an end game. Quick. I could barely function with all my injuries, and my uncle was too weak to help me even if I could cut the bindings and wake him.

Fighting in the field was a lot different from the trials when I competed for my family's company. There, I had to gain political and public support and beat the other competitors. It was all about flash and glitter and endearing myself to an audience while proving my skills. Armageddon had been watching, and I had the comfort of knowing he would have stopped them from murdering me, even though it was against the rules.

With David or Justum Venerit as he called himself, I had to find a way to stay alive while defeating him. I wasn't even sure how to do that since without magic, I couldn't vanquish him.

The calm, detached part of myself, the one that the darkness enhanced, already had the answer. If I couldn't vanquish my enemy, I had to kill him.

As simple as that.

Just like my uncle assured me, we all made the decision when the time came, and that time was now. Resolve filled me with confidence in my choice. No more fears, no more worry.

David Novato couldn't be vanquished. But he could be killed.

And I was just the girl to do it.

CHAPTER THIRTY-ONE
I Make a Choice

PULLING OUT EVERY CRYSTAL and herb bag I could reach, I threw them at David hard and fast. All I needed was for something to distract him enough that he didn't realize how close he was to the edge of the cliff. My right side was killing me. I thought adrenaline would eventually kick in and I would stop feeling the pain, but so far, that turned out to be a myth. There was no way I could hold him down and kill him with my bare hands because of my injuries, but I could still kick him with enough force to push him over.

David Novato bellowed as he slammed into the ground. I had a few more Flash-bangs in my pocket, made of the blue volcanic glass the Andersson brothers had collected. They responded to the magic we had cast inside them almost happily, as if they recognized their element was all around and wanted to show off.

He wasn't close enough to shove over the rim into the

magma pit. I ran and kicked him, stomping as hard as I could on his ribs. He was blinded by the smoke but still knocked me down with one of his wild swipes. I rolled to the side so he couldn't grab me and slammed my boots into his ribs again.

He slid away from my attack, closer to the edge.

I leaped up and drew my leg up to stomp him again when I heard the one voice that could distract me from my fury.

"Lia!" Peter shouted.

Anger and resentment boiled up inside me. He sounded concerned. Like he cared. Like he was still my best friend. I could even see his Light almost leaping from his skin, trying to reach me.

Except it couldn't. Suppressing magic must have been an innate ability for David, instinctual even. Although I had smashed him to the ground and kicked him half to death, his anti-magic spell was still working. There was no way for Peter to flood me with enough Light to make me question what I knew needed to be done.

I didn't even know why he bothered. Peter was taking his orders from my aunt too seriously. "Come on, Lia, stop. Let us help you," he said.

Instead, I stomped down again and broke several of David's ribs. Good. It was time for him to understand what pain was like on the receiving end.

Three figures made their way closer, difficult to make out because of the smoke from my herb pouches. My team, done with their own battles, coming to interrupt mine. Dark swirled within me, fighting against the other elements, dragging down my balance. Justifiable vengeance was all that was on my mind. And trying to finish before my team could stop me. This was my fight, and I would end it myself.

The entire world dimmed. Or maybe the darkness inside me could still blind me even when it was stopped from getting out.

Especially if it was stopped from getting out.

No tears fell, not from regret or the darkness. I stomped David's ribs again, and then I plowed my boot into his temple.

The movement knocked me off-balance, and I fell beside him. I jerked away so he couldn't grab me, but he was moving too slowly, his hand instead lifting to his head. He was losing consciousness. I shifted my weight onto my good side and pushed myself to my knees, cautiously scooting closer to hover over his body. I leaned against him when I realized he wasn't responding to my proximity and lowered my hand to his throat.

Then squeezed.

I couldn't remember ever reading one lesson about how to choke a man to death. There were probably books out there somewhere, but none were in my workshop library. I would have seen them.

Choking a man was hard to do. I wasn't quite sure I was restricting his air flow enough. And my hand tired quickly. By instinct, I tried to draw strength from the Earth I knelt on.

And it worked. Apparently, David's ability to negate magic finally stopped when he was almost completely unconscious.

"Peter, untie Ged," I heard Harris shout.

I was glad Peter was the one ordered to do it, diverting his attention from me. I needed the Dark to keep my mind on my goal. I was afraid he would realize his magic was working again and flood me with Light.

Of course, now that magic was working, I could vanquish David. It would have shocked me if somebody told me that when I was seventeen, I would be willing and able to murder a man. Because now I had the choice of taking him out magically, choking him while he was unconscious would be murder.

The darkness had enough of a pull on me that I almost did it, anyway. But I wasn't a Rector for nothing, and all the training I received to balance my dark side finally won out. And who knows? Maybe my father's spirit reached out to help me fight it off. He was the only one who knew what it was like to be a Rector and control the forces tearing me apart. Something inside me was telling me how. Maybe it was him.

I loosened my hand from David's throat and instead shifted it to his chest, over his heart. I did it to hold him down, but also to draw his magic through our contact.

"Lia, honey, I need you to listen," Harris said. "You must let him go. We'll tie him up and take him in. Trust me, you don't want to do this."

Oh. He couldn't see I wasn't choking David anymore. I didn't answer Harris, though, because vanquishing a magician was not easy. It took just about everything I had left in me to drag David's magic out of him. I couldn't look away. I couldn't alter my focus. I had to stay where I was, doing what I was doing, without wavering. That was how the spell worked.

Magic was a part of the magician, enmeshed in their soul. It took incredible power to rip it out, and mine was fading. I had been through too much, hadn't rested the way I needed to, was losing my will as the Dark was used up.

But I still had enough left to toss up a shield and stop the others from getting any closer. I did it without thinking, Seth and Harris swearing loudly from the other side.

"Well, at least we know the magic is back," Seth said. I warmed when I heard his voice. He really was a good kisser, and he liked me. Not like Peter. Seth wasn't fake with me. I could feel it when he held me.

Unfortunately, that positive thought pushed more of my darkness away and its hold on me broke. That weakened my resolve, but I pictured my uncle, brutalized by a madman, battered and bloody. Then I dug deep into my magic.

David Novato would not rise again with magic inside him. I was going to rip it out and burn it before his eyes.

Maybe that was a little dramatic, but I was still pissed off at what he had done.

"Lia," I heard Armageddon call, finally awake. His voice was so raw and weak. "Sweetheart, let him go. It's not his fault."

The darkness crept back. I loved my guardian, but he was an idiot. David made the choices he did on his own. He was responsible, and he would pay for it.

That was when I made a mistake. The most important

rule while engaged in battle was never let anything distract from performing a spell. "Yes, it is," I shouted. "He knew what he was doing. He used the life force around us to keep you bound. Nobody does that by accident."

To vanquish a magician, I had to connect to their magic and shred it. I understood how his power worked inside David because at that moment, while I was tearing apart his soul to get at its source, it was almost like I was in his memory again. It gave me a sense of his spellwork. He could do magic with opposites, too. It was like using the Fire element to create Water magic. David used the life force in nature around him to kill the magic flow. That meant it worked without a trace. No wonder nobody had any idea it was even possible.

A double mistake. Peter heard me shout. I shouldn't have told them the source of David's ability, shouldn't have created a shield to keep them away. Peter was too clever and knew me too well. He realized the magic was back, and he betrayed me.

Again.

His Light poured into me. "No!" I screamed. I needed to vanquish David. And if not, then I had to kill him. It was my duty. My job. It was who I was. It had to be done.

But I couldn't do it with Peter's Light pushing out the darkness. The element of Dark was what my family had used to generate our strongest magic for thousands of years. Dark was what gave us power over evil magicians.

Peter swept it away in an instant.

Blindly, I reached for the chunks of lead in my pocket. My wrist was in agony, and I fumbled, managing to unzip it anyway and grasped a ping-pong ball sized lump in my hand. I forced my magic through the lead, using it to flip a switch, seized Peter's Light within me, and turned it into darkness.

I needed to work fast. Leaning into the effects of the lead, I amped up my strength. It twisted and changed the Light Peter pushed into me, strengthened the Dark flowing out.

Bracing my hand back on David's chest, I heaved with everything I had.

Armageddon and Peter broke through my shield and tore me away. It felt like my head was exploding when they did. I didn't know why they wanted so badly to protect the man who kidnapped and beat my uncle. It infuriated me. I shoved my magic outward, trying to force them back so I could finish what I started.

I knocked my uncle off his feet. I felt terrible about that, but he kept going anyway and yelled at me. "Let him go, Lia, now!"

Armageddon wrapped his hands around my wrist and tugged. I slid away from David, losing my link, losing my ability to vanquish him.

I dropped the lump of lead, and the Light once more became Light, my will to fight leaving with the darkness. It also cleared my vision. I thought the smoke still obscured the glow from the magma in the clearing. I thought it was still hiding us.

Instead, it had been my own fury that was blinding me.

Then I noticed Peter was on the ground, lying face down. I was angry. I was hurt. I was betrayed.

But the clarity the Light forced on me made me realize that regardless, he was still my best friend. I was so dumb to let Peony's letter infuriate me. I never even gave him the chance to explain. The Dark had ruled me, and I allowed it. I was so stupid. Nobody could pretend that well. Peter was my friend, a true one, and I was a fool to believe otherwise.

Since I was suddenly trying to move away from David instead of towards him, Armageddon let me go. I stumbled a few steps and knelt beside Peter. I strained until I saw a trace. My magic. In him, around him. Then a flash of insight. A chunk of lead in my hand. Opposite magic.

Peter always got Light back from me. A perpetual renewal. Always. Except that night. When I pushed back, I knocked my uncle down. But with Peter, it knocked him out. Instead of renewing him, my darkness slammed into him. An attack on his magic.

An attack on his soul.

I never could tell how much Light was inside him, but I was sure my Dark didn't belong. And in my quest to save Armageddon, I had almost lost Peter.

I sighed. The common sense that had disappeared when I read the letter from my aunt finally returned.

Peter was my best friend. Not just because he was doing his duty, but because he cared about me. As much as I cared about him. And I repaid his care and friendship by hurting him.

Darkness leaked back into me at that thought. I sank into myself, nearer my center, closer to the near-balance that was my natural state. All of that extra Light, given to Peter, the only way to help mitigate the damage I had caused. Without his Light, I was left with my almost perfect balance and cold, harsh reality.

When he woke up, I would apologize. And he would forgive me because that was just who he was. I didn't deserve it, but I was glad he was there for me. And he deserved to be happy. I would help him however I could, too. I owed him everything, including my job. Because no Irregular would be allowed to remain on the team if they disobeyed a direct order from their boss. And Peter stopped me from vanquishing David against my uncle's orders. I was in a lot of trouble, but he diverted the damage I was about to do.

Darkness continued to flow into me. It tasted like ashes and regret.

"Hey," a voice interrupted my thoughts. I turned, and Seth was standing there beside me. "Come on, he'll be fine."

It was still hard for me to let it go. Not with all that Dark swirling around, getting stronger. But circumstances changed again. Harris was using physical restraints to bind David's unconscious body. Armageddon, standing firm as he transported evidence back to the castle for further investigation. And me, wondering how I could be so sure I was doing what was right when I couldn't see past my darkness.

"I screwed up this assignment big time," I blurted. I was embarrassed when my eyes filled with tears.

Seth reached down and slid his arms around me, avoiding my injuries as best he could. "Baby, you're fine. You saved your uncle. He can deal with David how he wants, so no harm, no foul. Peony can heal him. Peter will wake up soon and be at full strength by morning light. You're the only one who thinks you failed."

I dropped my forehead onto Seth's chest. He smelled good. I wondered for a moment if he could still smell my strawberry scented shampoo.

Recognizing how foolish I was acting, I grinned against his shirt. The darkness lifted a little, and I gazed up at him. "Thanks," I said. It was hard to tell what the look in his eyes meant because they were so dark. But I stopped wondering when he lowered his face and kissed me.

I guess he wasn't mad at me for my tantrum after all.

Good. I leaned in and kissed him back. It felt wonderful. Clean. And it wiped away the image of the truck driver hovering over me. I shoved that thought out of my mind forever. Seth filled the emptiness and erased my uncertainty. I deepened the kiss, tugging on his shirt since my side hurt too much to lift my arm around his neck. He pulled me closer, and I felt a jolt of electricity shoot all the way down to my toes.

The sound of thunder rumbled directly above our heads. We jerked apart, startled, looking for the source.

"Excuse me, but can you explain exactly what you think you're doing with my niece?"

CHAPTER THIRTY-TWO
Imbalance

"I'D GIVE ANYTHING TO hear what he's saying to Seth," Harris said, a smug look on his face. He grinned as he handed me an open water bottle. I would need two hands to twist off the cap myself and that wasn't going to happen anytime soon. I glanced around while I took a sip.

David and his henchmen were still unconscious. Harris and Seth moved them all together to the side of the clearing in front of the cave overhang. Drag marks led to each one, caused by the spell they used to move them. It was easier to leave their feet connected to Earth and use it to shift them than it was to carry them.

The surrounding area where Armageddon was held had already been wiped clean of magical evidence. My uncle had tossed the chair they had tied him to into the magma pit where it burned to a crisp. Then he took my new boyfriend out of sight behind a mound of volcanic glass for a chat.

"I'm sure whatever he says, it'll be terrifying." I thought

about how much I had resented my uncle's interference in my life and snorted. It didn't matter anymore. I was just glad he was alive and mostly in one piece.

A bolt of lightning lit up the sky, the boom of thunder so loud we ducked. For one second, I had the urge to save Seth from my uncle. He could be a tad overzealous when protecting his family.

Warmth filled me at the thought of somebody caring about me that much, and the light part of me increased.

Deciding my boyfriend could take care of himself, I turned towards Peter. He was so silent and still that I was beginning to worry. I had finally figured out I overreacted. There was a lot I needed to make up for, and I was less certain he would forgive me the longer he was unconscious.

The truth was, Peter had proved countless times that he was truly my friend. He put my interests before his own, and I repaid him with an act of disloyalty. I wasn't sure I could forgive myself. How could he?

Lowering myself to sit beside him was awkward and painful. Harris hovered over me for a moment, probably ready to catch me if I were to crash to the ground in a heap, then turned his back so he could handle sentry duty.

I touched Peter's chest, feeling for a heartbeat. It was faint but even.

"Can you hear me?" I whispered into his ear. My eyes were glued to his face, but he didn't respond.

I spread my fingers so my hand covered his heart. My aunt could heal his body, but I was afraid of what I might have done to the magic in his spirit. Reaching into the core of his being wasn't exactly easy. But I was so used to receiving his Light, and vice versa, that it felt like I was coming home to a place of warmth and welcome instead of the usual struggle.

He had so much goodness inside him. The Dark that had poured out of me and into him lingered, but it was having a hard time finding refuge.

As always, I couldn't read his balance. But even though his deepest levels were infused with light, he wasn't all good. He probably wasn't even eighty percent good because he was way too exciting. Still, there was something about his spirit that seemed to repel Dark. The real problem was how much I had depleted him and the unwelcome nature of the darkness that knocked him out.

I used a thread of Light to explore the damage. I could sense what was mine by the trace, and sort of folded my magic around it. With a snap, I jerked the Dark out of him and back into me. My mood instantly changed. He was so pale. I hated myself even more.

My mother once told me that the Rectors might have a lot of darkness, but our hearts were all good. That was why she married my father. And that was why she had faith in me. Even though it would always be a struggle, she said she knew I would never turn evil. Considering what had happened on my first assignment, I wasn't so sure.

An emptiness within Peter caught my attention. The Dark I attacked him with had left a hole behind.

I pulled magical strength from the cinder rocks that blanketed the floor of the enormous semi-cave around us and used it to bolster my power. Taking a deep breath, I held it and counted to three, then ripped out some of the

Light that clung to my heart and hurtled it into Peter. I almost fainted, collapsing on him, but the other magic inside me cushioned the magical blow. I traced my Light as it diffused throughout his body, finding a new home there.

He woke.

"Lia?" Peter sounded confused. I guess I couldn't blame him. It was probably pretty weird to wake up lying in the dirt with my face smashed into his chest. "Honey, are you okay?"

My tears soaked Peter's shirt. The dried cinders crunched dully as he lifted his arms and hugged me to him. Thunder echoed in his chest as his heart sped up, no longer thready and weak. He touched my hair, resting a hand on my head, comforting me.

That was his first instinct. To protect and comfort. Even after everything I had said and done, he remained true to our friendship.

The Light I gave him, the Light I used to heal the damage I caused his spirit, flowed from him freely. Like always, he was filling the void inside me. Guilt also flooded me. I couldn't bear it. The darkness rose up, clawing at my heart.

I was lost.

"Good, because I'm starving," I heard a voice say.

I opened my eyes. I knew exactly where I was - the infirmary at Castle Laurus. I spent a lot of time there when I was injured last spring before connected to my magic and ascended into my powers.

It was also where Peter and I had become best friends.

"Well, hello there sleepy head," the voice said. I turned and saw that Seth was sitting on a chair beside my bed. I smiled at him even though it was a pathetic attempt. For a second, I couldn't figure out why he wanted to be there. Then I remembered. We were dating.

"Hey," I said. I shifted on my elbows, propping myself up, and besides a slight twinge, there was little evidence I had been in a battle of any kind. My aunt must have healed me in my sleep.

"Peony went to grab us a food tray. Silly her, she left me in charge while she was out." Seth waggled his eyebrows at me like a cartoon villain and a giggle slipped out of my mouth. He grinned at my reaction and then leaned over to kiss me.

All in all, it wasn't a bad way to wake up. The image of how the sky looked before I passed out over Peter's body told me what type of lecture my uncle gave Seth, but since he was sitting beside me, obviously Armageddon had let him live.

Seth pulled away slowly and then smoothed my hair away from my face, tucking it behind my ear. "How do you feel?"

"Like my knees are made of jelly. I'm glad I'm lying down or else that kiss would have knocked me over."

Seth threw back his head and laughed. He seemed happier, less standoffish. I guess our exchange in the safe-house had changed things. "I love how honest you are," he said. "And funny. Now tell me how your wrist and shoulder feel. Also, your ribs, since Peony said three of them were broken."

"Wow, that jerk really messed me up. I hope David feels proud of himself for smacking around an opponent half his size," I scoffed.

"Well, he lost, didn't he?" Seth sneered. "So I guess he can't be too proud. Here, do you want me to tuck a few more pillows behind you so you can sit?"

"Yeah, thanks. Where's everyone else?" I didn't want to sound ungrateful for the welcome. Kissing him was quickly becoming one of my new favorite things. But I wanted to lay eyes on Peter and make sure he was better.

"It's teatime, so they're off eating in the dining hall. Peony said you would wake soon and let me stay to greet you."

"What about Tian and Reg?" I had been worried about them since we left the castle grounds.

"They went home before we got back. As soon as Peony stabilized Tian. They had no idea if anybody would - or could - attack a second time. They're fine. We'll probably see them pretty soon. Armageddon is calling in all the agents for reports."

Made sense. And I was still housebound, so everyone would continue coming to us. "How long was I out?" I hated getting injured. Especially passing out. It was so disconcerting.

"Two days. A little longer, actually, since when we transferred you here it was still nighttime."

"Wow." I yawned as I ran my hands through my hair, hoping it wasn't sticking out too badly.

"Yeah. You're a real sleeping beauty. So tell me, Beauty, are you ready to get up?"

I nodded. He steadied me as I swung my knees to the side and sat on the edge of the bed. I had on one of the white cotton gowns Peony kept on hand for her patients, which were shapeless and embarrassing.

"Okay, let's do this thing," he said. Seth stood as firm as a rock while I climbed to my feet. I swayed as the blood rushed from my head, and I felt like I would faint again. But I got a grip on myself and regained my balance.

"Head rush," I explained. "But I'm okay. A bit weak."

"Good job, though. You want to sit on the chair?" Seth asked. I nodded my response, and he hovered as I shuffled over to where he had been sitting when I woke, collapsing with a sigh.

"I feel like I just got back from the moon and I'm trying to get used to gravity again."

Seth stared at me for a second, then burst out laughing. "I bet."

As I walked from the bed to the chair, Seth had found a way to touch my hip, my back, my shoulder, and my arm. He was touchy-feely, but I didn't mind at all. I still felt like I was trying to make up for all the years I was separated from my parents, far away from family while I was working diligently in world-renowned boarding schools, searching for a way to connect to my magic. I may have received a stellar education, but magicians could be closed off. Even my parents.

Things were different now, and I couldn't get enough contact with the people in my life. I guess I would receive a lot more casual - and not so casual - touches now that I had a boyfriend again. Which really wasn't a bad thing.

A thought struck me, and I let out a soft sigh. How I got to the point where I didn't think about Chas unless it was by accident, I had no idea. I had thought we would be together forever. I had even vowed to get him back.

Then he betrayed me. And the scary part was, I no longer felt bad about it. I still hated Clarissa. There was no growing past that. But I kind of stopped feeling anything for Chas. Except for maybe pity for having such a crap family and being such an idiot that he turned his back on the rest of us.

"Oh, I'm so glad you're awake," Peony said. She walked into the infirmary pushing a tea cart loaded with goodies. She was always a welcome sight, but the pile of raspberries and sprigs of basil butting up against a block of cream cheese and croissants made my heart practically leap for joy.

So I liked the food at Castle Laurus. Sue me.

My aunt leaned over and hugged me. I wasn't much taller than she was, so she didn't really need to bend to embrace me while I sat.

"I'm glad I'm home," I told her. "Missions are okay and all, but you guys are better."

Peony straightened and eyed me closely. "Thank you, sweetheart. I love you, too. Go ahead and eat while I let Ged know you're awake. You two have a lot to talk about."

She bustled off, and I sighed again. That statement probably should have worried me, but I shrugged and piled cream cheese, raspberries, balsamic reduction, basil leaves, and thinly sliced red onion onto a croissant. I was starving and goodness knows how many berries would be left once

387

my uncle arrived.

"Lia, you are the weirdest person I know," Seth said. He was eyeing my sandwich, suspicion all over his face.

"Yeah, but that's why you like me," I quipped as I cut my heavenly teatime snack into pieces.

Seth snorted, but then winked at me. Then he groaned as he shifted his attention to the infirmary door. "Ged and I aren't seeing eye to eye right now," he said casually. I raised an eyebrow, but he shrugged. "I'm going to join the others so you two can talk."

"All right," I said. I took a sip of sweet iced tea. Heaven. "I'll find you later."

He gave me that quirky half-smile and my heart fluttered. His eyes, his eyes. They made me want to drop everything and spend all day kissing him.

"Baby, you need to stop looking at me like that or I'll never make it out the door." Seth strode back to where I sat. To my delight, he grabbed me by my shoulders and gave me a deep, long kiss. We broke apart and Seth briefly touched my cheek before darting off.

Although my uncle could walk silently, the sound of his footsteps echoed down the hall.

Seth may be worried, but Armageddon's bluster didn't scare me. The benefits of being the niece of the most powerful magician in the world knew no limit. The only thing I really had to worry about from my guardian was protecting my food. A giggle escaped my lips.

Then I popped another piece of croissant sandwich into my mouth.

We ended up in my uncle's study.

Armageddon had handed me a bundle of clothes and told me to meet him there, so I used the infirmary's bathroom instead of going up to my bedroom. He seemed to be in a hurry, and now that I was conscious again, I wanted to talk, too.

"That was your mother's favorite color when she was a girl," my uncle said when I walked into his study a short time later.

"You know, now that you say that, I don't think she ever told me." I sat in a chair across from Armageddon's desk. I was wearing a light, buttery yellow t-shirt. I never knew my mother liked that color. I felt a twinge of sadness that for all the love we shared, there were things we never had to time to do.

Like get to know each other.

"You look lovely. Make sure you show your aunt, she may allow you to wear something other than brown and gold."

We both had a laugh. Peony had impeccable taste, but she was always trying to play up the gold in my hazel eyes. And was heavy-handed at times.

"I'm glad you're back," I blurted. I didn't realize I was going to say that, and it sobered us up.

"I am, too. I've spent the last couple of days upgrading our defenses. We shouldn't have to worry about David telling anyone how he got through them. Regardless, we now have mechanical traps. It won't be as easy to cross the borders anymore. They can't be tuned to ignore the occupants the way the spells can, but we'll work around that. It's more important to be safe than to skip across the

389

border wherever we choose."

"True." I didn't want to bring the mood down, but I really wanted to know what he planned to do with David Novato. I didn't have to ask, though. Armageddon knew where my focus was.

"I've got David under lock and key but we've come to an understanding. Unfortunately, a truth spell won't work on him. We can't ensure he's being honest with us. Even your aunt has been unable to break through his defenses. He not only can control his ability to disrupt magic, but he has an impenetrable natural shield."

I grunted. I had an urge to jump up and run to the dungeons to give the guy another kick in the ribs. Armageddon and I weren't in agreement about how to handle him. I knew what it was like to be David's prisoner, felt everything he did to my uncle while I was using the Blood-of-my-blood spell. The pain had been agonizing.

What I didn't feel was Armageddon's overwhelming guilt about what had happened to David after his parents were killed. Armageddon did. That was the difference. Honestly, I might have felt sorry for him, too, if it weren't for the whole kidnapping-my-uncle thing.

"I can help with that," I said. "He taps the life force in nature. It isn't all that different from blood magic, and that can be disrupted with lead. I'll work something out."

"Excellent. We'll speak with Mort and Peony about that tomorrow," he said. I was glad he was willing to utilize the talents of his agents. Even apprentices like me. Maybe I could make up for some of my faults. Armageddon stood and then walked around the desk, slipping onto the chair next to me. "We need to review your assignment."

I groaned. Time to confront my emotional meltdown. And I really didn't want to. I squirmed, but then let out a noisy sigh of capitulation. "Fine. Let's talk."

"The guys filled me in on the events leading up to your separation."

He didn't go on, so I felt obligated to provide more details. Harris may not have written me up, but there was no way he would have hidden anything from my uncle. Armageddon was great at interrogations, and I wasn't any more immune to his tricks than anyone else. Sitting beside me indicated the informal nature of his inquiry, which meant Harris kept his promise. There would be no official reprimand.

"I don't hate Peter," I said. I wanted that to be clear. "I was totally out of control, and I feel awful about it, but I realize now how stupid I was. I wish to go on assignment again, but," and then I stopped. I didn't want to say it. I fiddled with the silver star necklace that was once again around my neck.

Armageddon waited patiently.

"But I need to learn more self-control first," I continued. "I completely lost it. I don't know how my father balanced his darkness. He was always so calm and reasonable. I feel like a train wreck that's hitching a ride on a wrecking ball that's on fire." My voice shook, but I pressed on. "I could have gotten myself killed. Worse, I could have gotten the rest of my team killed. Or you. Or maybe all of us. And then what would Aunt Peony do? She would have lost everyone, and it would have been my fault. It wasn't my skills or ability that won the day. It was luck. I'm sorry."

I swiped at my eyes with my fingers. Then just like the gentleman magician he was, Armageddon handed me a handkerchief. I dabbed the tears off my face. It was hard to not sob like a baby, but I wanted to. I had been pushing the consequences of my actions out of my mind, but the fact was, I deserved to be sanctioned. Or even run out of the Irregulars.

"Listen, sweetheart, I've had my own struggles with self-control. I want you to come to me when you feel the upheaval, and we'll work through it together. I'm sorry I wasn't here for you like I promised."

That made my gentle flow of tears disappear into a torrent of sobs. I felt so bad about everything that had happened. I had missed my uncle so much when he was gone. Although I tried hard to never acknowledge it, I had been terrified I would lose him the way I lost my parents - right when I needed him most. Thankfully, he didn't die. But he hadn't been there, either.

My uncle waited patiently until I finally regained control of myself. "It's not your fault," I hiccuped. "I'm the one with the issues here. I really want your help if you think you can fix my brain and stop me from doing evil things."

Armageddon laughed. "Honey, you're not evil. Trust me, I know quite a bit more about that subject than you despite the load of Dark you carry. This isn't about evil or killing. It's more like emotional overload."

I snorted. "Oh, fabulous. So you mean I'm hormonal?"

My uncle shook his head ruefully. "I guess that's what

it sounds like, but I wouldn't imply such nonsense. We'll figure it out. You won't have to wear your star necklace by the end of the year," he pledged.

"I don't mind. I love stars." I stared out the window blindly, not thinking. Just letting my mind drift.

"As you wish." Armageddon leaned back, relaxing. Waiting.

"I was going to kill him," I confessed. "David Novato wasn't going to get back up. Ever. When I realized I couldn't vanquish him, I was perfectly able, willing even, to execute him."

I was worried about what my uncle would do, but I should have had more faith than that.

"You're a good agent, Lia. Never doubt that. And there's nothing wrong with being a decent person incapable of killing, but there aren't any Irregulars like that. Do you understand? We all have to do what's needed, even if that means ending a life. You're a young lady of action. I can't imagine you would prefer to sit on the sidelines while those around you take all the risks."

He was right. I could never. "So much Dark inside me is a weakness. It causes so many problems. It might keep me from doing a good job. I may be a danger to the other agents." My voice caught in my throat. "I'm afraid I'll lose myself."

"Your darkness evens you out," Armageddon reassured me. "You're logical, methodical, and able to see how events and people fit together. It's a struggle for you to maintain your balance, but it's your greatest strength. Even when you're out of control, you're still good. Remember, you were critically low on your stores of Light when you attacked David, but in the end, you let him go. You could have stopped us from removing you, and if you embraced the darkness, you would have. The fact you didn't go under the dark while in the grip of your overwhelming fury shows who you really are."

It sounded convoluted, but it also made sense. The part of me that was scared of who I was let out a final burst of fear, then was gone.

"Thanks, Uncle Ged." The corners of my mouth lifted into a genuine smile.

"No problem. Now, on to more urgent matters." He abruptly straightened in his chair, looking at me intently. No wonder his enemies were intimidated by him. "Tell me all about you and Seth."

I gulped.

CHAPTER THIRTY-THREE
The Truth

PEONY ARRANGED FOR US to dine formally. It was funny how the upper class always went with structured events while trying to regain our equilibrium. Considering we knew all the rules, I couldn't blame her. There was comfort in knowing what was expected.

I made my way upstairs to take a shower and change into something nicer. I guess my aunt would have to wait to see me in yellow.

"How are you doing, pipsqueak?" Mort asked. He was sitting on a bench down the hall from my room, reviewing a stack of papers. I noted he wore his formal vest. Either he had just returned from his law offices, or he had already changed for my aunt's supper.

"I'm okay," I said as I sat beside him. My shower could wait. He was there to talk, and I had questions I needed answered.

Mort set the documents aside, slipping them back

into a manila folder before locking them in a black leather briefcase. "Good to hear. I've been reviewing the agent reports. I'm interested to see what you have to say."

"Ah. That's right. I have to fill out an after-action report," I said. Thoughts about what to add or omit flitted through my mind.

"Indeed. I'll run through the process with you in the morning. The sooner we can file with the Council, the better. The magical showdown at Lassen reinvigorated the volcano, and they're concerned there will be an eruption."

"Oh, that's fabulous." My father used to talk about marathon meetings he had with the Council. I hoped I didn't get summoned. I wasn't as patient as he was. Plus, I felt bad. Mount Lassen had been simmering before I got there, but I knew I was directly responsible for the increased activity. The potential consequences made my blood run cold.

"Nothing for you to worry about, Lia. We'll take care of it before anything major happens." Mort sighed. "Armageddon told me about your Blood-of-my-blood spell. He said he used your connection to give you insight into David Novato."

So that's why he had been waiting for me. Good. That was exactly what I wanted to discuss.

"I saw what happened to his parents." I hesitated, wondering how to ask him about my uncle killing people. Every time I pictured the bodies of David's parents as he tried to wake them, I trembled. There had to be a good reason. Something they did, a deed that put them on the wrong side of justice.

"Are you sure?" Mort asked. "You were looking through a little boy's eyes. David Novato explained what he saw during his interrogation, and events unfolded differently than he remembers."

That was the problem with eyewitnesses. They only observed one part of what transpired. Sometimes, believing their own eyes was to their detriment. It was our job to put the pieces together. That's why we talked to as many witnesses as possible during an investigation. My heart lifted. I backed my uncle, always would, but it was still difficult to compartmentalize what he did to David's parents, from my love, admiration, and trust.

Maybe I wouldn't have to anymore. "What happened?" Turns out, that was the only question I had.

Mort nodded his approval. It was hard to understand that we didn't always know what we thought we knew. Questioning everything, being open to the concept that we may believe in facts that weren't real, was painful. But I was willing to go there.

"Ged was hunting down the remnants of a small faction," he said. Magicians constantly made deals and formed alliances. Sometimes for nefarious purposes. It kept the Irregulars busy busting them up. "There were only a few left. I was investigating a line of inquiry with their known associates while Ged followed a trace. I don't know how he managed since the female magician of the duo was skip-transporting."

My stomach clenched at the thought of transferring from place to place in rapid succession without stopping. It was a way to interrupt a trace when the magician didn't connect to the right elements to perform a Trace-burn spell. I was so glad I didn't have to resort to such extreme measures because I would probably puke by the time I made a third transfer.

"And he found them at a tiny gas station in the middle of nowhere," I said.

"Yes. There was only one car in the lot, and a motorcycle belonging to the employee inside. He was a mundane. When Ged got there, he distance-transferred the man to safety in a nearby town."

"Oh, wow." It was policy to evacuate the helpless, but it took serious power to transport another person without going with them. My uncle never ceased to impress me. And he performed that spell in the heat of a chase requiring the constant use of magic depleting his reserves. I wondered if I could ever match his skill level.

"It was already too late for David's father. The male magician had transferred in too close, and they both died."

How horrifying. Magicians were careful to use transfer spells in select locations. If they had been skipping around, running from agents of the law such as Armageddon and Mort, they wouldn't have been looking before they leaped.

"I remember an explosion."

"Right after Ged arrived," Mort explained. "The woman was desperate. She just lost her partner in their last transport. She set his body on fire. Ged shifted David's father out of the store to a safe place up the hill. Your uncle wasn't sure about his status at the time and needed to get him out of there fast. Then he followed the woman. She had an incredible ability to control Air and Fire. Her balance was eighty percent dark, and she was a true sociopath. She caused the explosion, trying to catch Ged inside when it happened."

The trembling started again, this time in reaction to the danger Armageddon had faced so many years before. My mind recognized he was fine, he had made it through without a scratch, but a small part of me still lived in that moment, still remembered the heat and the sound of shattering glass and David's mother screaming.

"David's mom was terrified," I said. I felt compelled to speak for the one person who was no longer around to give her report. "She wanted to protect her son and threw his dad's jacket over him, hiding him."

Mort rubbed his temple. He looked so grim. And sad. "At that point, three more magicians joined the fray. Armageddon arrived in time to see a flash of light coming from the car right before one of the new arrivals yanked her out through the window, snapping her neck in the process."

"So it wasn't Uncle Ged's fault," I stated emphatically. I knew it. He never would have hurt the innocent.

"If you asked him, he would tell you it was. Ged takes responsibility for his missions and any collateral damage."

What an ugly phrase. I hated when we had our classroom discussions about that. It was such a cold, awful way to describe the death of human beings who had done nothing wrong. But it happened, and we needed to be prepared to handle it.

I wasn't sure if I agreed with my uncle, though. He was right about so many things, but I was in his head and felt how his guilt made him willing to let David punish him.

If he had allowed that to happen, my aunt and the rest of us would have been the collateral damage. We would have been the ones who had to live in a world without him, and all the people under his protection rendered vulnerable by his willingness to "take responsibility."

Not sure how to process that, how to balance it, I heaved a frustrated sigh. I wanted to be as good a person as my uncle. I wanted to accept my responsibilities the way he had done with Peter, saving the child of an enemy who died fighting against him. But I never wanted to be in a place where my guilt got the better of me.

Maybe that wasn't fair. Armageddon had been drugged and beaten. He was exhausted and not in full control of his faculties by that point. That wasn't his fault, either.

The anger I felt, the fear of losing the rest of my family, finally dissipated. He didn't leave us. That's what mattered.

"Then Uncle Ged caught the remaining magicians," I said.

"Yes. He vanquished the woman on the spot and sent her to the Council for processing. The others transferred again. He was worn out and stayed to clean up the mess. Your uncle transported a message, and I came to help. He wanted the area cleared as quickly as possible. Then we hunted down the rest together."

Irregulars were required to clear away all evidence of a battle. Armageddon had several large warehouses sitting empty, ready to accept the transfer from agents in the field. The rubble would have been pushed into nothingness. That's why everything had disappeared, and why my uncle used Earth to move David's mother out of the way next to her husband until everything was over. The deceased were always transferred last when there was time to send them for processing with respect and care.

I leaned back, releasing the tension in my shoulders. "Thanks for telling me, Mort," I said.

"No problem, kiddo. You needed to know. It's vital for an agent to have the full story." He stood and picked up his briefcase. "Go ahead and get ready for supper. I have a few more things to wrap up before we eat."

"Hey, hold up," I called. Mort turned back as I rushed to his side. "Have you heard anything about the ambush? When we ended up on the bottom of the river? I thought Oberon was behind it, but I guess it could have been David Novato."

"Oh, it was the Taines all right. We have all the evidence we need," he said. The look on his face was the same as my uncle's when the sky split in two. "Their time has come."

Mort gave me a curt nod. I watched him go, thinking about how Armageddon wasn't the only one who was intimidating when he was angry.

I was just glad his fury was on my behalf.

CHAPTER THIRTY-FOUR
Surprise

SUPPER THAT NIGHT WAS a subdued affair. Probably because I was flat out too drained to steal anything from my uncle's plate. And Peter had no idea that I was done being a lunatic, so he didn't talk much. He must have thought being cautious was a good policy for the evening.

"Are you sure you're feeling all right, honey?" Peony asked. She looked so concerned, her beautiful face filled with warmth and love. I was so relieved that she made it through the battle at the castle with no lasting harm. I don't know why I had been so angry about her concern for me in her letter to Peter. She was always looking out for me.

"I'm fine. I guess I'm just not feeling up to being good company tonight. I'm really sorry."

Seth, who was sitting in the chair beside me, leaned closer and kissed my temple before whispering in my ear. "Would you like to go for a walk after we're excused? It's nice out."

I looked up from my plate and caught Peter's eye. He was across from me, next to my aunt. Hoping he would respond, I smiled at him.

Joy of joys, he smiled back. We didn't even need to talk. All was right in the world because Peter was my best friend, and always would be.

"I'd love to," I said, turning my face to Seth. That helped me avoid my uncle's gaze. My conversation with him had not been comfortable, and I didn't want to set him off again. Seth was only four years older than I was. Not that big of a deal. But Armageddon hadn't agreed.

I smoothed the skirt of my teal summer dress. I selected it in honor of my aunt and all the efforts she made for a formal meal.

"That's a nice color on you," Seth murmured. His lips were still close to my ear. I wondered what it looked like to the people watching us and blushed.

"Thank you. You clean up pretty well yourself."

Seth chuckled and straightened in his chair. I nibbled my raspberry sorbet. It was crisp and refreshing and tasted faintly of mint.

"Sir," a castle messenger said as she entered the room, interrupting the last moments of our meal. "There are visitors at the gate. The guards asked that I fetch you right away."

With that, supper was over. Armageddon hurried out, an eyebrow raised in curiosity. We filed out more slowly, but none of us went upstairs to our rooms. We wanted to know who had come to see my uncle and congregated in the sitting room right outside the dining hall.

A crack of thunder sounded in the distance. That didn't bode well.

When Armageddon returned, he looked both angry and harassed. "Lia, I need you to join me. The Taines are here and demanding to address you. Mort is negotiating parley as we speak."

I groaned. I didn't want to see the Taines again, especially if Chas was with them. Or even worse if they dragged Clarissa along. Honestly, Oberon was beyond annoying.

The Taines had to know we had evidence tying them to the ambush. But anyone could invoke the terms of a parley and remain safe. Most mundanes learned about it from pirate movies when enemies wanted to speak without killing each other. Magicians used it to facilitate negotiations, or else nobody would get any business done. Of course, we attached a spell to it.

"All right, I'll meet them." I heaved a long-suffering sigh just to make it clear that I was only doing it because I had to.

Armageddon laughed. It was wonderful to hear that sound again. And I was happy my sarcasm helped eased the tension. "So accommodating," he teased.

"They came to Rector Enterprises, too. I'm so sick of them." I made a mental note to speak with my uncle later. I wasn't sure there had been time for him to read my report on the mandatory visit to my company.

We shuffled towards the door. Mort joined us, and he, the Andersson brothers, and Peter took up a position at our backs. My aunt stayed behind, her lips pressed together in annoyance. She would hold the terms of the parley spell, and by Council edict, the holder had to stay away from the magicians involved in the negotiation. That was a rule left over from the good old days when all you had to do was kill the holder of the parley to break the spell and then the battle was on. Or they were the ones who killed since they weren't under the spell themselves.

Knowing the Taines, I wouldn't put it past them to take a shot at her, anyway. It wasn't like they believed in honoring traditions. Not unless following them sucked for the rest of us.

Armageddon and I walked down the steps and out onto the drive together. The others waited near the door, close enough to help if needed. The sun was sitting low in the sky and was thankfully shaded by the trees in the west. I would hate to sit there squinting when my greatest enemy arrived, much less my ex-boyfriend. If he came. At least I was dressed nicely and looked good.

A carriage with the Taine coat of arms emblazoned on the door pulled up. The driver reigned in the horses before they could kick up dust onto our clothing, which I appreciated. I wondered if a driver that polite and accurate wanted to stay in the employ of the Taines and planted a mental reminder to check on his situation later. It would annoy Oberon to lose him since good carriage drivers were hard to come by.

And I definitely wasn't above getting in my digs where I could.

I lost the smirk on my face when Chas was the first person to disembark. It turned into a scowl when his father,

Oberon Taine, followed, and then Chas's four brothers.

Not that it mattered. There could be twice as many Taines and half as many Irregulars, and we could still beat them.

"I greet you," Oberon said. He walked up to my uncle and shook his hand. My skin crawled. Better him than me.

"What can I do for you, Oberon?" Armageddon asked. He always called Oberon by his first name, much to the man's annoyance.

Oberon wanted to come across as powerful and fearless, but he wasn't so brave that he didn't use my uncle's magician name out of respect like everyone else. "Armageddon, we've come to discuss important business with your ward. I demand my right to address her in person without your presence."

I was having a hard time not growling at him. Being alone with Oberon was the last thing I wanted to do. His nastiness clung to me like a film whenever we interacted.

"You may visit with her under that gazebo," my uncle said. Obviously, he didn't want me alone with my biggest enemy, either. The gazebo was at a distance so we could be private, but Armageddon could still monitor things. Not like they could hurt me since the spell for the parley was in effect. At least, not with magic. Emotional manipulation was still on the table, and Oberon excelled at that.

Oberon nodded his agreement, and all six of the Taines turned to join us.

"Tell your sons to stop, Oberon. You won't outnumber her so greatly." Thunder rumbled in the distance, a long, sustained booming peal.

"Fine. I only need the escort of one," he said.

Of course, it was Chas he dragged along. I was so sick of Oberon throwing him in my face. He was the reason Chas and I were no longer together, and yeah, it hurt. A lot. At least, it used to. But I was to the point where I wanted to get over him already. And Oberon's actions were more annoying than usual because he thought I still cared.

Darkness welled up inside me. It didn't bode well for them. Even if I couldn't harm them magically, I wasn't above throwing a fit. Use my temper for another purpose besides getting angry at my friends.

Chas's brothers stayed behind, standing around and glaring at my uncle and friends in the distance. I snorted. They were probably worried they would look as useless as they actually were.

I climbed the stairs leading to the shaded gazebo and stalked over to the opposite side of the small covered building. I turned to face father and son, my teal skirt swishing against my legs. "What do you want?" I snapped.

"Tut tut, my dear. No need to be so gauche. Where are your manners?"

"I left them in the ring beside the smoking wreckage of all your hopes and dreams," I said, referring to the fact I had rendered him unconscious, winning the battle for Rector Enterprises.

Oberon's nostrils flared. I wasn't sure how Chas felt about my rudeness because I refused to look at him.

"Hardly." Oberon glared at me, but I looked him in the eye and stood there acting bored. I wasn't remotely afraid of him, and he knew it. So he changed tactics. "Why don't you go for a stroll with Chas, my dear? He can relay my message. You two are old friends, aren't you?"

He knew we were a lot more than that, thanks to Chas telling Oberon our private business. No wonder I was so irritable with Peter. The poor guy was bearing the brunt of my anger at the Taines, and I hadn't even realized it until that moment. "I'm not interested in a walk. Tell me what you want now, or get off our property."

Oberon's eyelid twitched. Chas remained perfectly still, staring at his shoes.

"Fine. I'm here to give you a warning, Mirabilia." I hated when people used my full name, which was probably why he did it. "We have filed paperwork for protected neutrality with the Council today. We promised to help a certain individual avoid being intimidated by your connections while they conduct their business. We are more than happy to sponsor their case since we only want to do what's right according to the laws of our kind."

I was flabbergasted. Since when did any dark magician, much less a Taine, care about the law? What was he up to now? My mind scrambled, trying to remember all the reasons a business competitor could file a petition for protected neutrality. It kept them in a position of safety while a magician had business before the Council. The neutrality was enforced by the Irregulars.

Awkward.

"Of course," I murmured. I fell back on conventional manners, but Oberon was aware he had rattled me.

"I'm here as a courtesy." Oberon oozed with smugness. A petition like that wasn't common, but the rules were clear. No action could be taken against the petitioner or the clan sponsoring them. Oberon had just assured himself months of safety from our retribution.

"I see. Well, thank you for your time. You may go now." I cut off any possibility of further conversation. I wasn't required to listen to more than the reason for the parley, and the darkness inside me was blossoming. Besides, he would never tell me the reason for the petition since it wasn't required by law. He wasn't a helpful type person, prone to handing out information like candy. He only wanted me to know so we wouldn't take him down before we heard about their new protected status.

Even though I had my silver star necklace on, and the spell of parley was held in effect by my aunt, I suspected that my magic could burst through all that if I wanted it to. Which was pretty cool. It would hurt Peony if I did, so I merely turned my back in defiance as they left, their boots stomping on the wooden stairs.

But I was wrong. They hadn't left. At least, one of them hadn't.

"My father said you're with somebody new," Chas said. I didn't know how Oberon found out so quickly, but I pushed that aside for the moment so I could listen to what my ex-boyfriend finally had to say. "I'm glad you've moved on. I want you to be happy." His words pierced my heart - he sounded like he meant them.

"I don't care what you want," I blurted. My balance shifted further into the dark. I wasn't sure if I was angrier at his presumption, or at my childish reaction.

Chas recoiled. He had never heard that tone of voice

409

from me. "Well, it's still true," he said. "I never wanted to hurt you. I really cared about you, you know? But I didn't think it would bother you for this long. I mean, we only dated for a few months. But still. I want everything I did to be worth it."

A bolt of agony shot through me. He was right. He hadn't been my epic, forever love. But he shouldn't pretend it wasn't special, either.

"I didn't want your help, and as it turned out, I didn't need it. I'm glad you feel good about yourself, but that doesn't change the fact that you had no right to make decisions for me. Now, do yourself a favor, Chas. Don't come back here. I may not attack you under the protection of the parley, but the second you leave, you're fair game. Your family has been my family's enemies for centuries. Try to remember the Taines are the ones afraid of the Rectors. Stay away, or else I'll make sure you know why you've never been able to beat us."

I was furious. I was filled with darkness.

And I was full of pain.

In my anger, I also forgot that the petition had provided them another safeguard. I didn't think about that until after the words were out of my mouth. Fortunately for my dignity, Chas didn't think of it either. I stormed past him and was halfway up the path before he caught up. I was so full of Dark I didn't even care who he was anymore. The way I felt, Chas wouldn't stand a chance if we ever met in a dark alley somewhere. And unfortunately for him, they were right when they said love and hate really were opposite sides of the same coin.

At that moment, I hated him so much that the only thing that saved his life was the silver star around my neck. It stopped me from accidentally wiping him out of existence and kept my aunt safe as the holder of the parley spell. Thankfully.

I whipped around again. I couldn't decide whether to call him a name or spit in his face.

Chas looked sorry. He looked sad. And he looked like he wanted to say more, but Peter slipped his hand in mine, breaking the tension. I hadn't even realized he had come to my side. Then Seth took hold of my other hand, and the three of us stood there, staring Chas down, linked and ready to cast a spell.

The guys didn't know what Chas had said, but they were my team, not his. Their presence was a reminder that it didn't really matter Chas was once an Irregular. He turned his back on them, too. We were now allied against him.

Chas's lips tightened. Then his focus shifted. Harris had joined us. Then, surprising me, Mort. Chas had nothing to say. He dodged around us, then strode off, probably unable to face Armageddon taking my side, too.

My ex-boyfriend climbed into the Taine carriage where the rest of his family waited and latched the door behind him. I heard a thump on the roof of the vehicle, and the driver took off. The horses thundered down the drive until they exited the property through the main gate. Shortly after, it disappeared from view in a flash of light.

"Thanks," I said.

"Don't mention it," Mort answered. "He pisses me off, too."

A grin split my face, and I laughed. Mort was the best.

We walked back to the castle together. I was sad when Peter dropped my hand. He always filled me with such warmth and peace, and it had staved off the effects of the confrontation.

"How are you holding up?" my uncle asked once we reached his side.

"That wasn't fun," I said, avoiding personal conversation about my emotions as we entered the foyer. There were too many people around for me to talk about my feelings. If I could figure out what they were. "The Taines filed a petition for protected neutrality."

Thunder sounded again. "Always one step ahead of the law," Armageddon said. He turned to Mort, who was not only a good friend and my uncle's second in command, but also our lawyer.

"I'll make that our top priority," Mort said. He was answering my uncle's unspoken instructions. I used to think they were so tuned to each other that they didn't need to speak. But then I found out Mort could read thoughts. That explained so much. But it didn't take a mind reader to know Armageddon wanted him to dig up the reason for the petition so we could prepare our case against Oberon.

Mort went inside, taking Peter with him. I wished Mort had let him stay. Peter could help me sort out my feelings. He had been there for me right after Chas's betrayal, and nobody knew me better. And I wanted to tell him my apologies. His smile hadn't been enough to erase my guilt.

Armageddon turned back. "We can talk about this later when we have more details."

I nodded my agreement. Sometimes an agent just had to wait. Hopefully not too long, though.

My uncle headed for the study to join Peony. She needed to know what had happened and that she could drop the parley spell. Harris gave his brother a nod and then took off upstairs. That left me alone with Seth.

He slipped his hand back in mine and tugged me towards the castle doors. "How about that walk?" he asked, looking down into my eyes. I stumbled.

Why couldn't I ever be the graceful heroine?

But Seth didn't seem to mind. In fact, even though he was amused, he slid his arm around my waist to steady me and looked happy to do it.

Maybe embarrassing myself upon occasion wasn't such a bad thing after all.

We drifted back outdoors. I wanted to shake off all the drama and Seth was a great distraction.

It was twilight. It always took so long for evening to come in the summer. I missed seeing the stars. Even though magicians stayed up late, we were usually inside the castle in our workshops or gathered together when they came out at night. I finally had a warm and loving family, one I had wished for my entire life, but it was nice to find a minute alone, too.

Sure, I was with Seth, but he seemed to know I wanted a moment of silence and left me to my own thoughts. It was a nice thing to do.

Besides, I had no idea what to say to him. I guess we were in the awkward stage. So I tried to look like I was too immersed in my thoughts to interrupt.

And I did have a lot to think about. I couldn't avoid it any longer. I had loved Chas, so much, and yet I was ready to attack him the moment darkness tipped my balance. What kind of person was I? How does somebody move on from the love of their life?

Seth pulled me closer and leaned down, kissing my cheek. I tilted my head, and that movement to accommodate him was enough to show that I was interested. We kissed. For a long time. It felt good and helped me regain my equilibrium.

"Come on," Seth murmured. "We can see the stars better on the other side of the trees."

I went with him, knowing he was right. Also knowing it offered more privacy than we could ever find indoors.

"Sounds great," I said. We walked hand in hand through the wooded area until we came out the other side. Thousands of stars greeted us.

"I like how far out of town we are," Seth said. "Harris and I live in the city. It's nice, but there's so much light pollution we never see the stars like this."

"It's amazing," I said. And it was. Enough that my thoughts flitted away from Chas. Enough that I managed to avoid thinking about the Taine family and petitions and ambushes entirely.

"Amazing," Seth agreed. I smiled up at him. He really was a wonderful distraction.

I leaned into him for another kiss.

It wasn't until hours later that I thought about anything more important than how silky Seth's hair was when I ran my fingers through it. In fact, I was still having a pleasant dream about stars and kisses when everything faded, and I was left standing in a dark room with my mother.

"Don't trust him," she said.

"Who?" I asked. My mother had been trying to warn me for weeks, and it was long past time to figure it out. There was no way she meant Chas. I could never trust him again.

"He's here to destroy you," she said.

My heart thundered in my chest. I loved my mother, and I missed her, but I wished she had left me alone to my sweet dreams. The look on her face terrified me.

"Please," I begged. Communication with the dead was so frustrating. I was supposed to use my intuition to understand messages from my guardians, but I was terrible at it. "Tell me who and I'll be on my guard."

She reached for me, slow and graceful in that dreamlike way. I stretched out, trying yet again to clasp her hand. There was too much space between us, and I couldn't reach her.

My mother sighed. Her frustration made me smile. It was like looking into a mirror.

"I'll never understand the rules," she said. The quality of her speech changed, and suddenly we were having a real conversation instead of a dream trance. "What is the harm in a hug now and then? But it's not the time for that discussion. I must hurry."

There were so many questions of my own that popped into mind. And what was it about those dreams that made it so hard to touch my mother's hand? I didn't spend enough time with her in life. Was it really too much to ask to get a hug, a hand squeeze, a sign of affection while I was asleep? Who made the rules, anyway?

"I love you," I blurted, interrupting her. I knew she was dead, died with my father in a car accident, an assassination that had orphaned me. But her spirit was there, right there across from me, and I wasn't going to lose my chance to tell her something I didn't say often enough when she was alive.

She smiled at me, and in response to my declaration, her entire being was infused with light. She was so bright I had to squint my eyes. Her aura blended with the light behind her, and I realized she was fading.

"Don't trust him," my mother said urgently. There was no time left to say more. Again. "Don't trust Adrian."

My sleep pattern changed as she disappeared in the final seconds of my dream. My mind lifted towards consciousness, the last pieces of the dark dream-room disappearing around me. I opened my eyes and stretched. Time to start another day.

Wait.

Who's Adrian?

Want to read more about Lia and her friends?

Visit

www.tjkellybooks.com/books

for a book release schedule and ordering information about the rest of the series. Sign up for the newsletter to receive notices of upcoming books and exclusive content.

You can follow T.J. at

www.facebook.com/authortjkelly

www.instagram.com/authortjkelly

www.twitter.com/authortjkelly

www.tjkellybooks.com

About the Author

T.J. Kelly writes Young Adult, Fantasy, Paranormal, and Sci-fi novels. Destiny called on her thirteenth birthday when her mother asked the local bookstore owner to choose thirteen books a girl her age might like. The resulting pile of sci-fi and fantasy novels was her first love. When she can tear herself away from reading and writing, T.J. watches movies, asks countless questions, and bakes treats. Originally from California, T.J. now lives in Texas where she's hard at work on the Armageddon's Ward series.

9 781948 744034